THE RAVENS CRY :
SECRETS OF THE PAST

CHLOE V. HAMLETT

The Village of Hellow Wood, first settled by early settlers, wherein the Manors stand at each quarter' and the Ash of the Wirehes yet grows. Here divalleth folk of craff, lore, and the keeping of secrets. Drawn in the reign of Queen Elizabeth.

Dedication

I had this story in my head for a long time but finally pulled the courage to start writing it. I wrote this book with the message of never giving up, no matter what life throws at you, you always have friends and family around to lean on.

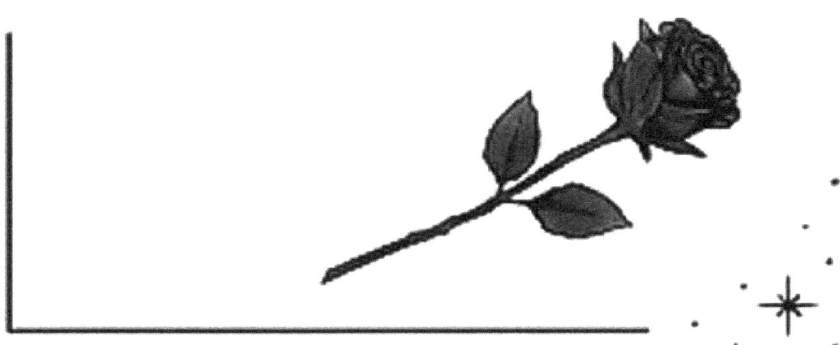

Acknowledgement

My family and friends are what inspired me through this story; the characteristics and ways of certain characters have been molded after loved ones. Some of the events that take place in the story are based on my life events that I wanted to share in a creative way. "In the quiet moments and the hardest days, it's the love of our family and friends that reminds us of who we are and who we're still becoming".

Table of Contents

Chapter One

WELCOME TO HOLLOW WOOD

VILLAGE

"The trees remember what the villagers forgot, secrets sink deep in Hollow Wood."

-E.L

Welcome to Hollow Wood village, my name is Clover Brinford, and this is my story about my gift that I at first thought was my curse. A curse of being able to contact and communicate with the ones who are no longer part of this mortal world. I grew up here in this small village called Hollow Wood, where the roots run just as deep as the history of this place. I am a descendant of one of the founding families that built this village so many moons ago. At the heart of our village is the oldest building still standing, held up by the rocks and stones my ancestors constructed. On the large stone arch as you enter the hall, you can still see the initials of the people who built it once construction was completed. We hold town meetings and founders' parties for us all to come together and celebrate the growth of the village, its history and traditions we still celebrate to this day, to also celebrate the people who have come and gone whether it be they moved to another home or succumbed to deaths touch, their bodies sent to take their final resting place with their families in our local cemetery just outside the village on the hill. Our village hall has had a few upgrades over the years, as it's a very old building. The old original stone floors take you through the small entrance hall to the main

part of the hall that opens with tall walls and big, strong beams that keep the roof sturdy. The four founding families' flags were draped at the back of the hall over a small, raised stage. Back in the old days, the windows would have been wooden shutters, but part of the upgrade of the hall consisted of some large decorative stained-glass windows that were installed with the founder's coat of arms embedded into the glass. The view as you look out through the houses that were built around Hollow Wood Hall, you can see the fields and beyond that the woods that surround the village. When the sunlight shines through the stained-glass windows, the room comes to life in a burst of colours.

When entering Hollow Wood village, it's a village where modern time has no place, as you walk through the main road of the village with old stone and beamed cottages on either side, some still had their traditional thatched roofs. It has obviously grown and expanded over the years, with new people settling here and making it their home. Everyone who lives here contributes to the working of the fields and field equipment, the farm animals, and the wildlife. We have everything a small village would ever need; our local baker, Ruth, a tall, younger lady with long blonde hair, always wore her hair in a side plait. She took over the shop when her mum passed away and inherited all the secret recipes. Just like her family before her, she and her father, Nick, run the shop together. She makes the best bread, pastries and cakes you have ever eaten. You can tell it's cooking and restock day as you can smell the scent of her famous pumpkin bread cooking in the stone stoves out the back of her shop, the sweet aroma of the cakes as they come fresh out the oven to be decorated with icing and fruits grown and picked from our fields. She has a lovely seating area covered by a white metal gazebo decorated with flowers outside the front of her shop, where you can sit and have a cup of tea with your friends and enjoy something nice from the menu. I always get her famous toasted pumpkin bread with three melted cheeses and ham: it's delicious. Just up from Ruth's is our local post office run by Gary, his wife Lucy, two sons, Jake and Paul and a daughter called Hayley. They are a lovely family, all with red flowing hair and the brightest blue eyes. My grandfather Axel used to have a job working for them. The most trustworthy post people who are guaranteed to get your letters to loved ones or parcels sent out safely to the neighboring towns' post office. They still use a horse-drawn cart to take them out to where they need to go, the wooden cart with large, round wheels pulled by a massive black shire horse called Troy. He is huge with a long, black and white flowing mane. We also have a row of small shops that sell things from antiques, clothes to food and furniture that were supplied and made by people around the village.

4

POST
OFFICE
POST OFFICE
POST
OFFICE

We also get to meet new people traveling through to visit our village due to the amazing scenic walks, our woods and field footpaths for the nature lovers, history buffs who want to learn more about our ancient village always take the opportunity to visit Antler Manors famous decorative open library, with towering shelves built floor to ceiling holding an abundance of books filled with tales and history of the past preserved in their pages. Ghost hunts started up in the area by villagers letting out their dwellings to be investigated in the hopes that the voices of the past would come forward to speak. Over Halloween, we always have a big party in the pumpkin patch field, the large corn maze carved out to terrify the inquisitive adventurer. A live band playing all the Halloween classics, hay bales placed everywhere to sit on, so you could relax and enjoy Ruth's cooking. There is always a Halloween spooktacular King and Queen chosen for the best costume. "I will win that one day, like my mum did, that's where she met my dad." It's my most favourite time of the year when the Halloween decorations come out around the village, warm pumpkin lanterns line the street, each one carved with their own personality. The trees at that time of year are all reds, oranges, and browns with a cool nip in the air, and the creeping fog that descends onto the fields gives it the perfect setting for a Halloween party. When looking for Hollow Wood, it is very rural with one entrance road through the woods into the village and one exit road back through the woods on the other side. The woods surround our village, keeping the world's problems and craziness at bay. We share the land with the wildlife, from deer, foxes, birds that sing in the morning, the frogs Croke as the night draws in, and the silent winged owls grace the sky's hunting, their prey that hides in the tall grass. Hollow Wood becomes even more enchanting at night as the warm lamps are lit through the streets, lighting up the cobbled tracks. You can hear laughter and merriment as we congregate at our local pub.

Our local Inn, called the Three Headed Raven, is run by Robert and his wife Fran. They are the biggest characters, always up for a drink and a chat. Both have rosy cheeks and a bright smile as they go about their day, greeting new people staying in the Inn, serving the local people coming into the Pub they run alongside the Inn. It always has the best atmosphere there with cozy, comfy padded chairs, a fire roaring and crackling when it gets cold. The smell of roast dinners and hearty stews cooking in the kitchen, you can hear Fran singing as she cooks. She has such a beautiful voice; she sometimes sings with the local band when we have parties. Robert, with his welcoming, cheeky personality, who always did front of house, joked and had a good laugh with the punters. Fran and Robert, one night, rang the pub bell to announce that Fran was pregnant with their first child. They were finally blessed after trying for so long, coming to the conclusion that it wasn't going to happen for them, but they were overjoyed. So here we go, let's get this tale started. Now you know a bit about Hollow Wood and the people who live there. I have set the scene of my home and where this story takes place. I'm taking you back, way before I was born or even thought of. I want to introduce you to my grandfather, Axel Brinford, a larger-than-life character who was born to rebel. I feel I take after him in so many ways. He was into the rock n roll scene in the late fifties, very much ahead of his time. He was tall with light brown wavy hair and was always seen with a cigarette in his mouth and a cold beer in his hand.

Even though he had the persona of a rock n roller, he had the kindest green eyes, which are our family trait, he had such a sweet way about him. I wish I had known him in life, but I got to know him in death. Being the music lover he was, he went to a rock 'n roll festival that took place in a massive field that was happening in a couple of towns over from our village with his mates. There were so many bands playing over the weekend, it was non-stop music and dancing like no one was watching and singing like he was the one on stage who everyone was here to see.

ANTLER
Axel Brinford

Axel was never meant to blend into the background. Tall and broad-shouldered, with a cheeky smile that always seemed to hide a secret, he carried himself with the restless energy of someone meant for more than the quiet halls of Antler Manor. His green eyes glittered with mischief and curiosity, always searching for the next thrill. A black leather jacket clung to his frame, paired with stone-washed jeans worn in all the right places, clothing that looked both rebellious and lived-in, like he was halfway between flight or fight. His warm sun kissed skin carried the colours from spending days outside and his tousled hair refused to be tamed, always giving him a roughish, windblown look. He smelled faintly of earth and his favourite fragrance of old spice. When Axel ran away with the circus, it wasn't out of defiance, it was out of hunger. Hunger for adventure, for stories he couldn't find in books, for laughter that echoed under the striped tents, for danger strung high above the ground building that large circus tent. He was the guy who climbed faster than he thought, who balanced where no one else dared, who made strangers feel like old friends. In the circus, Axel wasn't a runaway heir; he was the daring adventurer, the charming rogue, the green-eyed misfit who could vanish into the crowd yet command it in the same breath. The manor would always call him home, but for a time, Axel belonged to the wild music of fiddles, the smell of sawdust and the strange family of performers who welcomed him as one of their own. When he returned home and integrated back into his everyday life, he would find himself at the music festival.

He left his group of friends and the rowdiness of the crowd to go buy a drink. Being young and full of life, he embraced that weekend with his friends by drinking a lot and not sleeping, but little did he know he would also find the love of his life that night. Just one glance shared, and that's all it took. My grandmother's name is Velina Shaw. She is also part of a founding family that built the village. She left home in search of a bigger adventure beyond the boundaries of our small village. She would always come back and visit her family and friends, as they all went to the local school together, which was called Hollow Wood School. She travelled in the same circle of friends as Axel, but they never really saw each other in that way until the night they found each other at the festival.

When they all left Hollow Wood School and went their separate ways to different colleges in different towns in search of different futures, they never forgot each other or the friends they made from going to Hollow Wood School. Velina finished college and got a job in the local village shop, but she wanted more, she hungered for more. She was in search of her dream, and that was to become a big-time model in the big city. She saved all her money and worked her last shift, packed her bags and left on the midnight bus to the neighbouring town of Hale with her best friend Julie Cast, who also shared the same dream. They bought a one-way ticket to the big city to stay in a model scouting hostel. They shared a room with two other young ladies, hoping to stand out and get modelling jobs booked for magazines, billboards, and runways. As she worked and grafted away, she had her big break working for a high-end beachwear company and eventually became the face of the magazine called Sun & Sand, strutting out on the catwalks to promote the new fashions as they came in. As time went by, she found herself receiving an invite from one of her childhood friends back home to come to a festival to blow off some steam and catch up.

After her photo shoot in the big city was done, she ran back to her new apartment that she shared with Julie, which overlooked a beautiful park. They both started to get ready for the festival, clothes being flung on the floor until they found the perfect outfits. She found her favourite dress hung at the back of her wardrobe; it was tie-dyed with bright colours and sequins that followed the flow of the dress, which sparkled as she walked. Velina had naturally long, wavy hair that she entwined with beads, feathers, and plaits that fell down her back. Once they were both ready, they waited for the driver to pick her and Julie up to take them to the festival. When they both got dropped off, they looked for the VIP area that was set up near the drinks tent. It was set up for them by the company they both modelled for, with a large teepee filled with rainbow fury beanbags and fairy lights near a small grove of trees in the field. It was built away from the craziness of the crowd but still close enough to enjoy the bands as Velina craved space after being in the madness of the big city.

There was hay bales with furs placed atop them spaced around a dancing fire that appeared to move to the music. Star lanterns streamed across the branches of the small grove of trees, reflecting small stars everywhere. My grandfather Axel said to me, "It was like dancing in the stars, and that's where I fell in love with your grandmother." They both left their group of friends to get a drink from the drinks tent. Velina recognised Axel waiting in the queue and invited him back to her camp. With her VIP access, she had her own bar window with no queue to wait in; she ordered the drinks and led Axel back to where she was camping. They spent the night catching up with each other and talking about their achievements. They seemed to click immediately, as if no time had gone between them, and feelings grew fast as they flirted and giggled, they sat close to each other in front of the fire. Axel's ears pricked up, he heard one of his favourite songs starting with one of the bands that was covering. He gently took Velina's hand and asked her to dance with him. She bashfully smiled, stood up and took his hand to dance. As they swayed together under the star lanterns, the music consuming them both, Axel, lost in Velina's eyes, he lip-synced part of the song to her, "I can't help falling in love with you."

They spent the whole weekend of the festival together and were inseparable. It was then that Axel knew it was her he would marry one day. They thought at first it would be hard to start up a long-distance relationship, but the love they felt for each other made them want to make it work. Velina, not wanting to leave Axel, begrudgingly returned to the big city to her apartment. She felt so giddy from that weekend at the festival with him. Everything she did or saw reminded her of him, which caused a little smile to appear. Axel felt the same way when he got home; he could not concentrate on anything, and he came to the realisation that he just wanted to be with Velina. So, he packed a bag, didn't even think twice about his job or responsibilities and headed out the door to the big city to the address Velina had given him before she left him at the festival to go home. He hopped on the bus and just willed for the journey to go quicker so he could see Velina again. The bus stopped in the town of Hale so he could buy himself a train ticket. It was early morning when he left home, so he estimated it would be midday by the time he got there. Once the ticket was bought, he had to wait half an hour for the train to come, which felt like an eternity. Velina had an early morning photoshoot to get to, which was going to take up most of her day due to all the outfits she had to model and hair and makeup changes, but she wasn't work-focused when she turned up. Her work colleagues tried to get her to focus because all her pictures were just not coming out the way the photographer wanted. By this time, Axel had been sitting on the train for a little while and was coming to his stop. He hustled off the train, spying a flower stand that caught his eye, which was filled with beautiful-smelling flowers. He noticed that they had Velina's favourite, so he bought a bunch of dark red roses with long stems. He walked to the front of the train station and hailed a taxi to take him to Velina's apartment; thankfully, it wasn't too far from the train station, as the taxi pulled up to the building after a short drive through busy city traffic.

He gave the taxi driver the fare and ran up to the building's front door. He was so excited to see her, but nervous at the same time, as she didn't even know he was coming. He pulled the door open and started to climb the stairs to the top floor. When he made it to her door, he smoothed his hair and readjusted his leather jacket, checked his breath with a short burst of air into his hand, before knocking on the door. He could hear footsteps approaching from behind the door and he felt like he was holding his breath. The sound of locks unhooked, keys turning, and the door slowly opened. It was not Velina, it was Julie who was home on her day off. Julie was so happy to see Axel standing there, red-faced and slightly out of breath from climbing the stairs.

He said in a joking tone, "Bloody hell, I need to give up smoking." He puffed his breath as they had a little laugh together before Julie told him Velina was at a photoshoot. She told him, "Not to worry, her photoshoot is taking place at the Sun & Sand store, which is just around the corner from our apartment." Julie grabbed her bag, denim jacket and keys and told Axel to follow her as they made their way back down the stairs, across the street, and a couple of roads over to the Sun & Sand studio. Axel felt so lost and overwhelmed in the big city compared to Hollow Wood, but Julie was walking with such confidence. Axel tried not to look like a lost tourist as he followed behind her, tripping over his own feet and dodging people in the busy crowds. They got to the building, and Julie opened the door with her security access key. She took Axel through the shop. It always closed early on a Sunday, which was the day photoshoots normally happened. All the lights were off in the store; only the natural light from the street window shone through, silhouetting the hanging beachwear on its hangers.

It was quiet with no people in the store shuffling through the bikinis and swimsuits, no sound of beeping from the tills. Axel looked up above the counter and froze when he saw a large poster of Velina wearing the latest in fashion bikini. He felt his heart speed up, his face flushed. Julie giggled and pulled him away from the poster and said, "You are going to see the real Velina in a sec, she is just behind that door."

Julie quietly opened the door and waved to Franky, the photographer. He was a middle-aged, short, slim-built man who had seen it all in his profession, working his way up in the model industry. He was a very flamboyant character with spiky black hair, rocking his trademark round black mirrored glasses. Julie skipped up to Franky and gave him a tight hug, wrapping her arms around his shoulders and planting a kiss on his cheek. She wanted to let him know she was there with a guest who knew Velina.

The shiny black floors of the photoshoot room picked up the flashes from the cameras, setting the room alight like lighting flashes. Julie and Axel approached the beach scene that had been set up with sand, palm trees and the ocean backdrop with lighting rigged above to imitate the sun. Franky was looking a bit frustrated, standing with his hip popped and arms folded across his chest. He spoke in hushed tones to Julie, "I don't know what else to do. I'm all ears if you have any suggestions. Velina is not modelling how she normally does." Franky wanted her to smile and show she is excited to be at the beach in her new beach wear. Julie, returning to the hushed tones, explained to Franky the situation between Axel and Velina, which made him smile and laugh a bit. With this new information, he concocted a quick little plan to get Velina to snap out of it and make her smile and glow for the photo rather than looking like she was far away in her own mind. Axel was watching in awe as Velina posed, the cameras flashing away, but she couldn't see him behind the lights and flashes from the camera. She had her hair curled and pinned up high on her head, she was modelling a red bikini and a black sheer shawl draped over her shoulders. She was trying her hardest to concentrate and look the way Frankey wanted her to. Franky approached Axel and pulled his attention away from gazing at Velina by snapping his fingers together next to his ear. As he spun around feeling startled by the snap Franky asked him, "On my count, can you walk onto the beach set to get Velina to snap out of this daze she is in?" Axel agreed with a gulp and a quick head nod as he got himself ready to walk onto the set with his flowers for Velina in hand. Franky gave Axel a little nudge. He took a deep breath and walked out of the dark behind the cameras. Velina looked over when she noticed the movement; her face lit up. She was overjoyed to see Axel standing there in her world with red roses being presented to her, seeing his smirk appear across his face. Franky captured the perfect shot of her, her beaming smile with rose-blushed cheeks, that photo made the cover of Sun & Sand. Her poster of that photo still hangs up in the store to this day. It was the most iconic picture that was taken of her. From that day, Axel moved in with Velina and Julie. He adjusted to living in the big city, and he got a new job at the Sun & Sand shop to be near Velina; they became quite the celebrity couple of the time.

After living and working up there for a few years, Axel's parents contacted him as they needed him back home; they were getting older and needed him to take over the estate of Antler Manor. He spoke to Velina about possibly moving home to Hollow Wood. He didn't want to leave her but was willing to keep it long-distance if she wanted to stay with Julie and keep going with her modelling career. Axel and Velina were both in their early-thirty's by then she felt she had got all she wanted from her life as a model, so she agreed to move back with him, she wanted to slow down and find some peace back in the country, the big city was getting

too much and the new presence from younger upcoming models
was making Velina feel like she wanted to take a step back. She
would forever be immortalised as a legendary model at Sun &
Sand due to her professionalism, and everybody loved her who
worked with her. After the conversation with Axel, she broke the
news to Julie that she was leaving to go home very soon. They
shared the tightest, longest hug. Both of them started to cry. Velina
reassured Julie that she would always be there for her, no matter
what, and would still come up to the big city for the big monthly
sales, which was their tradition together. After a full day of being
on their feet, they would go out for a big glass of wine after all the
bargain hunting to admire their purchases and have a good gossip.
They both grabbed a glass of wine each after parting from their
hug and walked over to the back wall of their apartment to admire
the collection of photos and memories they made together as
roommates, in the middle of the photos of the parties the night life
and the glamour there preserved in a small wooden frame was their
one-way bus tickets they purchased together all those years ago
kept safe behind the glass. They both signed the tickets when they
had made it as successful models and found their dream, but it was
time for Velina to start a new adventure that took her home to
Hollow Wood. After telling Sun & Sand that she was stepping
down as the face of the company, they threw her the biggest
leaving party the company had ever seen and had her most famous
photo hung up in the shop, never to be taken down. After a few
weeks of packing and saying their final goodbyes, they hired a
moving van, loaded all their belongings and said goodbye to a very
tearful Julie. They left the big city that morning and made their
way home to Antler Manor.

Chapter Two

WELCOME TO ANTLER MANOR

"The Manor stands like a memory too stubborn to fade, its walls thick with whispers."

-E.L

They had unpacked and got themselves settled within the walls of Antler Manor, Axel's ancestry home. He left Velina to familiarise herself with the long halls and multiple rooms of the manor, he walked into the village to ask for his old job back at the post office. Velina was so happy to meet Axel's parents again and get to know them more, as they will all be living under the same roof.

Antler Manor stood proudly at the edge of Hollow Wood, its silhouette rising above the treetops like a sentinel of another age. Built of pale stone veined with dark marbling, the manor carried the weight of centuries in its bones, weathered yet unbowed, as if the land itself had claimed it as part of its legacy. High-pitched roofs crowned with slate tiles gleamed in the rain, and tall chimneys reached skyward like watchtowers, often trailing ribbons of smoke that curled into the air. The main façade was stately, its double oak doors flanked by carved pillars that bore carvings of stags, vines and feathered wings, symbols of the Brinford lineage. Windows rose tall, their glass panes catching both moonlight and morning sun, so that at certain hours, the manor looked alive with fire. At its entrance, a grand staircase swept down from the upper floor to the foyer, inviting guests into the ballroom just beyond, where chandeliers and mirrored walls reflected centuries of celebrations and sorrows alike. Yet the manor was more than grandeur. It was a living maze of history. Hallways stretched long and echoing, their walls lined with ancestral portraits whose painted eyes seemed to follow your every move. Velvet curtains breathed faintly in drafts, and floors creaked as though remembering every step ever taken upon them. Some doors opened to sunlit bedrooms filled with warmth, while others concealed secrets: dust-choked studies, locked attics and forgotten wings that hadn't heard laughter in decades. Behind the manor sprawled its grounds, a mixture of tamed beauty and wild enchantment. The gardens brimmed with roses and ivy, beyond the trimmed hedges, the land sloped into forests where magic walked and where the Brinford family's past seemed to stir with every rustling leaf. At dawn, Antler Manor was golden, its towers blazing in the rising sun. At night, it loomed silver and solemn, a silhouette cloaked in shadow, with its stag-carved doors and star-shaped lanterns casting faint halos of light. It was both home and fortress, both sanctuary and stage, every stone humming with the weight of stories long kept, and of new ones waiting to be written. The coat of arms of our family is stitched onto a royal blue flag with a pure white stag in the centre, gold flowers entwined around the large horns. It was hung in pride of place over the large wooden door, intricately carved with the stag being the forefront of its design. The large ornate wooden front doors with large metal work antlers for the handles were carved by my four-time great grandfather, who was also named Axel.

The large domed greenhouse clung to the side of the manor like a jewel box of living things. It was built for my fourth great-grandmother, Eve Longbow, married name Brinford. She was a healer and a practising white witch; she had to keep that side of her secret from the villagers who wouldn't understand her gift. She grew all the herbs and plants she needed in her greenhouse, making her remedies and potions. Eve loved spending time inside the greenhouse; it was where she could be completely herself, its glass panes glowing warmly whenever the sun struck them. The greenhouse was upheld by white-painted metal beams, their surface softened by ivy that curled and wrapped around them in spirals, as if nature itself claimed the structure as its own. Where the beams bent and crossed overhead, blossoms had been trained to weave along their lines, so that even the skeleton of the green house was adorned with life. Inside, the air was thick and heavy with the fragrance of herbs, flowers and damp growing soil. Lavender, rosemary, sage and thyme brushed against the scenes, mingling with the sweetness of blooming roses and the sharper tang of rarer plants Eve herself had coaxed into thriving. In summer, the heat beneath the glass became a living presence, a warm embrace that carried the mingled perfume of a hundred maybe more flowers in bloom. Drops of condensation slid down the panes like liquid light, glimmering in the sun. Rows of wooden tables and earthen pots filled the space, each one brimming with carefully tended plants, some small and humble, others strange and rare. Copper watering cans caught the light, their polished curves gleaming like hidden treasures among the greenery. A pair of wicker chairs rested in a quiet corner, often draped with Eve's shawls, where she might sit and write in her spell book while listening to the leaves rustle in the warmth. At the far end, wide patio doors opened onto a flagstone terrace; beyond, the manor grounds unfurled in all their grandeur. From this threshold, Eve could step out with a steaming cup of herbal tea, the scent of her greenhouse still clinging to her, and watch the morning mist lift from the grounds or the twilight sun melt into the horizon. The seating area was framed by pots overflowing with trailing ivy and fragrant blooms, a natural extension of the sanctuary within. The greenhouse was Eve's sanctuary, a place where earth, sun and magic wove together. Every leaf seemed to carry her touch, every bloom a whisper of her craft, turning Antler Manor not only into a home of stone but into a living, breathing heart of green.

Some of her original gardening tools have been left untouched in her wooden gardening box; we place flowers in there for her on her birthday. She also loved to breed ravens, which she called her familiars. Their generations from her original ravens still nest around the grounds of Antler Manor to this day, roosting in the large trees. Eve always carried a regal grace about her; she had a unique birthmark on her cheek in the shape of a small red heart. She was always given strange looks by the elders of Hollow Wood and a streak of jealousy from the younger ladies. Eve Longbow was a woman both haunting and beautiful, her presence like the hush before a storm. Her long hair, dark as raven wings, flowed in silken waves down her back, sometimes braided with sprigs of herbs or charms of her own making. Her eyes held deep, unyielding fire of survival, a dark onyx, touched with a faint ember-glow when her magic stirred, as though the flames that failed to consume her lived within her gaze. Her skin was pale like shining pearls that contrasted the coldness of her past. Eve's garments spoke of her duality: flowing gowns of forest green and deep black that moved like shadows, their hems embroidered with protective runes and raven feathers that brushed lightly against her steps. Around her throat, she often wore a simple chain bearing a stone of smoky quartz, a talisman of grounding and memory. There was always a sense of mystery about her. The air seemed to change when she entered a room, carrying with it the mingled fragrance of burning sage, wildflowers and lavender. Ravens often circled overhead or perched nearby, their black eyes reflecting her will as though they were both companions and guardians. Eve Longbow was not just a witch. She was the fire that survived, the raven that rose, and the legacy that would forever shape the Brinford bloodline.

Eve Longbow

SENIOR AXEL BRINFORD

My four-times great-grandfather Axel remarried after poor
Eve was taken. He had two children with a lady called Chrissy
Hughes, who looked like a very stern woman in her portrait that
hung in the entrance hall, with her hair always pinned up in a
pristine bun; her two children she had with Axel their names were
Axel junior and Missy. Unfortunately, Eve was arrested and
burned at the stake by the villagers when she was discovered to be
a witch, her wedding ring in the unique shape of a star, which was
made for her by her husband, he had the skills of a blacksmith and
metal worker. To this day, the ring has never been found. The ring
was suspected of being stolen from Eve before she was taken to be
executed. As lavish as Antler Manor sounds, it was so homely with
memories captured in photos hung along the long hallways.

The founding families built these properties over time, and
they put together a village council to help things run smoothly in
Hollow Wood, to help people if any problems arose. There are four
founding families in total, all their descendants still reside in the
properties made for them over the generations. As I mentioned we
have my family the Brinford's under the coat of arms of the white
stag in Antler manor, we have the Shaw's also my family on my
grandmothers side under the coat of arms of the Doe they live in
Gold Wheat Manor, the Wicker family under the Fox they live in
Hunter manor and finally the Hench family under the coat of arms
of the Barn Owl they live in Luna Manor. All stunning coats of
arms to be proud of. The Doe stitched onto a lavender-coloured
flag surrounded by wheat sown in gold thread, the fox, the clever
hunter, stitched in rich red on a black flag with emerald-green
stitched bushes, and finally the Barn owl stitched in silver on a
navy-blue flag perched on the crescent moon. The flags also hang
at the entrance of each property; the founding families adorned

these wild creatures to show what they specialised in to help the village run and thrive.

The stag meant wisdom and leading in helping the village grow and fixing quarrels. The Doe was growing crops and harvest to make sure food was made and distributed fairly. The Fox was the hunter to provide safety and meat to the village, and the Barn Owl was to nurture new life, keeping people healthy and safe in the dark hours. Now you are all caught up on the founding families. Let's get back to my grandfather. As some time went by, Axel and Velina made Antler Manor their home. Axel worked at the local post office, he was known by all the village and loved by all the village.

He could go anywhere, walk into anywhere, and there would be someone who knew him. He told me, "I saved a whole month's salary to buy the perfect engagement ring for your grandmother." He was on his way to the nearest town from the village called Hale to visit Ted's Jewellers to buy the perfect ring. But on the way, he was going to be unknowingly side-tracked, as Axel walked down the country lane happily whistling in the sunshine and feeling the warm breeze blow against his face with blue skies for miles, he noticed something ahead of him, there was a small wonky wooden stall set up on the side of the road under a very large old tree. The villagers named the tree the witch's ash, a large, dominant tree stealing the skyline.

An old lady with long, wiry silver and black hair spilling out from her hood sat behind the stall under the shade of the large stand-alone tree. She sold herbs, trinkets, handmade woven baskets, and birdseed. The old lady called out to Axel as he went to walk past her. He was shocked that she called him by his name to come closer. As my grandfather was on foot to the town, he left the road and cautiously approached the old lady. He said hello to her politely and asked how she knew him. She coughed, wheezing slightly and slammed her hand on the stall, shaking its contents, saying to Axel, "I saw you in my Ravens eye, you must take heed of my words, young man". Suddenly, out of nowhere, like it had plummeted from a portal in the sky, a large jet-black Raven with feathers so shiny and black they almost glistened blue with long flapping wings, squawked and landed on the old lady's shoulder, knocking loose dust that puffed into the air. This spooked Axel; he was ready to bolt. The old lady lifted her hands slowly to reassure him and pleaded with him to stay as she had a message for him. He took a deep breath of warm summer air and slowly approached the stall. He gently held the old lady's outstretched, Boney pale hand that cracked as her fingers wrapped around his wrist, what looked like dust or ash sprinkled from her robes as she slowly poised herself and leaned over the table towards him.

    She looked up at Axel Perring from under her hood, her
complexion Gray and ash in colour with dark eyes that almost
looked black. She had aged, wrinkled skin, matured from the
passing of time. Her high cheekbones framed her face; Axel could
see she had a very regal grace about her. She gently turned Axel's
hand palm up and placed a four-leaf clover that had been preserved

in amber tree sap. Her words to him in a soft voice with a slight crackle were "keep that clover close to you, if you are ever lost in this life or the after, look for the clover and it will keep you safe and bring you back to the right path." She released his hand and leaned her weight on the table. He was polite and closed his grip on the clover and put it in his leather jacket pocket.

Little did he know that that clover was going to be particularly important to him one day. Axel thanked the old lady, and he asked her if she was ok and if she needed help with anything. The fear he first felt was long gone. She nodded her head to him in thanks as she slumped down into her chair. She wished him well in picking an engagement ring. Axel looked up at her in shock. He never mentioned to her why he was going into town. He awkwardly thanked her again and hurried away, but the Raven took flight from the old lady's shoulder, flying overhead, following Axel. The shadow of the bird's large wings flapped above Axel's own shadow.

He entered the hustle and bustle of the small town and made a beeline for the local jewellery shop. He lost sight of the Raven and refocused on the task at hand. Buying the perfect ring. As he entered the shop, hearing the doorbell ring above his head, he started scanning the glass cases searching for the perfect ring to jump out at him. His search got interrupted by Ted Backster, the shop owner. Axel and Ted were old schoolmates, so he was hoping for mates' rates on the chosen ring. Ted, with his short blonde hair always styled and spiked up with gel, is a big man with broad, strong arms, wearing his usual comfy workout clothes. He was a very cheerful man and always ready to help make a sale. He said to Axel that he has some new rings that have just come in, they are top of the range and of the best quality. But Axel's eyes were distracted by an old, standing wooden case with vintage rings displayed inside. There, in a small blue box that matched the colour of my grandmother's eyes, was the perfect ring, sitting on a black velvet cushion. The shining diamond that sat atop the silver band was shaped in a star, which reminded him of the night they met. He told me he always said to Velina before they went to sleep, "Goodnight, my love, I will meet you in the stars," and my grandmother would reply, "See you there," with a cheeky wink.

    This ring was so beautiful, the shining star-shaped diamond that glinted under the down lighter in the cabernet, sat on a pure silver band engraved with leaves and vines, the design representing the stars in the heavens and the foliage of the earth. It almost had some sort of hold on him; he couldn't look away or even listen much to what Ted was telling him. The shopkeeper looked a bit hesitant to sell him the ring; he said it was found in his family home's loft; it had been up there unknowingly for years and years. He was doing some sorting out up in his loft one day when he found it hidden under a broken floorboard, surrounded by a circle of salt. Next to it was a small red leather journal. Ted thought it was too beautiful to be hidden away, never to be seen or worn. Ted had ignored all his scenes not to move or touch the ring, but he took it anyway and put it in the vintage showcase in his shop, not a week before Axel was coming in to buy an engagement ring.

But what Ted had known about the ring was very vague, he said there was a small entry written in his ancestor's journal, John Backster wrote it once belonged to a healer who was found out to being an evil witch, she was taken from her home and burnt at the stake next to a giant oak tree not too far out from the village. His ancestor John took the ring from her and hid it in the loft under the floorboards, surrounding it with salt to stop the power of the witch from coming back and blocking the magic the ring held. In the journal, it was mentioned that her last words of warning to John before she was taken, "My gift will not die with me".

There were very few details written in this small journal entry, but it shed a bit of light on how the ring came to be in Ted's possession. My grandfather didn't believe in supernatural stuff; he called it a load of rubbish. He didn't even know that this was the missing ring his own ancestor had made for his beloved Eve over three hundred years ago. At that time in Axel's youth, he didn't know anything about his ancestors. He lived in the present. He only started researching his ancestors after his parents had passed away, discovering the origin of the ring and Eve when he took full control of the estate.

Even after all Ted had told him, he was adamant he wanted that exact ring, but the shopkeeper tried showing him others that looked similar. He didn't want to turn Axel down; the vintage display case was meant to be only for display and not to be sold. My grandfather had made up his mind against Ted's attempted refusal, and, not wanting to let it go, he begrudgingly sold Axel the ring. As he gave Ted a firm hand shake for the accepted sale, he left the shop with the ring safe and secure in his pocket and the clover the old lady had given him in the other, a chilly wind whipped up around him sending a shiver up his spin, it was in the middle of the summer but he ignored the chill and continued on his path home. Suddenly, the Raven had made itself present again, squawking at him very excitedly and sitting on an old stone post attached to a small stone wall, ruffling its feathers.

He felt amazing about the ring and even got used to the presence of the Raven following him home, hearing the flaps of the large birds' wings above him; he just wanted to get things in motion and propose to Velina, start their married lives together. As he was walking back up the road, getting closer to home, he noticed the wonky old wooden stall had gone along with the old woman. The Raven flew over him and perched on a tree branch, the wood swaying from the impact of the landing. The witch's ash tree rose like a skeletal sentinel against the summer sky, its aged ashen wood with spider-web cracks warped as though lightning had struck it a thousand times but never felled it. The bark split in jagged fissures, oozing a dark resin that clung like coagulated blood. Its branches twisted outward like withered arms, crooked and pale like bones, reaching towards the sky as if to claw at the moon. No leaves dared to grow there, only brittle tufts of shadows that seemed to quiver in the wind, though the air remained still. Ravens often perched among their upper limbs, their eyes glinting like embers, their cries sharp and hollow, as if echoing from beneath the earth. At night, the tree breathed a low groan, a sound that rattled from its hollowed heart, carrying with it the stink of damp soil and old fire. Those who lingered near swore they heard whispers threading through the bark, hissing voices in tongues half-forgotten, coaxing, warning, promising. To stand too close was to feel the tree pulse, like a heartbeat but not your own, as though something within waited to be fed. Axel did not linger; he carried on up the road and entered the pathway that took him down to Antler Manor.

As Axel walked down the drive shaded by the large trees, he could see Velina out front on the green grass playing with Tex, the puppy they got together was a beautiful black Labrador with chocolate brown eyes. He was nearly coming out of the puppy stage but still had big, heavy puppy paws, as he excitedly noticed Axel's presence and bounded over happily barking to greet him. Velina wasn't far behind as she ran up to Axel. She threw herself around him and hugged him tight, kissed him fast and welcomed him home. He mentioned to her that he wanted to host a big party at the manor and invite all the founding families and their friends from the village to celebrate, but he would not tell her what they would be celebrating. My grandfather was terrible at keeping secrets. He said he was bursting at the seams wanting to tell her everything. He had no doubt in his head that she would say no when he asked her. He told her to go shopping for a knockout party dress and get ready for a night she would never forget.

As the week went on, invites were sent out, and decorations were going up everywhere in the main hall where the party was to take place. He wanted star lanterns hung everywhere, like the night they found each other. The day of the party had arrived, as he was walking around talking and joking with the staff, the family started flooding in from Gold Wheat Manor to greet Axel and his parents, Hilary and Axel senior.

They were all in on the secret and knew what was coming. You could feel the excitement and anticipation in the air. As everyone was shown to their rooms to start getting ready for tonight, Velina's sister, my Aunty Pearl, burst into Velina's dressing room with champagne and two glasses in her hands. She was already a little tipsy and so happy to see her. But she froze and stepped back from diving on Velina to give her a big hug; she was stunned by how beautiful and grown-up her little sister was. She looked stunning and so elegant in her dress for the party. It was a long silver fish tale gown with lavender lace that draped over the satin silver fabric, her long satin silver gloves that reached her elbows had beaded antlers sewn over the tops of the gloves, her long light blonde hair had gems entwined into the curls.

Aunty Pearl, feeling so much pride and joy for her little sister, started to weep happy tears; she placed the champagne and glasses on a side table. The maids who were helping Velina get ready left the dressing room to give them some privacy to catch up before all the mingling began. The party that was only a few hours away from beginning sent a flurry of excited butterflies fluttering in their stomachs. They both stepped apart to admire each other's dresses they had chosen for the coming celebration. Pearl really wanted to tell her the big secret, but she kept her cool and kept the secret to herself. Pearl was wearing the Doe family colours, a beautiful lavender silk dress that was figure-hugging and simple with no embellishments and pearl white kitten heels. Her hair was a darker shade of blonde than Velina's, it was pinned up with a few soft curls falling by her ears, her make-up was simple with a soft blush and a slight rose tint to her lips. The maids returned, they both had their final checks that their dresses, makeup and hair were perfect.

Velina shaw

PEARL SHAW

After having a little pause, they held hands to turn and look in the mirror for a second, they both took a deep breath before they both poured themselves and the maids a glass of champagne to cheer the night ahead. Breaking the chatter in the room, there was a knock at her dressing room door, one of the maids hastened over to answer the door to whoever was knocking. Behind the door was Julie, who came running in with an excited squeal to give Velina and Pearl a hug as she hadn't seen either of them for a while.

She joined in having a glass of Champagne with them, finding another glass from the cabinet. Julie was so glad she had made it in time, as her train route had an issue; she was transferred onto a bus that would take her longer to get back to Antler Manor. Julie was such a tiny young lady with long brown straight hair that was always so shiny with her doe hazel eyes and long winged eyelashes, she looked so glamorous in her long, short-sleeved dress that was covered in silver sequins, she was literally a walking disco ball. Julie hugged them both again before taking her leave to join the party in the main hall, letting Axel know that she had made it in time for the proposal.

Before Velina and Pearl made their way to the top of the staircase to be introduced to the party, they thanked all the maids for helping them get ready as they left the peace and quiet of the dressing room to make their way to the main hall. Everyone was now here, talking, laughing, and dancing to the music. Axel was mingling and waiting for Velina to make her grand entrance. With their heels clicking and echoing down the long hallways, hearing the rustling of the fabric brush across the floors, they remained hand in hand until they saw Gregary, the master of ceremonies, waiting poised for them both so he could introduce them into the hall. He bowed his head at Pearl and Velina and said, "Let me know when you are both ready."

Chapter Three

A PROPOSAL UNDER THE STARS

"Love under starlight is the oldest kind of magic; it binds beyond blood, beyond death"
-E.L

Velina and Pearl were the last two to attend the party as Axel wanted everyone present before her entrance was made. Velina was very thankful to have Pearl by her side, as for some reason she felt nervous about tonight, but also excited as if something tremendous was going to happen. They both stood silent side by side, holding hands in the dimly lit, quiet hallway, listening to the muffled merriment and music happening beyond the large, closed wooden door. Velina looked to the master of the ceremony standing with such poise in his Navy blue buttoned-up jacket with the white stag surrounded by gold flowers stitched on the breast, his pearl white gloved hand rested on the door handle, ready to open. Velina gently nodded to him to introduce her and Pearl's arrival, the large gold ornate door handle clicked down as the heavy wooden door was slowly pulled open, the light and noise flooded into the hallway with impressive brightness and volume. The music continued but was hushed so people could hear the master of the ceremony announce them into the party. Pearl was to enter first, she faced Velina, took both her hands and squeezed them gently to give her confidence and comfort, "You look beautiful," she released her hands and turned towards the light of the main hall and descended the grand stair case, Axel was waiting at the bottom as he took Pearl's hand he placed a gentle kiss atop it and lead her to her husband Jack. Axel took his place back at the base of the stairs and straightened up his bow tie. He took a deep breath, his eyes were fixed on the top of the stairs, waiting for Velina to appear. When Velina heard her name announced, she took a deep breath and straightened herself up, smoothed her gown and confidently entered the hall, she paused at the top of the grand staircase, her gloved hand resting lightly on the polished banister as the scene below unfolded in a shimmer of gold and crystal. The great hall glowed with glittering light from chandeliers strung high above, their brilliance dancing across polished buffed floors. Velina could smell the enticing blend of perfume, wine and candle smoke. For a moment, Velina simply stood there, bathed in the glow, heart fluttering before she began her graceful descent.

She could see so many familiar faces, her family from Gold Wheat Manor, friends from the village and her friends she worked with in the big city, as her eyes scanned the room, seeing everyone smiling and looking up at her in awe. She glanced to the bottom of the stairs and locked eyes with Axel, who looked so smart and handsome in his navy-blue tux with gold flowers on the cuffs.

He had the cheesiest, biggest smile on his face. Velina started
to descend the grand staircase slowly and gracefully with a smile

matching Axel's, trying not to cry tears of joy to see how everyone looked so beautiful, all dressed in their best finery. The music from the live band, the smells of the delicious food filled her senses. When she reached Axel, he took her hand, he bowed and gently kissed the top of her gloved hand, with a cheeky wink, he glanced up at her and said," Will you dance with me in the stars again?" Velina looked overjoyed as Axel led her through the crowd of the party to the centre of the dance floor. The grand dance hall of Antler Manor stretched wide and resplendent, a chamber built for both spectacle and whispers. Towering glass windows lined the far wall, their arched panes gazing out over the rolling grounds and gardens beyond. By day, sunlight spilled through them in radiant sheets, scattering across the room in shards of brilliance. By night, the glass turned black and reflective, mirroring the glow of firelight and the stars outside, as if the heavens themselves had crept in to dance. From the main entrance, a sweeping staircase curved down into the hall, its polished banister gleaming like dark honeyed wood, every step inviting with stately grace. Guests descending felt as though they entered not just a room, but a stage, every movement, every glance, magnified beneath the watchful light. Lining the walls, vast gilded mirrors captured and multiplied the shimmer of the chandelier that hung from above. The chandelier itself was an antique marvel: a branching constellation of crystal and iron, heavy with history, its candles flickering like captured stars. Light cascaded down and reflected through the mirrors until the hall seemed an endless gallery of brightness. The floor was the crown of the room, polished to a glass-like sheen, flecked with veins of gold that caught the light and sparkled with every step. At its centre lay the symbol of the house, the white stag etched in marble and inlaid with pearl, its antlers spread wide in noble grace. To dance across it was to tread upon the very heart of

Antler Manor, the spirit of the family watching silently. Though magnificent, there lingered a hush to the place when empty. The echoes of past laughter and music clung to the walls, the stag in the floor seemed to guard those memories as if the hall itself knew more secrets than it dared to reveal.

Velina followed Axel into the centre of the grand dance hall, her gloved hand resting gently on his arm. The room seemed still, hushed, as though even the mirrors and chandelier held their breath. She tilted her head, curiosity glimmering in her eyes, but Axel only smiled that cheeky, knowing smile of his. With a subtle nod of his head, Axel gave the signal to the staff. From high above, the ceiling began to stir. Slowly, delicately, star-shaped lanterns descended, drifting down on wire that seemed invisible like constellations falling from the heavens. One by one, their warm golden glow blossomed, casting the hall into a dreamlike light. Shadows swayed across the mirrors, the gold-flecked floor caught every flicker, until it seemed as if Velina and Axel were standing inside a galaxy spun just for them. Velina's lips parted, her breath catching at the sight, but before she could speak, Axel took her other hand and drew her close. Their song began to play soft, familiar, and achingly sweet. He placed his hand at the small of her back, and she leaned into him, her blue eyes shimmering with the lantern light. As they swayed together, the stars circled them, hanging low enough that their edges brushed against Velina's hair, sending golden sparks dancing across her. Axel lowered his forehead to her, the world shrinking to nothing but their rhythm, their laughter, the glow of their private universe. "You've always been my light," Axel whispered, his voice low and steady. Velina's smile trembled, her heart racing in perfect time with his. Together, they spun beneath the falling stars, their love written in every step.

When the song was coming to an end, Axel slowed the dance to a stop and smiled at Velina with his kind green eyes, lit up with the reflection of the stars. He put his hand in his breast pocket and presented a small blue box that matched the colour of her eyes.

Velina suddenly knew what was happening, and an excited panic took over her. Axel knelt on one knee and opened the box, revealing the glistening diamond ring that had now been returned to where it was made all those years ago. It was to have its moment of glory once more. Axel took a deep breath, smiled and said, "I'm not a man of many words, but I do believe action shows love above empty promises of it. I promised I would love you for eternity, so I will put that into action. I will not say till death do us part because I will always find your beautiful soul and love you not only in this life, but I will always find you in other lives we have. I will keep that promise in my actions to do so. Velina Shaw, the love of my life will you marry me?" Velina could not stop her tears. She knelt with Axel and said in the happiest confident voice she could muster, "I do, I do, I do". She wrapped her arms around him and hugged him so tight that she knocked the air out of Axel. He excitedly took Velina's hand, removed her glove and placed the ring on her finger, which was the perfect fit. They both stood together to a roaring applause as everyone faded back into the room, and everyone congratulated the newly engaged couple. The music played through the night, and everyone was dancing, singing and celebrating together, even Tex, in his little navy-blue bow tie, was barking and excitedly wagging his tail, getting all the attention from the guests mingling through the crowd, pinching left over food from people's plates when they were not looking. As the night went on into the early hours of dawn, people started filtering out to go home and congratulating Axel and Velina as they left, it was time to end the party and get some sleep. The family and friends who remained after everyone left to go home to the village returned to their rooms to relax and get changed into their comfy's to reflect on the amazing night they had.

The last notes of music had long faded from the grand hall, leaving only echoes and the faint shimmer of candlelight clinging to the chandeliers. Guests had drifted away into the night, laughter and farewells carried out through the manor doors until silence settled over Antler Manor once more. Yet for Axel, the night was not over. Velina's hand rested in his, her eyes still shining from the lantern-lit dance hall that had bound their hearts closer than ever. Newly engaged, she was radiant, her smile soft, her gaze full of trust and wonder. Axel squeezed her hand gently, that mischievous spark in his green eyes returning as he whispered, "There's one more surprise for you, my dear". When the great hall doors opened, Velina gasped softly. A trail of lanterns lit the path ahead, their golden glow swaying gently in the cool night breeze. At their feet, rose petals, dark red, velvety and lush marked the way forward. Axel led her down the lantern-lit trail, the world around them hushed, as though even the earth had stopped turning. The path ended in a small clearing, where a soft blanket had been laid out beneath the open sky. Around its edges bloomed long-stemmed red roses, her favourite, their fragrance rising in the dawn air like a secret blessing. Upon the blanket, a chilled bottle of champagne rested beside two crystal glasses and a bowl of ripe strawberries glistening with dew. They sat crossed legged together, poured themselves a glass of champagne and clinked their glasses. The echo of crystal reverberated into the coming dawn, the strawberries sweet against the taste of the champagne's bubbles, their laughter light and unguarded in the quiet of the approaching dawn. Above them, the stars began to fade, and the horizon glowed faintly with the blush of the sun. Axel leaned close, his cheek brushing hers as he murmured, "I wanted our first sunrise as an engaged couple to be ours alone." Velina nestled into him, her heart beating in time with his. Together, they watched as the first rays of sunlight broke across the sky, gilding the roses, the lanterns, the love they now carried into forever. As the light grew, so too did destiny. Though they could not yet know that in these tender, golden hours of morning, my mother was conceived, weaving another thread into the Brinford/ Shaw legacy.

As some time went by and they started to plan the wedding together, Pearl more or less lived at Antler Manor to help her little sister plan and organise the big day. They would visit the local florist to see all the options for the bridal bouquets to be made. She decided she wanted to blend the colours of her house and the new family she was marrying into. Velina and Pearl took a stroll through the village after placing the order for the flowers she had chosen. On their way to speak to the local vicar, she was such a fun character; she had short brown hair with warm golden-brown eyes. For a small lady, she could out-drink a full-grown man under the table.

She had a kind listening ear for anyone seeking solace in her church. She lived in the cottage on the grounds of the church but was always seen mingling in the village and taking part in the events. The church of Hollow Wood Village stood as the oldest sentinel of the settlement, its stone walls weathered by centuries yet unbroken, as though time itself had chosen to pass by. Built by the first settlers, a monument to survival and devotion. Though its structure had been carefully reinforced over the years to ensure safety, most of its bones remained original, the same stone laid by hands long turned to dust. Inside, the air carried a cool, ancient hush, tinged faintly with the scent of old wood and wax. Towering arches rose overhead, their curved spans etched with intricate carvings of twisting vines, celestial symbols, creatures both sacred and strange, each a testament to the artistry and hidden beliefs of its builders. The arches drew the eye upward, toward a ceiling that seemed impossibly high, as though lifting the spirit closer to the skies. Rows of polished wooden pews filled the nave, their surfaces worn smooth by countless generations of villagers who had knelt, prayed, or wept there. But it was the stained-glass windows that gave the church its soul. Tall and radiant, they filtered the light into pools of shifting colour, washing the stone and pews in crimson, sapphire and gold. In the morning, the windows poured fire and glory into the chamber, while at dusk, they cloaked it in somber twilight hues. When the sun struck just right, the beams of coloured light wove themselves into a living tapestry across the floor, turning the old church into a place not of earth but of the other world. To step inside was to be humbled by age, by beauty and by something unseen yet ever present. The church did not merely hold worship; it held secrets, its stones heavy with prayers, fears and unspoken promises of Hollow Wood's first people.

The gravestones and crypts, ancient and new, were greatly looked after with care by the grounds' night men, Jerry and his son Carlton. They would always plant wildflowers around the grounds of the church. You could hear the bees hard at work collecting the nectar, the hare's tall ears bounding through the flowers and foliage, at night, the family of hedgehogs foraging and snorting through the grass looking for the food that Carlton always left out for them to eat. In a place for the dead, it had so much life, as you walked around seeing and hearing the sights and sounds from the wildlife that called that place their home. As Velina and Pearl approached the church doors to enter, they were startled as the doors flung open right before they reached out for the door handle. It was Shelly setting up the church for the day and getting everything ready for the kids' club that was to take place later that day. All three of them were a bit startled but soon laughed as they warmly greeted each other. Shelly invited them both into the church. The rays of colour from the sun shining through the stained-glass windows, light that shone through the Church at that time of morning, almost looked like magic as the dust kicked up by the doors being flung open looked like glitter in the rays of the light that shone down over the pews.

They followed behind Shelly as she led them to her office space through an old door at the back of the church, concealed by a heavy maroon velvet curtain, to discuss dates and availability of booking the church for the wedding to take place. Shelly said her and Axel would have to come up together at some point to finalise some paperwork, but the date was booked. It was to be an early autumn wedding when the leaves on the trees turn orange and red, when the cool air and dark nights start to loom. Velina wanted the legal part of her wedding to take place in the church, but for the actual ceremony, her free spirit longed for her actual wedding to take place in the woods just beyond the church. There's a clearing where she played as a child with her sister; it was her happiest place to be. Nothing would be more perfect than to have her wedding ceremony and after wedding celebration in that place. Just like the church, the rays that shine through the holes in the tree canopy look magical with the forest surrounding you and the smell of nature, and the noise from the animals going about their daily life. As they sat in the comfy red high back padded chairs opposite Shelly at her desk, drinking tea and eating lemon biscuits, having a giggle together, Velina suddenly started feeling hot and queasy, she asked Shelly where the bathroom was. Shelly hastily pointed to another maroon velvet heavy curtain behind them. Velina launched up, ripped the curtain to one side, burst through the door and was immediately sick. Pearl and Shelly stood together and went to Velina's aid. Pearl asked if she was sick or feeling unwell. The strange thing was that Velina felt fine after she was sick; she felt fine that whole morning until that point. She slowly walked out of the bathroom, looking a bit pale. Shelly was there waiting with a glass of water for her. Pearl jokingly said, "You're not pregnant, are you?" with a giggle after her quip. Velina's giggle in response trailed off to a look of questioning on her face as she held her stomach and looked at Pearl and Shelly. In a quiet, calm voice, she said, "What if?"

In a lost haze between panic and calm, she did the maths in her head from now, if she was pregnant, to autumn when the wedding was to take place, she would be 3 months pregnant. Having a baby out of wedlock, even though she was engaged to be married, was something her family did not tolerate, so she pleaded with the vicar and her sister to "please don't tell a soul about this until I can confirm if I'm pregnant or not." Shelly walked over to Velina, who was hyperventilating a bit by this point, already feeling her parents' anger coming down on her. Shelly placed her hands on her shoulders. She calmly but forcefully looked her in the eyes and said, "Nothing that has been spoken in this room today will leave these four walls, under God's eyes, I will not speak of this potential little miracle until you say I can". Shelly sat Velina down and told her to calm herself, take some deep breaths to steady herself from having a panic attack. Pearl sat in the chair next to her and placed her hand on her knee in comfort, "I will say nothing to mum and dad about this. If you are pregnant, this is your news to tell when you are ready. Oh my gosh, I could be an aunty," In an excited squeak. They sat together for a little time, chatting about the wedding to keep Velina's mind distracted from the little life that was potentially growing inside her. After finishing up at the church with Shelly, Velina and Pearl took a slow walk through the village, making a beeline for the village doctors' surgery to get herself tested. Velina had a knot in her stomach; she couldn't decide if it was excitement or fear at the prospect of becoming a mother. They both walked through the old wooden door that was left open to let the fresh summer air into the waiting room, the smell of surgical cleaners filling their senses. The surgery was small but very well-equipped in the reception room with light blue walls and a tall window at the back of the room overlooking the fields. Velina approached the sliding door at reception and knocked to get the attention of the receptionist.

Chapter Four

THE LONG WAIT

"The womb is a cradle of fate, where new magic stirs before it has a name. Even before the first heartbeat, the legacy had already begun."

- E.L

(KNOCK, KNOCK, KNOCK) On the sliding door, you could see a haze of movement behind the cloudy glass that had the coat of arms of the owl perched on the crescent moon etched into the clouded glass. A figure approached the door, took a seat and whipped the sliding door open to an anxious Velina and Pearl. It was Enid Hench, the head of the house at Lunar Manor, part of a founding family. She is a very glamorous young lady with short, bleach blonde curly hair and her trademark red glasses that had red beading attached to them, so they hung around her neck. The Night Owl surgery has been run by the Hench's since the beginning of the village's infancy. Back in the day, Eve Longbow would practice her medicine there and provide healing herbs to the surgery that she grew in her greenhouse before she was taken and burned at the stake. The new surgery had been rebuilt over the original foundations and pre-existing structure, as it started to become unsafe. They managed to keep the original bricks and stones; they were incorporated into the new building. Enid shuffled some paperwork away and directed her focus to Velina and Pearl. She softly asked how she could help them and which one of them needed the help. Velina took a step closer to Enid and asked in a hushed voice if she could speak to a nurse or a doctor in private, as she did not want the locals sitting in the waiting room to pick up on why she was there. Velina faked a cough and gave Enid an intense stare in the hopes she would pick up the signal to keep things discreet. Enid picked up on how uncomfortable Velina looked and directed her to come through the staff room door to the right of them to have a word with her brother, Frank Hench, who is the head doctor at the surgery. Enid closed the sliding door and walked around to join Velina and Pearl in the staff room. She asked them to take a seat on the sofa while she went to find Dr Frank.

Enid left Velina and Pearl sitting in the staff room as she walked down a small length of hallway attached to the room with old wooden polished floors that gently creaked in some places, small white framed windows either side of the hall, one side looking into the Doctors small central court yard filled with potted flowers and cushioned benches placed around a small water fountain, the other side overlooking the fields, white net curtains hung up patterned with summer flowers. Enid approached the head surgeon's door at the end of the small hallway and gently knocked, turned the old brass doorknob in the shape of an owl, with a small click and creek, and she slowly pushed the door open to find Frank sitting at his desk in his office, tall oak wooden bookshelves surrounded the room, filled with large rustic medical books. One single window looking into the courtyard, next to the window, an old wooden door with large iron hinges covered by a dark green heavy velvet curtain, a warm lite desk lamp that illuminated a sea of paperwork stored in metal trays across the large oak desk with owls and trees carved into the wood. Frank removed his round spectacles and peered up at Enid with a warm smile, "Hello, sister, what can I do for you?" Leila, a beautiful young barn owl, Franks' desk companion during the day, woken from a slumber, opened her round, dark, blinking eyes as she turned her head to face Enid. She rustled her feathers and stretched her light brown golden wings. Frank calmed her by stroking the soft white feathers under her beak. She gently nibbled his fingers, looked over to the door at Enid with a slight look of annoyance from being woken, then flew over to rest in her perch box next to the window to go back to sleep. Frank arose from his tall back desk chair, his back cracking as he straightened up and stretched out his limbs from leaning over his desk, lost in medical paperwork. Enid informed him that Miss Velina Shaw was in the staff room and needed to talk to him about something, but she hadn't disclosed it yet.

Frank informed Enid to let Miss Shaw know that he would be with her shortly as he removed his casual knitted cardigan to put on his doctor's long white coat and grabbed his medical bag. Enid closed the door behind her and rejoined Velina and Pearl in the staffroom. She offered them a drink. Distant creaking came from the hallway by heavy footsteps as Frank walked into the staffroom with a smile on his face. He cheerfully greeted them, saying, "Hello, ladies, I hear you wanted to see me. What can I help you with?" Frank came over and sat on the sofa next to Velina. He placed his medical bag on the floor, and he looked up, waiting for either Velina or Pearl to speak. Velina smiled and shook Frank's hand, "It's me who needs to talk to you. I have a sensitive matter I need help with, but I want to keep it as private as possible. Thank you for meeting me away from the people in the waiting room." Frank reassured her and placed a kind hand on her shoulder, "Whatever you need help with will remain private, I promise." Velina came straight out with it and asked Frank for a pregnancy test, as there had been signs. He smiled at her and removed his hand from Velina's shoulder, opened his medical bag and handed her a small plastic pot. He informed her to go to the bathroom to provide a urine sample. He said he can test it to see if she is really with child, the results will be given in two weeks. Velina took the pot and proceeded to the bathroom. Pearl chatted with Frank whilst they waited. Enid returned to reception to get back to what she was doing before Velina and Pearl came in. A few moments later, Velina reappeared and gave the pot back to the doctor. He informed her he will be in touch in the next two weeks to give her the results. Two weeks to Velina felt like a lifetime away, but she accepted Frank's words and kindly thanked him as he showed them to the door and wished them a joyful day, "try not to stress too much over the next two weeks, as it will go quicker than you think".

Velina and Pearl walked home to Gold Wheat Manor to spend the rest of the day there, having a laugh, listening to their favourite music and making small clay pots in the cabin they share in the grounds of Gold Wheat Manor. They provide small decorative pots to the local shops with their coat of arms stamped on the bottom, once they have been painted and decorated, they are distributed to a local shop in the village to be sold to tourists when they come through. Doing a hobby like that helped Velina keep her mind occupied by the incoming news about her results. At the back of the cabin-like structure, there were patio doors that looked out over the farm and fields where the horses grazed in the green grass. Pearl took the pin off the record they were playing so she didn't miss any of her favourite songs and left Velina alone in silence as Pearl took a set of made pots to the kiln. Out of nowhere, a loud peck sound cracked on a glass panel of the patio door that startled Velina. She flung her head around to see a large jet-black raven pecking and flapping at the glass, excitedly squawking. Velina approached the patio door and tried to shoo the raven away, but it just settled on the floor. The bird looked up at her as if it had something to say. She approached the patio door, knelt on the floor and tapped on the glass. The raven rustled its shining black feathers, hopped up to the glass and mimicked the taps back to Velina. Velina chuckled, stood and turned away to call for Pearl to come see this cool tapping raven, but when she turned back around, the raven was no longer there, but in its place was an old woman standing right up at the glass. Velina froze as her gaze lifted towards her, her breath hitching when she saw the figure silhouetted against the glass. Draped in a long black robe that swallowed her shape, her face hidden in shadow. One thin, boney-pale hand was pressed flat against the glass, leaving a faint print of heat that seemed to generate from her palm. The pane trembled with the weight of her silence, and Velina's chest constricted, an icy dread crawling up her spine.

 The old woman's head remained bowed with long white and black hair falling from her hood, ash sprinkled from her robes as the breeze whipped around her, coming off the fields. Velina, finally finding her voice "Pearl…" she whispered at first, then louder, more frantic, "Pearl, come back in here now." she yelled and backed away from the door Then, with a sudden, unnatural snap, the old lady's neck cracked when she whipped her head up. They locked eyes for a moment. Her eyes were not human but twin orbs of polished onyx. They gleamed like wet stones, reflecting the faintest light while swallowing it whole, shifting as if something moved deep within their depths. For an instant Velina swore she saw her own reflection vanish inside them, consumed. Velina turned her head away from the ghost like woman to yell for Pearl, but when she looked back at the door, the old woman had disappeared; all that remained was a cloud of ash floating in the air and a strange Symbol smudged onto the glass left where the old lady's Boney pale hand was once pressed.

Pearl came rushing into the room, which felt like an eternity for Velina as she was waiting for her to come back when she yelled. It was as if time stood still and sped up. She was shaking and looked so pale as she grabbed Pearl tight, she started crying with fear, she pointed at the door and said she saw some sort of ghostly figure there, a tapping raven, she was speed talking. Pearl hugged her tight and glanced over Velina's shoulder to see the strange symbol smudged onto the glass. Pearl reassured Velina, sat her down on the stall and slowly approached the patio door to inspect it to see if this ghostly figure had gone. The ash that was floating in the air had been blown away by the breeze but left behind in the ghostly figure's wake was a single black raven feather stuck into the wood of the porch outside the patio door.

Pearl inspected the symbol, which was in the shape of what looked like a butterfly with a circle drawn around it. Pearl grabbed a cloth from her workbench, opened the patio door, and wiped the ash residue away, but the symbol had been burnt into the glass. Pearl's eyes frantically scanned around the fields, but there was no one in sight, only the horses. Pearl walked back inside, grabbed Velina, and both of them hastily left the cabin to return to the main house to compute what the hell they had just witnessed. As the sun started to descend behind the trees and darkness fell over Gold Wheat Manor, the sky started to glitter with stars. Velina decided to stay at her ancestral home that night with her sister, they sat in the kitchen together, the heart of the house where the family would come together to cook, chat and have a good laugh, it had large open windows that overlooked the fields they work on with the stables in view and the two resident donkeys peach and fuzz at the base of the garden singing to them in the sound of a yell when they were hungry. In the middle of the kitchen, there's a large marble top island surrounded by seating stools with a large blue clay fruit bowl in the middle that was always filled with bright, ripe fruit. The kitchen had a high open ceiling with large beams entwined with dry barley wheat that reached from one end of the kitchen to the other. With a hot cup of tea and chocolate biscuits to dunk, they tried to understand what had happened in the cabin, the shape of the symbol burnt into their minds as well as the glass panel.

After that night passed and a little time had gone by since the incident at her home. Velina was feeling so tense as Axel still did not know about the news Velina was so desperate to hear from Dr Frank. As the following day came, she was expecting the call from the surgery to hear the news, informing her whether she was pregnant or not. As she sat in the snug room looking out the window to a stormy, rainy day, Axel was at work, and his parents were visiting friends in the big city. Still not being able to get that symbol out of her mind, she just wanted to understand what it meant. So, to keep her mind occupied, she visited Antler Manor's famous library. The library of Antler Manor was less a room and more a sanctuary, a place where time itself seemed to hesitate at the threshold. The ceiling stretched high above, a mural unfurling across its breadth: painted forests dense with emerald canopies, delicate willows trailing their silver-green fingers, emerging proudly from the shadows of painted trees, a great white stag peered out. Its eyes followed the room with quiet majesty, as if it held the spirits of the Brinford line who guarded every story kept within those walls. From floor to ceiling, towering bookshelves encased the chamber like the walls of a castle. Each shelf was heavy with tomes and journals, their spines rich with gilt lettering and worn leather, the smell of parchment and ink perfuming the air. Some volumes held stories of adventures and wonder, while others cradled the whispered words of ancestors handwritten journals inked by candlelight, waiting for future generations to discover their secrets. A ladder to lift a reader toward treasures hidden high above. At the heart of the room, a grand fireplace roared, its mantle carved with oak leaves and curling vines. The fire crackled with a gentle, golden warmth, its light spilling across the floor and chasing shadows into corners. Before the fireplace stood a large, comfy sofa, plush and inviting, deep enough for two to curl up together or for one to stretch out with a book in hand. A woven rug sprawled before the hearth, its pattern reminiscent of tangled roots and forest paths. Tall windows, their frames arched like cathedral glass, overlooked the sprawling grounds of Antler Manor. By day, sunlight streamed in, casting golden bars across the shelves; by night, the windows opened the room to the hush of moonlight and the watchful glitter of stars. Often, the reflection of the fire met the view of the gardens, making it seem as though the manor itself was wrapped in both flame and starlight. The library was a place of enchantment, a hall of memory and imagination where every corner promised discovery, every page seemed to breathe with a life of its own.

The librarian Dart, an extremely high-energy thin man who's more comfortable being lost in the pages of an enjoyable book than out and about in public. Velina entered the library, and he nervously but cheerfully greeted her. Dart, who stuttered over his words, sometimes trying to talk faster than his brain could keep up with, asked Velina if she needed any help looking for a book. Velina smiled, thanked Dart and asked him if there was anything in the library about symbols and their meaning. Velina took a seat on the comfy, long, cushioned sofa by the large open fire that had been lit as the day was damp and chilly. Dart placed the books on the coffee table in front of her that he found on symbols. Velina grabbed a book from the pile, got comfy in the corner of the sofa and started to read. She scanned through the pages but had no luck;

they were all about Morse code and code breaking. It was not the sort of symbols she was hoping to see. She thanked Dart as he took the books back to return them to the shelf. Velina left the library and went on a wander around the manor. She found herself in the greenhouse listening to the rain pattering on the glass roof, admiring all the various kinds of flowers, herbs and the sweet smell of her tomatoes growing on their vines. Velina stumbled across Eve Longbow's wooden gardening toolbox with her initials carved into the wood. Next to her initials was a small, strange-looking symbol of a seven-pointed star.

Velina rushed to the floor to get a closer look at the symbol. She ran her fingers over the shape in wonder and confusion as to what it meant; it had the same style as the one that was burnt into the patio doors' glass at the cabin. She looked over her shoulder to see if anyone was around. When she was happy, she felt alone. She started to rummage through Eve's gardening box. Once it was emptied, she noticed some chipping in the corner of the box as if something had been picking at it, so Velina picked at the area, and the bottom of the box lifted away. Her hand was shaking as she gently lifted the bottom of the box out to reveal a hidden compartment that had a very dusty old leather book. On the cover of the book was another symbol on the top, taking up the whole front cover. There were three circles, the top circle being the biggest, the middle being a bit smaller, and the bottom circle being the smallest, with a line straight down the middle. Velina could not believe what she had discovered. She gently removed the heavy book from the hidden compartment, replaced the bottom of the box and put the tools back roughly where they were found. She hurried out of the greenhouse with the book in hand. Velina returned to the snug room. The rain was pouring now, so she placed the book on the coffee table, lit a fire in the fireplace, took a seat and gently opened the book to see that the first page was empty. She started flipping through the pages, but the whole book had nothing in it. She sighed and closed the book with disappointment. She threw it on the coffee table and pushed it away as she slumped down on the sofa. She looked up to see the spine of the book facing her and noticed one more symbol, which seemed to be glowing through the thick layer of dust. She sat back up abruptly and picked the book up again, examining the spine. She gently brushed the dust away to reveal another symbol, which was glowing a soft blue. The glowing symbol had a horizontal line with a half circle underneath it with an arrow pointing down; it almost resembled an upside-down sunset beneath the horizon line of the ocean. Velina felt a strange feeling come over her, like she was no longer alone in the room. She closed her eyes, took a deep breath and brushed her finger up over the symbol. Something within her soul made her say, "reveal my words in the light of sunrise."

A gush of cool air that came from nowhere made Velina feel a power she had never felt before; her engagement ring seemed to vibrate with energy. She opened her eyes and looked down at the spin of the book; the symbol had changed. It was now glowing a warm gold; the half circle was now sitting on top of the horizontal line with the arrow pointing up. She opened the book with haste that was once empty, now filled with pictures of herbs, rituals and daily notes written by the hand of Eve Longbow herself. Velina scanned the pages until she came across a page with so many symbols and written underneath each one was its meaning. She hoped the one she was looking for was in there. Then, at the bottom of the page, she could not believe it, there it was, the shape of the butterfly with a circle drawn around it; the meaning of the symbol was for protection. "The ghostly figure was sending me the symbol for protection. She wasn't there to hurt but to protect." She glanced down at the page again, and two symbols started glowing a light pink. One was a human stick figure with a round circle for the stomach, and the other was an egg shape with a small circle sitting inside the egg; both meanings were the mother and fertility. Right then and there, Velina knew she was going to be a mother. She felt overjoyed, she placed a loving protective hand on her stomach and said, "I can't wait to meet you, my baby girl Orenda". The phone rang next to her which made her jump, in pure panic she slammed the booked shut swiped her finger down the symbol on the spin of the book and she said "with the darkness of night hide my written thoughts" she still felt confused how she knew what to say, she put the book in the drawer of the coffee table and composed herself to pick up the phone. As she predicted, it was Doctor Frank with her results. He said with joy and congratulations to Velina after what must have felt like an exceedingly long wait, your results are that you are pregnant.

Chapter Five

BREAKING THE NEWS

"She braced for their disappointment, but not once did she doubt the life growing inside her. She thought they would see disgrace. She felt the miracle. She stood in front of them unafraid."

— E.L

Axel chose the wrong day to walk home when the heavens opened it had been a long day at work at the post office, it was his turn to take Troy the shire horse to town with peoples parcels and letters in the large wooden cart with the hard seat that made his bum and legs go numb, him and Troy journeyed to Hale post and delivery Depop to drop everything off before returning home in the rain, poor Troy was not impressed with his long wet main that stuck to his large neck. After drying off Troy and giving him an extra carrot for braving the rain, Axel trudged home as fast as he could. Seeing the dry safety of home, he ran into the house out of the rain, clutching his jacket close to him. He burst through the door but was startled to find Velina standing there staring at him. She looked different to him as she stared at Axel in silence. He went to give her a kiss, not getting too close as he was dripping wet from the rain, he asked if she was ok. She looked up at him and said, "I have something to tell you," In a very unsure voice. Axel straightened up and became concerned," You are scaring me, love. What do you want to tell me? Are you ok?" He placed both of his hands on her shoulders to comfort her. She looked up into his eyes and said two words that would change their lives forever: "I'm pregnant." Axel's face went pale with water droplets falling down his cheeks. Unblinking, he said, "Come again." Velina repeated herself slowly, "I.... am.... pregnant" as if she was talking to a child. Axel's eye began to become as wet as his rain-soaked body, a smile flew across his face, in a burst of excitement he wrapped his arms around Velina laughing and shouting "IM GOING TO BE A DAD AND YOU ARE GOING TO BE A MUM AND TEX IS GOING TO BE A BROTHER" he was overjoyed and all Velina's worries just washed away like the rain falling into a flowing brook. He immediately said to Velina," Go pick a room, any room in the manor, for our little miracle to thrive, I will fill it with everything you and our little one would need. You name it, bottles, nappies, a crib, toys", he was speed talking and getting so excited, Velina laughed and kissed him mid-sentence "will you help me pick the room for our little girl." Axel looked confused. "How do you know it's a girl?" Velina placed her hand on Axel's heart. She gently took his hand and placed it on her stomach. "I just know, say hello to Orenda."

Once the news was broken, Axel wanted to tell everyone he knew, but there were still Velina's parents, whom she was feeling a bit nervous about telling. Axel said he would be at her side when they told them just in case things went south. Axel said, "Besides, we are pretty much married already," in a joking voice. Velina smiled and put it to the back of her mind for now. She was content with just the two of them knowing for now, "We will cross that bridge when we get to it, but for now, it's just you and me who know. Let's go pick a room." Axel linked Velina's arm into his and led her up the stairs to find the perfect room to start brainstorming designs and colours for when baby Orenda arrived. Axel did look a bit confused as to how Velina came up with such an unusual name, but she was adamant that's what she was to be called. "I don't know why it just feels right for her." They wandered the hallways, entering and leaving room by room, until they saw the perfect one. It was the last room at the end of the hallway. The hallway was lit by a large window at the end, letting the sun flood in through the panes of old, slightly rippled glass. To the right of the window was an old wooden door with a large decorative brass handle that clunked when you turned it. This was a room Axel had completely forgotten about. It was filled with dust and old furniture covered in large white blankets; the room was dark, starving the space of light as the wooden shutters had been closed for the longest time. Velina said she had such a good feeling in this room, she flung open all the dusty shutters to let the light illuminate the hidden beauty of the room. The panoramic views were stunning from this angle of the house; you could see the grounds where the ravens were nesting in the trees and the lush green grass. Axel started pulling the dust blankets off the covered furniture. The more things were unveiled, the more they discovered this room was meant for a baby. They found a dust-covered crib, a beautiful, ornate chest of drawers and an old rocking chair. Velina looked up at the crib, imagining her baby girl in there, as her eyes glanced over the wooden slats of the crib, her blood ran cold. She could see an outline of a baby's name carved and painted into the wood of the crib. She leaned forward and brushed her hand over the letters, watching the thick layer of dust crumble away under her touch, feeling the carved letters of the wood, to reveal the name Orenda.

Orenda

Velina lost all the air from her body. She stepped back from the crib fast; the heel of her foot got caught on an old, ragged rug that was covered in so much dust you could barely see the pattern. Axel stretched his arms out and grabbed Velina before she fell to the floor. He cradled her and calmed her with a tight hug. Axel looked up at the crib in amazement, seeing the name with his own eyes, "Have you been in this room before? How is that name on the crib? That's the name you plucked from somewhere?"

Velina was shocked, but the name still felt right to her. She calmed herself down in the embrace of Axel, and they both stood together and agreed to call this a very weird coincidence. Axel said in a joking voice, "Hey, at least we won't need to buy a crib." Velina giggled and playfully hit his arm. Over the coming days, they worked together in the room cleaning, washing down the walls, freshening the paint and getting all the furniture looking brand new again. A couple of times, getting distracted by having a paint war when Velina got Axel on the nose with some pink paint.

When the room was finally finished, the windows were gleaming with new fold-away shutters, so they didn't obstruct the stunning view. The room was a very soft pink with beautiful flowers that Velina had painted herself around the corners of the room. Axel took the crib and fixed the broken slats; he repainted it ivory white with the name coated in the same soft pink as the room. Velina had gone into town and bought some comfy soft cushions for the rocking chair to support her back. They added the new addition of a bookshelf filled with stories of adventure and magic that they could not wait to read together with their little girl. Axel playfully leaned his elbow on Velina's shoulder, with both looking at how amazing the room looked. Axel teased Velina, "This better be a girl after all this hard work." Velina pushed Axel off her shoulder and gave him a tight hug with tears welling in her eyes. She said, "I'm one hundred percent sure" through joyful sobs. Axel pulled her close and kissed the top of her head. They took one last look at their hard work and retired to go have a cup of tea and a well-deserved slice of cake that Axel had picked up from Ruth's bakery.

Night drew in, after a long day doing the finishing touches in Orenda's room, it was finally time to get some shut-eye. They both snuggled down in bed together and drifted off, but Velina's dreams were to be disturbed. It was a quick flash of a dream where she was awake, walking around Antler Manor during the day, but it had a different feeling to it. The decorations were different; all the pictures she had taken with friends and family had disappeared from the walls. Velina found herself standing at the top of the stairs overlooking the main hallway. She saw Eve Longbow walking through the hallway, smiling to herself and holding her pregnant belly, a small bump peeping out from her long white nightdress; her long black flowing hair fell loose and free down her back.

Then the front door burst open, and angry villagers came pouring in, grabbing at Eve. Hearing her screams, Velina jolted awake, sweating and scared. She took a deep breath and looked around the dark room in a panic, but there was nothing she could do but sit up and calm herself down. She had a drink of water she kept in a jug on her bedside table. She quietly got up out of bed and walked over to the window to let some air in the room. When she pulled the curtains back to unhook the window latch to push it up, there sat on the ledge outside was the biggest raven she had ever seen, just looking out over the grounds. It didn't even flinch when Velina opened the window; they both just stayed there for a little time in silence, looking out across the dark grounds illuminated by the moonlight. After a little time, the raven turned its head to look at Velina, and with a strong beat of its wings, it flew off into the dark. She watched the large bird disappear into the night. She started feeling her eyes getting heavy, so she closed the window and returned to bed to hopefully get some undisturbed sleep. The following morning, she arose a lot later than usual. Axel did not want to disturb her and left her to lie in. Velina awoke. She was unsure whether to tell Axel about the dream, but she could not dwell on it, as today was the day she would be telling her family that she was having a baby; she hoped it would go well.

Velina sat up in bed, stretched her arms and back out to wake her muscles so she could get up out of bed. The room was still dark as Axel didn't open the curtains in the hopes of letting Velina sleep. She leaned over to her bedside table and turned her lamp on. The room lit up in a warm glow, and Velina's mind went back to her dream from last night. She was trying to understand what she saw and why she saw it. She wanted to learn more about Eve Longbow and her life here at Antler Manor. Her inner thoughts are racing, "Is she trying to contact me? Does she need help? Is she trying to send me a message?" Her thoughts were disturbed by the bedroom door opening and Axel slowly entering, balancing a tray filled with all of Velina's favourite breakfast treats.

He made her blueberry pancakes with a warm pot of syrup on the side, croissants, and pain au chocolat, all sweet as sugar, which was what she was craving. He placed the tray on Velina's lap and leaned in for a kiss, cheekily pinched one of her croissants and climbed back into bed. Velina laughed and playfully hit him on the arm in protest of the thievery. He asked her, "How are you feeling about breaking the news to your family today?" They were invited for dinner at Gold Wheat Manor for a family catch-up. Velina shuffled uncomfortably with a mouth full of blueberry pancakes, saying, "Fine, absolutely fine," following a big gulp. The morning rushed on by, and the time was getting closer and closer to them having to leave. Velina found herself sitting in the baby's room alone on her rocking chair, just prepping herself for how today may or may not go. She heard a knock on the door; it was Bailey, one of the maids, informing her that Axel was waiting downstairs and ready to go in the car. Velina took in a big breath, stood abruptly and followed Bailey to the car outside, where Axel was waiting for her, holding the door open. Every footstep closer to telling her family she just wanted to get it over and done with, so it's out in the open, she could deal with whatever her family's response was.

They pulled up to Gold Wheat Manor and were greeted by Pearl, who was standing outside having a smoke. She gleefully skipped over to the car and gave them both a hug. Velina pulled Pearl in close and said, "We have something to tell you". Pearl's eyes lit up, already knowing by Velina's hushed, excited tone what she was going to say. Before any words even left Velina's mouth she said, "I'm going to be aunty Arnt I?" Velina nodded at her with a smile saying it's a little girl, Pearl screeched and Velina grabbed her arm to shush her laughing saying "be quiet and act natural we need to tell mum and dad next, I'm glad you are happy". Pearl said, "I'm more than happy, I'm elated for you both, and so will mum and dad. Just own it when you tell them."

They all straightened up, took a breath, and entered the house to start the get-together. Everyone was there Velina and Pearl's parents, Craig and Crissy and Axel's parents had returned from visiting their friends in the big city. Craig is a big man with a warm glow to his skin and a strong build from working outside on the land, in his booming voice cheerfully saying "grubs up everyone get comfy" he proceeded to carve the meat to pass it around the table, everyone leaning in to spoon all the veg onto their plates. As they all started eating and laughing together, Axel stood and clinked his glass to ask for everyone's attention. The room fell silent; all eyes were on Axel as he gently pulled Velina up to him. "We have some exciting news to tell you all." Craig's voice boomed in a jolly tone, "Out with it, stop leaving us in suspense." Velina looked up to her parents. The words came flooding out, "We are expecting, and it's a girl." Everyone remained quiet, all eyes turned to Craig, who locked eyes with Velina. His face expressionless as he slowly stood pushing his chair out from behind him, the sound of wooden chair legs on hard stone scraping across the floor sounded louder in the silence of the room. He walked the length of the table to them both.

He bypassed Axel, ignoring him and placed both his hands on his daughters' shoulders; both their eyes met in a quiet moment. A tear rolled down his cheek, the warmest smile crept across his face as he pulled Velina in for the tightest hug, and the floodgates opened. He started laughing and wiping the tears away as he said, "I'm going to be a grandpappy." he turned away from Velina, who was also tearing up through smiles, and he grabbed Axel and gave him a tight hug as well, saying, "Whatever you need, I'm a phone call away." Velina's mum walked over as well and hugged her as if she wasn't ever going to let go of her. She said, "I'm so proud I can't wait to meet her and spoil her." Craig grabbed a glass of beer and raised it high above his head, and bellowed, "Congratulations to you both and the newest little member of the family, my beautiful granddaughter." Everyone started cheering and joining in on the toast. A few months had passed since that day, Velina was definitely starting to show now and feeling Orenda move and kick as if she was desperate to join the outside world.

Velina's dreams have been still lately, but that curious raven still seems to follow her around when she leaves the house or goes for a walk around the grounds. Axel was at work, and Velina found herself at home alone, so she thought she would go and read some more of Eve's book that was now concealed in the drawer of the coffee table in the snug room. She opened the drawer and carefully removed the old leather book. She brushed her finger up the glowing symbol on the spine, saying, "reveal my words in the light of the sun rise." The words and images appeared as they bled across the pages. She got cozy on the sofa and started reading through the spells and the ingredients until she came across a very strange spell called the life protection spell. There was an image of a woman who resembled Eve; her pregnant belly was transparent, revealing the baby with a soft glow around it. The spell's instructions were to find an object dear to you, which will be the vessel that holds the life you wish to protect. The life and soul will be kept dormant and safe within the object until it senses your wish to release the soul into a new host in the form of a baby.

Velina's eyes could not leave that page; she noticed on the image of the pregnant lady who resembled Eve, on her wedding finger was a ring in the shape of a distinctive star. Velina's eyes bulged as she looked down at her own hand to examine her own ring. The soft vibration from the ring triggered again, but she didn't feel alarmed; she felt a warm comfort as she realised this ring once belonged to Eve. She sat there for a moment, eyes examining the page again to read the logistics of the spell. The ingredients that started the spell were to steam a certain combination of bone, herbs, plants, and a strand of the mother's hair.

The steps were one healthy pinch of an ancestor's ashes to represent life, death, and rebirth, one healthy pinch of earth powder, a blend of ground roots, tree bark and soil from your home ground, for stability and the nurturing aspect of life. Two pinches of gold/yellow powder made from dried marigold or turmeric, linked to the sun's energy, for success and life force. Two pinches of floral powder made of ground petals from your garden, like roses, jasmine and lavender, representing love, vitality, and flourishing. One strand of the mother's hair is to be combined in a pot of hot steaming water; the fumes must be inhaled through the mouth and nose to prepare your body to transfer the baby's soul and spirit into the chosen vessel, which must be worn on the body or kept in a safe place. Velina thought that somewhere in this house must be Eve's apothecary of spell ingredients, but she had no idea where to start looking in this massive old house. Velina closed the book, placed it on the table, and leaned back on the sofa. Her eyes began to feel unnaturally heavy, she looked to the window and saw the raven flapping at the glass, its large silhouette blackened by the sunshine, as Velina slipped into an unnatural sleep.

Chapter Six

THE DREAM OF EVE LONGBOW

"If she dreams of me, then the hour is near. I do not come to those who are safe. The blood remembers what the magic stirs. That is why I return in dreams."

- E.L

Velina felt strange; she was asleep but awake, lying down but walking, dreaming, and living in these different surroundings she had woken up to. She sat up, placed a protective hand on her belly, and looked around the room. She knew what room she was in, but everything looked different. She slowly stood and cautiously left the snug room and followed her senses along the hallway and down the main staircase. Everything had a strange glow and blur to it as if Velina didn't belong in this time but was given a rare behind-the-scenes access to a time that wasn't her own. She found herself at the entrance of the greenhouse. All the plants looked different. Velina's tomatoes were not in their usual soil beds, but in their place, growing were some herbs that Velina had never seen before. She entered the greenhouse and wandered around, examining everything and looking for anything unusual. Her ring started to vibrate as she approached the back corner of the greenhouse. She noticed a loose metal grate on the floor as if it hadn't been latched properly. She heard footsteps behind her; it was a man she didn't recognise. He didn't resemble anyone from the Brinford family, but he strangely resembled Ted Backster, who owned the jewellery shop in Hale town. He had the same face shape and build as Ted with blonde shoulder length hair, his clothes looked strange, definitely not from her time, he wore a brown waistcoat overtop an off white shirt with a matching pair of smart brown trousers; he looked truly angry with his sleeves rolled up and a gleam of sweat settling upon his brow, his nostrils flaring with his sharp eyes fixed on the loose grate in the floor. He approached the back corner of the greenhouse and walked straight through Velina as if she wasn't even there. He pulled the metal floor plate up to reveal a set of stairs that led down into something. Velina hurried down behind this Ted-looking man to see what he was up to and why he knew this hidden staircase was there, but no one from Velina's time had any clue about it. The stairs led down into a hidden room, the walls covered in chalk-drawn symbols and a large wooden oak cabinet that was filled with bottles, pots, and stirrers. The room flickered and danced to the light of candles placed on candle holders on the walls around the room. There in front of her was Eve screaming in pain, holding her pregnant belly. This man stood there shielding his face from the light as aggressive, unnatural winds whipped around Eve.

He was yelling out for her to stop this demon magic and get her condemned soul and that devil's spawn growing inside her back into her cell, but he couldn't walk forward towards her from the aggressive wind that was whirling around the room that seemed to intentionally hold him back. Eve yelled back in anger, "John, you are no friend of mine anymore. I showed this place to you. I trusted you, but your perverse intentions were made clear enough; I dread to think what would have happened if Axel hadn't been here that day. Is that what it is? You betrayed my trust because I didn't fall for you. I healed your children when they were sick, I stitched up your hand when you cut it while building your jewellery shop, I was your wife's maid of honour, I'm not the monster here, you are." John yelled in response. "I LOVED YOU, but you were too wrapped up in Axel to see it. If I can't have you, no one can. You probably used your dark magic and weaselled your way into my feelings. This is not natural. When you burn, I will cleanse my soul of you. You are not natural, the things you do are not natural." Eve spoke through gritted teeth, "Your infatuation with me isn't love; you made that clear when you pushed your intentions on me. Your dark thoughts are yours and yours alone. When I burn, you will also burn for what you nearly did to me. What's natural about burning a mother and her unborn child? I swear on all the spirits and Mother Nature herself, I will have my revenge," she knelt again in pain, gripping her belly as she clung onto the edge of the table. The light intensified around her; the spell began to activate and create a heavy steam that rose up from the cauldron around her face. She looked up to see that Axel had broken free from his guards as he barrelled down the stairs and lunged his whole body at John Backster, cracking his fist right against his jaw. Blood sprayed from John's nose, but he fought back just as ferociously by body slamming Axel to the ground and calling out for the guards. Axel grabbed a loose rock that was on the floor and smacked John over the head with it, which temporarily knocked him out cold. He dropped the rock and scrambled over to Eve by passing through the wind and light as if it gave him permission to pass. He wrapped his arms around Eve to take her away, but she was too weak to move as the spell had already started. She asked Axel, "Please just hold us as we are whole for a short time, you, me and Orenda." She was sweating, her damp, dark hair clung to her face as she hugged Axel tight. They could hear the guards coming through the greenhouse to recapture Axel. John was steering as he placed a weary hand on his head, seeing the trickle of blood fall onto his fingers.

Axel said to Eve through tears rolling down his face, "Let me see your beautiful smile. I want that to be the last thing I see before I'm taken." Eve stilled herself and gave Axel the warmest smile, placed both her hands on his cheeks, and softly kissed him. She wanted to keep this moment forever and asked him, "You must carry on living for us, your eyes will see this world for me, your ears will listen to our favourite song, as long as your heart will beat, then so shall mine, so please live for us. I love you, Axel." Axel stared at her taking in every feature of her face the flecks in her dark eyes the cute curl of her lips as she smiled up at him, "I love you I will always love you please wait for me with our favourite song playing when it's my time to join you" She laughed through tears and said in a soft whisper "I promise" They heard the guards clattering down the stairs Axel turned to Eve and said "I will distract the guards as much as I can so you can complete the spell you are doing to keep our daughter safe" They had discussed the plan back at the prison cells where they were both being held in, they made their escape so Eve could get the ingredients to perform the spell. But from leaving the prison, John had noticed their absence, he hunted them down and started fighting with Axel whilst Eve carried on back to Antler Manor to perform the spell. John thought he had bested Axel by seizing him with the guards he had yelled for and ordered them to hold him in one of the rooms at Antler Manor whilst he went and got Eve. As Axel was outnumbered, he was dragged away yelling for Eve and saying "I love you" Eve's tears turned to anger as the light intensified even more, she screamed and waved her hand towards John, a strong gust of wind sent John flying back to the ground in disbelief as a supernatural wind held him there, he tried to wriggle free from the phantoms grip. Velina, watching all this happen and powerless to help, all she could do was observe and take in all that she saw. All she wanted to do was to help poor Eve and Axel, but these were shadows of past things that had already happened.

Velina approached Eve, unaffected by the light and turbulent winds that surrounded her. Eve was leaning over a black cauldron, heavily breathing in and sniffing the steam that arose from the pot. Velina noticed the star wedding ring floating over the cauldron, and Eve was yelling and repeating the words "I PROTECT THIS LIFE THAT GROWS INSIDE ME, BUT MY BODY IS NOT LONG FOR THIS WORLD SO I OFFER THIS RING TO HOLD YOU AND PROTECT YOU SO YOU WILL GET THE CHANCE TO LIVE ONE DAY". Eve's cries of pain from performing such a powerful spell "ORENDA LIVE IN ANOTHER TIME I WILL FIND YOU AND I WILL NEVER STOP LOVING YOU I WISH I GOT TO HOLD YOU IN MY ARMS" the light started to move from her pregnant belly and whirled around the ring like a cyclone as if the ring was sucking the light from Eve into the star diamond. Then the room went silent, the light disappeared, and the wind unnaturally stopped. Eve slumped down to the floor her weight leaning against the leg of the table, she looked up at John Backster and spoke with a weak shaky voice but still finding the power of her words, "My gift will not die with me. You can burn my body, but you won't burn my daughter, she is safe from you and all those ignorant Villagers". Velina noticed that Eve had broken shackles attached to one of her wrists. John Power walked over to Eve and wrenched her up by her wrist; he snatched the ring that had fallen into the pot. He flickered off the liquid from the ring and shoved it in his pocket. He leaned in close to Eve, centimetres from her face and said, "Whatever dark, disgusting magic you have put in this ring, it will never see the light of day. You might have somehow escaped the cell you were in, but you can't escape the fire that's coming for you in the morning." He yanked her away, kicking and screaming with what little energy she had left, calling out for Axel, but he had been detained and heavily guarded to make sure he didn't intervene again. John dragged Eve out of Antler Manor and threw her into the back of a horse-drawn wagon, locked up tight by a large, heavy padlock and rode away down the drive. With all this happening, Velina was crying and calling out for Eve, but she felt like she was being pulled away from this reality, dissolving from the dream. She woke up crying and saw the raven still tapping at the window.

Velina stood and hurried out of the snug room, down the main staircase and into the greenhouse. She knew exactly where to go, to the back corner of the greenhouse. She yanked the metal grate from the floor, a burst of dust and bits of metal paint flaked to the floor as the dark void appeared before her, and a soft gust of air blew up in her face. She hurried to the kitchen to grab a torch and returned to the greenhouse to proceed very slowly down the dust-covered, uneven stairs. She felt like she floated down these stairs in her dream, but in reality, it felt cold and damp with uneven earth under her feet, cobwebs hanging everywhere. The torch lit the way down the stairs, and she started seeing the symbols on the walls and the familiarity of the large cabernet that now looked old, rotten, covered in dirt and dust, filled with bottles, pots, and stirrers. Velina glanced around the room that had small cave-ins with piles of rock and mud on the floor. The room felt so quiet and still with an incredibly sad tone in the air as Velina shuffled through Eve's belongings and old books that she cherished in her life. She heard Axel calling out for her. She called up to him to come to the greenhouse. She stood at the top of the stairs with the torchlight shining up so Axel could see where she was. He looked around in wonder and confusion as he followed Eve down the dark stairs. He looked around the room and tried to take it all in, "How did we not know this was here?" He glanced at Velina and asked what she had found out and how she had found it. Velina didn't know whether to tell him in truthful detail how she found this room and about Eve or make up a believable story, so she didn't sound insane. Velina took a deep breath and asked Axel to follow her to the snug room to show him Eve's book and tell him the one-hundred percent truth. If Eve could be truthful with her Axel about herself, then Velina could be truthful with her Axel. They both sat on the sofa in the snug room, and she placed the book in Axel's lap. She had forgotten to use the spell to conceal the words, so everything was there for him to read.

Axel turned the pages, trying to make sense of the words and images. She explained everything to him about the ring, the book, her dreams and how Orenda came to be. She truly was a miracle baby that was conceived over three hundred years ago and was to be born in the year nineteen sixty-nine. Once they had finished talking Axel looked at Velina not saying a word and lent down to gently place his head on her belly and softly pressed his ear to Orenda, "hey little one in there, you may or may not be aware of your beginning and how magical you are, but me and your mum will love you and keep you safe no matter what, Eve if you can hear me I want you to know that your love and protection for her will be amplified through us" He lifted his head to meet Velina's gaze who was smiling and tearing up, he kissed her and pulled her into a tight hug. They both got distracted by a tap at the window to see the large black Raven as it stared at them both for a moment and then flew away. The presence of the Raven was a comfort to them now, as it would show up every now and then over the months of Velina's due date, getting closer and closer. Time moved on from that day as Velina found herself slowly walking around the manor. By this time, she had forgotten what her feet looked like, and her back ached something terrible, but the glow she had confirmed that she was completely content and happy. She walked into Orenda's room and sat in the rocking chair, taking the weight off her feet as she admired the room and could not wait for it to be used. At this time, Axel had taken full control of Antler Manor's estate with his parents retiring and taking it easier. In that new responsibility, he had started to dive deep into his ancestry and researched everything he could find on Eve and Axel. He left his study to go find Velina to see if she was ok and if she needed something. He knew exactly where she would be as he walked into the baby's room to find her relaxing in her rocking chair, listening to some music on the radio.

Axel giggled to himself as he watched Velina rock in the chair to the music with her head leaned back, looking up at the ceiling, singing to herself. She didn't even know he was standing there watching her until she heard a prominent out loud giggle and snort. She looked over at him and laughed, her face flushed with embarrassment. He approached Velina and knelt on the floor next to her to discuss their wedding that they had rescheduled for a later time when Orenda was older and could be a part of the ceremony. Velina didn't want to feel rushed; it helped that her parents were fine with her getting pregnant before she was legally married. It gave her more time to get the decorations right and send out the invitations; there was also the big job of picking her wedding dress, which she definitely would not be able to fit into at the moment. Axel then trailed off and started to inform Velina of all the information he had found out about Eve and where she came from. Velina sat up straight and said, "Tell me what you have found." He cleared his throat and proceeded to tell her all he had found. He even found their wedding certificate; they got married in the local church. He also found out she was a local to Hollow

Wood village, and she worked at Night Owl Surgery, providing them with her lotions and healing remedies. I also found out she was hired here to become a maid at Antler Manor. Velina giggled and said, "Ahhh, that's how they met, he fell in love with the maid." Velina said she wished she knew of a way to see into Eve's past, as papers don't hold the details, just the record of her actions. She then grinned and looked at Axel with a face full of mischief, "what if there's a spell we could do together to see into her past, there must be something in her book and the apothecary to achieve that" Axel looked concerned and felt uneasy with the idea "there may well be but should we be messing around with that? we don't really know what we are doing". Velina scoffed and called him scaredy pants. He straightened up, not taking kindly to the insult on his bravery, "ok, little miss Witch, let's see what you got, let's do it, but I'm following your lead through this."

They both stood together, Velina a bit slower on her feet than Axel, he was trying to put a brave front on and hide the fact that he felt absolutely terrified "are you sure you will be ok doing this spell especially how far along you are" Velina placed a comforting hand on her belly and examined her ring which felt like it was humming again like the speed of a hummingbird's wings pattering against her hand. She said she had never felt stronger and more capable of doing magic, which strangely came very naturally to her, considering she had never practiced the art before. She had no fear or doubt in her abilities; her fast thinking to learn these spells as she discovered them just made her want to learn and do more. It was almost as if this path was inevitable for her that she found herself on. She looked at Axel and rubbed his arm to reassure him that she felt absolutely fine with performing the spell, but they had to actually find it first; such a spell might not even exist. She said to Axel, "The magic from our baby, whose blood she also shares with you, that is what's giving me this strength." Axel felt in his pocket the clover preserved in tree sap that he keeps near him at all times, remembering the warning foreboding words of the old woman he met at that old little stall underneath the witch's ash tree. He took it out and asked Velina to hold her hand out, he placed the clover in the palm of her hand, when Velina's hand made contact with the clover her head violently shot back, her eyes wide staring up to the celling, a vision filled her mind's eye of the moment Eve found this clover in the fields of hollow wood, she was sat leaning against a tree in the tall growing corn with the sun on her face, as she cut the peace of sap away containing the clover from the base of the tree and examining it with a smile on her face, her dark eyes almost glowing from the rays of the sun. Velina's head fell forward, gasping for air as Axel comforted her, "What the heck was that? What happened to you?" She closed her hand around the clover and thanked Axel as she placed it in her pocket and told him what she saw. She kept none of her magical happenings from Axel anymore; he was very intrigued when he was told what had happened.

Chapter Seven

SPIRITS INTO THE MIRROR

"Do not flinch when the glass ripples. It means they have heard you. Mirrors were never made just for mortals alone. They are windows for the waiting.

- E.L

They entered the snug room together like two excited children up to no good and removed Eve's book from the drawer of the coffee table. She swiped her finger up the symbol on the spine of the book, reciting the spell to reveal the words. They started researching to find a spell that resembled what they wanted to accomplish. Velina shouted out loud, "AH HA, look at this spell, it's called a glance of the past, that sounds like what we want." Axel nodded and looked at the ingredients they would need to perform the spell. It says you need a mirror for scrying, preferably from the time you wish to observe, a pestle and mortar to crush up the plants and herbs of mugwort and bay leaves. This will help you fall into an open trance so your spirit can fade into the mirror. Axel left Velina to familiarise herself with the spell, and he went to go and find the stuff she needed for the spell to work. He came back with a small bag of the plant and herb, a large ornate mirror that was original to Antler Manor with stags and golden flowers carved into the old wooden frame, age spots and smudged like smoke that spread across the glass, making you think about the countless number of people who have glanced into this mirror, examining their reflection. He leaned the mirror against the coffee table so it was propped up right in front of them, so they could both sit on the sofa and see their reflections. Velina grabbed the pestle and mortar to start crushing the plant and herb together, adding some of her spit and asking Axel to do the same as she did; to spit into the mixture so she could combine everything into a paste. Once it reached the right consistency, she dipped her finger into the bowl and smeared it under Axel's eyes and then her own. She took his hand and warned him, "Do not let go of my hand or your spirit may get stuck in there and become disconnected from your body. I am your magical anchor, so you can get back to your body". Axel nervously nodded and gripped her hand tight, lacing his fingers with hers; her skin felt unnaturally cool to the touch. Velina glanced into the mirror and informed Axel to do the same as she drew a symbol onto the glass of the mirror in the shape of a cross with arrow heads at the tips pointing outward. The symbol started to glow a soft green; she informed Axel to keep eye contact with his own reflection. They stared past the glowing symbol into their own reflections' eyes until the world around them started to fall into darkness. Hers and Axel's eyes went cloudy, milky white as their spirits detached and floated up from their bodies, they glided for a moment getting used to the feeling of weightlessness as they felt pulled like a magnet through the mirror, flying like ash caught in the wind.

SPIRIT SCRYING

INGREDIENTS:

- A pinch of dried mugwort
- Two bay leaves, crumbled
- A mortar and pestle
- A drop of spit from each participant
  A mirror—preferably from the time
  you wish to see.

CRUSH THE VISION BLEND

Combine mugwort
and bay leaves
in the mortar.

Grind into a
fine mixture.

Add the spit of each
participant and
mix thoroughly.

Their cloud-like forms opened and adjusted their eyes to the surroundings. Standing hand in hand, they turned their heads around to see a smoke-like portal, seeing their bodies sitting on the sofa with milky white eyes staring out blankly. It gave them both a shudder to see themselves; the disconnect from their own vessels made them feel like they were standing at the edge of a tall cliff, looking down over the edge, feeling that strange flip in their stomachs, trying to ignore the compulsion to jump. They took a slow walk around to figure out that they were in the main entrance of Antler Manor. They saw Eve rushing around with her long black hair pinned up under a bonnet, her maids uniform a long dark royal blue dress with a white apron and the white stag embroidered on the front, she was carrying way too much for her small arms, and she tripped on the edge of the large rug, she went flying forwards, her bucket and clothes streamed out in front of her to be met by Axel senior at the base of the stairs leaning forward to catch her. Axel giggled and said to Velina, "You both have bad habits of tripping over rugs and giving me and that Axel a heart attack."

Velina laughed and joked, "Don't make me let go of your hand," in a playful tone. They watched the moment Eve and Axel met for the first time, both blushing as he lifted Eve to her feet and helped her pick up all the cleaning tools from the floor. Eve was so awkward in her youth, but she was to grow into a beautiful, regal woman. Velina felt so sorry for her knowing her fate, but this moment was so precious to see. Axel senior insisted to Eve that she accompany him to a founder's ball that the founding families held once every ten years to celebrate the growth of Hollow Wood. Eve looked flustered and curtsied to Axel. She said, "Thank you, sir, for the invitation, but I am just a maid, I'm not a lady or Duchess or anything; I don't even own a gown fancy enough for the founder's ball." Axel took her hand, gently lifting her chin with his thumb and forefinger, stealing her eye contact, making her cheeks blush, "I don't care for titles and for the gown, I will happily buy you one." She didn't know what to say or how to say it, "Thank you, sir, it would be an honour to accompany you". Axel senior still holding her gaze gave her a wicked smirk and let her chin free from his grip, "call me by my name no need for calling me sir, and you don't need to curtsy to me. Now you know me, can you tell me your name?" Eve feeling more and more flustered with this interaction, she wanted to gain some kind of upper hand "my name needs to be earned, fight for it" she leaned in close to him feeling him leaning towards her as she sternly took her cleaning bucket from Axel's other hand and walked away with a devilish smirk that floored Axel's jaw. He watched her walk away as he continued his daily routine, but his thoughts were only concentrated on her.

Velina and Axel watched as everything started to go misty around them, and the room began to change. As things started to come back into focus, they were now standing in the middle of the village in front of a shop. They jumped back quickly as a horse and carriage pulled up just in front of them. It was Eve and her fellow maids she worked with who were tasked with helping her pick a gown for the founder's party. They all filtered out of the carriage and entered the shop. They were greeted by Martha, who took the letter that was presented to her by Eve. She was instructed to break the seal to read the contents.

The letter stated that Eve was a special guest of Axel's at tonight's founder's ball, and she needs the perfect gown. If you could help her and put the costs onto Antler Manor's account, the fee will be settled. Martha looked at Eve up and down, circled her a couple of times, then took her hand and whisked her away into the aisles of gowns. "I have the perfect gown for you." Her fellow maids were left to admire the dresses and try on the jewellery that was hanging on the hooks. A little time went by; the maids had been joking about trying on the different veils, pretending they were marrying a wealthy king from a faraway land. They heard Martha call from the back, "Ladies, take a seat, she is ready." They hurried and took a seat on the sofa to see Eve in her new gown. Martha opened the curtain for Eve, who stepped out into the room. Everyone went silent in awe as they all admired how beautiful she looked. Eve turned and looked in the mirror at her reflection. Her face dropped, fiddling with the fabric of the gown between her fingers, she looked a little downhearted. Martha noticed the change in her mood, "Dear, what's wrong?" Eve turned to Martha and gestured to herself, "I'm nothing special, look at me, I'm just a maid in a fancy dress." Martha looked at her and gently turned her away from the mirror. Martha removed Eve's hair from her bonnet she was still wearing and undid all the pins.

Her hair dropped down in flowing, loose, shining black curls. Martha left Eve for a moment as she disappeared out the back. She grabbed her makeup bag and applied a dusty pink blush to her cheeks, a soft red stain on her full lips. She brushed a golden powder eye shadow across her eyelids, so her dark eyes popped. Martha slowly turned Eve back around to face the mirror. Martha smiled with pride at her. "I don't see just a maid, I see a beautiful young lady with regal grace and dominant presence." Eve looked at her reflection in the mirror and examined herself with harsh judgment. She had never worn makeup before, she could never afford it, and she never had the chance to do makeup with her mother, as she lost both her parents to a plague that swept the area when she was a child. She looked at herself up and down in disbelief, her eyes welled up as she turned abruptly to give a hug and thank Martha for her help. Axel and Velina noticed the room starting to go smoky again as they looked around to see where they would end up next. Things started coming into focus. They were inside the main village hall, the stain glass windows reflected rainbows of light streaming through the coloured panels from the setting sun, the large, tall candles that were placed in tall gothic black candelabras were being lit by the staff making their way around the room, the band was playing music their ears had never heard before, it sounded ancient and haunting.

The hall was filled with people dressed in flowing gowns, the men dressed in smart suits, as they danced and laughed together when everyone turned to hear a bell signalling that the ceremony was about to begin. Everyone parted to clear the dance floor as the founding families made their entrance one by one to take their places under their family flags that were hung at the back of the hall. First in was the Wicker family from Hunter Manor, who took their place under the flag of the Fox. Then the Hench family from Luna Manor, who stood under the flag of the Owl, Next was the Shaw's from Gold Wheat Manor, who took their place under the

101

flag of the Doe. Everyone was waiting for the members of Antler Manor to make their entrance.

The Founders Ball glowed with life at the heart of Hollow Wood Village, the grand hall shimmering beneath the light of the candles. As the Coloured beams still fell across the polished floor, washing the guests in shifting hues of ruby, sapphire and emerald. At the centre of it all, beneath the towering banner of the white stag, Axel Brinford entered with Eve on his arm. Her gown drew every eye, black beaded lace cascading over a full skirt that caught the candlelight in glimmers like scattered stars. The corset hugged her form, each bead stitched with care, shimmering as she moved. Long black silk gloves climbed to her elbows, sleek and elegant against the pale glow of her skin. Together, she and Axel seemed less like guests and more like royal figures stepping up to their throne. Axel leaned closer as they walked, his cheeky smile curving when he caught her sideways glance. "Careful," he murmured low enough for her alone to hear, "you're stealing more attention than the white stag itself." Eve's lips curved, playful fire flickering in her dark onyx eyes. "Then perhaps they should change the flag to something more eye-catching." She teased back, her voice soft but edged with confidence. As they took their place beneath the great banner, the whispers in the hall swelled, every gaze following them. Yet to Eve, it was only Axel's warm hand at her arm, the quiet thrill in his smile, the unspoken spark dancing between them that made the moment feel like theirs alone.

They were the only two that represented Antler Manor as Axel senior's parents had passed away. They stood there proudly together; all eyes were on them both as the ceremony began. The vicar entered the room wearing his long white robes with gold stitching, holding a large golden goblet embellished with all kinds of jewels and stones. He said, "Welcome, everyone, to our founder's ball held every decade. Here before us are the founding families who will drink the waters from our stream held by the founder's goblet, made by the hands of the original families who supplied each metal and material to make this goblet, materials cultivated from their own lands when their homes were built.

This goblet symbolises unity and peace. Each member will drink to keep the treaty of peace. If one family does not drink, this breaks the promise of unity." Axel and Velina walked around to stand closer to Axel senior and Eve, who were holding hands and looking forward, waiting for the vicar to approach them with the goblet. The vicar handed the goblet to each family until he got to Axel and Eve, who both sipped the water. Everyone in the hall cheered when Eve lowered the goblet from her lips. The music started, and the founding families met in the middle of the dance floor to begin the founders' dance. All the ladies stood on one side and all the men on the other. A beautiful tune started playing; it had such a dreamy sound, with the violins starting the tune, then the harp joining in the sound. The men bowed to the ladies, and the ladies curtseyed to the men. They stepped together and apart a few times, lifted the palms of their hands up together, but not touching. Eve and Axel's eyes were locked on each other the whole time. They spun around, then they came together into a flow of spinning steps as they turned around the room. Others started to join in, and the dance floor filled. The room started to disappear into smoke again. Velina and Axel reappeared in the entrance hall of Antler Manor. It was dark; only a couple of lanterns were lit to shine out by the front door.

The carriage wheels rumbled over the stone path, lantern lights swaying with each bump as the horses carried Axel and Eve home to Antler Manor. The night air was cool, fragrant with pine, but inside the carriage, warmth and wine lingered between them.

Their laughter spilled out into the quiet as the coachman slowed to a stop before the main entrance. Axel hopped out first, a little less steady than usual. He offered his hand with a grin that bordered on mischief. Eve took it, though her own balance faltered, and together they tumbled out in a graceless heap of silk and polished boots. By the time they staggered through the double doors of Antler Manor. They collapsed onto the marble floor of the entrance hall, breathless with laughter that echoed against the high ceilings. Her black-beaded gown sprawled across the floor like spilled ink, his jacket askew, but neither cared. Axel, still chuckling, propped himself on one elbow to look at her. Candlelight from the hall sconces lit her face, and for a moment, the laughter softened into something deeper. "You know," he said, his voice warm with wine and conviction, "you've officially been fired." Eve raised a brow, lips parting in amused protest. "You're far too dangerous to be a maid. I want you as something more… the lady of Antler Manor." Eve's smile turned sly, a spark of mystery dancing in her gaze. "And yet," she teased, "you still don't even know my name." Axel let out a laugh that rang rich and full through the hall, then, without hesitation, took her hand as though he were already certain of his fate. "Then tell me," He whispered, "the name of the woman I've just asked to marry me." The manor around them seemed to hold its breath as their laughter blended once more, wine-drunk joy tipping into the heady certainty of something much greater: love at first sight.

The silence after his words hung heavy, broken only by the distant tick of the great hall clock and the flutter of candles along the walls. Eve, still sprawled on the polished floor beside him, gave him a dangerous smile. "You are bold, Axel Brinford," she murmured, her voice like velvet over glass. She tilted her head, studying him as though weighing his soul. "To ask for a lady's hand before you even know the name that shapes her." Axel shifted closer, his green eyes alight with certainty, no hesitation. "I don't need to know your name, but it would make life a lot easier," he said, brushing a stray curl from her cheek. "I already know you". Her gaze locked with his, sharp and teasing, but softened by the blush of wine and the thrill of the night. For a moment, she considered keeping the secret, letting him burn with wanting. But something about the way he looked at her completely undid her, breaking down the walls she had so carefully built. "Very well," she whispered, her lips grazing his ear as she leaned in close, "my name is Eve." The sound of it fell between them like a spell, ancient and undeniable. Axel drew back just enough to see her face, his smile breaking wide and unrestrained. "Eve," he repeated, savouring it. "You've just ruined me." She laughed, low and rich. He pulled her against him on the marble floor, uncaring of propriety. In that moment, Antler Manor no longer belonged to the Brinford's alone; it had found its true lady as Eve accepted his proposal, taking the star-shaped diamond on her finger.

The room started to turn to smoke again as Axel and Velina could see the inside of the church appearing through the mist. They sat in the pews; they could see Axel up front, dressed in his finery, a navy-blue suit with gold flowers around the cuffs, waiting for Eve to make her appearance. Velina leaned in and said to Axel, "I can't wait to marry you here." Axel kissed Velina on the head, and they both stood to see Eve entering the church with her long black lace veil covering her face. Eve's dress was beautiful but different compared to other dresses of the time. It was a flowing lace gown, but the colour shocked people into stunned silence as it was black with small glittering black beads following down the shape of the lace that shone from the light beaming through the windows. Axel looked so happy and overjoyed to see her, his face beaming as Eve approached him. She held black orchids for her wedding bouquet, long, draping dark flowers that complemented her dress beautifully. Velina looked around the church at all the faces. Her gaze froze; she spotted John Backster sitting with his wife. A flash of anger grew inside her blood as she knew what was to come from him.

The room started to fall dark as if someone was turning the brightness down around them on a dimmer switch, in the middle of the scene before them a bright red slash appeared in the middle of the room as if something had cut through the canopy of a tent, no one was reacting everything was still happening around them, but this thing had torn into the reality. Red-hot lava melted out of the slash as a humanlike creature slumped free from the slashed void. Axel and Velina stood to leave the confines of the pews. They backed away as this strange, intimidating thing started standing before them, skin growing over the features of the charred, cracked body. It contorted, jerked, covering its face, roaring in pain as it turned away, slumped over, clothes started to appear on its form, it whipped its head around to reveal John Backster's face. He straightened up, cracked his limbs, stretched his fingers out, and he readjusted his clothes as he took a sinister deep breath of the air. He snapped his gaze towards Velina and Axel. He approached them like a hunter stalking its vulnerable prey with his sharklike eyes fixed on Axel. Axel, tightening his grip around Velina's hand, whispered, "We need to get out of here now." Velina didn't hear Axel's words, muffled by anger through gritted teeth. She said, "John Backster, how are you still alive?" He laughed with a villainous giggle, "I wouldn't say alive." His eyes were blood shot and cloudy as he held his head in pain, he stretched his neck again and slinked up behind them both with supernatural speed, he leaned between them to whisper in Axel's ear "it's time to die" he shoved his whole body weight down on their clasped hands and broke them apart, the wedding vision disappeared into a cloud of black smoke dissolving the scene around them into nothing. Axel's human spirit could not exist for long in this reality; he would die. Velina was his anchor back to his body. Velina's spirit was slung shot back into her body, but Axel was still stuck in there.

The mirror shimmered like black water, its surface rippling as Axel's spirit strained it. His reflection no longer matched him; it twisted and warped. He pressed his hand to invisible glass, feeling stuck and drowning in the smoke that surrounded him. Velina's palm pressed against the mirror on the other side, her blue eyes glowing softly as she fought to keep him tethered. Then John's presence poured in, thick and suffocating, like tar spilling into a river. The smoke coiled around Velina's arm, pulling with a force that rattled the very mirror itself. "No!" Axel shouted, voice echoing strangely in the mirrored, smoked chamber he found himself in. His eyes searched as he heard Velina struggling against John's smoke, but John's dark laughter reverberated through the void. With a violent wrench, Velina pulled back away from the smoke that gripped her wrist, seeing it repel back into the mirror.

 She could see him running around in the heavy smoke, coughing as the atmosphere strangled his lungs. She banged on the mirror and called for him to follow her voice to find the portal. Axel could hear Velina and the banging, but the smoke made everything echo around him and confused his sense of direction. He found it harder and harder to breathe; he started to cough as he fell to his knees, and he crawled aimlessly, trying to figure out where the portal was. He lay on the floor with his breath becoming increasingly laboured. He looked up to the sky and shouted to Velina through heavy coughing, "I love you." he could hear John Backster's laugh echoing again through the smoke, seeing a dark shadow figure darting around him, disturbing the smoke as he rushed past, making the blackness heavier and thicker. John's figure loomed out of the smoke, his charred skin cracked and glowing faintly with ember-light, black tears searing down his hollow eyes as his true form burst free from the gloom. His voice rumbled like the roar of a furnace yet carried a sharp clarity that struck like blades. "Eve thought the fire could hold me?" he spat, laughter curling with smoke. "Centuries in that inferno prison, but still, I stand before you! The flames licked my bones, tore at my soul, but they could not end me. No… they forged me. I am the smoke that seeps through cracks, the shadow that refuses to fade away. I am eternal." He stepped closer, the mirror-glass trembling as his presence pressed against it. His gaze cut into Axel first, his grin widened into a cruel, stretched smirk. "Your family cursed me. Your bloodline raised its hand against me again and again, and for that, every Brinford will choke on their pride. You built your manor legacy on love… Well, I will grind it to ash. Axel, I'll rip the laughter from your spirit and make it scream. And you, Velina, his precious anchor, you'll drown in the same smoke that carried me out of my prison."

The darkness surged higher, twisting around him, embers flaring in the swell of shadow. His words rang out, each one seared with venom. "I will not stop until every Brinford name is carved into the earth as nothing but a memory. The Raven's cry will be the last sound your bloodline ever hears." His laughter followed, sharp and unrelenting, as the smoke closed in tighter, swallowing the light.

Spell for Lost Souls

Prick the finger with
a compass-tipped pin

Draw a triskelion
in blood.

Eve Longbow
the White Witch

Velina could hear John's maniacal laugh echoing through the mirror. She could feel heat rising through her body as she became enraged. Velina grabbed Eve's book to find a spell to help Axel guide his spirit back to his body, back to her. She flipped through the pages with their hidden flapped compartments; pages folded within pages. In some parts of Eve's book, you had to turn it back to front to read the words. She found a spell to give lost souls direction. Velina proceeded to follow the instructions. She knelt in front of the mirror and cut her finger with this small decorative pin that was tied inside the book by a piece of twine; ruby blood flowed from the cut; she drew a triskelion symbol onto the surface of the mirror, which was a symbol of three combined swirls. Axel peered into the distance with squinted eyes and heavy breath; through the suffocating smoke, he could see a faint light, a glowing rope that lurched out to him, and it wrapped around his wrist with gentle guidance. With what little strength he had, he slowly got to his feet and followed the rope to the glow in the distance like a beacon of hope.

The laughter from John went quiet; it was replaced with anger, "NO NO NO NOOOO" being called out with a violent growl. Velina pressed the palm of her hand flat on the surface of the mirror, and her other hand held Axel's hand, hoping the spell would work. A minute went by, which felt like an eternity. Everything went silent as she closed her eyes; she put all her concentration and magic into the symbol. She could hear her own heart beat pounding in her head, then she felt Axel's body Jurk he fell back on the sofa coughing and grabbing his throat breathing in heavy the clean air, Velina let go of his hand and quickly ended the spell closing the portal, John was locked in there by swiping salt over the mirror and saying "with this salt I cut the magic, our spirits returned to their vessels". She turned around and pulled

Axel up. She gave him a glass of water to help clear his throat. He grabbed her to give her a hug and said," Promise me we will never do that again." She agreed, leaned into him to hug him back, then suddenly she felt her legs become very wet, her eyes went wide as she realised her waters had broken, baby Orenda was on her way.

Chapter Eight

YOU'RE HERE TO TAKE HER OR

GIVE HER BACK.

"No curse can root where love has already bloomed."
-E. L

They both sat for a second, stunned as Velina squeezed his hand to alert him that Orenda was on her way. Velina laughed and smiled, then doubled down in pain as her contractions started. Axel shouted for one of the maids to grab their bag they had put together with bits they thought they might need. He called Derek, their driver, to bring the car around to the front of the manor to take them to the night owl surgery; by this time, it was dark out with the full moon shining. He grabbed the phone to call Frank at Luna Manor to inform him he needed help as Velina was going into labour. Frank said, "Congrats to you both, I will meet you both at the surgery." Luna Manor was the closest founding property to the village, not far from Night Owl Surgery, which was built at the back of Luna Manor's grounds, which then proceeded onto the street of Hollow Wood village's main road. He took Velina's arm to pull her to her feet, taking advantage of the time in between each contraction to walk to the car. They left everything out in the room as it was; they didn't have time to pack all of Eve's stuff away. Axel slammed the door behind him in haste, a bit too hard; the shudder from the slam rippled over the old wood floors and vibrated the table that had the glass of water on it, it that was already teetering on the edge of the sofa side table as it tipped over and spilled, the splash of water fell over the mirror, washing the salt away. The mirror started to crack, flicking small shards of glass to the floor. Dark, thick smoke seeped from the lightning splits across the mirror that poured out like a heavy waterfall. The black smoke whirled and grew with intense force as the form of John Backster, the Molthera, strode out of the dark vortex of smoke. He took a deep breath, his hollowed-out eyes examining the room as he tried to figure out where he was. He heard commotion outside, so he slunk up to the window to see Axel guiding Velina into a big metal contraption that he had never seen before, which moved with no pulling force of horses.

John looked over the grounds and recognized where he was. Antler Manor, he prowled around the room examining the pictures in frames, his light cat like movements floating over the floor, he picked a photo up that had Axel and Velina together laughing and smiling, he examined the image in confusion wondering how the image looked so smooth and what paint they used, he threw the photo to the floor with disregard and looked to the light that was shining under the door. He walked over to the door and disappeared into a dark cloud of smoke that oozed under the crack of the door to reappear on the other side. He was then confronted with Axel from his time in a large portrait, with Eve sitting in a chair in a long black gown beside him, holding his hand. He approached the old painted portrait and stared up at it for a moment, the face of the man he wanted to kill and the woman he wanted to possess. He lifted his hand that disappeared in a dark swirl of smoke, and a long black claw took the place of his existing hand. In a rage, he slashed his claws across the painting in a fit of rage. He stormed out of Antler Manor to find anything, anywhere or anyone he knew. If he couldn't kill Axel from his time, who had long passed away, he would kill his descendants. He walked out of the manor. He was startled by a large black raven that swooped out of the darkness, flapping, pecking, and scratching at him. He swiped his charred hand with angry force and sent the Raven plummeting to the ground with a hard thump. He leaned down to examine the Raven; he looked into its dark eye that was wearily staring up at him, almost looking like fire and rage in its eye. He said in a questioning tone, "Eve, is that you in there?" The large dark bird, in a panic, opened its large wings frantically to fly away into the night. John watched the Raven fly away in confusion he thought "it can't be her it's just a stupid bird "he carried on down the driveway recognising the large flag flapping in the wind at the entrance, he looked up at the proud stag and wrinkled his nose in degust, a hot splash of larva shot from his mouth as he spat on the floor in front of the flag the ground steaming from the heat when it hit the gravel, he powered walked away in anger down the dark country road.

Axel and Velina parked out front the main door of the surgery that flung open as warm light flooded the dark street, Axel was helping a very sweaty panting Velina out of the car, the nurses helped her into a wheelchair and hastened her away to the delivery room where Dr Frank was waiting for them with another nurse Hayley Hench his niece who was training to be a nurse ready to assist him with the delivery of the baby. Axel took a seat in the waiting room with his hands clasped together tightly, leaning on his knees. He wanted to be with her when their baby was born. Things had started to change by this time; it was more acceptable for fathers to be with the mothers when their babies were born. All it took was one scream from Velina he stood, power walked into the room to see everyone's eyes look up at him, but he ran to Velina's side to hold her hand, he placed a cool wet rag on her

head, she was very sweaty by now with her legs up and Dr Frank
showing his niece how to check how dilatated she was. Velina held
on tight to Axel's hand. She smiled up at him, thankful for the cool
rag he gently stroked over her forehead. Movement at the window
in the surgery caught their eye, it was the Raven, sitting there
looking a bit dishevelled but calmly watching. This gave Velina a
bit of calm for some reason. Whilst all the commotion was
happening in the delivery room, little did they know they had
another unknowing onlooker slinking around them at the other
window. It was John in his smoke form; his face appeared forward
through dark swirls of smoke as he looked through the window,
seeing the scene, clocking the Raven, he had a scuffle with back at
Antler Manor. He scoffed at the scene, so he blew onto his hand,
pushing a dark cloud through the open crack in the window that
floated over to Velina, who inhaled the dark mist through her nose,
which made her cough. The nurse noticed the window slightly
open, and she rushed over to close it, thinking something had
blown in off the fields. By this time, John had disappeared back
into the darkness with an evil grin across his face.

As time went on through the night, it reached early hours of
the morning, Velina was ready to push. Axel held tight onto
Velina's hand, she was yelling out in pain as she breathed deep and
pushed on the advice from the doctor. Frank excitedly said, "The
baby's head is out. Keep going, Velina, you are doing amazing."
Axel felt a bit lightheaded and overwhelmed by Velina's cries and
the cheers of encouragement from the nurses. He leaned forward to
see Orenda's head out; he leaned back to tell Velina. She wasn't
really paying attention to him, as all her focus was on pushing.
Before she knew it, they both heard the first cries of their baby girl
as Dr Frank lifted her away to clear her throat and wrap her up in a
small purple blanket. Velina felt the universe go still as she held

Orenda for the first time in her arms; she had stopped crying and was stretching out her tiny fingers. Axel started crying, looking at his two girls safe and together. Velina just naturally started to breastfeed Orenda, who was happy to have some milk after the ordeal of joining the outside world, but little did they know the black mist from John passed through Velina into Orenda as she drank. Once she was done feeding, Axel reached his hand out to Orenda. She wrapped her little hand around his finger with the smallest, tiniest smile on her face. By this point both Velina and Axel were crying with joyful tears, the nurses took Orenda and passed her to Axel, he walked over to the window with her the sky was showing signs of dawn approaching, the Raven was still watching through the window, he said in a hushed tone "Welcome to the world little one" she had hold of his finger again "Eve if that's you please be at ease that she will be safe and loved" The Raven moved closer to the glass and Axel lent down so Orenda was at the same level of the Raven, he watched as he saw a single tear fall from the Ravens eye as it ruffled its feathers and flew off into the morning sun as it rose over the trees. They offered for Velina to stay overnight in the patient's quarters, but she just wanted to get home to get Orenda and herself cleaned. Once the doctor was happy that Velina was fit enough to leave, Axel pushed Velina and baby Orenda out in a wheelchair, helped her into the car and drove them all home to Antler Manor.

They pulled up outside their home, and Axel went around to open the door for Velina, who was holding onto the baby. She looked so tired, and Little Orenda looked very sleepy, too. They slowly entered the house; they made their way up to Orenda's room. Velina slumped down in the rocking chair, holding the baby, she would rock back and forth with her, whilst Axel got the baby basket, which had all her newborn clothes in it. They fitted her in a cute purple baby grow with small white stags embroidered into it. Orenda wriggled and giggled as they tried to put the outfit on her tiny body. As Velina was dressing her, she noticed a small black vein that appeared across her tummy. She looked up at Axel and pointed it out to him. She said, "I will call the doctor. I don't know what that is." Axel looked concerned as they had only just got home. He examined this black vein as Velina called Frank; he freaked out as it grew in front of his own eyes. He and Velina began to panic as she cried down the phone at the doctor to please hurry to come check the baby. A little time went by; Axel was waiting and pacing in the main hallway for Frank to come down the drive. He would hear the gravel being disturbed, whilst Velina stayed upstairs with Orenda sitting in the rocking chair with her, singing her songs. Frank arrived at Antler Manor and was greeted by an incredibly stressed Axel. They rushed upstairs and calmed their demeanour before entering the room to see the baby. Velina stood calmly, placed Orenda on the changing table; she unbuttoned her baby grow to reveal the black spider cobweb that had spread across her little tummy. Frank looked concerned he got his stethoscope out to listen to her heartbeat. He breathed warm air from his mouth to warm it up and placed it on her chest to listen. He said, "Her heartbeat sounds laboured, not as strong as it should be." He recommended that Velina try to feed her to keep her strength up whilst he did some research on this black vein that he had never seen before. Frank rushed to Antler Manor library; Dart jumped into action to provide Frank with every book he needed on strain viruses and rashes on babies.

Velina got Orenda ready to have some more milk, but she wasn't interested; she just wanted to sleep. Her little rosy complexion started to turn the colour of ash. Velina delicately passed Orenda to Axel and asked him, "Hold her, I have an idea. I need Eve's book." Axel looked down at his baby girl, who was asleep but looking very pale. Velina ran out of the room to the snug to find all kinds of chaos. She noticed the clover covered in sap on the floor, she picked it up and put it safely in her pocket. She noticed the claw marks slashed across Axel and Eve's painting, the cracked mirror with the salt washed away by water that was once in the cup resting on the sofa side table. Velina put two and two together very quickly and realised that John had escaped from the mirror; he is somewhere in Hollow Wood, and he could still even be in the Manor somewhere. Tex appeared behind her in the doorway, barking as if he was trying to tell her something. She followed him out of the snug and across the hall to hers and Axel's bedroom. There was a frantic tapping at the window. Tex started scratching at a floorboard and crying. She rushed over to open the window to allow the Raven to fly in; it rested on the back of a high-backed chair. Velina knelt and ripped the floorboard up, causing her fingers to bleed. There in a small space was a little wooden box. She lifted the box out from the compartment in the floor to examine it. She unhooked the small latch, the lid popped open, releasing a small puff of dust. Inside was a small, jagged amethyst crystal tied to a piece of thin rope that made it into a necklace, also some sage held together tied by a string. She looked up at the Raven, and it squawked and took flight. Velina and Tex weren't far behind. She entered Orenda's room, Tex and the Raven, waiting by the window just outside in the hallway. She placed the box on the baby's dresser and tried to hurry Frank out, who had returned from the library; the spell she needed to do had to be done fast.

Whatever John had done to her, Velina had the remedy. Frank solemnly stood from checking Orenda's pulse again, he told Velina and Axel, "her heart is very weak, and there's nothing I could find in the books about this. I have never seen this before. If that spreads, I'm sorry to say she will pass in the next twelve hours." The best thing you can do is make her comfy, feed her sugar water if she won't breastfeed, it will help keep her strength up." Frank took his leave from them; Axel stood at the window looking out as it started to rain with dark, heavy clouds looming over Antler Manor. The room felt so dark and weighted like he could not breathe. He looked over at Velina, who was frantically removing a necklace from an old box that she whipped over her neck. She lit a small stick of sage and started wafting it around the room. Axel just let her be if she thought it was going to help. Orenda was resting in her crib, her little chest barely moving up and down as the black veins started creeping onto her face. The Raven flew into the room and settled on the side of the crib, looking down at her. Velina leaned down and picked Orenda up in her arms. She felt so small and delicate, as if one wrong move would break her. Axel sat on the window seat and leaned his head back. He felt his eyes uncontrollably close as he drifted off. Velina started to recite the spell, holding the crystal around her neck to the black veins, saying, "Purify, clean, expel." She repeated it until the black veins started to drain away, and the crystal absorbed the dark smoke that was spilling out. A burst of hope surged through Velina with every black vein that disappeared. She left the sage burning for a while and rested once she saw there was nothing left on her little body. But Orenda was still so weak, she still refused milk and barely took the sugar water. Hours went by, and it was dark out. Velina's hope started to falter as Orenda's face started to pale again.

She rocked in the rocking chair, not taking her eyes off Orenda for a second, taking in all her little features, her long lashes, and her soft, fuzzy brown hair. Axel was still unconscious, propped up on the window seat with Tex beside him. The moonlight was shining through the open shutters, illuminating Orenda's tiny pale face and the dark circles that had appeared around her eyes. She wrapped her in her blanket, but Velina could still feel her breath on the top of her hand that was resting over her little body to keep her warm. Velina tried to get her to drink some sugar water, but she was too weak. Then the room started to feel strangely warm, and a still peace came over Velina as a teardrop fell from her cheek and landed on Orenda's. She looked around the dark room and said, "Please, whatever you are, I know you are here to either take her from me or give her back. Please don't take her, let her live." She looked around the room. The Raven had gone. Axel and Tex were still asleep. She looked over to the doorway, and there, blocking the light from the hallway window, was a cloaked figure that had appeared. It gracefully floated over to her, the hooded figure said in a soft, grateful voice, "Can I please hold her? I never got to when I was alive," Velina looked up, searching with her eyes to see through the layers of dark fabric and nodded to her.

The figure leaned over Orenda, she placed her bony, pale finger on her little head, and gently pushed back to make Orenda's mouth slightly part, she blew a warm, growing mist into her little mouth. Orenda took a deep sigh and started to stir. The figure removed her hood, revealing her dark eyes and ash-pale skin. She placed her hand on Velina's heart, and the figure dispersed into a mist and dissolved inside Velina's body. Velina felt like she had fallen asleep for a moment, like she wasn't present. Eve opened her eyes through Velina's and glanced down at the baby. She wept and lifted Orenda to her face and said in a gentle voice, "You will never be terrorised by John again, not as long as I'm here and your mum and dad. I wish I could hold you all the time and be the one you take your first steps to and be the one you call mummy for the first time. I will always love you no matter what," she leaned down and kissed her cheek. It glowed, and a small red love heart birthmark appeared on the skin of Orenda's cheek.

In a burst of energy, Eve's spirit separated from Velina, reappeared in her cloaked form, she doubled in on herself and faded in a shroud of ash to reveal the Raven that flew out of the room. Velina, through tear-filled eyes, felt the room go back to normal; everything came back into focus. When she looked down at Orenda, she held the sugar water bottle. She was drinking fast and noticed the small red love heart mark on her cheek. She laughed and cried all at once. She didn't know what else to do, she called over to Axel, who was coming out of his sleep along with Tex, she called him over to see Orenda's colour come back to her cheeks, her finally drinking the sugar water and making all kinds of little squeaking sounds as she lapped up the mixture.

They both walked over to the window to see the moon shining across the grounds, and the clouds had broken to clear, star-filled skies. In the distance to their disbelief, it almost glowed as it walked across the green grass, a pure white stag grazing. Following behind the proud stag that lifted his head was a pure white doe and a small white baby fawn, stumbling around trying to find its footing. They didn't look real. White stags were thought to be extinct from the hunters, but nature always shows its resilience to the terror and aggression of humans. Velina lent her weight against Axel with Orenda yawning, and she chucked the empty bottle to the floor. Velina left the window to place her safely in the crib to rest, now that the nightmare had passed. Velina clutched the clover still in her pocket and placed it on the dresser to stay in Orenda's room. She ripped the crystal that still hung around her neck, placed it in a glass jar, and filled it with salt. She pressed the lid on to prevent whatever that was seeping back out, she locked it

away in a small chest that she found in Orenda's room and asked
Axel to place it in the loft to be forgotten about.

Chapter Nine

BEFORE THE STORM

"The air held its breath, and so did they. Before the storm, there is always silence; in silence, the soul listens."

-E. L

Time swiftly moved on from that night, and the fear of John Backster lightly subsided over the years with a protective watch from Eve, who always sat at Orenda's window on guard, squawking and flapping her large black wings in the warm sun, or taking her rest in a large bird box Axel had built in the cedar tree overlooking Orenda's room. At Antler Manor little Orenda was flourishing and thriving, walking and talking, at the age of ten she was doing well at school particularly in art, in this time, Axel had lost both his parents to old age they both had passed barely a week between each other at Antler Manor in their bedroom, they both adored Orenda and were happy for the time they had with her watching her grow and get stronger and stronger. Antler Manor was fully owned by Axel now, so he took it upon himself to learn all he could about his ancestors and heritage. He would spend hours and hours in the oldest part of the library reading through years and years' worth of old family journal's, the writing in elegant decorative swirls across the old age stained pages, until he came upon an entry from Axel talking about a familiar name John Bakster and the blite he bought to his and Eve's relationship the entry said, "Axel Brinford, Journal entry Oct 27th, 1815 On this being a Tuesday I have had a ferocious scuffle with the vagabond John Backster who I found intimidating my dear wife Eve in her apothecary room. I was working in my office organising all the payments to pay for the new baby's furniture when I heard a very distressed scream. I bolted to find my poor Eve pinned to the floor with John Backster holding her down. The anger inside of me left his face bloodied, and my knuckles also. My staff came to my aid, hearing the commotion and threw the vile beast out of our home. The last thing I heard him yell from down the driveway was, "This isn't over, you don't deserve her." I'm glad this day is over; Eve and the baby are both settled, but she is shaken. She got on well with the Backster family." The bottom of the journal entry was signed by Axel Brinford.

Axel removed his glasses and rubbed his tired eyes as he looked up to see Velina approaching him with a nice hot cup of tea. He smiled at her and prompted her to sit next to him to show the entry he had found about poor Eve. Velina's eyes teared up when she noticed the date the entry was written; it was three days before she was taken by John and the villagers to be burned. She said, "Have you read on to see if the journal explains about the fire and how she became a Raven and how John became that creature?" But it did not. The journal had missing pages torn from the book, but on the last page was the statement written by Axel's hand in sharp handwriting, "When will this torturous life be over? I want to be with Eve and Orenda, but I promised them I would live". Axel closed the journal, and he took a sip of tea, feeling a heavy weight on his shoulders from reading those words. He said to Velina "I'm going to take a stroll to the church to place some flowers on my parents grave and Axel's when I pick Orenda up from school so we will be a bit late" Velina gave him a kiss and pinched one of the bisect sitting on the saucer under the tea cup she said "I will cook your favourite meal tonight bangers and mash with bake beans" Axel smiled he rubbed his hands together almost tasting and smelling the food already. He grabbed his coat and bag and walked out the Manor door to pick up Orenda from school, waving goodbye to Velina, who watched him walk away from the front door. She looked overhead to see Eve flying over the trees following Axel's root. Axel could see the shadow of Eve's flapping wings above his own shadow, which always gave him comfort as he left the drive of Antler Manor to start his short walk to Hollow Wood School to pick up Orenda and go to the florist to buy some flowers for the graves. He wished he knew where Eve's remains were buried so he could leave flowers for her, too.

Axel approached the school, waving and chatting to the other parents waiting for their kids to come running out. He could see all the happy faces from the kids running out the doors carrying more stuff home than what they were sent there with to show their parents. He looked up to see Orenda's smiling face running towards him, carrying her art set she took everywhere with her, her face looking up at him covered in paint. The teacher hurried out behind them to inform the parents that it was arts and crafts day. By the looks of all the paint-smudged hands and faces, they all had the best time. He picked Orenda up and gave her a big kiss, getting some not-quite-dry paint on his mouth. He laughed and smudged it across his lips, saying, "Now I have green lipstick" as he pouted at her. Orenda giggled as Axel put her down and placed all her school bits in his backpack, making sure he wiped away all the paint from him and Orenda. She took his hand and followed him to the florist Heather & Stella's flower arrangements to pick some nice flowers for Nan and Granada's grave; she got to pick what they put on there. As you entered the shop, the smell from all the flowers filled your nose, occasionally seeing some bees that had found their way into the shop, buzzing over all the distinct types of potted plants and bouquets, but no bees this time of year, it was too cold. As

Axel scanned through the shop, he was startled by Heather, the florist. She shared the shop with her best friend Stella; it had every kind of plant imaginable until he noticed a bouquet of long-stemmed dark red roses that he purchased for Velina for when they got home. Orenda came running over, carrying two small pots of busy lizzies for her grandparents' grave. Axel made the purchase and left with Orenda as they made their way to the church, which was only a short walk outside the village on a hill by the woods. They walked past Ruth's bakery; he promised Orenda they would get some pumpkin bread on the way back to go with dinner tonight. Her face lit up as pumpkin bread toasted with cheese was her favourite.

They approached the church gates, unhooked the large metal latch and gave them a big push; they squeaked as the old iron hinges swung them open. It was noticeably quiet that day, no singing birds, no wildlife going about their business, no grounds keepers or Shelly the vicar walking around the church, just the sound of the breeze rustling the remaining leaves in trees every now and then. Axel got a chill up his spine for some reason, but thought it was just the cold October evening air coming in. Eve landed on a gravestone, the sound of her wings startled Axel, which made Orenda giggle as she greeted Eve, giving her soft wings a pet. The Raven looked at Axel in confusion as to why he was so jumpy. He took the two flowerpots from Orenda and placed them on the graves, giving a little prayer in his head to them. Once his visit to his parents was done, he proceeded with the Raven and Orenda in tow to the older part of the church yard where the headstones were all leaning and covered in age spots, cracks and moss, the old carved words still just about visible. He placed a small bouquet of lilies on Axel's grave. He looked up to see the Raven sitting on the stone as a small tear fell down her beak and trickled onto the writing. Eve squawked. She flew over to an incredibly old, short, wide-trunked, leaning tree. The canopy of branches hanging down low, almost making a den entrance that was covered in ivy and moss, the Raven started scratching at something and flapping her wings, beckoning Axel and Orenda to come over. They carefully stepped over the overgrown foliage to the area the Raven was scratching and pecking at to reveal what looked like stone hidden beneath the brush. Axel directed Orenda to sit on an old stump, with Eve hopping on the floor around her feet. Axel began to pull up the weeds and brush until he started to uncover an above-ground stone coffin with the lid askew, slightly revealing the inside, but it was too dark to see in there.

He kept clearing until the old stone coffin was completely clear and out in the open. The coverage of the foliage had kept everything very well preserved and intact from the elements. The carved words were clear on the side of the stone coffin, saying, "She is not dead, just sleeping."

Axel froze, examining the words and looked up at Eve, who had her beak pointing to the floor. He asked her, "Is this unmarked coffin yours?" The Raven looked up at him. She softly squawked in agreement. Axel took a single dark, long-stemmed rose from the bouquet he bought for Velina and placed it on top of the stone coffin. He said, "Eve, I'm sorry I had no idea you were here all along under this tree. I will talk to Shelly and make sure this is cleared and taken care of in your memory." Eve shed another tear and hopped on top of her coffin, so she was eye level with Axel and lightly pecked at his fingers as he stroked her feathers. As it got darker, it was time to get home and to also grab some pumpkin bread before Ruth's shop closed for the night. They hurried down the church pathway back through the village to enter Ruth's bakery, instantly feeling warmth from the crackling fire at the back of the shop. He said to Orenda to go pick a loaf whilst he took a seat in one of the cozy wooden booths. It was very comforting inside Ruth's shop, all the wooden dark-stained booths carved and varnished with crimson flower-patterned cushions displayed on the benches, fresh flowers placed on each table, with warm, glowing, flickering flames from the melted yellow wax candles. He looked up to Ruth appearing from out the back hearing the jingle of the beaded door curtain, being politely greeted and apologised saying "Hello Axel sorry I didn't hear you come in and Orenda oh my gosh you have grown so much" Orenda came running over to Ruth at the till and asked her, "I would like this loaf please" she emptied her pockets which had a small amount of lose change, defiantly not enough to cover the cost of the bread. A small pony toy was pulled from her pocket as well that she placed on the counter along with a small handful of loose change. Ruth looked over to Axel and giggled, nodding her head as if to say This is fine. She took the change and the small pony toy and said, "This will take pride of place, sat on my till so it can keep me company." She bagged the bread in a brown paper bag and passed it to Orenda, who was beaming with pride at her first purchase for her dad.

Axel took Orenda's hand, her other clinging onto the warm loaf; they thanked Ruth and left the shop. By this time, the street was quiet; everyone had shut up shop and gone home, and they felt they should do the same. A cold breeze was blowing down the main street, making the shop signs sway and creak. An unnatural, heavy fog started to settle around them, so Axel pulled Orenda in and told her to stay close to him. Eve was flying above, losing sight of them under the heavy mist that cloaked the ground. Out of nowhere, the wind whipped up as heavy snow started to fall from the dark grey clouds. Axel picked Orenda up. They ran to Hollow Wood Hall to take shelter, which was in eyes' view, with the outdoor spotlight shining out so he could see where to head for through the snow and wind slashing at his face and eyes to wait for the worst of the storm to pass so they could go home. He shoved the heavy wooden door open, placed Orenda and the bouquet of red roses down, he hurried back to the door to try to close it behind him, but bits of snow and wind pushed in around him through the gap of the almost closed door. He just about managed to close it, blocking the craziness of the storm outside away from them. He checked on Orenda to make sure she was ok and not hurt. He dropped his bag on the floor, took his coat off and wrapped it around her to make sure she was warm. He sat her on a chair next to the radiator, which was thankfully still on. When they both settled, they were disturbed by a sound of crying and whimpering coming from the main hall beyond its closed door. He looked at Orenda and told her to stay by the radiator so he could go check it out. He slowly approached the main hall door, pressed his ear against it to listen, and he could definitely hear a woman in there crying. He slowly and carefully pushed the door open, gently saying in a soft voice, so he didn't spook her, "Hello, are you ok in there? Do you need any help? My name is Axel. I'm just taking shelter from the storm. Are you doing the same?"

He slowly pushed the hall door open wide and stepped in to see a figure covered in a shawl. He couldn't see her face, but she was a large, wide-shouldered lady; from the back view, she was rocking backwards and forwards in a chair at the front row, crying. The wind and snow hit heavily against the windows. Axel was afraid the glass would break. The hard pattering sounds from debris hitting against the hall outside, which echoed around the room, was very overstimulating to hear over the whimpering from the woman who hadn't reacted to Axel's words of comfort at all. He slowly walked down the aisle with rows of chairs left out on either side of him. He approached her closer until he got to the front row of chairs, where she was sitting, her face still hidden by the shawl and the rocking motions. He asked again, "Ma'am, are you ok? Can I help you?" He got closer to her step by step and reached his hand out to place it on her shoulder in the hopes of comforting her and stopping her from the aggressive rocking. He noticed as he got closer, there was a red shining puddle of blood on the floor in front of her that grew with every drop. He placed his hand gently on her shoulder, and she froze; the room fell silent for a moment, only hearing the commotion from the storm outside. In a sudden flash of movement, she spun around and screamed in Axel's face. She flung her shawl around Axel. In a panic, he fell back to the floor and tried to remove the tangled shawl that wrapped around him. He threw it aside and looked up in horror to see it was Ted Backster's face staring back at him, but he didn't look right, his eyes were red with blood flowing from his tear ducts, but it wasn't Ted's voice it was a voice he recognised immediately, "Hi Axel we meet again but this time you won't get away from me" he jumped to his feet to run to Orenda who was still out in the entrance hall sat huddled by the radiator. Axel scrambled to get to his feet, but Ted's body was on him in a flash, with John's voice laughing from within him. Axel pleaded with Ted, "TED TED mate, wake up, it's me, Axel, don't let him control you."

Ted's eyes flickered for a moment, his pupils appearing behind the blood in his eyes. He looked terrified; he was breathing heavily. He lifted Axel to his feet but pushed him away, saying, "Get out of here, please get away from me as fast as you can and don't look back." Axel thankfully nodded to Ted and ran for the door as he heard Ted starting to scream in pain behind him, trying to fight John from within to stop him from taking over his body again. Axel didn't look back, though; he slammed the hall door behind him, grabbed a mop from the cleaner's cupboard and slid it through the door handle to barricade John in there. He knew it would not hold him forever, but hopefully long enough to get away. He grabbed Orenda, who was huddled up by the radiator, clutching the bread and roses. Axel took her hand, pulled her to him, and started walking fast with her. She looked worried, confused and put the brakes on because she didn't want to go out in the storm. Axel knelt to her level, looked her in the eyes and said, "Honey, we must go. It's not safe here anymore. I will carry you and shield you as best as I can from the wind and snow, but we must leave." She went to remove his jacket that was massively too big for her to give it back to him, but he pressed the jacket back around her and said, "No, you keep that on and stay warm." Axel lifted her, and she pressed her face into his chest and pulled the jacket around her to brace herself to feel the snow and wind. He held on tight to her, trying to ignore the roses that were tickling under his chin. He pulled on the door handle, it flung open with force against the wind, he stepped back for a moment, then pushed on out into the cold and wind. He searched the skies, his eyes scanned the area for any sign of Eve, but she was nowhere in sight. He hoped she was ok and took shelter somewhere safe from the storm. He was just about ready to run into the snow when he heard a blast behind him, black ropes of smoke wrapped around his ankles. He dropped Orenda to the side of the hall's porch; the red roses and bread were flung to the floor; he told her to hide behind some wooden crates that had been left there from a delivery. Before Orenda had a chance to respond, Axel was dragged back into the hall's entrance.

Before she hid, she peeked around the open door to see Ted's blood-soaked face with red, dead eyes holding up an unconscious

Eve by her talons, her long black wings dangling down, and her dad on the floor, constricted by black smoke. The final words she heard from Ted before she hid were "It's time to die."

Chapter Ten

FIRE IN HIS BLOOD TIME JUMPS

BACK.

"I gave him fire to destroy him, but to also make sure he remembered. Curses do not always bind the body. The worst ones burn the soul."

-E.L.

Ted was opening his jewellery shop, going about his daily routine, the sun was shining, he had done his family duties and was ready to make some sales when he saw Doctor Frank Hench walking down the street towards him. It was exceedingly rare to see him in town and not hunched over his desk, lost in medical paperwork. Ted called over to him to wish Frank a good morning and have a little chat with him. "Morning, doc, how's the family and the surgery doing? I need to book in and get my back looked at." Frank walked over to Ted and said in a very tired husky voice, "No problem, just give me a call when you want to come in and I will get you sorted. You're getting old, mate, that's the problem." They both laughed together. Ted looked at Frank, who appeared very drained and upset by something. He asked Frank, "You, ok? You look down". Frank had been with Axel and Velina not long ago, giving them the news no parent wants to hear that their newborn baby's life is already coming to an end. He explained to Ted what happened the night before; he hadn't slept because he was just reading and researching illnesses in infants, trying to identify what the hell that was. Ted placed a hand on Frank's shoulder in comfort and said, "You are the best Doctor. If you can't help the poor little soul, then no one can." He told Ted he was going to call in on them later this afternoon, but he needed to get some sleep first. He came into town to change his surroundings for a bit to clear his head and mentally prepare himself for two grieving parents. Ted said goodbye to Frank and asked him to send condolences to Axel and Velina for him. He watched Frank slowly walk away in the direction of the car park, and he continued to open the shop. It was early morning; he went around turning the case lights on until he got startled by a figure standing behind his reflection in one of the glass cabinets.

He spun around to be greeted by no one. He thought he was tired, but when he turned back around to finish turning the light on, he looked up again, and the figure was standing right behind him in the reflection.

He screamed in pain as he felt a deep pressure plunge into his back. Black smoke filled the air around him, and he could not understand what was going on. His eyes were wide with panic, the pain built up in his entire body as everything went black, and he fell to the floor with a hard thud. He woke from the feeling of someone nudging his arm and asking him to wake up, Are you ok? Do you need an ambulance? Ted's eyes flung open, he jumped to his feet, breathing heavily and panicking, clasping his chest, holding onto his desk for support. In himself, he felt strange, like he was wearing clothes that were too tight, but he had made them fit. His skin was tingling like he was covered in small magnets. He leaned forward and started taking big, deep breaths. By this time, the lady who woke him up was out the door and running to a pay phone to call for an ambulance. She came bursting back into the shop to try and calm Ted and tell him that help is on the way. She sat him down at his desk and offered him a glass of water and a cool, wet rag for his head; he was burning up and sweating. Moments later, she heard the sirens in the distance coming in to aid poor Ted, whose eyes were now going very bloodshot. The ambulance team burst through the door with a stretcher for him, just in case he could not find the strength to walk. In the meantime, the lady told Ted she would contact his wife as they went to the same morning mothers' book club after the children had been dropped off at school. Ted, in short, gasped for breath, thanked her and handed his shop keys to her to lock up for him. They loaded Ted into the back of the ambulance and rushed him off to the night Owl surgery as fast as they could to get him treated for whatever this mysterious illness was that had taken him. They pulled up out of the back of Night Owl surgery, where the emergency staff were ready to jump into action. They pulled the stretcher out with a very poorly looking Ted upon it; he was greeted by Frank, who joked with him, "Didn't realise you were this desperate for a doctor's appointment." Ted mustered up the strength for a laugh and a smile, then completely passed out.

They rushed him into the theatre immediately, they attached a drip to him to hydrate Ted as he was abnormally sweating, his mouth was dry and cracked as if he had been trekking in the desert for days. Frank was astonished when he took Ted's temperature; it was reading one hundred and ten Faren Height. He shouted for more staff to bring cool towels and all the fans to try and get his temperature down, as he was dangerously burning up, but from what he couldn't fathom. Ted was starting to come too, but he was still asleep, unable to open his eyes, where they felt heavy and sore like he had small bits of gravel stuck in them. Then he heard a voice not from the commotion happening around him but from within his own mind. His body started shaking and going into shock, then he heard a very stern angry voice within him say, "TED, WILL YOU CALM DOWN THE SOONER YOU SUBMIT TO ME, THE FASTER YOU WILL HEAL." Ted's natural response was to cry out loud and tell the voice to "leave me alone, GET OUT, GET OUT". The surgery staff thought Ted had come too and was telling them to get out. They tried holding his big arms down as he flung them around wildly, trying to get rid of whatever was talking to him in his mind. Frank had no choice but to give him a sedative and hoped that keeping him cool and resting his body, which was working extremely hard to survive, would help him. He grabbed Ted's hand and pinned it to the bed. The staff helped and tried to keep him still. Frank injected the top of his hand he held on until Ted went limp. Ted drifted into a deep slumber and by doing so, John could take full control of poor Ted's body without a fight. Within seconds, Ted stopped sweating and shaking, his colour returned to his face, and he just slept. Frank left all the fans running, but removed the cool, damp towels from him just in case he went the other way and was too cold and left him to sleep but kept a close eye on him throughout the day.

Ted's wife, Crissy, burst through the surgery door demanding to be taken to Ted, asking, "Is he ok? What's wrong with him? Where is he?" Doctor Frank's sister Enid, who always manned the reception, pointed to the door on the right. She rushed back into the staff room to inform Crissy that Ted was stable, but he's under a strong sedative, so his body doesn't have to work so hard, so he can rest. She said, "He will be staying here tonight so we can monitor his progress, but he is stable." She gestured for Crissy to follow her and took her to the room where Ted was resting. She could see him sound asleep on a white hospital bed through the large glass window; the fans were blowing around him to keep him cool. Crissy asked if they knew what was wrong with him, but they couldn't give her a confident answer, as they had never seen symptoms like that before. She thanked Enid and left the surgery, as she had to go pick the children up from school to also inform them that Daddy is not feeling very well and must spend the night at the doctors. After saying goodbye to Crissy, Enid went to find her brother in his office, who had passed out from exhaustion at his desk. He was being guarded by his beloved owl, Leina, who looked up at Enid when she peered around the door. She crept in to see books flung everywhere, each one open to a different page showing all kinds of diseases and viruses. Leina flapped her large white wings, which woke Frank abruptly. He sat up straight, muttering something about black veins, but he shook his head and removed his glasses that were sitting crooked on his face. He looked up at Enid, in a panicked tone, he asked her for the time, as he had to be at Antler Manor to check up on their newborn baby. Enid glanced down at her watch. It was five o'clock, so Frank rushed to his feet, opened the window wide for Leina, kissed his sister's cheek and yelled, "I will be back later." Enid laughed to herself, rolled her eyes, and looked over to Leina and said, "What are we going to do with him?" The owl shook her head in some kind of agreement and took off flying out the window.

Frank ran to his car, chucking his medical bag on the passenger seat, firing up the engine, and driving as fast as he could to Antler Manor, expecting to see and hear the worst. He pulled up through the gates, driving down the lengthy driveway towards the Manor. He parked up, took a deep breath, and prepared himself for what he was going to encounter behind the large decorative wooden door looming in his peripheral vision. He grabbed his bag and approached the door; he rang the large bell to hear hastened footsteps clipping across the stone floor. The door flung open to a maid who was smiling and laughing, not the greeting the doctor was expecting, but he asked how the baby was doing after his visit the day before. The maid gleefully said to Dr Frank that baby Orenda had made a full recovery and is resting in her bedroom with her mum and dad. She was told to inform Frank that they would be in touch with him soon to book an appointment at the surgery for a full check-up on her, but for now, after a very taxing night, they were all resting. Frank smiled and laughed out loud in relief at the news that the baby was ok and said to the maid, "Thank you for informing me and please let Velina and Axel know how happy and overjoyed I am for them." He left Antler Manor with a new pep in his step. Ted was stable, baby Orenda was doing well, and he could not wait for them to come down to the surgery so he could meet her properly. Frank made his way back to the surgery to check on Ted and clean up his office. He finally went home to have some proper sleep in his bed and not propped up on his desk. He could not wait to rest his head on his nice, comfy pillow and not a hardback medical book. He also needed to refix his glasses that were now bent at a funny angle due to falling asleep with them on his face. They still served their purpose but sat at a wonky slant on his nose.

Ted's eyes flew open; he felt the cool breeze from the fans blast frigid air over his face, which gave him a slight shiver. He looked around the room, trying to focus on something, but his vision was blurred, and he felt groggy, as if he had just gotten over a very rough flu. He went to wipe his face with his hand, but his movements felt strange, as if his brain was sending all the right signals to his arm to lift his hand, but no movement occurred. He led there for a few moments thinking to himself "what if I'm paralyzed? Am I going mad? What was that voice I heard?" Then his arm started to lift without his control, he was confused as he saw his arm jutting up and it was stretching out its fingers, then

138

betrayed by his own hand flung back on him and gripped around his neck. A voice echoed out in his mind, "Don't scream or make a scene. I need you alive, and you're the only one I can bond with. My name is John Backster. I am your ancestor. I want to show you something. I want to show you how I became this monster. An image flashed in a circle of fire in Ted's head of a humanoid figure that was covered in cracked, burnt skin and dark smoke pouring out of the caverns of the creature's chest. There were no eyes, only sunken dark pits where droplets of lava trickled out like falling fire tears. Ted gasped and said out loud, "Who did this to you?" A dark voice growled in his head, just one name: "Eve Longbow." Ted's eyes went wide, and he realised who he was talking about, "the witch who was married to Axel's ancestor? I found your journal in my. (He paused and corrected himself.) Our loft, your journal, was put with a ring that belonged to the witch. Upon reading what you wrote in your journal entry you were very vague." John scoffed and said, "thank you for releasing it from the circle of salt, in doing so you not only released whatever magic that ring held but also released me from my fiery prison that she condemned me too." Ted asked John "what did you do to piss her off that much?" He heard John scream in anger in his head, "I HAVE DONE NOTHING WRONG. I JUST WANTED WHAT WAS MINE. SHE WAS MINE AND SHE CHOSE THAT IDIOT AXEL OVER ME. I will show you what happened to me."

Ted sounded confused as to how John could show him these things, so he asked in a very hesitant voice, "How can you show me what's been and gone? Do you mean you have a hidden journal concealed somewhere?" John went quiet in his head for a bit as if he was up to something coiled in the inner fabrics of Ted's head. He could feel a strange sensation pulsing in his temples as he strained against the discomfort of the humming. He cried out, "WHAT ARE YOU DOING IN THERE?" John's voice appeared out of nowhere, telling him that he was making room in Ted's head for this one memory of John's he wanted to show him. John told

Ted to close his eyes and breathe steadily, as merging his memories with John could cause some pain; he just wanted this to be over and have his life back, but now he has an unwelcome hitchhiker boycotting his body. He felt his eyelids close against his will, but shouted to John, "Wait, if you show me this and I help you to do whatever it is you need, will you leave me so I can have my body and my life back?" John went quiet in deep thought, then said in a deep, menacing voice, "Anything?" Ted, now close to tears, said, "Yes, anything, just please get out of my head when it's done." John agreed to these terms: "We have a deal, but if you do anything to sabotage me, I will not hesitate to end you, whether you're my blood or not. I want vengeance."

Ted promised he would not get in the way of his plans and submit to John taking control of his body when he needed it, but the thought of what John wanted to do made him feel sick. He lay there in pain whilst John was placing the memory in his head, his temples continued to throb, his heart was racing, but he kept his eyes shut and breathed deep, long breaths out of his mouth and through his nose as John instructed. Ted was very thankful for the fans still going, the soft hum from them almost became a calming white noise for him to blank the horrors that were happening to his body. He heard John's voice appear loudly in his head, which made him jump. "My memory is ready, it will feel like you are in a dream, but this is no dream, welcome to my nightmare."

Chapter Eleven

CURSE OF MOLTHERA

"I cursed him, Molthera, for he would melt his skin but never his sin. To curse a soul is one thing. To let it linger is another. The Molthera is both. Beware the ones who burn without smoke. Their time is still coming."

-E.L.

Ted's body tensed, his eyes flickering beneath his lids, looking around at a place that was familiar to him, but it felt different, looked different. He was in his home at Hollow Wood village. He recognised the large fireplace in his living room, but the furniture was different, and all his family photos were missing. John's voice made itself present in his mind, telling him to leave the house and walk to the witch's ash tree just outside the village. Ted poked his head out the front door that was ajar to see all the villagers wielding torches and chucking bales of hay and large branches on the back of a horse-drawn cart. He looked up to see John standing on the edge of the cart containing the materials, yelling orders at people. But Ted was distracted by the sound of crying coming from upstairs inside the house. He left the door entrance and followed the sound up to the master bedroom. The door had a large lock on the handle, so he took a deep breath, and he felt his light form pass through the large wooden locked door. He could see John's wife. He recognised her from an old family painting; she was tied to a chair; she was facing out the window, where you could see the witch's ash tree with its large branches reaching skyward, its lush orange autumn leaves glowing in the low setting sun in the distance. Her tears were uncontrollable; she had bruises on her face and arms. John's voice echoed in Ted's head, "She was disobedient to me, she helped Eve and Axel escape their cells; she had to be punished. So, I gave her a good beating and tied her up facing the area her best friend was going to burn." Ted tried to control his thoughts and regretted his choice of helping this monster with whatever plan he had in mind, but it was the only way to get him out of his head. Ted wanted to help John's wife, but there was nothing he could do about it, as this was only a memory of things that had already happened. He looked out the window, and he could see people gathering around the large tree, building what looked like a pit for a large fire. Then Ted's thoughts clicked; this was the moment Eve was going to burn.

He hurried back down the stairs and out the front door to see that the cart was now full to the brim with flammable kindling. He could see John with his son standing next to him, holding an inflamed torch up. All the villagers were gathered around John, chanting and cheering at him that he had flushed out the witch who had enchanted Axel. Axel was in chains mounted on a horse with two riders on either side of him to make sure he didn't bolt. John raised his hand to silence the crowd and gestured to his guards to bring forth Eve, who was bound by the hands and feet. She had been put in a white hessian dress that hung from her small frame. John approached her and grabbed her long black hair that was blowing in the breeze. He leaned in and inhaled the scent of her hair and then tore a chunk of it straight from her scalp. She cried out in pain as John lifted the hair up and yelled, "LET'S BURN THIS DEMON TO HELL." The crowd cheered as Eve's tear-filled eyes looked up to Axel. She mustered up a smile for him, and he returned a smile to her, as weak and sad as it was. The crowd started moving as they made their way through the village towards the witch's ash tree. It hadn't been dubbed that name yet; at the time, it was just a large tree outside the village where families would go for picnics and gatherings. They all filtered around the tree and started piling the hay and wood around a large single pole jutting up from the ground. Eve looked up to Axel, took a deep breath and sent her inner voice to him. Axel's eyes looked to her in shock as he could hear her voice, clear as day. "My love, I will always be around, but not in a way you can see me as I am now. I have a plan, but please don't fear me. Always remember us when you first caught me at the bottom of the stairs that day, don't remember me like this." Axel looked over at Eve and gave her a nod, knowing that that would be the last time he would hear her voice like that. He mouthed to her," I love you." John's eyes were everywhere; he caught the final tender moment between Eve and Axel, a diabolical plan manifested in his head.

John ordered his guards to remove Axel from his horse and to bring him up to stand by his side. Axel was protesting the whole time, not taking his gaze away from Eve, and neither her gaze was away from him as they soaked up as much as they could of each other's presence before the inevitable end. John's son was still standing quietly, holding the flaming torch aloft above his head. Once the construction of the branches and kindling was completed, he yelled for his guards to tie Eve to the large wooden pole that stuck out from the centre of the stacked flammables. She didn't scream or even look at John; she was calmly breathing deep as if she were meditating. They slammed her back against the wooden pole and tightened the knot around her wrist and tied another length of rope around her chest. She leaned her head back against the wooden pole and looked above her to see a large black Raven perched atop it, squawking and looking down at her as if they were communicating to each other. John looked on in horror, seeing this silent back-and-forth conversation between Eve and the Raven, he picked up a large stone and threw it at the bird. The stone hit just below, falling into the kindling below, sending the raven flying up into the large tree, flapping its large wings in protest at him. He leaned in close to Axel and ordered the guards to remove his shackles but hold onto him in case he tried something. He snatched the torch from his son and aggressively rammed it into Axel's hand; Axel's eyes went wide in realisation of what John was asking him to do. John raised his voice to the crowd and said, "Axel must be the first person to set this demon ablaze to break the spell she holds over him. If he doesn't, then he is too far gone; he must burn with her also." Axel dropped to his knees he sobbed and pleaded with John to not make him do this. "please please John don't make me do this I can't I can't" in between sobs and uncontrollable tears falling from his eyes he heard Eve's voice in his head once more "My love its ok, it must be you to do this, set me free so I can set you free, never forget how much I love you" Axel looked up at her and nodded he straightened up and took slow somber steps towards her and raised his arm holding the torch.

Ted could not believe what he was seeing, what a monster John really was, which made him feel even more ashamed of having this asshole in his family tree. He knew to himself that whatever Eve had planned for him, he deserved it. He looked to Axel with his shaky arm holding up the torch, and he plunged it down into the wood, and the fire blazed almost immediately. He dropped to his knees in front of Eve, who just smiled at him through the flames that started nipping against her dress. Eve slowly raised her gaze to John, reciting a curse in her head she had memorised from her spell book. The page itself was on fire but never seemed to burn. Her head shot back, her eyes were on fire as her gaze snapped to John. Her words were loud and very clear,

"LET ME BE THE MONSTER YOU THINK I AM," a high-pitched scream barrelled from deep within her chest as her long black hair ignited in fire that whirled in the wind. The ropes fell from her and shrivelled away into the flames below. John's eyes went wide in terror as he lifted his pistol and fired right at Eve, where it struck her stomach, but the shot had no effect on her. She was standing up straight as she lifted her arms, her fingers dancing, manipulating the fire as it swirled around her. The crowd backed away and took cover behind the wagons and carts. The horses were whinnying in pure panic as the heat thrummed and pulsed in the air. Eve spoke the curse, "JOHN YOU WILL BECOME A CREATURE OF YOUR OWN MAKING. FIRE COME TO ME LEND ME YOUR RAW DESTRUCTIVE POWER," she screamed again as she directed her hands in John's direction, sending flames roaring at him that latched onto first his clothes, then burned deeper to attack his skin. Eve said, "YOU WILL BURN FOR ETERNITY." Eve recited the spell, the fury burning from her lips, "by fire's tongue and shadow's breath, I cast thee down to living death. Let flesh be charred, let soul be torn, by curse of ash, a beast be born. Crack the skin and hollow the eyes, smoke shall rise where mercy dies. Let pain be fuel, let fear be flame from this day forth, forget thy name. Molthera arise, unholy and true. Your world shall rot and burn around you." John screamed and fell to the floor in uncontrollable pain. The fire burned his skin, and black smoke started bellowing from canyons that clawed across his chest. His eyes sank back, replaced by empty dark holes where more black smoke poured out. John stood there not moving for a moment, as the flames relentlessly attacked his body.

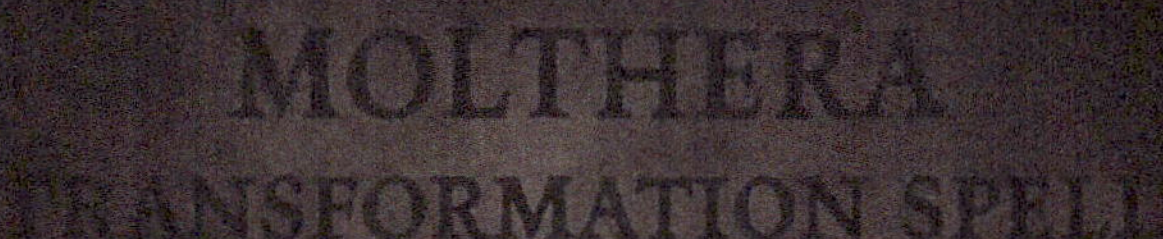

MOLTHERA
TRANSFORMATION SPELL

By fire's tongue and shadow's breath,
I cast thee down to living death.
Let flesh be charred, let soul be torn,
By curse of ash, a beast be born.

Crack the skin and hollow the eyes,
Smoke shall rise where mercy dies.
Let pain be fuel, let fear be flame,
From this day forth, forget thy name.

Molthera rise—unholy and true,
Your world shall rot and burn
around you.

When Eve's magic started to falter, Axel was still on his knees in front of her but was unaffected by the heat as if he had a protective shield around him. He looked up at Eve, seeing her long hair that was ablaze, whipping in the wind, her dark, beautiful eyes replaced by fire that burned so intense, but he remembered her words, "Please don't fear me," so he stayed in his spot watching what was happening to John in disbelief. He knew Eve had power, but not this much. He looked back towards her. He started seeing her become unsteady on her feet. He knew she was getting low; the spell was coming to its end. He had a bit of hope that Eve could come back from this and survive; they could run away together and live somewhere else, far away from here. The flames dissipated from around John, leaving a charred mess curled up on the floor. Eve had one last thing to do, so she stepped down from the platform that was still engulfed with flames. She gracefully walked past Axel towards John, who was now gasping for air. Eve stood over him and said, "You destroyed my life, your family's life, you poisoned everything you touched. You are now one of the lowest life forms, a Molthera, a creature that deserves to burn." She took a dagger that had fallen from John's waist belt and held it up until the blade of the knife started to glow a furious yellow and red with heat. She slashed at the air, and a cut had appeared in the open space that hung there; inside was dark with glowing embers spitting out from it. She waved her hands towards John, who looked lifeless. Flames lifted his limp body towards the slash in the air and tossed him in. You could hear him scream out as he fell into the dark fire, "I WILL KILL YOU ALL IF IT'S THE LAST THING I DO." Eve closed this portal slash with a whip of her hand, and just like that, as if someone had turned off a light, the flames dispirited from around her, her long, wavy black hair fell down her back again, and her dark eyes looked towards Axel, who was already on his feet, running to her aid.

He cradled her against his body and held her close to him; she was sweating, the beads falling down her face as she looked up at Axel. He made a joke for her, "remind me not to get on your bad side," he giggled through tears. Eve looked at him and giggled as she placed her hand on his cheek. She said to Axel, "I'm dying, my love. I used too much power; I can feel it in my spirit. I need to put on one last show, though." She leaned up and kissed him softly and held his gaze for a little while, seeing the villagers slowly creeping out from behind the wagons and carts. Eve got to her feet wearily, holding on to Axel's arm as they stood together slowly, she looked back at the large fire she was originally tied to that was still burning strong. She glanced up at the tree where the Raven was still perched, she nodded in its direction; she got a large wing flap in response. She asked Axel to find the ring that John had taken from her and keep it safe, but she didn't know where he had hidden it, as they both knew what a precious life it contained inside it. She glanced at Axel and said, jumping over her words in tears and frustration, "This is goodbye now. I wish it didn't have to happen this way; we should be at home now getting excited to welcome our baby. I love you I love you I love you I'm sorry my love" She kissed him again and with what strength she had left pushed him away, she ran full force at the inferno and leaped into the air as time felt like it had slowed down, the Raven meet her pace and flew towards the flames as their bodies collided together, the fire exploded out and lurched up to the sky. The villagers stood frozen in fear and wonder, their torches sputtering low as the fire roared higher, devouring the wooden stake where Eve Longbow had once been bound. Heat licked the air in waves, crackling with hunger that promised nothing but ash. Eve did not scream; the glow with something fiercer than rage and resolve pulsed around her. With one final breath, she opened her arms to the flames, her silken skin melting away as the fire consumed her whole. The blaze wrapped her body, swallowing flesh and bone, yet from within the pyre came not death's silence but a pulse of power. The crowd gasped as the fire surged upward, bursting into a shape that was not human. From the very core of the inferno, wings of molten light unfurled. The Raven, her Raven emerged, vast and radiant, feathers gleaming like obsidian kissed by flame. Twice the size of any earthly bird, it rose unscathed from the fire that should have destroyed it, eyes burning with Eve's own immortal gaze. The villagers stumbled back, some clutching their mouths in horror, others dropping their torches as the bird spread its wings wide. Ash rained down like black snow, stinging their eyes, yet none dared look away. The last thing the villagers saw was the Raven vanishing against the moonlit sky, unburnt, eternal and vengeful. Leaving them trembling with the knowledge that what they had tried to destroy had only been reborn anew.

All that was left was Eve's body, a lifeless, empty shell burning in the flames. The villagers didn't know whether to be happy or sad, but they all stayed in silence and watched as the fire burned through the rest of the night. As the flames died down, Axel was still on the floor where he had fallen from when Eve pushed him. He saw the ashes from the pit in the ground fly up into the air and settle onto the tree, turning it a discoloured grey. All the leaves fell to the floor and blew away in the wind. He heard a Villiger call the tree the witches' ash, and the name stuck since that day. After that night, the villagers made a song in memory of Eve Longbow and the tales of the horrors that took place that night.

The Ballad of Eve Longbow

In fire she fell, but ash bore wings,
The mother lost, the raven sings,
Her love undone, her soul unbowed,
She walks the wind—no longer cowed.

They feared her hands, they feared her name,
So cast her body into flame.
But witch-fire burns beyond the pyre,
And vengeance wakes with wings of fire.

Eve... Eve Longbow... they whisper still,
Through broken trees and breathless chill,
Protecting one, avenging all,
She answers every justice call.

So mark the night and heed her cry,
She is the wind, the wrath, the woe—
The fire they sparked... long ago.

Ted felt exhausted from everything he had witnessed. John's voice appeared in his head again, "You see why I want revenge; this isn't my memory now because I was in the black hole. This is what my son saw. I had to mesh mine and his memories together to show you the full night". Ted played along; he didn't want John to catch on to how disgusted he felt. Ted watched Axel stand in somber silence and walk to the pit that was now just full of ash. He removed his jacket and lifted what was left of Eve's remains that were falling everywhere; he had to gather them up and bundle them in his jacket. He walked off in the direction of Antler Manor. Ted's eyes snapped open, he was back at the surgery led on his bed with the calm hum from the fans blowing over him again. He took a deep breath to be greeted by Frank, who was happy to see him awake. He just came back from Antler Manor to tell Ted the baby was well and was alive. Ted heard John's voice say, "dammit, I thought I killed it, guess I will try harder next time, but I need my strength for the big finale." Ted shuddered at his cruel words but was a bit relieved to know John was going dormant for a while. He looked up at Frank and asked him when he could go home to his family. He just wanted to hug his wife and kids. Frank examined Ted, took his temperature, and told Ted to follow the light from the torch in front of his eyes. He followed those instructions with no problems. Frank told him to "rest up tonight, and we will see how you are in the morning to go home, but no working, you must rest. I'm still trying to identify what illness came over you as I have never seen it before." Ted nodded and thanked him and did not take long to fall asleep. He was truly tired. Frank turned all the fans off but kept one running for Ted through the night. The sun shone through the window into Ted's room through a small crack in the curtain, which woke him up. He squinted his eyes and sat up, stretching, looking around the room. He waited to hear John's voice, but nothing; it was quiet, and he didn't know whether to feel relieved or unnerved.

Frank walked into Ted's room looking a lot fresher now that he had shaved and put on some clean clothes. He gave Ted the good news before he could even finish his sentence. Ted's wife and kids came running into the room, jumping on him in bed, all of them laughing and so happy to see him awake and looking like his old self again. Ted lifted his arm out of the cranage to make sure his drip was not pulled out with the onslaught of hugs and kisses from his family. They all backed off from him, making sure nothing was caught on them, and Frank said that the drip can come out, and you can go home and rest. I have written you a prescription to give to Enid on your way out for some pills that will help. Frank swiftly and professionally removed Ted's drip, and he waved him out of the room so he could clean up and put all the fans away. Ted handed Enid his slip of paper. She smiled at him and was glad to see him back on his feet. She handed him the pills, wished him well and said in a week, give us a call to come back in for a check-up, but if anything feels strange from now till then, don't hesitate to come back in. Ted thanked her, put his large arm around his wife and left the surgery with a big smile on his face, watching his children playing and chasing each other out the reception door. They walked home, the fresh air he inhaled through his nose and out his mouth. They walked back into their home and excused themselves to go get changed and cleaned up. His wife went to the kitchen with the kids to make some breakfast for them all to sit and eat together. Ted retraced his steps from the memory and made his way to the master bedroom, where he could still see, in a shadow, John's poor wife tied to the chair. He sat at the end of his bed and said, "I don't know if you can hear me or if you're even here. I hope you're not, and you are at peace. I am sorry for the pain my ancestor put you through, but I also want to thank you, as I wouldn't be here with my beautiful wife and kids if it weren't for you. I hope you're at peace," He looked out the window, seeing the witch's ash tree in the far distance and a beautiful white butterfly fluttering at his window. He smiled and nodded his head.

Chapter Twelve

POSSESSION WITH INTENT TO KILL.

"When intention guides the cursed hand, possession becomes murder."

-E.L.

Over the years, Ted never heard John in his head; he was hoping it was just a side effect of the illness that came over him, which made him go a bit delirious. But he always felt wrong for some reason, like having an injection and the feeling you get after, when your arm feels sore and uncomfortable, like something that is sitting within him, ready to make itself known once more. He never had another illness like the one he had that day all those years ago. In that time, he and his wife were expecting their third child, which they were overjoyed about in their advanced ages. It was getting cold by this time; the time was getting closer for him to go pick up the kids from school. The day was clear but a little chilly, so he grabbed his jacket before kissing his wife goodbye and telling her he loves her. He looked in the mirror in the hallway to put his cap on and noticed his eyes were going very bloodshot. He brushed it off to all the overtime he was doing at the shop in preparation for the new baby to come. He took the short walk to school to see his children running out at him, waving a painting in the air they worked on together, followed by the teacher shouting out to the parents, it had been arts and crafts day. Dry paint stained their hands as they jumped around him in excitement from the praise he gave them. He told them it would be framed and hung in the house when they got home. He looked up across the road to see

Axel arrive to pick up Orenda, who had green paint smudged across her face. Ted gave out a little giggle seeing Axel pick her up to kiss her and getting green paint on his lips. Ted overheard Axel tell Orenda they were going to the florist to buy flowers for the graves. He was going to go over to say hi, but in all the madness of the other parents and kids, he thought he would catch up with him another time. He was walking the kids home when he started getting a very intense headache, nothing, some painkillers and a big glass of water couldn't fix.

He unlocked his front door; the kids kicked their shoes off, running along the hall to find their mum, who was sitting in the living room resting having a cup of tea. He caught a glance in the mirror again, removing his hat, seeing his eyes getting very red and watery, and the headache was starting to consume his thoughts. He called out to his wife he was going to the doctors and not to worry he will be back soon, he heard her call out from the living room "ok love hope you are ok" a swell of dread filled him as he poked his head around the corner of the living room door to see his family talking and laughing about their day, but he had this sinking feeling that that would be the last time he would see that. He stood there for a moment, soaking in the scene and the happiness he felt until his headache pulled him away. He pressed his hands to his temple as he closed his front door behind him and headed in the direction of the doctors until a voice echoed in his head, "It's time to fulfil your promise to me." Ted froze in fear, hearing that all too familiar voice ring in his mind as tears started to fall down his face. His legs spun him around to face the other way, taking him in the direction of the florist. The feeling of your own limbs not obeying you made Ted feel very uneasy, but there was nothing he could do but keep his mouth shut and follow in silence. By the time they reached the florist, he and John saw Axel and Orenda leave the shop; she was carrying two pots of busy lizzies in her hand and catching sight of Eve's black wings flying above them. Ted could feel his emotions rise in anger against his will at the sight of Axel and the large Raven flying over, but he knew in himself these feelings did not belong to him. John aggressively instructed poor Ted. "Follow them like a cat stalking its prey; they must not know we are watching them. Look in your backpack, I have put a shawl in there to wrap around your face." Ted felt unnerved. He didn't remember doing this, but sure as hell, he reached in and found the shawl that he had taken out and wrapped around himself. He followed behind them, but not too close, watching as they momentarily paused outside the bakery, then continued onto the church. He watched from under his shawl as it flapped around his face in the wind that was slightly picking up.

He quietly cut ahead of them and entered the church from a different gate, his presence there caused the wildlife to flee, knowing what he was harbouring inside him was the purest form of evil. There were no groundskeepers tonight, no Shelly, as he knew she was at a family function, as she came into his shop earlier that day to buy her sister a bracelet. The churchyard fell eerily quiet; he felt so bad disturbing everything, but he didn't have a choice. He ducked down behind a bush that had a clear view of the entrance gate. He saw movement as he watched Axel and Orenda push the heavy gate open. He heard the iron hinges creak loud as they echoed across the graves, ringing his ears. He could see Axel was anxious by the way he jumped in response to the Raven that landed on a headstone nearby, and hearing Orenda's little laugh. He stalked them quietly, listening to the conversation in confusion as they were talking to the Raven. He didn't understand, but John cleared things up immediately. "Don't you remember the vision I showed you at all? That Raven is Eve, the witch; she somehow must have hijacked the bird's body like I'm doing with you." Ted's eyes narrowed in concentration as he watched Axel under a tree pulling up roots and foliage, revealing an old stone coffin. John's voice growled in his head, "So that is where Axel buried the witch; her remains get to be at peace, yet I'm this." Ted knew John deserved the punishment he got, but he didn't let on for fear his wrath would backfire on himself. He watched Axel place the rose onto the stone coffin. The night was drawing in, and the wind was picking up more. He looked up and noticed the clouds rolling in dark and incredibly low. He saw Axel and Orenda leaving. He waited for the Raven to disappear, his body jerked up uncontrollably, and he power walked over to the stone coffin. John's mocking voice reading the side of her grave "she is not dead just sleeping, isn't that the truth, I wanted to wait until tomorrow on her so cold death anniversary but I can't wait, tonight is the night he dies along with her and if the kid gets in the way she will have to be disposed of as well".

Ted felt terrified that he couldn't kill Axel and Orenda; he wouldn't. The thought of his family filled his soul with grief, but also some peace, knowing that they had a great support system around them, but that dark voice rattled a warning: " Remember Ted, don't get in my way, or you will also die tonight." Ted quietly agreed and let John take control of his body as they walked to the village hall. Ted felt very confused as to why they were heading towards the village hall, but he let John do what he had to do. They entered the hall, thankful for the shelter from the storm. It was really picking up by this time; they could hear it hitting against the walls outside. John turned the hall's porch light on, which lit the fast-growing snowy ground across the road from the bakery. He burst through the main hall doors and walked to the back of the room, onto the stage, and lifted a hatch that led to the cellar below.

He pulled the string that had a brass handle tied to it, and with a loud click, the room lit up, and to Ted's horror, the room was set up with an old dentist chair in the middle of the room that had straps attached to it. Hanging from the walls were all sorts of things, from clippers to hammers and wrenches. It was a horrible scene, and hanging in the corner was a large bird cage. He knew who that was for. He couldn't understand how all this got here without his knowledge or anyone else's. John spoke up, "There's a reason you have been so tired lately. When you're asleep, I can take one hundred percent full control of your body without you getting in my way. I have collected this stuff over the past few months whilst you slept." Ted's face dropped to the floor; he noticed droplets of blood. He checked his nose, but nothing. Then his vision started to falter, and the room went black.

John blinked aggressively as the blood poured from his tear ducts onto the floor. He stood straight and stretched his neck and arms, wiggling his legs to make sure Ted's subconscious had gone dormant. His attention was disturbed when he heard a loud bang slam against the cellar window.

He unlocked and opened the hatched window, looking out across the grounds that were at his eye level, and to his disbelief, there huddled on the floor was the Raven that had been brought down by the fierce winds. He stretched his arm out the window, the ice biting at his skin, but he couldn't quite reach the bird or fit his body out enough to lunge for her. He grabbed a heavy crate that he moved with ease and stepped up as he grabbed the bird by the feet and dragged her in. He shut the window behind him but forgot to lock it as he felt the joy of holding the bird in his hands. He threw her limp body in the bird cage. He left the cellar to hear commotion at the hall's front door. It was Axel who was batted in by the light shining out through the storm. He ruffled the shawl around his face and took a seat in the front row, and started to put on the theatrics, smirking to himself. He lifted his voice as feminine as he could and started to rock back and forth, crying and whimpering, letting the blood fall from his eyes to the floor and pool at his feet. The anticipation and pure excitement fed his performance as he heard Axel approach him and try to comfort him until he felt his hand on his shoulder. He froze for a moment in contemplation on how to play his next move. So, he screamed and wrenched up, he threw the shawl at Axel's face that startled him and sent him flying to the floor, dazed and confused. "Hi Axel, we meet again, but this time you won't get away from me." He watched Axel jump to his feet to make a run for it, but John, using Ted's powerful body, pinned Axel down. Axel pleaded with him, "TED TED mate, wake up, it's me, Axel, don't let him control you". John's grip began to loosen as he lost control. Ted regained his body long enough to get Axel away from him and try to stop John from getting control again. He watched Axel's face nod to him in appreciation and run for the door, once it was just him and John alone together, he heard his voice erupt in his head "HOW DARE YOU I HAD HIM. You are no good to me anymore I warned you to not get in my way" Ted argued back " I won't let you kill any more people, what Eve done to you, you deserved it, she's not the demon you are" John's anger bubbled within as to Ted's horror he watched his own large arm rise against his will to his neck and began to squeeze with unnatural strength.

Ted gasped and pleaded with John to stop; the veins in his head bulged, his breath wheezing with every inhale John's grip tightened down more. Ted struggled against him until everything fell away, with a loud crunch, John's fingers boring deep into his neck, which John had snapped. His body lay there for a brief moment, limp and lifeless, until it started to jerk to life, black

162

smoke bellowed from his mouth and wrapped around Ted's lifeless body until it was lifted to a standing position. With a loud crack, his head was pushed back into place by the smoke. His eyelids slowly opened, blinking until John focused in on the hall door. He thundered towards it with black smoke bellowing from his hand as the door blasted open, seeing Axel just about to run into the cold of the storm. He flung dark, smoking ropes that wrapped around his ankles, yanking him to the ground. He did not see the child, which he didn't really care about; he sent a dark smoke hand that crept across the air to retrieve the unconscious bird from her cage. The smoke hand returned, lifted her to John's hand and with the other, he yanked back hard on the smoked rope that was wrapped around Axel's body. He dragged him back inside the hall's entrance. In John's glee, his face covered in dried blood, he looked at Eve, then back at Axel, lying on the floor covered in smoke, jolting and kicking, trying to break free. He could not believe he had actually pulled it off. Eve's eye slightly opened, greeted to the mayhem that was around her, but she remained dangling there as she spied Orenda's face peeking around the door. She closed her eyes and concentrated on her, trying to muster any power to send her a message. She connected to her spirit briefly but long enough to tell her to run home and alert her mum. From behind her closed eyes, she heard John bellow, "IT'S TIME TO DIE."

Chapter Thirteen

IT IS MY TURN NOW.

"Power does not always pass gently; sometimes it rises in flames
and says, ' it's my turn now"

- E.L

Axel was falling unconscious from the pressure of the black smoke that was crushing his body, his eyes slowly blinking into darkness. He glanced to see Orenda running into the cold, still wearing his jacket that she pulled in tight around her, which looked like a large dress on her small frame. He breathed a sigh of relief knowing she got away, but before he succumbed to the pressure, he looked up to see Ted's blood-soaked face. There was nothing of his friend in there anymore, he could tell, but when he glanced up, he saw Eve in his grip, which was the last thing he saw before the world fell to darkness. In what felt like only a few seconds, he had closed his eyes from passing out. He slowly opened them, blinking into a bright light that was shining in his face. He squinted, trying to take in his surroundings. The room reeked of rust and damp rot; echoing was the distant sound of the storm raging outside. When he went to stand, his arms and legs were tied down. He felt fear coursing through him, his ragged gasps as he felt his body tight against the cracked leather of the old dentist chair. He caught a shadow; he heard movement. "Ted, is that you? Please be you. Help me out of this." But Axel heard no response, just the stalking cat-like movement behind the light stalking his every movement, trying to release himself from the chair. He heard a guttural growl from behind followed by a deep chuckle "keep trying all you like

Axel (the name left his mouth with a disgusted tone in response of speaking his name) those bonds are tight you will never get out" another deep laugh growled from behind the light until he heard a click, the lights cut out and the room went dark. His eyes blinked fast, trying to adjust as fast as possible to scan the room for an exit. He saw John, but not as Ted anymore; he was in his full Molthera form with black smoke cascading from the cracks in his chest. The black pits where his eyes should be, focused in on Axel with a carnal hunger to kill. "It's my turn to live now I have Ted's body at my disposal, yes I will have to put up with that family of his but I'm sure a few around the house accidents can remedy that" another laugh crackled from John as spurts of lava spat from his mouth.

Once the light was restored, Axel struggled aggressively against his restraints when he noticed Ted's lifeless body slumped against the wall in the corner of the cellar. He cried out for his friend, but there was no response. John informed him, "Don't waste your breath, Ted is dead. I warned him not to get in my way, but he disobeyed me. That's the result for people who disobey me." He aggressively pointed to Ted, but his hollowed-out eyes fixed on Axel. He stood up straight and started to walk over to the wall that had every tool hanging from large hooks on the old web-covered stone wall. His burnt, cracked fingers gently brushed over each tool as he smiled to himself, "I'm going to enjoy this, it will be slow, I want to have fun, burning in my pit for all those years gave me a hunger that no curse will subside or neuter me. Eve may have won the battle, but for sure she will not win the war." Axel looked up with tears in his green pleading eyes to see Eve caged up. She was pecking at the metal bars and trying to get out to call for help. Eve had come to, a black iron cage rattled violently now as she thrashed inside, her feathers matted, her eyes bright with fury and fear. John loomed near, no longer a man. His skin split with fire-veined cracks, smoke curling from his seared flesh. The Molthera. His eyes, now hollow pits, leaked slow rivulets of molten sorrow. He whispered something unintelligible, the sound burning the air itself. "Time to die", he hissed, tilting Axel's head up to force his gaze towards the cage. Eve screeched, wings flared wide, but the bars shimmered with something ancient, warded iron. She was trapped. Helpless. All she could do was hope Orenda got to her mum in time and that they were sending help. Axel's eyes welled with his green eyes shimmering light like the northern lights as he accepted his fate. He quietened himself, picturing his family clear in his mind; he wanted them to be his last thoughts.

John threw the hammer to the floor, unimpressed by it. The clang of metal hitting the floor startled Axel, sweat dripping down his face as he caught sight of the hammer lying on the floor. John approached him again and said, "I want to feel your pain in my fingers." his cracked hand lifted in the air and faded away in dark smoke as long dark claws grew. Axel started to shake, seeing them getting closer and closer to his neck and feeling them settle there for a moment when they were disturbed by a loud bang from above them. Someone was here; his eyes lit up with hope as he yelled and screamed out to whoever it was. John stomped up the stairs from the cellar, not giving a care to how he looked, knowing the sight of him alone would send whoever it was screaming away in terror. Axel started to struggle again, taking in the opportunity to escape, but the bonds were so tight. He heard a shuffle sound from behind and a whip of cold snow air rushing around the room. So many sounds were happening around him, there was a fight going on upstairs with loud bangs going off, and he thought whoever it was they were putting up a great fight. He felt a small, gentle hand grasp his as his face spun down to see Orenda placing the clover sealed in sap into his hand. He couldn't believe his horror and relief knowing she was there, holding a large pair of scissors to cut through the leather straps. Eve was hopping up and down at this point in joy to see Orenda Freeing Axel from the chair. Before the last bond was cut, they saw a form rolling and crashing down the hard stone stairs. A mass of long hair whipped around as Velina and Axel's eyes met. Velina's eyes looked different; they were glowing white with light veins creeping down her cheeks. She was under the influence of an extraordinarily strong spell to help her fight, John. She smiled and lifted her hand up towards the stairs, creating a barrier of light that John was running at with all force and might to break.

Velina cried out for them to hurry up and get a move on; her nose trickled with blood as she fought with all her might. Orenda cut the final bond, and Axel stood to his feet, feeling uneasy as the blood flowed back to his limbs with a harsh tingle. He ran over to Eve, who was frantically pecking at the lock. Velina cried out to Axel and Orenda, "Move." She lifted her other hand towards Eve's cage, and another beam of light shot across the room, hitting the lock loose but not free. Her strength started to fail; she cried out to Axel to get Orenda out of there through the window. He grabbed Orenda up in his arms and lifted her towards the window. He pushed it open and forced her small body through and told her, "No matter what you hear in here, don't look back, RUN." He closed the window behind him and went to help Eve whilst Velina was fighting with every ounce of power she had. He locked his finger through the gaps in the cage and pulled with all his force until the light behind him faded and dark smoke engulfed the room. He turned to look for Velina, who was out cold on the floor, shrouded in dark smoke that was creeping around her. He lunged for her, but the smoke lifted her first and pinned her to the wall. A sound of tutting and footsteps walked down the stairs towards him. John was wagging his finger at Axel and told him, "Step back or I will rip her limb from limb." Axel gritted his teeth and clenched his hand around the clover tight in his palm. "Leave her alone, she has nothing to do with this." John looked up at him with fake surprise and shock. "Oh, but she does, she is a descendant of our dear Eve over there. Another witch, another demon." Eve hopped about in her cage, kicking at the door now with all her might, and it started shaking loose. Axel pleaded with him to spare her life; "take me, I will die at your hands, please let her go." John smirked and scoffed, "What is it with these women that makes men act like total fools. You would give your life for this thing." Axel got down on his knees and cried out. "Yes, I would." John nodded silently in agreement and lifted Velina's body towards the window that was flapping open and closed because of the wind whirling outside. The shadows placed Velina on the cold snow that filled the ground and dispersed away into the wind.

Axel stood and walked towards John with his arms up and then turned to sit back into the dentist's chair. John Power walked over to Axel Claws up, ready to finish this, when Axel noticed the hammer on the floor had disappeared. Orenda stood up from the shadows, reaching up to the bird cage with all her might and bringing the hammer down onto the lock; the cage door flung open. Before Eve could fly out to Axel's rescue, John brought his claws down hard across Axel's throat, and ruby red blood poured out heavy as he gripped his throat, gasping. The clover concealed in tree sap fell from Axel's pocket to the floor, soaked in his blood. Two sets of cries called out from Orenda and Velina. Velina, who was bashing against the window trying to get back in, but it was being held closed by shadows. John laughed to himself, pleased to see the carnage around him and his dream finally fulfilled. His form immediately disappeared into smoke and crawled across the floor back into Ted. His corpse reanimated with a jolt and ran from the cellar, leaving the devastation behind him. Velina kicked hard against the glass until it broke, the shadows dissipating. She climbed down and grabbed Orenda to cradle her cries as Axel gasped for life. Eve flew from the cage down to the floor and whisked the clover up in her beak and threw it at Velina. She lifted her hand, caught it, seeing Axel's blood staining her palm. The raven flew up to land on Axel's chest. She outstretched her large black wings. Fire ignited in her eyes, suddenly more than a bird, more than a witch- more than anything. Eve's voice, echoing through the air like wind through the trees, spoke one final incantation. Fire and light blazed from the bird's wings as a pulse of light blasted through the room, making Velina shield her eyes. Suddenly, the room filled with light, and everything froze around them. She cradled her face down over Orenda's head, who was still sobbing into her jacket whilst clutching her mum's arms.

Velina never felt such power and stillness all at once until she felt a soft hand stroke her head. She lifted her gaze up to be greeted by a woman bathed in light with a regal grace to her, her long flowing black hair that had raven feathers wrapped in plaits fell around her shoulders, a beautiful black dress that gently swayed as she moved. Orenda and Velina stood and looked around the room. Eve examined them and took both their hands in hers; a tear fell down her cheek as she smiled at them. "I am sorry to break this news to you, but Axel's life has perished. But there is something I can do for him. I want to thank you for keeping Orenda safe and my memory when I was alive, clear of reckless words from people who just don't understand," she softly brushed tears that started falling from Velina's eyes in realisation that her partner was dead. "Please bring him back to us please Eve" The sobs got heavier

169

when she felt Orenda tightened her hug around her waist. She pulled herself together to be strong for her. Eve could see the strength in them, "you both are my blood I want you to be strong, this won't be easy I can give you a small moment of time to say goodbye to him then I must complete the spell." Velina grabbed her arm, stopping her from turning away "what will happen to you?" she asked in a concerned voice. Eve faced her again and pulled her in for a hug and then kissed her cheek "don't you worry about me I have lived a long enough life to see Orenda grow but it's time for me to be with my Axel" Eve knelt down to Orenda who peeked out from hugging her mum, she lurched forward and wrapped her small arms around Eve. She hugged her back and never wanted her to let go. "Orenda, it's my time, whenever you see a raven, think of me, won't you? I know you are going to grow to be a strong woman like your mum and powerful. Each witch will discover her talent as she grows," she kissed the heart-shaped birthmark on Orenda's cheek that tasted salty from her tears and cupped her face in her hands one last time. She stood and informed Velina to always keep that clover safe.

Eve looked around the room, flicking her light to see the mayhem of what John had left behind. Axel's lifeless body slumped back on the dentist's chair with his mouth agape. She informed Velina that we need to clear this place and get him to the witch's ash tree, where I can draw all my strength. Velina looked at Orenda and covered her eyes to lead her upstairs. The village hall was a mess with chairs flung everywhere, scorch marks on the floor, and rubble blown in from a hole caused by the impact of Velina flinging John into it in the fight earlier. She grabbed a chair and told Orenda to sit and stay there and gave her the clover to fiddle with whilst she waited. Velina rejoined Eve downstairs in the cellar, really seeing Axel properly for the first time. His beautiful green eyes, lost to the void of death, his cheeky smile that always made Velina smile, were gone. She stroked his face with a cloth she found on the floor to remove some of the blood so she could see his features more clearly. Tears fell down her face. "Eve, how are we going to get him out of here? What do we do?" Eve gracefully floated over to her and pointed out that the night is now still as snow fell through the broken window, followed by haunting moonlight. She glided her hands through the air over Axel's body as he started to float up above the chair. She gestured to a cupboard, the doors flung open, revealing white, clean decorator sheets stacked inside. She asked Velina to grab one and lay it beneath Axel's body. She whipped the sheet out as it splayed over the dentist chair, and his body descended back down on it. Eve grabbed one side, and Velina lifted the other, wrapping it around him and tying a knot in the fabric to stop it from falling open. Eve asked Velina to step back as she lifted her head back and closed her eyes, and whispered a spell into the void, summoning something to her. Light glowed from her long, elegant fingers, and the room fell silent. Orenda was sitting up in her chair, ignoring the absolute mess of everything around her, chucking the clover in the air and catching it in her hand when she heard a bang behind her. She panicked thinking John was back, so she ducked and hid beneath the chair, hearing what sounded like hoofs stomping behind her.

Chapter Fourteen

I DON'T UNDERSTAND.

"Some spells fail not because they were weak, but because evil
listened too closely."

-E.L.

Orenda glanced out from under the chair, and to her
amazement, she saw a large, proud white stag stomp past her; its
heavy hoofs vibrated the floor with each step. It almost glowed
where its fur was the purest white; its large antlers were thick and
very tall, almost as tall as Orenda when she stood. It descended the
cellar stairs. Thankfully, it was a wide passageway to fit the
humongous stag. Velina could not believe her eyes at what she was
seeing in front of her. Eve opened her eyes and greeted the stag
like an old friend and bowed her head to him. Velina, still stunned,
felt the compulsion to do the same. The stag's chestnut brown eyes
looked kind and soulful, as if it had lived a thousand lives with the
wisdom he held in them. He kneeled so his body was level to the
dentist chair, Eve, and Velina, as careful as they could, pushed
Axel onto the back of the stag that slowly stood to adjust to his
weight. As they left the cellar, holding onto Axel to make sure he
didn't fall from the stag, they climbed back up the stairs. Eve
looked behind her, and with a flick of her fingers, a spark of red-
hot fire bounced into the cellar, setting it ablaze. Velina understood
it had to be done, but she could not figure out how to break the
news of Axel's passing to everyone. Eve could see the stress in
Velina's face as they entered the hall to see Orenda looking up in
awe at the stag. It took a step toward her and lowered its large

172

head; she looked at her mum, who gave her an approving nod. Orenda reached her hand out to stroke the stag's head, feeling its soft fur brushed beneath her fingers. She thanked the stag for helping them carry her dad out of that horrible cellar. They walked through the village hall, smelling the thick smoke that was now billowing up from the depths below the stage. Once they got outside the hall, leaving it to burn, they started their short journey to the witch's ash tree. They took in the calm serenity after the snowstorm had passed, leaving everything covered in a snowy white blanket. The snow crunched beneath their feet, but Velina noticed that Eve was barefoot, and she looked fine; she didn't look cold at all as her long black hair whipped around in the soft, chilling breeze.

They saw the witch's ash coming into view in the distance, and she could see Eve tense up from the sight of it. From the village behind them, they could hear the fire alarms going off to put out the inferno before it completely destroyed the old structure. But they kept their focus forward on the task at hand. The stag stopped and glanced up at the large tree looming over them, the moon shining bright, silhouetting the branches that reached out to the sky. Orenda wrapped her dad's large coat around her tight as she watched the stag kneel to the floor with Axel balancing on its back. Eve and Velina worked together to lift him from the stags' back and gently placed Axel on the floor. They all looked up at the stag, who was looking back at them for a moment. Tears fell from the large animal's eyes as he turned and disappeared into the trees behind him. They all stood in silence for a fleeting moment, waiting for someone to say something or do something. Eve knelt and asked Orenda for the clover; she removed it from her pocket and placed it on Axel's chest as Eve instructed her to do so. She removed the sheet from his face, which blended in with the snow;

173

his eyes had begun to sink in. Eve looked up at Velina and said, "It's time for me to finish the spell. He may be deceased, but I have a tight hold on his spirit. I have come to the realisation that he has what it takes to help us destroy John; the link he has with that clover preserved in sap is the answer to killing him forever. But it is going to take a certain type of witch with a gift to aid him, to unlock the power that's inside this clover to stop him from the bloodshed yet to come. John is the Molthera, to sustain living in Ted's body, he must consume the essence of people, or he will burn the body out from the inside." Velina gasped in horror and held on tight to Orenda, who looked scared. Eve asked them both to step back so she could finish the spell, which was already unpredictable. She had never tapped into magic like this before; anything could happen.

Eve approached the large tree with its ashen colour almost aglow against the moon's light as it now shone a tone of red, its bare branches twisting outward. She placed a hand on the rough bark, and a soft, warm glow ignited from her fingers when they touched the tree pressing into the ancient bark. Tree magic is the most wild and unpredictable to control, but to wield it gives the witch her most untamed, pure power intensified. Eve's magic was the essence of fire and the fury and strength that came with it. To burn or purify her gift lit up inside her spirit. Her long, black, flowing hair that blew in the soft wind became locks of twisting fire; her form became transparent as light blasted from her entire body like a beacon that could have been seen from the outer stratosphere. She felt the pure wild free magic engulf her entire being, rushing through her veins as she strained to turn her face to look at Velina, Orenda and Axel one last time. Her feet started to leave the earth as she ascended the height of the witch's ash tree with light still pouring out of her with the intensity of the sun. She smiled at them below her as they looked up, shielding their eyes. Eve said, "You will have some time to say goodbye to him in one of your most precious memories together, but I don't know how long I can give you; this magic is too strong for me to control". Velina shouted a heartfelt thank you to Eve as the light started to consume her and Orenda; they both fell to the floor next to Axel's body. Eve strained again as the wild magic pulsed through her to give them as much time together as possible, her arms shaking, the veins in her neck perturbing as she held the light steady. Velina opened her eyes slowly. The room she gazed at was bright around her. She could not make out anything until she felt movement next to her, it's Orenda, but she looked different, she looked younger, her clothes had changed. She recognised what she was wearing immediately, her Navy-blue bell dress with golden flowers sewn onto the straps, with her little white shoes over her white lace frilled ankle socks. She held a small woven basket filled with dark red rose petals. Velina then knew what memory she was in as she looked down at her wedding dress on her body. She held her hand out to Orenda, both seeing the room fade away around them, to see the church's walls and old pillars appear before them.

As the familiar and comforting walls of the church surrounded them, the faces they loved so much started to appear. Axel's parents smiled at them both, which brought a tear to both their eyes. Velina looked up toward the head of the church, past where her family and friends were sitting, to see Axel looking a bit confused until he looked up and locked eyes with her. His smile, Velina soaked it up, thinking this would be the last time she would see him like this. Orenda broke away from Velina and ran for her dad. He scooped her up into a big hug. Velina approached him as he set Orenda back down. They both held hands and glanced toward Shelly, who was herself getting a bit tearful. Velina's dress shone in the setting sun as the light poured through the windows. She had a full-length gown that splayed out behind her as she walked with glittering beads that outlined the flowers and lace that trailed down the skirt. The bodice was form-fitting with the same glittering pearls that shone so brightly from her curly hair that fell down her back. Her ring in the shape of a star seemed to have a glow all its own as she pressed her hand on Axel's heart, and he did the same to her. They relived the moment together until Shelly called out, "This part of the ceremony is done. Would everyone leave for the woods for the second part to commence? Just follow the star lanterns that mark the path." Everyone filed out into the night and followed the lanterns along the path, leaving just Axel, Velina, Shelly and Orenda to finalise all the legal bits and leave for the woods themselves to finish the vows. Orenda ran ahead with Shelly as Axel and Velina locked hands tight. They did not speak, just walked together, watching the excitement of their beautiful daughter throwing the last of the red petals onto the floor in front of them. They came to the clearing that was lit up with so many star lanterns it would make the night skies themselves jealous; they gave Velina's dress a different kind of sparkle in this light. She could see all the happening under the light vale that kept an annoying barrier between her and her loved ones. Axel kissed her hand and left her at the beginning of the aisle as he took his place down with Shelly. Ted was there with him, smiling that massive grin he had. Velina's father walked up beside her and looped his arm through hers and led her down the aisle towards Axel. She could feel the tears rolling down her face as she never wanted this moment to end.

The trees above them were covered in small fairy lights that were entangled in fresh drapes of red roses that hung above their heads. The fire torches were lit around the seating area that had white drapes on the back of the chairs, which also had red rose posies tied into bows. She looked up to see the black bird perch covered in black crystals that Axel had made for Eve to sit on; she had pride of place at the front of the podium. As she approached the giant white metal gazebo that was covered in fresh red roses, the smell was so fresh, she turned to hug her dad, who was crying through his proudest smile, kissed her cheek, and he turned to take his seat. Axel took her hand; she stood in front of him, not being able to look away from those green eyes. Shelly started the ceremony until it got to the vows that they both made themselves. Axel went first, "Velina... from the moment I saw you under those star lanterns, dancing barefoot to rock and roll like the world was made just for you- I knew. I knew I was already yours. That night, the sky didn't hold a single star that could compare to the way your blue eyes lit up when you laughed. And I would've chased that light forever. So, I did. I left behind everything-every plan, every comfort, every version of who I thought I was supposed to be- Because nothing mattered more than telling you the truth: That I love you. Wildly. Bravely. Completely. Since then, you've given me a life I never dared dream of. You've given us Orenda- our wild-hearted miracle, with my eyes and her own fire. You've made our days louder, softer, and infinitely more beautiful. You are my home, Velina. In a world that always felt so fast, too big, too uncertain- you are my steady. My laughter in the chaos. My morning coffee and my midnight song. So today, in front of everyone, I vow what my heart already knows: That I love you with every part of me- Through the quiet, through the storm, through the grey hairs and the growing years. I will hold your hand when nights are long, and dance with you under the star lanterns when we're eighty. You, Velina, are my forever. And I will never stop choosing you."

Velina could not stop her smile, and she tore her veil off, which was driving her cuckoo by this point. Everything came into focus, and she placed her hand on Axel's heart and spoke her vows to Axel. Axel... There was a time in my life when I thought love had to be complicated to be real. But then one day, in the middle of bright lights, tangled cables, and a million posed smiles, you walked out from behind the camera, holding a bouquet of long-stemmed red roses like it was the simplest thing in the world... And suddenly, everything made sense. That moment stopped time. Not because of the flowers, or the surprise, but because it was you. You- this man who saw me not as a model, or a mystery- But as someone worth loving exactly as I am. You didn't just step into the shoot. You stepped into my life- quietly, boldly, completely when I came back with you to Antler Manor, back to the scent of the flowers in the grounds, the echo of laughter in the old halls. Back to a place that became not just a house, but the heart of our story. You gave me a life that feels like breath after holding it for too long. You gave us Orenda, our fierce, bright girl who reminds me every day of what we built together. You gave me a love that is wild and still, like firelight on winter nights. So today, I vow this to you: I will never stop turning towards you- in storms, in silence, in celebration. I will carry your heart when it's heavy. I will laugh with you when the world is light. I will grow wild with you in this home we made. I still blush when you surprise me with roses. Axel, you are the calm in my chaos, the real in all the noise, the man I prayed for before I knew how to use the words. I love you. Now, always, and even beyond that. Axel's smile was so wide, and both their eyes were full of tears, but they held it together until Pearl interrupted them and walked on stage with Orenda, who had put something together in secret for her mum and dad on their wedding day. Eve, still perched on her stand watching all the goings on, flapped her wings when she saw Orenda's little face light up when she glanced over, letting her know not to be nervous, and you will do great.

Pearl led her near Eve as she stood just behind her, so she was in front of her parents. Eve flew over ahead and landed on the metal gazebo so she could watch from a better vantage point. As soft instrumentals of "can't help falling in love" began to play in the background, the guests fell silent. A gentle breeze stirs the petals scattered along the aisle. She pauses and looks at her parents, her voice steady and sweet. She held her piece of paper up to her face whilst the pillow containing the rings was tied in a safe bow hung from her small wrist. "Mummy, Daddy.... You always sing this song in the kitchen when you think I'm not listening. But I hear it. I see the way you look at each other. And I know what love means because I see it in our home every day. So here are your rings.... to remind you that no matter how big the world is, your love always brings you back to each other. And when I grow up, I want a love just like yours." She hands the pillow to Shelly, who has tears in her eyes, and is so proud of how well she delivered her little Surprise. Axel and Velina thought Ted had the rings. Pearl took Orenda's hand and led her back down to sit with her. Seeing how proud her parents were of her gave her the happiest feeling. Eve flew down and perched on the back of Orenda's chair, flapping her wings in joy. The music swells just slightly, the words soft whispers in the wind. Axel and Velina looked at their daughter, and Axel said. "You were our first of forever. And no matter how many years go by, we will always be your home." Her little face glowed with happiness watching them both up there. They exchanged rings and completed the ceremony, everyone cheering as they kissed under the roses. Eve flew over to a tree branch and pulled off a tied piece of rope, and the sky started raining red rose petals that fell everywhere. Orenda started grabbing handfuls of petals and spinning around, throwing them into the air. Velina and Axel laughed together as they danced to their song under the falling red petals. Orenda ran up to them and hugged them both as the three of them danced together. Velina looked out at all her loved ones smiling, laughing, and dancing under the falling petals, then she noticed everything started glitching around her, and her mind started to panic. She looked at Axel and kissed him deeply before everything started falling away. She just kept repeating to him, "I love you, I love you, I love you." She cupped his face. He also looked panicked and confused, seeing everything slowly disappear around him until his form was no longer solid. He slipped away from Orenda's and Velina's grasp like ash caught in the wind.

Eve screamed out in pain, the wild magic started to consume her as she lost control, and the light that was steadily beaming from her exploded in violent pulses. She cried out, seeing Velina and Orenda still unconscious on the floor next to Axel. She knew she had to bring the spell to an end, so she started lifting her hand. A small glowing portal appeared below her, coming from the base of the tree, and Axel's spirit form walked out, looking very confused as he glanced up at her. Eve felt strange as dark smoke started rolling around her waist. It grew larger as John's face appeared through the dark void of smoke as he pressed a very unwelcome kiss to her lips. He laughed as she jutted back from him, but her lips felt strange as black veins crawled up her cheeks from the corners of her mouth. She cried out in pain and anger, trying to complete the spell, but it was too late. The pulses of light consumed her as she faded back into the trunk of the tree. The tree shook aggressively, the branches breaking and falling all around them. The dark smoke had disappeared into the night; the spell was corrupted by his darkness. As fast as everything happened, the light faded, and everything went still. Eve's spirit had disappeared into the witch's ash tree. All that shone was the blood red moon, making the snow look like a sea of blood stretching across the still fields. There was nothing but stillness as Axel's body became rigid, still wrapped in the blanket. Velina and Orenda were lying on the floor next to him, their eyes closed in a stage deeper than sleep where there were no dreams. Their breath blew out like fog as the cold closed in around them both. Axel, now adjusting to his spirit form, kept looking up at the tree, feeling very lost and confused; he didn't even notice the mayhem behind him. He walked past the large tree and disappeared into the woods, not knowing his direction or mind.

Chapter Fifteen

WHAT IS HAPPENING?

"They will not know what is wrong at first. But magic always makes itself known in the end."

- E.L.

A small glowing light appeared from Velina's engagement ring that floated up above her and Orenda as they shivered from the cold, but they still never woke up. A soft dome fell around them both, shielding them, protecting them, stopping them from freezing to death. In the distance, there was movement. People were running across the road, up over the fields towards the witch's ash, being led by a very panicked barking dog. Tex had sniffed the family out and led the villagers to them. He ran over panting, leading them across the frozen terrain. He lay across Axel's body, whimpering in the hope he would open his eyes and play ball with him like he did all the time back home. He lifted his head and noticed Velina and Orenda also lying on the floor. He got to his feet and walked over to Orenda. He sniffed her and lay down by her side to keep warm whilst the villagers inspected the scene. They did not know what to think; they didn't know if they were all dead or if some were still alive. One of the villagers ran back to call for Dr Frank for help. The early hours of the morning were appearing in the sky as streaks of pink and orange, drowning out the dark sky as the moon took its leave. Understanding something clearly at last, the sun burst forth above the trees as its warm light cast golden rays shimmering through the morning fog. The villagers did not like the look of it, red sky in the morning, shepherds' warning. Frank grabbed his robe and stumbled out of his bed, hearing the frantic knocking at his front door. He swung the door open, seeing a young man panting in panic, asking for his help, "There has been a murder at the witch's ash tree, please follow me quickly". Frank ran for the home phone and called the police to alert them to come to Hollow Wood village under the witch's ash tree. He said, "Find us under the witch's ash tree and hurry", which was description enough for them, as the tree had a reputation of its own, known by all far and wide around the village. He quickly ran back upstairs to alert his wife and put on some trousers, also an extra-thick jumper to keep warm. He fumbled and grabbed his heavy winter coat from his wardrobe; he quickly kissed his wife and left. Frank ran back down the stairs, grabbing his medical bag he always keeps full and prepped by the front door in case of emergencies. He followed the young man back to the witch's ash tree, hearing sirens and flashing lights tearing down the lane, appearing from the road in the woods towards them. He looked to his horror, seeing the Brinford's all lying on the floor, he caught sight of the frosted breath coming from Velina and Orenda, but nothing from Axel, his ash skin and dark, circled-eyed face peering into eternity from the blanket that was wrapped around him.

Dr Frank made sure everyone stood back so as not to corrupt the scene as the police ran up, pushing the crowd back even further, but keeping Frank to the forefront. They banged metal spikes into the ground and pulled yellow tape across them, which put a barrier between them and the villagers. There was a photographer taking pictures of them and of the scorched ground, every little detail they could recall for future examinations. Suddenly, Velina jolts up, looking around in a panic, "Where am I? What's going on? Who are you?" Her questions came faster and more panicked. Frank knelt to her side as she spotted Axel. She crawled away, minding herself as she launched over Orenda, who was still not awake and Tex, who was keeping her warm. She throws herself over Axel, screaming and crying, demanding someone to tell her what the hell is going on. The police looked at each other, very confused, as an officer knelt to her. "We were hoping you could tell us what happened, miss. We have just arrived on scene." Velina searched and searched her memory, but the last thing she remembered was saying goodbye to Axel when he left to get Orenda from school. She was having a full-on panic attack as Frank told her to try and take deep, slow breaths and put your head down to try and calm yourself. She did that, but nothing was working. The more she tried to think, the less she could remember. Orenda's head peered over Tex's back as she looked over to her mum, who was hyperventilating on the floor. She then glanced around through half-open eyes and saw her dad. She screamed out loud, which scared Tex, but he stayed by her as she gripped his fur and cried into him. Velina instantly snapped out of her own panic attack and crawled over to her, lying herself over Orenda's head, and the dog as she cradled them both whilst Axel's body was lifted and taken away in a body bag. Orenda wrapped her dad's jacket around herself tighter when she felt the clover in her pocket. She gripped it in her hand and held it tight, the feel of it gave her comfort. Frank approached them both with a large blanket and draped it over them, saying, "I'm so so sorry for your loss." There was not much else he could do but stay with them and ask one of the officers to drive them home.

Velina looked up at him and thanked him for the blanket. She helped Orenda to her feet and walked her and Tex to the police car that took them back home to Antler Manor. When they pulled up outside, the officers said they would stay out front to keep watch

just in case the murderer was still lurking around. She thanked
them and proceeded out of the car. She looked up at Antler Manor,
which now looked so huge and empty. They approached the door,
which opened before they could even push on the large Antler door
handle, to be greeted by one of the maids who looked very
confused and concerned to see the lady of the house and Orenda
climbing out of the back of a police car. Velina looked back at the
officer with a dead stare in her eyes, to the one in the driver's seat
and asked if he could inform her maid what's been going on and to
pass the word to the rest of the house, as she just wanted to get
some sleep and rest and try to process what had happened. Her,
Orenda and Tex climbed the stairs together with their heads low
and their steps feeling heavy as they climbed. Velina took Orenda
to her room, which was now decorated perfectly for a young girl,
but she wanted to keep the flowers that had been painted in her
room by her mother. The name above her crib had been cut loose
into a door mount as you entered her room. Velina lifted Axel's
heavy jacket that swamped Orenda and inhaled his smell, the
jacket still had his scent on it, which smelled like his Favourite
cologne, Old Spice and mint from the chewing gum he always kept
in his pocket. Velina shook the coat to remove any debris before
hanging it on the back of Orenda's door. She turned to hear a light
thud fall to the floor. It was the clover concealed in the glowing
amber tree sap. Velina knew she had seen this before in Axel's
possession but could not remember how it came to be given to
him.

She lifted it in her hand to examine it for a moment until she
heard Orenda call for her to tuck her in bed. She held onto the
clover, putting it into her pocket and proceeded to comfort Orenda
as she wept in her arms before slowly falling into sleep from
exhaustion.

Velina slowly crept out of Orenda's room, leaving Tex asleep at the end of her bed. She glanced out the window before leaving her room, seeing the large birdbox outside nestled in the large cedar tree that overlooked her room. She felt she was searching for a memory that would just not come to her. She walked the long halls alone, the light from the sun showing her the way towards the kitchen, where she sat at the table and absolutely broke down. The staff could hear her whimpers but were unsure whether to comfort her or let her have some space to grieve. They were leaning their ears against the kitchen door, holding back tears of their own, listening to the despair from the other side of the door. They all looked at each other, all having the same idea and left the kitchen door to go to the greenhouse and pick some flowers to make a large, beautiful bouquet for Velina. Two other maids ran up to the master bedroom and drew all the curtains to black out the light, they fluffed up all the cushions, pulled down the duvet and laid Velina's pyjamas on the side of the bed for her, they filled the fireplace with wood and lite the fire so the room would be nice a warm, the cozy sound of the crackle and warm light dancing across the carpet. The maids heard scurrying up the hallway as three other maids carrying the large bouquet of white lilies and red roses placed them on the bedside table. They did the final checks, placed a tray at the end of her bed, atop the wooden tray containing small jam jars of different flavours and a mixture of breakfast pastries that were still steaming hot. They all hurried out of the room, doing the final checks to find themselves all huddled up in front of the kitchen door again, listening to Velina's cries. They were all whispering to decide who would enter the kitchen and try to lead Velina up to her bed to get some rest. Gary, who was a groundkeeper, leaned over the maids, listening in. He had come in from outside tending to the horses, wanting to get a drink from the kitchen and escape the snow to warm for a moment. The maids informed him what had happened to Axel, and you could see he had a large lump in his throat. He slowly pushed on the door and leaned around the corner to be greeted by Velina, "Ma'am, may I enter?"

Velina lifted her head and quickly wiped her eyes dry before composing herself, seeing Gary peer into the kitchen. He was a tall man with a long black ponytail and sharp features with ice blue eyes; he lived on the grounds to keep watch of the horses and help tend to the gardens. Velina responded, "Yes, please do come in. Don't let me stop you from your day." Gary removed his cap and placed it on the side, the maids all peering around behind him, all softly smiling at Velina, hoping they all don't overwhelm her. Gary approached Velina and placed a comforting hand on her shoulder. She closed her eyes and, for a moment, could imagine it was Axel's hand on her. She could feel tears building up in her eyes again when they were both distracted by the radio crackling, turning itself on as if it was sweeping through stations. It fell silent for a moment, then flicked back on playing Axel's and Velina's song they danced to together when they found each other at the festival. Tears started to fall from Velina's eyes as she smiled to herself. She stood to face Gary, who still had his hand on her shoulder. She awkwardly asked him if he could dance with her in the kitchen to this song. He didn't say anything but nodded his head and smiled at her, knowing how much this song meant to her. He gently pulled her into a hug; they started to sway together. Velina closed her eyes, picturing the moment she danced with Axel to this song for the first time at the festival, their whole lives ahead of them both. She pressed her face into Gary's chest, sobbing as she smiled to herself, swaying along to the song as it came to an end, then she glanced up at Gary to notice all the staff crying and smiling with her. They all came around her and gently led her away from Gary and the kitchen. They took her up the stairs to the master bedroom, where they helped her out of her clothes that had been torn and covered in blood. The maids carefully placed her clothes in a plastic bag that was provided to them by the police so it could be checked for evidence. Velina made sure the clover that was in her pocket was put on her bedside table. A hot bath had been filled for her with her favourite bath oils and salts added to the water. They gently helped her bruised body lower into the hot steaming water, the bubbles gathered around her as she lay back against her bath pillow. They cleaned her up and washed her hair with gentle care not to hurt her further. They helped her into her clean pyjamas that were made of soft silk. Once dressed, they led her to her bed, where she spotted the flowers. She cried again, hugging them all and thanking them before falling into her bed, feeling too tired to eat the pastries. The maids placed the breakfast tray on her dressing table and left her to sleep.

Orenda woke her eyes heavy and stinging from the tears she had wept before she fell asleep. It was about midday as she looked at the light pouring into her room, then noticed Tex still curled up at the end of her bed, asleep, the light snore that vibrated out of his nose when he exhaled. That gave her a little giggle; she felt comforted knowing he was there with her. She moved free from her covers and walked over to sit at her window seat, looking out over the grounds and, like Velina, spotting the large bird box. She looked at it, thinking hard, searching her memories, but nothing came to her. She stood abruptly, feeling the compulsion to paint. She loved painting and was exceptionally good at it. She pulled her paint box out from under her bed and grabbed an empty canvas from her arts and crafts corner in her bedroom. She laid down a paint sheet and placed her easel with the canvas secured on top.

She started painting something using dark colours, black mostly, she didn't even know what was happening, it was like her arm had a life of its own, streaking across the canvas in confident swipes. She stepped back; she surprised herself to see she had painted a large black raven with its wings spread out like it was about to fly right out of the canvas at her. She looked at the dark bird and felt sad, like she had some kind of connection to the creature she had just painted before her, but she could not understand why. Then she felt compelled again to paint in a soft gray across the bottom of the canvas. Whenever you see a Raven, remember me, won't you? A tear fell from Orenda's eyes as she looked lost into the painting, confused and frustrated with her lack of memory and why she feels she knows this bird. She felt a headache coming over her, and she returned to her bed to fall back to sleep as she felt more relaxed in her dream world, where she had full control of everything. She could see her dad walking through the woods, but looking a little lost, she felt the cool breeze around her in her dream, hearing all the animals around her foraging from the forest floor.

Her sleep was disturbed when she heard her bedroom door handle click, and the door swung open. She was snapped out of her dream world to see her mum peer into her room. "Just wanted to check on you, dear. How are you doing?" Tex was alert then as he jumped off the bed and ran over to Velina, licking her fingers. Velina stroked his head and diverted him out of Orenda's room to let him get some food and water. She entered Orenda's room, closing the door behind her, seeing the painting of the Raven and the words painted underneath. She was happy to see her painting, as it was something Orenda loved to do. But when she looked at Orenda, she looked confused and freaked out by the painting. "Mum, did you paint that bird? I didn't do that." Velina looked at her, concerned. "You must have done it, it looks fantastic." Orenda pulled the duvet over her head, feeling scared and confused as to how the painting got there. She felt like an intruder had entered her room and used her paints while she slept. Velina took a seat at the edge of Orenda's bed and placed a hand on her shoulder over the duvet that was covering her head. "I can remove it if you like. Maybe you were so tired you forgot you painted it." Orenda peeked out from under her duvet, accepting that that is what must have happened. Velina kissed Orenda on the head and told her to get dressed, as she had a surprise for her downstairs. Orenda jumped out of bed and got dressed in one of her favourite dresses, a light blue dress with daisies over it. It was a dress her dad had bought for her on her birthday. Velina picked up the dirty clothes from the floor Orenda had been wearing the night before and placed them into a plastic bag, one that the police men gave her, as Her's and Orenda's clothes needed to be tested for any evidence. She took Orenda's hand and led her downstairs to a sitting room where a small red velvet box was placed on the table in front of her. Velina gestured for her to open it. Orenda stepped forward and picked up the little box from the table and slowly lifted the lid. A smile spread across her face, seeing that Velina had had it taken into town to the local metal workers to have it designed into a beautiful necklace. The amber had been polished and shaved into a shiny oval shape with a beautiful silver metal work frame cased around the edge of the sap-covered clover. Velina lifted it from the small box, revealing a silver chain that pulled loose from the small cushion inside, and she placed it around Orenda's neck.

Chapter Sixteen

I GREW BUT NEVER FORGOT YOU.

"I miss my dad, but I still see him in my visions. The visions came in silence, flashes behind my eyes, stories my hands had to paint."

-O.B.

Time moved on in Antler Manor. The memory of my father is everywhere, but still no memory of how he died or how we were out there with him, hurt and bruised, but that's all. I miss him so much, all I want to do is tell him about my projects at college, my first job, earning my own money, about mum taking up her own hobbies in the greenhouse, growing more and more obscure herbs and plants. Some of them look so beautiful and strange, each having its own properties of either healing wounds or helping you sleep; I have read glimpses of my mum's journal with all her findings, and it's so fascinating. I am nineteen now. I go to Hale College, which is just a short walk from my home. My aunt Pearl moved in with us after my uncle Jack died, so my mum and Aunt Pearl kept each other company. It's great seeing my mum laugh again and truly feel it. I have taken up art and photography in pursuit of my dream of one day owning my own gallery to display and sell my paintings and pictures. But I have been struggling to concentrate lately. My dreams have been plagued by images of things I really do not understand. When I wake, I must sleepwalk because I have painted the images I have seen when my eyes drift off into sleep. I want to talk to someone, but I do not want to be looked at as mad. I see my dad with a white stag. I paint a large black raven a lot, something in that dark bird's eyes that is so familiar to me, but I can't put my finger on it. Orenda is now growing into a young lady with her own dreams and goals and has taken on the world with a strong family at her side, ready to help her where they can. At Hale College, they were getting excited about the coming Halloween party held at Hollow Wood every year. Each year, the event grows and becomes bigger and better. Orenda and her friends were excited about who would be crowned the spooktacular Queen of the Halloween Fancy Dress competition. Orenda had no clue what she wanted to dress up as while she packed to go home for the weekend to help her mum prep her stall at the event, selling her herbs and remedies. She was having a laugh with her friends in her dorm room about one of them wanting to dress up in large mustard and ketchup bottles before heading out the door and coming home.

Once she reached the white gates of Antler Manor, she was greeted by a very old and slow Tex who was plodding along out of breath, excited to see her, and slowly wagging his tail. She walked down the drive on a cold Autumn Day, slowing so Tex could walk beside her, listening to the ravens around her flapping their wings and squawking to each other. She felt Tex lick her fingers in want of some head scratches before they reached the door and entered the warmth of the manor. As they entered, Velina ran out from the kitchen with her antler manor apron on, smelling of all the herbs and brews she had made and bottled for the Halloween fair. "Orenda, my dear, welcome home." She gave her a big hug and took her through to the kitchen whilst the staff took Orenda's belongings to her bedroom. Orenda took a seat at the kitchen island, watching her mum pour Navy-blue wax seals over the small bottles, stamped with the head of the stag, then putting them all in small black premade boxes ready for tonight. She wanted to raise money for local charities in the area, and she also found it fun being at her stall and talking to everyone who approached. As Orenda leaned over and took a pile of flat black boxes and started putting them together for her mum, she needed advice: "Mum, I need some help?" "What's up?" Velina replied. "With everything going on at college and helping you set the stall up, I haven't had time to get a Halloween outfit together for the costume competition." Velina stopped what she was doing and had an idea. "Come with me, I think I might have something that will help." She turned the stove off and removed her apron, took Orenda's hand and led her up the stairs. They climbed the flights until they got to the hatch that led into the loft. Orenda was unsure what was up there, as it was filled with so much stuff, not to mention old dust and probably spiders. As she shuddered, she followed her mum up the stairs to the loft above that Velina had pulled down, as they climbed up she peered at the chaos around her.

Old furniture from generations ago was stored in the loft, covered in old white dust-covered sheets. Trunks and old bags stacked in the corner high, old suitcases and fake Christmas trees long forgotten. As light beamed up through the ceiling from the floor below, Velina pulled on the hanging cord, and the light clicked on, showing even more stuff. Thankfully, the loft was well insulated, and everything was kept safe and dry by the covers draped over everything. Velina walked to the back of the loft, pushing past all the clutter and furniture until she came to what looked like a rack covered in a zipped-up protector. She pulled the zip down and pushed the cover away, revealing a rack of old dresses. Orenda's mouth opened in amazement, seeing five dresses hung there, all black but each a distinctive style. Three of them looked very casual, like dresses you could walk around the house in, one was a black nightdress with a long, deep blue robe draped over top. But when she pushed them all to one side, she saw a stunning dress. It was a black beaded ball gown draped in black lace; it had a tight corset covered in black shining gems with a pair of silk gloves that hung from the hanger. Orenda walked forward and ran her hand over the details of the dress, lost in the sparkle; it still looked new. Velina said, "These dresses were stored up here a long time ago; they belonged to a previous lady of Antler Manor." Orenda carefully took the dress off the hanger and held it up to the light, seeing more and more detail. Her mum said, "Try it on, see if it fits, it looks your size. Go behind the rack and try it on. I will get a mirror for you." Orenda walked behind the rack to try the dress on, as she removed her clothes, being careful where she put them, as she did not want to get them covered in dust. She lifted the skirt of the dress and stepped into it, pulling the string tight and tying a knot. She eyed the corset, looking at all the lace, feeling lost on where to begin.

She loosened the black ribbons and pulled the corset over her head, then called for her mum to help tighten the corset. She walked out from behind the rack holding the ribbons tight. Velina saw Orenda in the dress, and a tear fell from her eyes. "That dress fits you perfectly, you look beautiful, I'm so proud of you." Orenda smiled at her mum and turned so she could adjust the ribbons. Once it was done, Velina took her to an old mirror she had found to show Orenda how amazing she looked in her dress. "You look like a powerful sorceress in that dress; I also found this in one of the old trunks." Velina lifted an old, crooked witch's hat that was lined with sequins and black beads that matched the dress very well. She walked away for a moment and brought back an old staff that had a black crystal set atop it to help finish off the outfit. It was from one of Velina's old Halloween costumes from when she lived in the big city with Julie. Orenda looked into the mirror and was incredibly happy with the whole outfit; it was perfect for the

Party. She felt her worries fade until she locked eyes with her own reflection in the mirror, for a split second, a woman's face took the place of her own. She had similar features to her and the same red heart-shaped birthmark on her cheek with long, black, flowing raven hair. Orenda blinked aggressively at her own reflection until her image caught fire in front of her with large black wings that were ablaze; they opened out behind her. She screamed and fell back into Velina. "What's wrong, are you ok?" Orenda looked back at the mirror, seeing just herself again with her mum behind her holding her up. "I must be tired, I thought I saw.... It's nothing, I need some food and sleep, I think." Velina rubbed her shoulder and grabbed her clothes from behind the rack and loosened the black ribbons of her gown. "Go have a shower and hang this dress up. I will ask one of the maids to clean and prep the dress for you for tomorrow night. I will cook your favourite tonight, mac & cheese," Orenda smiled and held onto her mum's shoulders as they descended the stairs from the loft, holding her dress up, so she didn't trip over the fabric and fall down the stairs. Orenda watched her mum walk away towards the kitchen. She entered her bedroom to remove the dress and draped it onto her window seat with silk gloves and a hat placed atop it and leaned the staff against the wall. She looked out across the grounds from her bedroom window, seeing the now moonlight pour through the trees, casting long shadows across the grass.

She entered her bathroom and turned on the hot water, steam bellowing from the gap at the top of the shower. As she entered, feeling the warm water over her skin, she reflected on what she saw in the mirror. She knew that face. She knew those dark eyes. But she could not place it. Once she was done in the shower, she entered her bedroom with her towel wrapped around her, seeing that her dress was gone and clean pyjamas had been placed on her bed for her. She plaited her long wet hair, got into her pyjamas and put on her favourite slippers fashioned on the ruby slippers from the Wizard of Oz. She entered the kitchen, smelling the familiar scent of cheese and pasta cooking in the oven and was greeted by her mum and Aunty Pearl, who were laughing over a glass of wine. Orenda smiled seeing the two of them together as they turned to see Orenda walking into the kitchen, followed by Tex, who waddled off to his bed by the patio doors. The radio was on. Music was playing, and the night felt good, like anything amazing could happen. They all danced around the island in the kitchen, laughing together and singing along with the radio. Orenda forgot how tired she felt; she just wanted to be with her aunt and mum tonight. It got to early hours in the morning, and they all started feeling tired. Velina and Pearl were very tipsy as they walked, leaning on each other, singing as they climbed the stairs to go to bed, leaving Orenda sitting in the kitchen alone, having a tidy before she went up to bed herself. Orenda looked over to Tex, who lifted his head, his cloudy old eyes watching her as she moved around the kitchen cleaning up. She looked back at him and walked over to sit on his bed with him. He lay his head back on her lap, wagging his tail, whilst she gently stroked his head as they both drifted off. Orenda started to dream she could see Antler Manor grounds in the spring when all the flowers were beginning to bloom, she could smell the fresh scent as it rode the breeze. She looked over towards the drive and saw Tex running after a butterfly, bounding after it with his tail wagging.

She felt a pit in her stomach as if Tex was running away from her, but she was so happy watching him play, not looking stiff like he usually does. She walked out towards him, and they both froze and looked at each other for a fleeting time. Tex's tongue was hanging out, panting from chasing the butterfly. A tear fell down

Orenda's cheek when she realised what was happening. He was passing on; he was resting now free from his old body. Tex ran to her as she leaned down to catch him. He licked her face excitedly, wagging his tail, then stopped and sat in front of her. He had a look in his eyes like he was happy and at rest. She could not stop the tears as she watched him walk away down the drive to eventually fade away from view. Orenda's eyes snapped open, still feeling the weight of Tex on her lap. He was not moving, but as the tears fell down her face and onto his black and grey peppered fur, she knew he was at peace. She gave his body one last hug. She gently placed him off her lap and covered him in a blanket, when she looked up and saw her mum looking very groggy and hungover as she walked into the kitchen. Velina looked at Orenda, who had red, wet eyes, then looked at Tex, who was covered in his blanket. She ran down to him, sobbing, gently removing the blanket to see his face. It looked like he was sleeping how he always did. Velina called for Pearl when she appeared at the door and saw Tex in his bed, tears fell down her face. They all lifted him up in the blanket and made their way out of the patio doors and into the grounds. They walked into a clearing where Axel is buried, surrounded by bushes of red roses that had wilted in the cold of Autumn. Orenda left them to go grab a shovel so they could bury Tex with Axel.

Once they placed Tex into his resting place, they wrapped him up securely with his blanket and his favourite toy, which was an old duck that squeaked when you squeezed it. They knew they would miss that sound when he was happy after he had had his dinner or breakfast. When the grave was filled in, they all stood for a moment in silence, each of them with tears falling down their faces. The wind blew cold as they made their way back inside, still in shock, but once Orenda told them of the vision she had when she fell asleep with Tex, that lifted their sorrows slightly. As the day went on, they prepped for the Halloween party to keep their minds busy and to lift their sorrows from Tex. They all drove up to the field, seeing all the hustle and bustle of everyone from the village hanging bat garlands, placing pumpkin lanterns everywhere, hay bales being placed for seating, and the fire pit being built. It was happening, they were led by one of the organisers to an area where the stalls were being built. Velina was happy with her spot as it overlooked the whole field and the festivity going on. Velina didn't dress up too much; she wore a long black dress and had a witch's hat on with an old broom. Once she was all set up and happy, she stayed at the stall talking and mingling with the other vendors as Orenda headed home to get ready. She entered Antler Manor to a quiet home; no Tex greeted her at the door. She wiped the tears that fell from her eyes and proceeded to her room to get ready when she bumped into one of the maids, who saw how sad she looked. She put her arm around Orenda, "Come on, Miss, I will help you get ready and look fab for tonight." Orenda was thankful for the company. As she was helped into the gown and laced up the maid whose name was Sally, her brown eyes cast a checking look over Orenda to make sure everything was perfect. She added a little extra blush to her cheeks and smoothed her hair out from the rollers that were placed in her hair to give soft, flowing beach wave curls. As her long, deep brown hair fell from the rollers, Sally ran a brush through to break the curls, then added some hairspray to set them in place for the night. She sprayed her with some perfume and guided her to the mirror, where she apprehensively looked, hoping not to see anything appear in her reflection. As she placed the witch's hat a top her head, she smiled as she was ready for the night ahead.

Chapter Seventeen

HALLOWEEN SPOOKTACULAR

KING AND QUEEN

"In this dress that my mum found in the loft, with a twirl of magic, and now I'm ready to dance the night away! Spooktacular Queen? Oh, I'm just getting started."

-O.B.

When Orenda hopped into the car to be taken to the Halloween party by the family chauffeur, she was helped in by Sally, tucking her dress in to make sure nothing got caught in the door. She waved her off, smiling as they left Antler Manor. Thankfully, the night was not too cold, but the fog had descended around the village; it had the perfect view for that night as the full moon shone out through the few clouds in the sky. As they drove through the village, it was deserted because everyone was at the party already, and a few people were walking up dressed in their best Halloween costumes with their children dancing and skipping ahead, swinging small pumpkin lanterns. She smiled to herself as she spied her friends from college walking through the village as well, seeing the two giant bottles of ketchup and mustard waddling through the street. She laughed out loud and asked the driver to stop so she could walk with her friends to the party. She shouted for them both to stop as she hurried to catch up with them. Thankfully, she wore her comfy black trainers under the gown, as you could not see her feet through all the fabric. "Kerry, Bella, wait up, never thought in my life I would be running after two giant bottles of sauce", they all laughed and took in each other's outfits. Their attention flew to Orenda's "Wow, girl, you look amazing, your dark glamours, Glinda." Orenda twirled the glitter and beads shining in the lantern lights as they made their way to the party. When they arrived and entered the field, they were greeted by music all around them, the smell of cooking and roasted chestnuts, pumpkin curries and baked loaves that were warm and toasted with melted butter. They walked up to the popcorn booth and got some toffee popcorn each, not risking spilling anything down their outfits.

As they spun at the sound of the speaker calling everyone to the fire mound, it was ready to be lit. She looked over and waved at her mum, who was having the best time with Aunty Pearl. They both looked over and smiled at Orenda, putting two thumbs up in approval of how amazing she looked. As everyone gathered the speaker who had his face painted like a skull wearing a smart black suite covered in cobwebs spoke over the microphone to the crowd "welcome everyone to the night of horrors, when the living and dead come together to celebrate Halloween or Samhain in the old Celtic ways, lets light this fire will you all count down with me?" The crowd cheered and started counting down from five. "FIVE, FOUR, THREE, TWO, ONE." A strong wind blew from nowhere, rustling through the crowd, making people huddle together. The flame that was lit on the wooden torch surged and sputtered, which made the holder jump. He threw it to the floor in front of Orenda, where the flame extinguished. The wind calmed down and went still, and the crowd hushed as Orenda picked up the extinguished torch. She looked at it for a moment, still seeing the embers crawling through the wood as they reflected in her eyes, she could not look away. She felt heat surge through her body as the torch then ignited back to life in front of her. She held the torch away from her in case any of the embers fell on her dress as she looked up in the far distance, seeing the witch's ash tree silhouetted by the moon, surrounded in fog. She snapped out of the trance when the man running the ceremony leaned down to ask for the torch back. Orenda blinked and handed it over, feeling a little confused. She smiled at him, gave him the torch and stepped back with her friends, who gave her a weary look. The man spoke through the microphone again, "Sorry about that, folks, the spirits must be partying hard tonight, let's join them, shall we?" The crowd cheered as he threw the torch onto the fire, and it went up in an instant. The heat warmed their faces as they watched the branches and foliage burn away into embers that joined the stars in the sky.

When the cheering had subsided, the judges started walking around the crowd looking at everyone's costumes. There was every horror creature you could think of, from werewolves, Frankenstein's, monsters, vampires, fellow witches, and zombies; everyone had made such an effort this year to join in with this celebration. The fire torches were lit around the field as everyone danced, ate, and drank. When we got too hot and wanted a change of pace, we left the party goers to enter the scream corn maze that was a killer scarecrow themed this year. My two mates deflated their sauce bottle outfits and tied the loose costumes around their waists so we could all link arms to feel safer. As we approached the corn maze, there were two scarecrows with blood dripping from their stitched eyes and mouths hanging from two giant crosses at the entrance. We waited for our turn to enter as we pulled back the black, ripped curtain showing the two scarecrows in full view. As we approached the two scarecrows lunged down at us, roaring, growling and clicking their teeth as they laughed maniacally at us, screaming and running into the maze that was softly lit by flickering Eddison bulbs to show us the path. All we could hear ahead was another group screaming and laughing, hearing a distant chainsaw revving up. We all held on to each other tight, feeling our heartbeats in our heads as we came to a crossroad. The signs were two big arrows, one pointing left into the maze and one pointing right. One said left for death or right for torment, splattered on the sign what looked like blood. We froze in place, deciding which route to take, so we went with the right as we chose the logic that turning right was always right. We turned right, feeling our legs go jelly as the lights started flickering more down this road. As we looked, we saw a silhouetted figure where it was so cold we could see his breath blowing out like mist with an axe loosely held down by his leg. When the light went out and then back on, it moved closer and closer until this mutated scarecrow with large metal staples over its mouth lifted the axe high, screaming at us, which sent us running past him. We could hear him chasing after us as we reached another crossroad, and thankfully, he had darted back into the corn, waiting to scare the life out of the next group. As we panted, reading the signs, catching our breath, the two large wooden arrows said left for dark, right for dim.

They all panicked and ran left this time, holding onto each other's arms for dear life. The corn maze twisted and turned, still hearing the terror in the distance until all the lights went out. In the darkness, we took slow, unsteady steps, holding our hands out to feel where we were going. Until we started hearing heavy breathing and chains clanging together, we all agreed not to panic and run in the dark in case we fell and hurt ourselves, but the noises were all around us and getting more overwhelming with each step we took towards the lighted path again. We saw another sign, this one in the shape of a circle, saying you are near the end of the corn maze, follow the lighted path out. We looked at each other and took a deep breath, knowing we were about to meet the chainsaw scarecrow. They braced themselves, waiting for him to jump out at any moment; they all definitely had shaky legs; it was all still just the lights and walls of tall corn to show them the way. From behind, they heard a thud as the final chainsaw scarecrow crashed through the corn, screaming and revving the chainsaw. They all bolted from the maze, screaming. When they came tearing out the exit, the scarecrow backed off as they all fell to the floor on soft hay, laughing. They all agreed not to do that again. They heard over the speaker that the costume competition winners were to be announced for King and Queen, and to come up to the base of the stage to hear the results. We all gathered around, hearing the speaker take the mic again. "Everyone, you're all amazing, but there can only be one spooktacular king and Queen. Here are the results from our judges. Our Spooktacular king is...... DEAN WICKER dressed as a warlock. Come on up and take your crown and sash." Dean Wicker, who was a young man of nineteen, was a member of the founding family of Hunters Manor. He rushed up to the stage with his fists hitting the air as he accepted his crown and sash. It was now time to crown the spooktacular Queen. Velina held her breath and crossed her fingers tight for her daughter, willing him to call out her name.

Orenda closed her eyes and held her friends' hands tight in hers as she waited for the results. "Our spooktacular Queen is.... ORENDA BRINFORD, dressed as a beautiful dark sorceress, come on up here and be crowned my lovely. Orenda jumped with joy as she ran up the steps and accepted her crown and sash. She glanced over at Dean, who could not take his eyes off her for a second. He looked flushed in the face as he approached her and bowed, extending his hand to her. They could start the first dance as King and Queen. Orenda smiled bashfully at him and took his hand. He led her back down the stairs to the middle of the dance floor, which was lit up with flashing lights everywhere and a giant pumpkin disco ball hanging high in the centre of metal scaffolding that had Halloween decorations hung from it. She moved in close to him as he took her waist and held her hand. She settled into him, placing her hand on his shoulder, feeling a little awkward as the music started playing out over the speakers. Orenda looked up at Dean, seeing his dark eyes shining as he looked back into hers, getting lost in the green as the lights made the colours dance in them. They began to sway to the music, and all the awkwardness fell away. The song consumed them both as everyone watching them watched on in pride. Orenda's dress glittered and sparkled as she danced around the floor. Dean slowed the dance as the song was coming to an end. He could not resist doing an old Hollywood spin, then leaning Orenda back, she giggled at him. He pulled her back up slowly, meeting her gaze. He pressed a soft kiss on her lips, her cheeks flushed as she kissed him back. They came apart, hearing everyone around them cheering for them both. She caught a glance at her mum and aunt, seeing Velina smiling with tears in her eyes.

She curtsied to Dean as he bowed back to her and led her off the dance floor so they could chat together. They took a seat on a hay bale in front of the fire. They could hear everyone behind them cheering, dancing, and laughing. Dean wanted to get to know her more as they sat and chatted for ages about any and everything. A lady walked by holding a tray of caramelised apples, he waved to her and asked to buy two. They ate their apples together, enjoying the warmth of the fire as Dean got brave and held her hand. She smiled and squeezed his hand back, they both agreed to meet up with each other at the weekend in Ruth's Bakery for some food and to get to know each other some more. Dean held her gaze. "Looks like fate gave me more than just a crown tonight... it gave me the girl in the legendary dress that sparkles as much as you do. So... your majesty, shall we show them how it's done?" They both stood together and rejoined everyone on the dance floor and danced until the witching hour rang out on the church bells in the distance on the hill. When the party came to an end, they were already excited for next year's event as it always got bigger and better every year. The following day, Orenda spent most of the day in bed until she woke up in a panic, remembering she had made plans with Dean to meet at Ruth's bakery; she hurried to her bathroom, glancing at the time, seeing she had about half an hour until she had to be there. She had a hurried shower and threw on her favourite black jeans with a soft wool maroon jumper and a black bobble hat, and a scarf. She bumped into her mum, who was on her way to see if she was ok, as she does not usually sleep this late. In passing, Orenda rushed off, shouting she was meeting Dean at the bakery. Velina laughed to herself and shouted out for her, "Be safe and be back by five thirty, I hope it goes well, dear."

Ruth's bakery smelled like spiced dreams, childhood memories, fresh cinnamon rolls, sugar-dusted pastries, just a hint of vanilla that lingered in the air around them. Orenda walked in nervously, smoothing the sleeves of her jumper, her hair still a little damp from her shower when she rushed out. She spotted Dean sitting near the window table, with two hot drinks and a smile that crinkled just right. "You made it", he said, standing a little too quickly and nearly knocking over the hot chocolate. "I wouldn't miss it", Orenda replied, eyes flicking to the treats lined in the display case. "Are those cinnamon stars?" He grinned, "Ruth said they're for magically promising first dates." Dean gave her a cheeky wink and bought them two cinnamon stars each to go with their hot chocolates. Orenda laughed and removed her hat and scarf. "Well, I'm glad we are starting out with something enchanted." They talked for hours about things that didn't feel like first date topics. Orenda told him about learning to shape and grow wild brambles with her mum in Antler Manor's greenhouse. Dean admitted he once accidentally set his sock drawer on fire trying to light a single candle, but his clumsiness knocked it over. Ruth, from behind the counter, smiled knowingly, seeing how fast they became so comfortable in each other's presence. The bakery buzzed around them, but it felt like they were in their own little world together. As the candle on their table burned low, Dean leaned in just slightly and said softly, "I'm really glad I met you, Orenda." She smiled, brushing sugar from her lip. "I think the cinnamon stars agree." Outside, the weather started to change as the rain rolled in, pattering down the glass windows next to them. She knew it was time to leave and go home, but the rain was putting a stop to that, and she did not mind in the slightest.

Chapter Eighteen

I CALL UPON THE WHITE STAG. Time

jumps back

"The forest held its breath. Then, the stag answered. To summon the white stag is to be seen by magic older than language."

-E.L.

It was dark, but Axel could see that dawn was not far away. He was walking in the woods but had no memory of why or how he got there. He fell to the floor, clutching his head, seeing John's face flashing in his mind in bursts of fire. One minute, he looked normal, human, then his features contorted, his eyes shrivelled into his head, and smoke bellowed out cracked, melted skin; he looked like something flung fresh from hell with empty dark pits where his eyes should be and fire running through his veins, covered by charred, cracked skin. Axel felt it in his soul that he had to be stopped. He was aimlessly walking through the woods until he found himself in a village that felt oddly familiar to him. He followed the streetlights that were being extinguished one by one to indicate that the day was starting. He glanced around, seeing people leaving their homes to go to work and start their day. His eyes locked onto a front door that he felt compelled to approach. He got up to the door and went to knock, but his hand fell through the wood. He panicked and stepped back, examining his hand, feeling his finger with his other hand, but when he tried to knock again, the same thing happened. He held his breath and took a step forward as his body passed through the solid wooden door. He looked around, feeling like he knew the house he had just stepped into. He looked at the wall, seeing the faces of a family smiling back at him. He leaned in and looked at their faces, trying to remember who they were. He knew that he knew them, but he couldn't think straight. He heard a loud thud followed by a scream that came from upstairs, a clattering sound of children's feet thundering down the stairs towards him as they pulled open the front door and ran from the house, crying. He could hear commotion coming from upstairs, so he followed the sounds. He walked the stairs, but strangely not feeling his feet connect to the floor as he climbed to hear the sounds getting louder. He turned onto the top landing and looked towards a closed door where he could hear crying from a woman and yelling from a man behind it. Axel held his breath again and passed through the door to see a woman on the floor holding her arm in pain and a large, muscled man aggressively pointing his finger at her and telling her to never disobey him again and teach those children respect. Axel flew at him but fell straight through his body. He felt so frustrated that he couldn't help.

He looked at the man's frowning, angry face, his features twisted in aggression, then a name escaped Axel's mouth. "Ted? You are Ted? But you're not Ted, you are John the Molthera." Axel knew he had to follow John's every move; he could not be trusted. He stood and swung a punch at him, but his arm fell straight through his face. Axel felt so frustrated, he shook his hands and tried again, but the same result. He could see John's face through Ted's. A small glowing cluster of veins started to appear on his neck. John grabbed his neck and stormed out of the room, so Axel followed him. He followed him out of the house and back through the village to a bridge where the water runs under it. John panicked and frantically looked around, noticing a man who was sitting under the bridge with a ragged old blanket covering him. John approached this man like a big cat stalking its prey. He slowed his approach and looked down at his hands, seeing the glowing veins heat up under his skin. He was determined to hold onto this body and get another chance at life, so he continued his hunt as he crept off under the bridge to strike up a conversation with this man. Axel followed him, feeling noticeably confident now that he knew for sure he could not be seen. John stalked up to this man and kicked the side of his foot that stuck out from the blanket. "Who are you? What are you doing under this bridge?" John asked in a voice filled with annoyance. The man jerked and glanced up at him, seeing the glowing veins beneath his skin that were illuminated more intensely in the shadow of the bridge. He threw the blanket off him and said, "I am a homeless man just passing through on my way to Hale." John laughed to himself and crouched down to be at the same level as the homeless man. John's arm reached out fast as lightning and grabbed the poor man's throat as he slowly stood, lifting him up off his feet with impressive strength. The man twitched and gasped for air, but nothing helped him; he was caught in John's grasp, and he was not letting go. John pulled the man closer to his face, squeezing his hand tighter around his neck until the man's body went limp. Axel cried out, but he knew he could do nothing about this. Axel watched as dark smoke bellowed from John's mouth into the homeless man's chest, like there was a connection between them.

The glowing veins that were all around John's neck started to fade away as he pulled back the black smoke and chucked the remains of the body that now looked disfigured and dried like a prune that had been left to bake in the hot sun into the water as the current took the poor man away downstream. He rolled his shoulders, stretched out his arms and took in a deep breath as he cracked his neck, almost like he was adjusting a new fitted suit to his body. John chuckled to himself and walked away like nothing had happened. Axel fell to his knees, sobbing in frustration that all he could do was watch and observe this horror. When he looked up, he saw a figure appear under the bridge. He straightened up and walked towards the figure that just appeared out of a mist, then became a more solid form. It was the homeless man who stood there at the water's edge watching his body disappear downstream. Axel approached the man and placed a hand on his shoulder. To his surprise, his hand did not fall through him. He said to him "I'm sorry my friend there's no comfort I can give you after what just happened. What's your name?" The man looked up at him confused and just said "Nick my name is Nick" Axel closed his eyes and felt a warmth go through him as he looked up to the other side of the flowing water running under the bridge to see the pure white stag staring up at them both. It crossed the water with ease towards them and lowered itself in front of Nick. Axel, by instinct, knew the stag had come to take him somewhere better. He helped Nick onto the back of the stag and watched as they crossed back over the water and disappeared into the trees beyond the bridge. Tears fell down Axel's face as he felt lighter by being able to at least help him in a small way. He looked around and followed the hustle and bustle of people living their lives, going about their day, when Axel took a seat out front of a baker's shop. The radio was playing music, so he sat and just listened until a particular song came on that triggered a memory in his head. He leaned back on the chair; he could see star lanterns and a beautiful girl he was dancing with to this song. He could feel her head pressed onto his chest as he just listened until the song came to its end, and the pressure of her head leaning on his chest faded away.

Axel came to a realisation from following John around for years and years, helping the poor people whose lives John had taken so he could live inside Ted's corpse. Watching Ted's body age with each year as it went by, seeing how he treated poor Ted's family, who thankfully made a runner one evening before he got back home from work. Axel is calling for the stag to take another person away, and another and another. Axel took note of every buried body, every piece of evidence that John had carelessly left behind. But he just had to figure out how to get him caught, how to give his evidence over. Axel had one mission, and that was to bring John down once and for all, but he just had to make a plan on how to do it. He had some inner thoughts, "Could the stag help him in some kind of way? But then again, who in their right mind would listen and follow a wild animal to random crime scenes?" It had been about eleven years since Axel had passed, and he had done everything in his power to remember where all these poor people had been disposed of. He even called upon the stag to mark the graves and leave pieces of wood so they could be easily found one day. John buried most of his victims in the woods that surrounded the village, so it was easy for him to get home quickly and unnoticed when he walked home from the jewellery shop. The police were on the hunt for a murderer who was him, but they kept coming up empty-handed every time, as John would always go for people who didn't have families or were homeless, so their roots could not be traced back to anyone. Over the years, Axel would find himself seeing people age around him, but he never changed, seeing new life entering the village. The baker had a new son who was working with her, and he now runs the shop while she pops in every now and then to talk to everyone or do some light baking in the evening to help restock for the day. The family that runs the post office, the sons have taken over the business, and they have their own children now. The daughter left a few years back to go travelling with her best friend.

He went for a walk around the village, he didn't really leave his usual spots, which were shadowing John or sitting out the front of the baker's, listening to the ever-changing music and people watching. He felt a strange pull to walk towards the exit of the village, where in the near distance he could see a large ash-coloured tree. It was during autumn, and all the trees were in flames of reds, oranges, and browns, so he followed the pull he felt. He approached the tree and took a long look at it as he followed the trunk skyward when he saw a young girl sitting on one of the branches, reading an old leather book. He walked around to the other side to see who she was, to see if he knew her from people watching at the bakery, but he had not seen this girl before. He felt a strong connection to her. He took in a deep breath, and his feet lifted from the ground as he levitated up towards the branch where she was sitting. He looked at her for a moment until she looked up at him, for a split moment locking eyes with each other, when he noticed she had one kind green eye and one that was so blue it almost looked white. She screamed out loud, which made him scream out, "You can see me?" The girl shuffled away from Axel and jumped down from the tree branch, twisting her ankle as she hit the ground. Axel floated down to her in a hurry. "Are you ok? Please don't be scared of me, my name is" but he was cut off when she looked up at him and said, "Axel?" Axel stepped back from her, "You know me? How do you know me? And how come you can see and hear me?" The girl stood but unsteady on her right ankle as she fell forward. Axel's automatic reaction to her falling, he leans forward and grabs her arm. He could not believe that he could actually touch her. He noticed the unique necklace that had fallen out of her black shirt. It was a silver-framed necklace; in the centre was a four-leaf clover encased in amber tree sap. She looked up at Axel and said, "Thank you for catching me. My name is Clover, Clover Brinford, and you are my grandfather. Your picture is on the walls at home."

Axel stabled Clover, then pulled her into an embrace; he could not control the tears that fell from his eyes with joy that he could actually hug someone, to hug his granddaughter. He put her back down on the ground and asked if she could fill him in on his life, as he had no memory. Only flashes from the past, but they are all jumbled, then he went on to tell Clover about John, who was squatting inside Ted's body. Clover could not believe it, as she knew John as Ted, but she always kept her distance as she had a bad feeling about him. Then out of nowhere, a large golden retriever came bounding up behind them. He was covered in water and shaking all the droplets everywhere. Clover laughed and pushed the wet dog away. She introduced him to Axel, "This is Jasper, he is my dog, he always goes and plays in the creek when I come here to read my book." He looked down at the wet dog who was staring right back at him with one golden brown eye and one so blue it almost looked white. Axel stared at them both, noticing they both had the same ice blue eyes. He then had a memory of a black lab called Tex. Clover informed him that Tex passed away at the old age of thirteen, and he is buried with your body in Antler Manor's grounds. Clover also told him that she had done some research in an old leather-bound book she found hidden in a drawer of the coffee table at Antler Manor that had a strange spell on it, to read and hide the words. Written inside, she felt she had a natural gift with this kind of practice and found a lot of information about different spells and history about witches, "it's said if you are born with one normal eye and one ice blue eye, it allows you to see the world around you as it is and the world beyond. I have seen

213

spirits for as long as I can remember, but how come I have never seen you around Antler Manor?" Axel explained that he had no memory of who he was when he was alive, but all he knew about was the man he had to follow and stop. Clover leaned against the tree, rubbing her ankle until she felt life come back into it again and asked Axel to follow her back to Antler Manor to see for himself where he once lived and had a family. He could see his wife, Velina, and his grown daughter, Orenda, who is in her early thirties now. Clover informed Axel that her birthday was in a few days when she turns sixteen, and according to the book, she found that as a witch, that's when your full powers come to light and can be harnessed fully.

They took a shortcut through the woods towards Antler Manor, where Axel felt like he was vibrating. He could feel some kind of magnetic pulse as he got closer and closer to the manor. He hadn't ventured this far out from the village before; he felt nervous butterflies form inside him. He placed a hand on Clover's shoulder to stop her as he felt like he was having a panic attack. Clover turned to look at him. "Can ghosts have panic attacks?" she asked in a teasing voice. Axel glanced up at her with his hands on his knees, heavy breathing, "Well, apparently they can," he said in playful annoyance. Clover grabbed his hand and pulled him towards the large white gates; the sign of the stag was displayed on the front. "Welcome home, grandad", he smiled at her. Recatching his composure, he glanced towards the large manor house set back in the beautiful grounds. Large cedar trees shaded the driveway. Clover pushed on the gate and took Axel's hand to follow her down the drive, but for some reason or another, it felt like there was a barrier preventing Axel from going past the gates. His head lowered as he took a step back. "I'm not meant to be here. I'm sorry, Clover, but I must go." Axel took off running back into the woods, leaving Clover standing alone at the gates, watching his form disappear from view. She called out for him, but he kept running away, so she closed the gates behind him and proceeded down the drive. Before she got to the front door, she crammed Eve's leather-bound spell book into her backpack before her mum opened the door to greet her back home. "Cloverleaf, I thought I heard you coming. I have cooked us all our favourite meal tonight, mac and cheese." Clover ran to her mother to give her a hug, then ran past her up the stairs to her bedroom, which was up in the loft. It was the size of a well-contained flat; it was decorated with all-natural wood and green draping plants hanging and climbing across the beams. She had star lanterns she found in an old box in the loft streamed across her four-poster bed, so when she lay down, she could look up at them. She had her own bathroom, mini kitchen, living room and bedroom with a flat roof garden that overlooked the whole grounds. She loved sitting out there when it was a full moon, just absorbing the mystical power it radiated. She would leave bottles of water out on the roof as well to collect moon water and to recharge her collection of crystals. She also loved being up there with the Ravens, especially if they were roosting and there were baby Ravens around, whom she would bring food home for them all after school.

Chapter Nineteen

WELCOME, BABY CLOVER. TIME

JUMPS BACK.

"Mark her name, for she carries all we could not finish. Welcome, baby Clover. She is not the first to bear the gift. But she may be the last to bear it alone. Let her be held and loved before she is needed."

-E.L.

Orenda was growing into a lady she was dating her boyfriend who lived at Hunter Manor his name is Dean Wicker a confident you man who carried the charismatic charm of the family, he had black hair that was always styled perfectly, a pale complexion with a sharp jaw line that was always hidden by stubble, deep hazel eyes that would almost look brown some days. He comes from an extensive line of hunters, part of a founding family in Hollow Wood. At weekends, he would either come stay at Antler Manor or Orenda would stay with him at Hunters Manor, but mostly, he would come stay with her as she hated seeing all the pelts and animal heads that decorated the main entrance. The blending of the founding family's never really happened in the past but in modern times the Brinford's blended with the Shaw's and now they blend with the Wickers, as Orenda and Dean were expecting their first baby together, They both would reminisce about how they meet at a Halloween event the village was holding like they do every year with a large party, music, food and drink, they always have a spooktacular King and Queen. Orenda had found one of Eve's old black dresses in her loft, so she went as a witch for the Halloween celebration. Dean's costume was a wizard with a large, tall, pointed hat that had gold stars all around, with a matching robe that swept the floor as he walked. They got voted the spooktacular King and Queen of Halloween that year and found love in it. Orenda had developed her own gift when growing into a young lady; it became abundant when she turned sixteen, but she tried to hide it from her mother in case she didn't understand. She could sleepwalk and find herself painting things that she saw in her mind. Some of her artwork was of her father and a beautiful white stag helping strangers climb onto the beast's back. Some were of an evil-looking monster with dark, hollowed-out eyes, veins that glowed like fire trying to burst from under its skin. She even managed to name this thing; it was called a Molthera. But the one thing that she kept painting again and again was a large black Raven sitting in the witch's ash tree. On her sixteenth birthday, she painted a baby girl with thick dark hair, a small love heart birthmark that matched her own on her cheek just under her left eye, but the baby's eyes were so strange, as one was green like an emerald and the other was like blue ice. She even knew in preparation to buy a small brush for the baby when she was born, so Orenda could brush her hair, she knew she would have a baby girl one day, and she would name her Clover.

"Hi there, this is where I come into the story. When my mum brought me into this world, I can tell you my story and theirs." Orenda was relaxing at home one day. She was very far along; the weather had gotten colder in the month of October, with a chill in the air. Velina had gone food shopping with Aunty Pearl, who had moved in after her husband passed away, so she could be with her sister. They were all each other needed; they would go on little outings together, have nice meals in new restaurants in the towns over from the village. But this day, I had clearly had enough and wanted to join the outside world even though I was a bit early, which was the polar opposite of my mum, who was late for everything. Orenda felt a sharp pain that flew through her body, so she got up and went for a little walk around the house. In her mind, she wanted to hang on for as long as possible, knowing Velina was coming home with her favourite snack, ginger nut biscuits. But the pain intensified, she felt wet trickling down her legs, her waters had broken. She grabbed the phone to call Dean, who had gone to work with his family at Hunter Manor, with the assurance Orenda would be in the same state as he had left her in the morning. When he got the news, he raced home to pick up Orenda to take her to night owl surgery. Once they got there, they were greeted by Enid, who wheeled a wheelchair around for Orenda, she took them through to the delivery suite where Dr Mack was waiting, Enid's son Mack took over from Frank when he retired from working in the main part of the hospital to focus mainly on admin now, to keep patients records organised and up to date. Orenda cried out in pain, grabbing her belly, sweat beading down her face as she got taken through to her room. They helped her onto the bed whilst Dean was dabbing a cool rag on her and holding her hand as she cried out for the pain to stop.

Dr Mack sat Orenda forward and gave her a spinal injection to help with the pain when it came time to push. Orenda lifted her legs so the Doctor could examine her. She could not believe it, but she was being watched by a few students to learn how a baby was born. But she could not care less, she just wanted this to be over. The Doctor instructed her to push, but nothing was happening; every push did nothing. After being examined again, Mack informed her she needed an emergency caesarean as the baby was stuck and facing the wrong way. So, the nurses upgraded the room and the equipment to get ready for the baby to be cut from Orenda. A screen went up, so Dean and Orenda were behind it, and the doctor got to work removing the baby. Once the cut was done and the baby was out, the room went into a panic as she was not breathing properly. Orenda was losing blood and going into shock. Dean stood up in a panic, not knowing where to go and what to do as his baby was taken away to another room to try and clear her airway and get her breathing. Dr Mack went back to Orenda, who looked very pale and drained, as he stitched her back up and wrapped her in warm blankets to increase her temperature. He attached her to a drip to get fluids back into her. Dean ran down the hall to find where his daughter had been taken to be greeted by a nurse holding her wrapped in a purple blanket that had small, stitched antlers on it. The baby was making all kinds of small squeaks as Dean took her from the nurse and held her close to him as he walked back to Orenda, who was sitting up in bed waiting to hear about the baby. Dean leant forward and passed her to Orenda, who was crying from relief to see she was ok and moving around. She looked at her little face, seeing the small love heart birthmark, but when she opened her little eyes for the first time, she was shocked to see the trademark green eye of the Brinford's and an ice blue eye. She asked the doctor to check her again, but she was perfectly fine. She was responding to sounds and following the bright coloured toys with her eyes as she stretched out her hands wanting to hold the fluffy dinosaur to her face.

Orenda held Clover up to see her eyes glancing around the room, but her vision locked onto something that was not there. Orenda followed her line of vision but saw nothing. It gave her the creeps a bit, so she asked the doctor if she could go home and get settled. Dean came in with a wheelchair after the doctor agreed that they could go home. Dean helped Orenda into the seat and wheeled her out the front to the car. On the drive home, Orenda asked Dean, "Do you think our baby can see things? She keeps looking at things when there is nothing there." Dean reassured her that she was just getting used to seeing all the different things around her and said that she would grow out of it. "I definitely did not grow out of it." When they got home, Dean opened the front door to be greeted by Velina, Pearl and Julie, who had come to Antler Manor when she was told that her best friend's daughter had gone into labour. She was the head of her own photography business, which was booming, and she moved back to Hollow Wood Village to enjoy the place where she grew up. She came running out and told her story to Orenda that she was in the pub at the time of learning the news, but when she went to leave, some idiot had blocked her car in, so she had to push her way out. Dented her car up a bit, but she could not miss her best friend's daughter coming home with her new baby girl. Julie took hold of Clover whilst Dean helped Orenda into the house. She immediately wanted to introduce Axel to Clover against the doctor's advice of telling her to rest the moment she got home. She straightened up and asked if she could have a moment alone with her dad and Clover. She took her baby from Julie and slowly walked through the main hall and out the patio doors into the grounds. She walked past a large hedge into a small clearing that had been planted with red roses everywhere. They were not as full and bright due to the cold, but there were some that had blossomed. She sat down on the stone bench that overlooked her father's gravestone. They wanted him here at Antler Manor so they could visit him anytime they wanted. She wrapped the blanket around Clover tighter to keep her warm from the October breeze and leaned forward to talk to her dad.

"Hi, Dad.... I have brought someone very special to meet you. Her name is Clover, your granddaughter. She has your quiet strength already. I can feel it in the way she looks at the world, like she's trying to understand everything before she can even speak words. I wish more than anything that you could hold her. That you could tell her the stories you told me, about how you grew up running away with the circus and your rock and roll years, and how you met mum. You would've loved her dad. And I think. No, I know you would've been proud of me. I didn't think I could do this without you, but your voice never really left me. You're in every decision I make; in every ounce of love, I give her. She is going to grow up knowing who you were, not just the legend, but the man. My father. The one who taught me how to stand when it was easier to fall. Rest easy, Dad. I'll tell her everything on your behalf." Orenda stood slowly, feeling very sore and made her way back into the manor, where she was greeted by her mum, who was listening at the door to everything she had said to Axel. She smiled and asked if she could hold Clover. Orenda passed her the baby so she could see her up close, but when Velina saw her eyes, something came over her. Her head reached back violently as her voice echoed, "When Silvered moon doth bleed its cry, and hushed winds through shadows sigh, A babe shall draw her first cold breath, Betwixt the realms of life and death. Eye of green earth, the world we know, of living flesh and sunlit glow, an eye of frost, the veil shall part, to glimpse the ghost and their still hearts. Mark thee well, this child of thread, whose steps will walk between living and dead. For she is the gate, key, and spell, where she doth tread, both realms shall swell". Velina's head fell forward. She felt faint and quickly passed Clover back to Orenda, who was shocked at what she had just witnessed.

Orenda had all kinds of things going through her head, "Does mum have a gift like mine? Shall I talk to her about it? I can confess what I have been going through with these visions I keep painting." Orenda opened the door to Clover's room, which was just down the hall from hers. It was painted a happy pastel yellow with farm animal stickers all over the walls. Dean was snoozing in the rocking chair when Orenda placed Clover down in her crib. She fell asleep immediately and left them both in there to sleep so she could go do the same thing. She grabbed the second baby monitor and tucked herself into bed as she drifted into a peaceful sleep. Her visions had calmed down a lot since Clover was born, as she had to be up a lot to feed her through the night, and when she actually did manage to sleep, it was a still, peaceful one. A couple of weeks later, Orenda plucked up the courage to talk to her mum about what happened when she held Clover; she would not let her dodge the question this time. She has her cornered in the kitchen with only one door; Orenda's body blocked her from leaving. "Mum, I need to confess something to you." Velina looked up at her with questioning eyes. "What is it you want to tell me, dear?" "I think you have powers, and so do I." Velina stayed still for a moment, then lifted her gaze up. "Yes, my dear, I think we are both blessed with some kind of gift. When you were a child, I would come check on you some nights when there was storms I would find you sat up at your easel painting all kinds of things but when I tried to speak to you it was like I wasn't even there" Orenda was surprised that she never questioned her about it but I guess it was lack of communication on both their parts. Velina explained "when I touch someone's hand I can read a person's soul; it just comes out I can't help it.

That's why when I go out, I always wear gloves. I didn't think I could read a baby's soul." They both embraced each other and promised not to keep anything from the other ever again.

Chapter Twenty

SPELLS. TIME JUMPS FORWARD.

*"Do not rush a spell. Magic has no patience for the unprepared.
The first spell you cast will hear you. Choose your words as you
would ally."*

-E.L.

As time went on, and clover grew into her own, she realised
her own unique way of seeing the world. She grew accustomed to
seeing the shadows and hearing slight voices that whispered into
her ear at night, but she decided to ignore them, in her frustration
of only being able to see and hear for a small moment, but she
wanted to see a full spirit. She had a fascination with the
paranormal but was getting tired of just seeing flashes of spirits;
she wanted to see a full manifestation. She took to going on ghost
hunts with her cousin, where they would delve into the world of
darkness to see beyond the veil. It was getting close to Clover's
sixteenth birthday, just being three days away, when she woke
from a nap and heard whispering. Jasper barked at her and wagged
his tail. He started getting excited, running to the door and then
back to Clover as if he wanted her to follow him. Clover opened
her bedroom door and followed a very excited Jasper down the hall
into a small, snug room that hadn't been used in a long while. She
sat on the sofa, seeing an old, cracked gold-framed mirror leaning
against the wall where Jasper was examining his reflection. Clover
leaned back onto the sofa and plonked her feet heavy on the coffee
table in front of her, and she heard a click. She quickly removed
her feet to lean forward, panicking that she had broken the old

coffee table, but just saw a drawer leaning out. She went to close it but saw there was something inside. She opened the drawer fully and saw an old leather-bound book sitting in there. She lifted it out, looking around the spin, seeing a strange symbol. She felt small jolts of electricity running through her fingers as she thumbed through the empty pages, feeling disappointed that there was nothing exciting inside. Jasper came over and sat beside her as he licked her hand to comfort her, so she stroked his head in thanks. She looked back at the book in her lap, seeing a small light glowing from the spine of the book. She ran her fingers up over the strange blue glowing symbol and something happened, it changed to a warm sunlight colour and the symbol had slightly changed seeing the arrow now was pointing up, the book flew open as it fell from her grip onto the coffee table, the pages flickering themselves until it stopped to lay still revelling old text written in beautiful swirling calligraphy.

The Bloodline of Ash and Echo

FROM EVE'S SPELLBOOK —TRANSCRIBED IN RAVEN INK

From fire she came, and silence she
broke, A Brinford child through
shadows spoke, With Eve's own gift
and grave-born grace,
She walks between both time and place.

She'll call the dead—they shall obey.
A fallen knight will find his way.
Through bonds of blood the beast shall
call.Molthera's wrath undone by call.

But trust not all the spirits say,
For liars dwell where shadows play,
Yet follow feathers, black as night...
The raven guards the final fight.

Clover leaned forward and read the dark, cracked page that had imagery of ghouls and dark mist streaked across, with a dark black Raven drawn in black coal, its eye that followed you as you read down the words on the page. Clover spoke out in a hushed voice as she read the words to herself. "The bloodline of ash and cold. From Eve's spellbook, transcribed in raven ink. From fire she came, and silence she broke. A Brinford child, through shadow, spoke. With Eve's own gift and grave-born grave, she walks between both time and place. When blood runs warm with ancient flame, and dead ones whisper out her name, the veil shall thin, the truth will unfold, as secrets rise from ash and cold. She'll call the dead- they shall obey, A fallen knight will find his way. Through bonds of blood the beast shall fall- Molthera's wrath undone by call. But trust not all the spirits say, for liars' dwell where shadows play. Yet follow feathers, black as night... The raven guards the final fight." A pulse of unknown power crawled through Clover's veins as she slammed the book shut and shoved it away on the table. "A Brinford child through shadow spoke? Is that me?" She looked at the book as if it were a cornered animal ready to bite her fingers off if she reached for it again, but she could not stop herself. She wanted to read and learn more from its weathered pages. "Who is Eve? Her name is in this book; it must have belonged to her when she was alive," Jasper barked and made Clover jump, so she closed the drawer and tried to make everything look untouched. She raced back to her bedroom, where she grabbed her bag and some snacks from the kitchen to make her way to her favourite reading spot. The witch's ash tree.

Luck

A four-leaf clover
concealed in amber

Grants protection
to the wearer.

And the fortune
to never lose one's way
in life.

But trust not
all the spirits say

Object of Power:

A four-leaf clover, sealed in amber sap
from the ancient Lifebark Tree.

Effect:

Bestows its bearer with unwavering protection
against misdirection, be it of foot or fate. The
wearer shall never stray far from their destined
path, even when all roads seem lost. When worn
near fhe heact, the charm awakens the "True
Compass"— a subtle guiding force of unseen grace.

Incantation (to be whispered at dusk:):

Clover caught in amber flame,
Guard my step and bless my name.
Let no road deceive my sight.
Guide me true by fate and light.

Instructions: Wrap the clover in silk before the
waxing moon. On the third night, seal it in amber tree
sap warmed by candlelight. Once hardened, thread with
hair of the one it will protect, or a strand of their thread-
bound fate. Wear close to the chest.

Caution: Do not break the amber seal. If shattered,
the charm loses its guidance and may invite wandering
shadows to trail the bearer.

The sun was shining through the clouds every now and then. It was a crisp October day with all the leaves changing to the beautiful fire oranges and reds of autumn. She and Jasper made their way out of the village that had been decorated with Halloween pumpkin lanterns ready for Halloween, as she walked towards the large Witches ash tree as Clover started to climb Jasper ran off to the creek to splash around. Clover got comfy on the thick branch and leaned her back against the trunk. She pulled the book from her bag and started to read when she saw a passage about a four-leaf clover concealed in sap. She pulled the necklace free from her black shirt and held it up to the image in the book. They were both the same. Clover read the information to herself, "a four-leaf clover concealed in amber. Grants protection to the wearer. And the fortune to never lose one's way in life. The incantation (to be whispered at dusk): Clover caught in amber flame, guard my step and bless my name. Let no road deceive my sight, guide me true by fate and light," she went on to read about her necklace coming to the realisation that Eve had made and spelled this necklace almost two hundred years ago. She took in a breath and let her necklace fall back around her neck as movement caught her eye to the right of the branch. She looked up to be staring at a ghostly figure floating right by where she sat. She locked eyes with him for a moment and screamed out in shock. In her hurry to move away, she leapt down and twisted her ankle. As she saw the figure float down to her, she realised who it was. The face she had seen in so many family pictures at home. It was Axel Brinford, her grandfather. He was being so nice to her and making sure she was ok, but he was definitely in shock that she knew who he was and that she could see and hear him. When Clover had the idea of bringing him back home, she didn't know how to tell her mum and grandmother that she could see Axel. But when they got back to the gates, Axel could not pass; there was some kind of barrier preventing him from entering. After watching him disappear back into the woods, all Clover wanted to do was research to find a way that would allow him to cross this shield that's up around the Manor.

Clover ran straight for the library and lit the fire so she could be warm whilst researching. The library has fallen quiet over the years since Velina closed it off to the public after Axel died; she didn't want people entering her home unless she knew them personally. When the fire was healthy, Clover walked to the oldest part of the library, the old, large dusty books that consumed the shelves loomed over her. At this time, she missed Dart, the librarian who had retired and moved down to a small cottage by the coast with his three cats. All she could see was volume after volume of old journals from her family. Until she found an old map of the grounds, she ran her hand over the spines of the well-preserved house plans that had been put into protective covers until her finger felt the same tingle she had when she opened the spell book. It was drawn plans from the year eighteen zero one. She looked at the map and sat herself in front of the fire, then opened Eve's spell book to find a spell that could help her look for whatever this map had concealed from her. She could feel it as she swiped her hands over the old, stained paper. She skimmed through Eve's book to find a spell called the hidden trail. She closed her eyes to concentrate, memorising the words in her mind. She spoke them aloud, allowing her hands to glide over the map, "What lies beneath, what sleeps unseen, let paths arise where none have laid. Guide my steps through soil and shade, by blood once spilt and vows once made, root and ash, hear my plea, unveil the way that calls to me." She opened one eye and glanced down at the map, but nothing happened. She sighed deeply, obviously missing a step. She read back over the page, noticing something she had missed. "I need a piece of tree root from the grounds." Clover stood and raced to the greenhouse, grabbing a handheld shovel so she could dig down to retrieve the root from the grounds.

She drove the shovel down into the dirt deep enough to chop a piece of root free from the earth and returned to her spot in the library. It instructed her to place the piece of root at the centre of the map; she lifted her hands over the old sheet that had curled edges and spoke the spell. It felt different this time. She felt heat pulsing from her palms as she opened her eyes and saw the piece of root wildly spinning by itself. She looked down at it in disbelief as it slowed, then stopped pointing in a direction. She lifted the map; it started to adjust her cores as it led her out of the house and into the grounds. It took her to the boundary of the woods. As she ventured deeper, she came upon an old cave entrance jutting out of the earth. She moved around it to make sure that this was where the map was leading her, and it for sure was. The root was fixed onto the entrance of the cave; it looked dark and not very inviting, but all the same, Clover felt safe entering. She closed the map and placed it propped against the cave wall as she descended into the dark. She looked behind, saying goodbye to the light at the mouth of the cave entrance and carried on down using the light that lit behind her until she came to an old wooden door. She clenched Eve's spell book against her chest and pushed the door open. As she peered her head around the door, she saw a stone-domed ceiling and a beam of light shining down from a hole in the roof. Vines had fallen through the hole over time, but something was illuminated in the centre of the room. A stone chest that had been carved with all kinds of symbols that Clover had no clue what any of them meant. She looked around, noticing wooded torches barely visible in the dark spaces the beam of light could not reach. She opened Eve's book again, using the beam of light so she could see what she was reading. She came upon a spell to bring forth light. "Let fire burn where shadows sleep." This short incantation set her hand ablaze, which startled her. She shook her hand in a panic, trying to extinguish the flame, but she then came to realise the fire did not burn her. She held her hand up and wiggled her fingers and giggled to herself as she walked around the circular room, igniting the torches. With each light that filled the room, she could see cave drawings all along the walls, amazing imagery of rituals taking place under a full blood moon, women dancing in flowers with their hair flying free. She paused when she stopped at an image of a woman surrounded in flames and a raven that was overlayed on her body.

She looked above the door and saw words carved into the
rock: "To all daughters with a gifted spirit, beneath earth's
watchful heart, you are safe. Let no fear follow you here. This is a
sanctuary. This is sisterhood. Within these walls, the witch is never
alone." As she walked around the cave, she could see wall
paintings of classes being held, paintings of single mothers coming
to them for help if they had been outcasts from normal society.
Clover felt so much comfort within these walls that she could feel
her heart warm; she felt an immensely powerful presence
approaching her in the room, and she was no longer alone. She
looked to the beam of light that poured down the centre of the

room, and she could see a figure beginning to form within it. She took a step away, feeling her back hit the solid wall behind her as she viewed a woman step forward from the light. Her gentle voice echoed off the walls as she approached Clover, "hello my sister it's been a very long time since life has been within these walls" Clover's mouth dropped open wide, she could not find the words to speak so the lady carried on filling the silence with her calm voice, "I sense a very powerful gift within you, it's not your sixteenth birthday is it? Your full power will come forward, and you can learn to harness it." Clover felt tears fill her eyes and her cheeks flush. The white witch glanced at her in confusion, "Why are you threatening to cry, dear? This is a joyous time in a blooming witch's life when her full power comes in." Clover finally found her words "I don't have anyone to teach me, I have a grandfather in sprite who can't cross the gates to come home, I have a monster I need to destroy, my mum and grandmother would not understand, I feel lost and overwhelmed" She fell to her knees as her legs gave way from beneath her feeling the tears now falling down her cheeks. The white witch calmed the young girl as she stepped from the light to comfort her. She knelt and pulled the girl into a hug, her scent was like forest flowers, her long white hair flowing in the breeze, the soft fabric of her white dress felt cool to Clover's face as she wept. The witch introduced herself. My name is Hazel. I was around before Antler Manor even had its foundations carved into the earth here, before this village even came to be.

She stroked Clover's hair for a time to settle her until she looked up at Hazel, noticing something familiar in her eyes. "You come from an extraordinarily strong line of women, each of whom possessed a gift. We would help in this world where they could not, but we were cast aside, named as demons to be burned and tormented for the gifts we have. So, I made this place for me and my sisters to find sanctuary away from the cruel world that condemned us." She went still for a moment, looking around the room as if she was remembering the happy times she had here when she taught women in need of help understanding their gifts. Clover then comforted her. She took her hand and held it in hers. Hazel smiled at the girl and touched her cheek. "It's nice to meet my descendant." Clover's eyes went wide. "You're my ancestor?" Hazel giggled at the girl's shocked face and explained "yes, my dear I am the bloodline you flowed from I am the elder white witch who started the original coven here until we were chased off this land by settlers, we scattered to the winds some stayed here and suppressed their gifts to fit into a normal life and others fled, I sealed this cave down with a spell so only witches and women in need can cross this threshold". Clover's mind came to a quick realisation when Hazel said this "how far does your spell spread on the land?" Hazel thought about it, "I'm not too sure why you ask?" "I think that's why my grandfather can't cross the gates to come home, he is not a witch or a woman needing help he is just a spirit, could you drop the spell, and I will promise to keep this cave safe" Hazel felt a bit hesitant at the request "I don't think it is my spell I only cast that around this cave. Clover, can you bring your mother and grandmother to me? I want to meet more of my descendants. I can also feel something in your blood that's not right, something is missing in you, and I fear your mum and grandmother as well.

Chapter Twenty-One

UNLOCK THE DOOR TO YOUR MEMORIES.

"When the time is right, speak the truth aloud. The door will open. You will finally see. Memories are spells in disguise- unspoken, unwritten, but waiting to be undone. What was taken can be returned. But only if you are brave enough to see"

- E.L.

Clover ran from the cave, her steps pounding into the ground. She saw Antler Manor appear through the hedges in front of her. She burst through the ballroom patio doors, ran up the grand staircase, and towards the kitchen in the hope her mum and grandmother would be in there having their lunch. She shoved through the kitchen door, panting, seeing both of them sitting there, they both turned to look at her in shock, being made jump by the loud bang against the door when she pushed it open. "Mum, nan, I can't explain right now, but I need you both to come with me somewhere so cool to meet someone awesome." They looked at her, then looked at each other. They stood willing to go along with Clover, as it sounded very important to her. They followed her as she led them back through the grounds towards the boundaries of the woods to show them the cave entrance. Orenda looked sceptical. "Clover, please tell me you haven't been down there. It does not look safe. What if the ceiling falls in?" Clover pulled both her mum and Nan's hands towards the cave. "Trust me, it's safe, just please come with me, this is important". They followed behind Clover as they descended into the cave, coming to the wooden door. Clover gave it a push open into the domed chamber, seeing that the torches were still lit and her book was where she left it. Orenda and Velina glanced around the room, seeing the cave drawings, the words carved above the door they just came through, then their eyes fixed on Hazel, who reappeared through the beam of light that shone from the hole in the ceiling. They both screamed and made a run for the door, but Clover blocked her body across the exit and shouted at them both to calm down and please listen to what she had to say. They paused to catch their breath and nerves; they spun to face Hazel. She slowly approached, assuring she was not going to harm them "sisters please don't fear me for I am your blood, and you are mine, rest yourselves I require to see your memories there is something off I can feel it." Velina and Orenda took a seat on the steps leading up to the stone box in the middle of the room and let Hazel enter their minds.

Hazel knelt behind them both and placed a gentle, soft hand on each of their temples. A bright light flashed in her mind as she stared, whizzing through both their memories until she came across a large, heavy wooden door that was in both their minds that was padlocked shut with heavy chains made of black smoke draped in front of them. She focused her full power on the locks and chains; they started vibrating until the heavy locks fell to the ground, releasing the black smoked chains to the floor. The doors exploded open, light spilling out as a wave of memories filled their minds that had been locked away from them. Hazel fell back from them, both taking in a deep breath from seeing all the memories, understanding exactly what had happened to them both. "You need to free Eve; she is your only hope in bringing the Molthera down.

That punishment is meant for the weak-minded to suffer, but I fear John is not. He was a monster before Eve did that to him; I think he is turning this curse into his superpower." Velina and Orenda sat quiet for a moment, not taking in anything Hazel had just said. Velina lifted Orenda's chin to meet her gaze and smiled at her with tears falling down her face. Orenda pulled her mum into a hug, remembering Eve, Axel, and the memories of John. They sat and hugged each other for a moment, then called over Clover to join the hug. Hazel smiled, seeing them all come together, realising their full combined power as a family. They all stood to face Hazel, regathering themselves, ready to hear what they had to do to win this fight to free Eve and to bring the monster down. Hazel waved her hand over the stone chest, and the lid popped open, letting loose a cloud of dust that wafted to the floor.

She lifted the lid to reveal a box filled with trinkets, crystals, and black wax candles. She said, "In this box are the most sacred items that help protect a coven against evil, but you will need a full coven to make the spell work. Five women are needed to cast the spell to free Eve's trapped spirit from the witch's ash, and with your combined powers, you need to unleash the Fire Raven within her. She will have the strength to kill John." They all nodded in agreement, feeling confident about what they had to do, but Hazel had to give one more thing to Clover. "You, my dear, I could sense your gift the moment you stepped into this room, when I looked into your eyes, one of green earth and one of ice blue to see beyond. You have the gift of spirit-wielding. If you call them, they will come to you and fight for you if John has any tricks up his sleeve. I am giving you this black crystal necklace that will be John's tomb for eternity that will hold him but it's your gift that will trap his undead spirit, Eve needs to land the killing blow to weaken him enough, you need to stab this crystal into his black heart". Clover took the crystal and placed it over her neck and silently agreed to what she had to do. Orenda stepped up towards them both and pleaded not for Clover to be the one who had to do this "it's too dangerous she can't I won't allow it I will do it" Hazel placed a calming hand on her shoulder. "She has the Clover around her neck to keep her safe; she is also protected by both of you, but yes, it is her gift that will destroy John for good." Orenda walked away in defiance, but she knew this had to be done either way. Hazel glanced up, seeing the moon's light fall through the hole in the ceiling. They had been in that cave until the night fell. "Happy sixteenth birthday, Clover. The midnight hand turned, and she informed Clover to walk into the beam of light. She stepped up and approached the beam, lifting her hand hesitantly towards it. Hazel assured it would be alright, as this used to be a ritual when she was welcoming the new witches' full power. Clover smiled and stepped into the light, feeling the cool air flow through the hole in the ceiling. She lifted her hands, feeling a power in her heartbeat as her vision was consumed in the moon's light. Hazel then approached the light with a red piece of chalk she lifted from the stone box in front of her and smudged two red lines under her eyes. She grasped her hand around Clover's wrist and informed Clover to do the same to hers.

Hazel's eyes went white as she looked up to the moon that was perfectly central over the hole in the ceiling. Clover's eyes did the same as she mirrored Hazel. The fire in the torches intensified as the flames roared higher. Hazel, with her long, sharp nails, cut a line on both her and Clover's arms. The blood flowed and entwined around their wrists, binding them together like a bracelet of blood. Hazel spoke the ritual chant that echoed through the walls of the cave. Velina and Orenda huddled close together, stepping away from the fire bellowing out from the torches. "By sky above and stone below. Your light is known, your power sown. You are one with all who came before, a witch in full, forevermore." Strong air whipped around them both as the moon moved away from the entrance in the ceiling and the ritual came to an end, the wind stopped, the flames calmed, and the blood bracelet binding them together trickled down their wrists, dripping on the floor. They both breathed deep as Hazel pulled Clover into a hug, congratulating her on now possessing her full uncapped power. Clover looked around the room, seeing her mum and nan, a look of pride washing over their faces as she stepped out from the beam of light, a young woman, a young witch. Hazel explained why Velina and Orenda's powers were late to bloom "as the ritual flows from the elder witch's being me, my power ignites the young one's inner power on their sixteenth birthday, your gifts will still grow naturally but this ritual just solidifies it faster within you". Clover felt like she was on top of the world and could not wait to test her new powers. Hazel warned her "this power is not a toy to play with as you are still at risk of summoning something bad." Clover wanted to be taught so Hazel said "please do come back and I can teach you; I can teach you all to harness your gifts as this is why I built this place. We can have a chat about the plan for releasing Eve as well." They were all eager to start learning, but they all felt tired after the day's adventures, so they bid farewell to Hazel and made their way home to Antler Manor to get some sleep. Before they all went up, Orenda quickly pulled Clover into the kitchen and asked her to close her eyes whilst she asked Velina to go get her present, she could not wait till morning to give it to her.

They instructed Clover to open her eyes, and she was met by a dark room; her mum had placed a homemade chocolate cake on the kitchen island with a number sixteen candle lit. Velina was standing with a package in her arms, wrapped in black glitter wrapping paper. Clover's eyes lit up with joy as they started singing her happy birthday. Clover leaned down towards the candles and made a wish. She counted to five, then blew out the small flames; the room fell dark around them. They all giggled in the dark room searching for the light switch when it was found and the light lit up the room. Everyone screamed in shock as Axel stood in the kitchen doorway. "Hey, Clover, happy birthday," he lifted his hand awkwardly and waved at them all, his ghostly figure looking more solid than it had ever been. Clover had wished her grandfather were here to enjoy her birthday with her; her wish was granted. Velina's eyes instantly welled with tears as she saw the unchanged, unaged face of Axel standing in the doorway. She walked up to him and placed a hand on his cheek; it felt cold, but it was him. With Clover's powers, Axel's form was no longer translucent, like he was part of this world again. He ran his fingers over Velina's face, which had aged, but her eyes were exactly the same. "See you in the stars, my love," Velina laughed and winked at him and said, "I'll see you there." Orenda ran over to him and hugged him tight like she would never let him go. Axel looked at her grown woman's face, remembering the small girl's face when he last saw her.

"I remember you... You were a little girl before I died, before I was taken from you all. Clover brought me back... and suddenly, it all returned. You. Your voice. Your laughter echoes down the hallways of Antler Manor. I saw you standing there just now. I didn't recognise you, not until I saw your eyes, the trademark Brinford green eyes. You have my eyes. You've grown into something fierce and beautiful. A woman who's faced storms I should have shielded you from. A mother, you are now a mother, Orenda. And I missed it all. (he choked his words) I missed your first steps as a witch, your first heartbreak, your first spell. I wasn't there to tell you you'd be okay. I wasn't there to fight beside you. And that... that is a weight I will carry, even in death. But if there's one thing I know now, it's that you didn't need me to survive. You became everything me and your mum dreamed you might be... and more. You didn't just carry our blood, you carried our strength, our love. You carved your own path when the world became hard. And your daughter, she carries the same spark, too. I see it. You gave her the world I never got the chance to give you. Orenda... I'm so proud of you. I may have missed your life... but I see your legacy. And it's glorious. You are not the little girl I was taken from. You are the woman I always hoped you'd become." Orenda just smiled, and she started to sob. She wrapped her arms around Axel, feeling like a little girl again. She whispered out just one word through her tears, "Dad." They hugged for the longest time. Orenda never wanted to let him go, but they parted. Axel turned to Velina and outstretched his hand towards her. "Will you dance with me?" She smiled and took his hand as he led her back through the kitchen towards the ballroom. He pushed open the door and asked her to wait at the top of the stairs whilst he descended to the bottom. Orenda walked behind them holding onto Clover's hand, seeing the smile that lit up Velina's face. Out of the corner of her eye, Dean walked through the front door early hours of the morning, coming home from a hunting party, seeing them all standing by the ballroom door.

Dean approached Orenda and gave her a kiss. She politely shushed him and pointed to look through the ballroom doors to see Velina descending the grand staircase towards Axel. His eyes went wide as he locked eyes with Orenda. She reassured him and said she would tell him the details later, but for now, just let them have their moment together. Velina reached the bottom of the stairs and took Axel's hand, that same cheesy grin that always set her heart alight. Axel glanced up the stairs, seeing Dean for the first time. He gestured for Dean to come down towards him. He felt nervous as he walked down the stairs to be eye level with Axel. Axel looked stern at him for a short moment making him sweat then laughed and gave him a big embrace. "it's so nice I get to meet you Dean please would you both dance with me and Velina it would mean the world to me" Dean smiled and looked up at Orenda who looked a bit bashful as she walked to the top of the stairs. Orenda looked at Clover. She smiled up at her mum and pushed her more towards the top of the stairs, where she saw Dean and her mum and dad watching her. Before she could descend the stairs, she looked up to the window to see Hazel peering in at them. Hazel lifted her hand and waved it in the air, her fingers elegantly dancing as pure magic spilled from her fingers. It glittered through the air and pushed through the glass as it first swirled around Velina. Her long hair fell from her tight bun and flowed down in loose curls; her dress she had worn the night Axel proposed to her formed on her body as the lavender lace settled around her. She looked up at him, and he was staring at her in awe.

Chapter Twenty-Two

LIVE IN THE MOMENT

"Live now, child. Magic is strongest when the heart is still present. Do not rush towards fate. Let the moment root you before it flies. Even in a life bound by spells, there must be time to breathe."

-E.L.

The magic moved from Velina and settled on Axel as his navy-blue suit with the gold flowers around the cuffs materialized on his body. He smiled and held Velina close to him. Once Axel was all suited and booted, the magic then moved onto Dean, a black tux appeared on him with a smart black bow tie, he lifted his hands, gob smacked at what he was seeing as the magic flew up the stairs to Orenda. It dances around her body curling her hair, small pearls appeared that entwined into her curls, as the magic fell around her, a royal blue dress formed that glittered as she twirled, it was in the style of a gown that flared out from around her waist and swept the floor as she moved, Dean who could not take his eyes off her just stared with his mouth agape. The magic was not done, it flew to the centre of the ballroom spinning like a suspended galaxy, it exploded, filling the room with glittering stars that hovered around them all. Orenda glided down the stairs, taking Dean's hand, then music filled the hall as they spun and danced together. Axel savoured this precious moment, seeing his daughter so happy, feeling Velina in his arms dancing in the stars with her, he could not contain his joy as tears welled up in his eyes. He glanced back up the stairs, seeing Clover sitting at the top with her dog Jasper, just smiling and watching everyone together and

245

happy. The white witch had faded away from the window as the sun poured in through the large patio doors, beams of light shining through the stars that were beginning to fade away, as well as their ballroom attire. Feeling lost in the magic, they all came back to reality and realised just how tired they all felt. They looked up, seeing Clover resting her head against Jasper sleeping away. Dean looked at Orenda and giggled as he walked up the stairs and lifted her up off the ground to take her to her old room, as he could not carry her up into her loft apartment. He placed her down gently on her old bed; she did not wake or flinch at all from exhaustion as she slept soundly with Jasper curled up at the end of her bed.

Axel looked around his old room with more memories flooding back to him. He turned to Velina, who was sleeping soundly in her bed. He walked over and sat on the edge, watching her sleep peacefully, seeing the rise and fall of her chest. He looks out the window, knowing he had to leave soon to follow John, as this was his tenth day from his last feed to keep secure inside Ted's body. He sighed deep and gently brushed Velina's hair from her face as a smile lifted across her mouth. He left the room, slowly closing the door behind him, but he then realised his hand fell through the door handle. He was out of range of Clover's power; he was a full ghost again. He sighed, not letting that ruin the feeling of happiness inside him as he left Antler Manor in pursuit of John. He rounded the corner to enter the village, seeing John out and about early, which was strange and out of sync with his usual routine; he should have been in the baker's by now ordering an almond croissant for his breakfast on a weekend. He was skulking off into the woods, which was strange, so Axel followed him. When they entered the woods, he noticed John stretching a lot, and his skin was sagging from around him. A blast of black smoke exploded from Ted as John as the Molthera, stood out in the middle of the woods, breathing heavily and stretching all his joints. He started talking to himself, pacing back and forth, the leaves and twigs crunching and burning under his feet. "I need to kill Eve for good; the next blood moon is coming up, I can use its power to amplify my own, I'm going to burn down that Witches ash tree with her trapped inside it". He outstretched his hands, black smoke bellowing from his palms to Axel's horror, John was creating a small army before his eyes, one by one, the bodies took form, all with sharp, black, long claws so long they almost scraped the ground. John used as much strength as he could, but he could only create eight of them; he felt he needed much more power to bring down Eve. "I will wait for the blood moon, harness its power and create an army so deadly that death itself will fear me." Axel's eyes went wide as he sprinted away from John, his feet almost flying across the forest floor, leaving him examining his small smoke army to inform everyone.

Axel flew through the door at Antler Manor to find Orenda sitting in the greenhouse painting. He ran in front of her, but she looked dazed, like she was not with it fully. He waved his arms in front of her, trying to snap her out of it. He walked back around to see what she was painting, and he was distressed to see she was painting a smoke army, a very large smoke army, with John standing up front, pointing to the witch's ash tree and the blood red mood shining behind the tree, silhouetting its large branches. Orenda finished, she robotically placed the paintbrush down and walked away. Axel examined the painting, trying to find any clues she could have painted revealing a weakness, but all he could focus on was the sheer size of the smoke army thundering across the field, ready to destroy poor Eve, who was still trapped inside. He thought, "Here we go again, ghost having a panic attack." He leaned forward and took heavy breaths, trying to find composure, when he heard a sleepy voice appear from behind him. It was Orenda following the sounds of panic from the greenhouse. "Dad, are you ok? I didn't realise ghosts could have panic attacks. I could hear your bellowing breaths from the snug room where I was taking a nap." He looked up at her and smiled, saying, "Clover is just like you." She entered the greenhouse, spying the canvas with the horrifying image painted across it. She took a step back and called for her mum and Clover to come see this. This time, Pearl was with them, ready to help in whichever way she could. They all examined the painting, red paint dripping down from the moon, where the paint had not dried yet. Velina said, "he is planning to strike faster than we thought. The blood moon is only six days away," Velina realised the date the Blood moon falls. "How poetic of him, it's the date when Eve was burned at the stake all those years ago at the base of the witch's ash tree".

They all rushed up to the cave to call upon the elder white witch. She came forward from the beam of light in the centre of the room to find a very panicked crowd standing in front of her. They explained John's plans to burn down the tree where Eve's soul was bound, Clover stepped forward "we need to start training now I need to free Eve as soon as possible or she will be killed" Hazel glided forward towards Clover "get ready to raise your own army to fight against John, we have the upper hand he does not know that we know what he is planning thanks to Axel and Orenda's painting" She asked everyone to gather around her "do we have a full coven of five women to start the spell to free Eve that's step one" Velina's gaze snapped up "we don't right now but we will" Velina walked away and pulled her mobile from her pocket and called Julie to invite her to the house. She left the cave to go meet her to guide her back up to the cave. Julie looked a bit confused about this whole situation when she entered the cave and saw the room before her with Orenda, Clover, Pearl, and Axel. At the sight of Axel's ghost, she screamed and ran into Velina, who held her still and tried to calm her. "Julie, it's ok, stop, stop, I will explain everything, but for right now I need your help, we need your help." Julie calmed herself and turned to face everyone, "ok, I… I'm calm. What the heck is going on here?" Velina sat Julie down on the steps "we need a coven of five women to perform a very strong spell we can't do this without you we need you to help us free someone who is very special to us all" Julie took a deep breath "ok carry on I need more info than that" Velina laughed and continued "I am a witch we are all witches accept Pearl the magic must of skipped her when she was born" Pearl stood slowly and lifted her hand to the beam of the light it was now raining outside and there was a small waterfall of water falling into the cave. She lifted her hand to the rain, manipulating the water, making it splash and dance to the movement of her hand. "I also have a gift, but I have never wanted to share this with anyone, I'm ready to fight I have been wielding water since I was a young girl" Velina stood in disbelief "why did you not tell me it was clear as day what I was" Pearl stepped towards her "I just never wanted to tell anyone it was my own secret to keep"

Hazel looked at them all, feeling proud and happy to see the space being used for what she intended it to be. She gathered them around her, "ok, class is in session." She first taught them all about crystals and their uses. Hazel sat them all in a circle so she could speak to them all. She placed an assortment of crystals on a table on top of an old cloth. "Sisters of magic, hear the call. By root and flame, by sea and storm, we gather not to wield, but to understand. Stone holds the memory of the earth. Each crystal, a whisper. Each glimmer, a voice that speaks in silence." She gestures to the stones and crystals laid before them. "Quartz for clarity, to strip away illusion, Amethyst for spirit, to open the veil, obsidian for protection, born of fire and shadow. Moonstone for intuition, glowing with the light of the inner tide. Rose quartz... for the heart, where all power begins." Hazel walks around the circle slowly, meeting each woman's gaze. "Clover, you call to spirits, let them guide your hand when choosing stones for balance and truth. Orenda, forged in legacy, let obsidian teach you where pain becomes strength. Velina, touched by memory and love, feels the warmth of rose quartz and knows your heart is your greatest shield. Pearl of waters breath, lapis and aquamarine will answer your voice when you shape the tide. Julie, you may be human, but you are still our sister. Every woman has a little magic inside her. When you hold a crystal, you will still feel the hum within you. They will teach you when you are ready". She returns to the centre of the room, voice steady and low. We do not command stone; we listen to it. We do not force our will; we walk beside it. Today, you do not learn to use crystals. You learn to hear them. Hazel lifts a single crystal, clear quartz, to the light, "in silence, power speaks, in stillness, it sings. Now listen.

"This lesson will help you on the battlefield and know that my strength will run through you all as well when the fight begins. We will now move deeper, not just into the crystals but into what they awaken within you. Magic is not in the crystals alone... it is in the harmony between crystal and soul. Labradorite, the stone of transformation, for witches who walk between who they were and who they will become. This enhances psychic sight, especially during change. It protects against energetic attacks also." Hazel gestures for Clover to come forward, as she steps into her ancestor's legacy, awakening ghosts' sight and ancestral fire. Hazel places the crystal into Clover's palm and instructs her to hold it tight. "Black tourmaline, the grounder for those who must stand firm when the wind turns bitter. Shields from dark energy, anchors the spirit in the body during deep spell work." She walked towards Orenda as she placed the crystal into her palm and told her to hold on tight to it. "I give this to you, whose strength must anchor others when the earth begins to shift." Orenda closed her hand around the crystal tight. Hazel returns to that table and proceeds to pick up another crystal, "Carnelian, the flame within, for courage, for blood memory, for the voice that demands to be heard. Ignites creative fire and passion, wakes the witch's confidence in her spellcasting." She offered the crystal to Velina as her heart led her back to old paths and towards new truths. Hazel retrieves another Crystal and gracefully walks towards Pearl. "Aquamarine, the voice of the deep, water remembers, and it speaks when called. It enhances communication, especially emotional truth. Connects to the tide of magic, within water wielders." Hazel places the crystal into Pearl's palm, whose control over water now seeks purpose and precision.

"Fluorite, the seer's lantern for clarity of mind, and focus to walk the veiled path, clears mental fog, strengthens magical memory and balances spiritual energy." She passes a crystal to Julie for her to hold onto; her quiet knowing begins to blossom into luminous guidance. Hazel now informs them that they will be learning the art of crystal paring. She instructs the women to each choose two crystals. One they are drawn to, one they resist. Sit with both in silence and listen. "What draws you may reflect who you are. What resists you may show what you still need to become. Remember, crystals cannot lie. It simply is. Let it show you what your spirit already knows. In every crack, a lesson, in every shimmer a truth." They all keep hold of their crystals that Hazel had given them, holding them close to their hearts before stepping up and choosing a second crystal that they feel they resist against.

Once they had chosen, they took their seats and sat there for a moment, closing their eyes and feeling the sounds all around them. The wind whipping through the hole in the ceiling, the sound of dripping water once the rain stopped, everything felt heightened around them, the energy thrumming around the room making them all feel a bit high. Hazel could see the magic was becoming too much, so she paused the class and instructed them to get some fresh air. She collected the crystals they left behind, realising they each had kept hold of the crystal that Hazel had given them. A smile flew across her face, "I haven't lost my touch, I still got it." She stood there for a moment, taking a breath herself feeling the pride and excitement of finally teaching witches again, not just any witches, but her bloodline.

Chapter Twenty-Three

PASS THE CLASS

Spells can be taught. Power cannot. That part must be claimed. Passing the class means nothing unless you understand why the lessons matter. The craft tests the hand, but more often, it tests the heart."

-E.L.

The lessons had been going on for a few days, to learn and prepare as much and as fast as they could, to stop John from killing Eve and unleashing his smoke demons. Hazel wanted them to join her on a hike. It was still dark out; you could see the moon in the sky still, but it was also approaching dawn. Hazel led them up and up through the trees when they came out into a clearing. The view was breathtaking; you could see sky and land for miles, and a streak of the sea in the distance. Hazel asked them to stand a foot apart next to each other, facing where the sun would be rising. "I want you to feel the dawn warmth in turn igniting your own power. Let your power rise within like the sun when it blazes the sky. Breathe deep and take in this clear air, fill your lungs." They all closed their eyes and lifted their chins up, breathing in through their mouth and out through their nose as they held the gifted crystals in their hands. Hazel instructed them to open their eyes, seeing the sun explode over the horizon, everything lit up in yellow and gold. They all felt a surge of power run through their entire bodies; they could feel the heat under their skin. They all had smiles on their faces, feeling invincible, then Hazel instructed them to take each other's hands and form a circle. Each grasped the hand

253

of a fellow witch next to them. They came together, all facing each other, as a surge of bright light exploded from within the circle, sending them all falling to the floor, feeling giddy and laughing, finding this small moment together to have a little laugh. Hazel knelt with them, giggling to herself, saying, "You guys nearly had it. To sustain a power circle as a full coven together, you can break any spell. But clearly, this is your first try, and the power overwhelmed you all. But do not worry, up on your feet, we will try again, but we will focus on something else until you can all withhold each other's power flowing through you all."

Hazel stood with the Horizon behind her as everyone sat on the grass, feeling the October wind fly over the hills but feeling thankful for the sun and the cloudless sky. Hazel started the next lesson, "You are not vessels to be filled, you are flame, already burning. The crystals do not give you power; they reveal what has always been yours. Today, you will feel the weight of your own strength... and learn how to guide it. The purpose of this lesson is to teach you how to use your gifted crystal to focus and amplify your natural magical abilities. Control your emotional surges while channelling energy, recognize when a crystal is echoing their strength back to you." Hazel instructed the group to form a wide circle this time, each with their crystal placed over their solar plexus, being held in their dominant hand. "Close your eyes, feel the crystal's energy, not as an object, but a mirror of your own strength. Breathe deeply, letting emotion rise, grief, joy, fear, courage, fury, whatever feels true. Let your energy rise. Clover felt her spirit flare, her eyes shot open; her ice blue eye was glowing white as she glanced around, seeing a haze descend around her like a soft mist. Hazel whispered telepathically to Clover, "You walk between the worlds now. With control... You could command armies of the forgotten." Orenda grips her obsidian hard; a faint tremor rattles through the ground. The air stills around her. She is no longer just a fighter; she's a centre of force. Hazel murmurs to her, "You are the shield and the strike. Let no one tell you otherwise." Velina's rose quartz glows warm, and for the first time in years, her aching heart softens. A ripple of protective magic spreads from her like a silken wave. Hazel gently says, "You love fiercely, that is your Armor. Not your weakness." Pearl holds her aquamarine; her breath synchronizes with the sound of a nearby water channel trickling down the hill. The moisture in the air begins to move at her command, forming water that dances around her body. Hazel nods to her, "You do not follow the tide, sister. You are the tide." Julie holds the fluorite to her forehead, her mind opens like a book, visions, old signs swirl in her mind. She understands things not yet spoken. Hazel smiles at her, "You are a foreseer of the knowledge of things yet to come."

Hazel ended the lesson for the day, seeing how tired everyone was, she said to enjoy the day that awaited them. Before they all retired to lie on the grass and rest for a time, Hazel had a final statement, "You know your powers do not come from these crystals. It comes from knowing who you are and who you will become. Use the crystal not as a crutch but as a companion on the path you already walk. The more you trust yourselves... the louder the crystals will sing." Axel and Dean appeared out of the forest, with Jasper running ahead to jump on Clover in excitement to see her. The wind had a bite to it, sharp with the scent of drying leaves and the woodsmoke of distant chimneys, but the sun softened it, turning the whole countryside into a garden quilt of fields and fire-hued trees. At the top of the hill overlooking the countryside beyond Hollow Wood village, blankets of fields and meadows had been spread wide over the horizon. Warm bread, apples, cheese, and slices of roast chicken were laid out in mismatched containers.

Dean had carried the basket and its contents up, but Axel could not help bearing the weight until he was in range of Clover's power. Clover sat cross-legged with a mug of hot chocolate nestled between her palms, watching her wonderful, dysfunctional family settle on the grass with her, eating and drinking and laughing together. Her mind drifted to Eve, imagining a beautiful black Raven sat with us, flapping her large dark wings. Pearl tugged a scarf tight around her neck and stretched out in the sun like a sleepy cat, her curls catching the light as they splayed out onto the grass. Julie was laughing quietly as she peeled an apple with her small, curved blade, the peel curling into a perfect red spiral.

Velina had brought a little cloth-bound book of poems and was led against Axel's chest, reading aloud in a half-mocking tone, dramatic and over the top, making Orenda snort into her cider every few lines. "Oh, fairest flame of Autumn's breath, take me, rake me, shake me unto death!" Orenda nearly choked, "Who wrote this stuff?" "Apparently, a very passionate druid from 1847," Velina grinned, flipping the page. "Shall I continue?" "Only if you want Dean to faint," Axel said, laughing and throwing a grape at him in jest. Dean laughed at Axel, "Velina, spare my sensitive ears, please." he was unwrapping a carefully packed pie and waved a spoon at them. "Don't mock the dead, Axel. Some of us are trying to eat in peace." "Some of us are the dead," Axel replied in a joking tone. The banter between them both gave Velina and Orenda a good giggle. "You two are like an old married couple," Velina jabbed Axel in the stomach. They all laughed, genuine, bright laughter, the kind of laughter that echoes like bells in the open air. Hazel stood a little apart, sipping tea from a carved wooden mug, her hair braided back, eyes soft with approval. She didn't speak, but the way she watched them made it clear, this was part of the teaching, too. Clover leaned against her mum's shoulder. "You ever think we'd get a moment like this?" Orenda looked out over the rolling hills, the dying leaves glinting like coins in the sunlight. "No," she said simply. "But I'm damn glad we did."

The wind rose briefly, lifting scarves and hair. Hazel started humming a song none of them quite remembered hearing before, but there was familiarity to it. Her haunting siren voice echoing across the hills, they all fell silent. The world followed in tow as her long white hair flowed in the cool breeze. "In fire she fell, but ash bore wings, the mother lost, the raven sings. Her love undone, her soul unbowed, she walks the wind- no longer cowed. They feared her hands, they feared her name, so they cast her body into flame. But witch fire burns beyond the pyre, and vengeance wakes with wings of fire. Eve... Eve Longbow... they whisper still, through broken trees and breathless chill. Protecting one, avenging all, she answers every pistice call. So, mark the night and heed her cry; she is the wind, the wrath, the woe. The fire they sparked... long ago. They all felt like they had been put under a trance. Her voice sounded so pure but equally haunting. They all burst into cheers and clapping for her, and she went a bit bashful as she had not had an audience for an exceptionally long time. Orenda sat crossed legged chewing a crisp apple, eyes scanning the horizon like she wasn't ready to believe they were safe, for now. Velina nudged her gently with a thermos. "Drink some tea before you start brooding about shadow armies again." "I'm not brooding," "you're always brooding," Dean chimed in. "That's just her face," Clover added in a bantering tone and smirk across her face. "She can't help it." Orenda took a dramatic bite of her apple. "I hope the Molthera is ready for the fight of his life. I'm ready to bring a hell of a storm to him." Laughter rolled through the group, and they all shouted together, "CHEERS TO THAT." Hazel, who had chosen a large flat stone as her perch, sat there with all the grace and poise of a perfect Lilly. She watched them all with the quiet pride of a mother watching over young play and thrive.

Julie, who was drawing a symbol into a dry bit of dirt with a stick she found, asked, "Do you think our crystals can feel this? Happiness?" Hazel nodded. "Absolutely. They remember everything. Just like the land does." Axel stirred then, his gaze lingering on Orenda. She was laughing now, really laughing, shoulders shaking, head thrown back. A strand of her hair was caught in the wind. "I missed this," he murmured. She turned towards him, brow lifting, "What's that?" His voice faltered, then steadied. "I missed... watching her become... her. The last memory I had of her, she was barely past the height of my waist, wearing my jacket that was very much too big for her. "And look at me now," overhearing his conversation with Hazel and Julie, she raised her mug in a mock toast. "All grown up and ready to fight for my family." "Yeah," Axel said quietly. "But now you're the kind of powerful witch any monster would run from." Clover leaned against him, her smile soft. "I can see how proud you are of her," "I am," he said, "of all of you." Pearl plucked a smooth stone from the ground and tossed it lightly into the air. "Can I just say... I didn't think I'd ever feel normal with other witches and being a witch." Velina scooted beside her and put her hand out to catch the stone before it fell back into Pearl's hand. "This isn't normal, it's better. This is a weird and crazy dynamic we have here, but in the famous words of the mad hatter, all the best people are." Pearl smiled and rested her head against Velina's and smiled.

Julie reached over and gently touched Velina's shoulder. "We're not just witches now. We are a coven." A hush settled over them, not solemn, but peaceful. The kind of silence that comes when everyone feels the same thing at once but doesn't want to say it aloud. Clover stood, breaking the silence, "I think we can do it, we should try the power circle again, but with dad and grandad in the circle as well." They all stood and formed a circle, Dean looking a little confused, but he followed what everyone else was doing. He stood in between Clover and Orenda when they all closed their eyes and lifted their chins up to the skies. They held their crystals in their hands and felt the power pulsing through them. They all opened their eyes and looked around the circle. They grasped each other's hands tight, all making a connection with the person next to them and their crystal. Each hand, they clamped their fingers shut tight as light burst from around them, exploding up to the sky like a supernatural beckon. They held steady. Hazel got to her feet in amazement at what she was seeing. The light started to flicker, all colours sending flares of energy dancing around them. Jasper was sitting beside Hazel, mesmerized by all the light. Everyone was smiling at each other as they held the power steady. They released their hands, the power fading away, they erupted into cheers and laughter, dancing and running around from the success of holding the magic steady and not letting it get out of control. Clover shouted, "JOHN, WE ARE COMING FOR YOU." From the success of today's lessons, they all packed up what remained of the picnic and made their way back down the hill to return to the cave to talk about plans and strategies for freeing Eve and defeating John.

Chapter Twenty-Four

STRATEGY TO FREE EVE

"Break the bark, not with blades, but with the bloodline, breath, and belief."

-E.L.

Dean and Axel were granted entry to the cave as the torches ignited, lighting up the domed room. Axel could not believe that for the years he lived at Antler Manor, he never knew this was on the land he walked. Hazel explained, "It was cloaked to you, but now that I have granted you access, you may now see it." He was amazed, along with Dean. They all sat around the room. Hazel lit a fire to starve out the cold, for the sun had begun to slip, turning from warm honey into the pale amber of early dusk. Shadows lengthened across the hills outside, welcoming the night air. With the inside of the cave glowing from the flicker of the fire, everyone gathered to keep warm. Orenda stood with her arms folded, lost in thought. Clover sat on the floor next to Jasper with her knees drawn up. Velina lit some candles around the room before taking her place next to Axel and entwining her arm through his and resting her head on his shoulder. Julie traced her fingers over old maps that were laid across an old stone flat-top table. Pearl leaned against the wall closest to the fire to keep the chill from her bones, and Dean was just walking, lost in the cave art around the room. Hazel, carrying a small wooden carved box, placed it on a table so everyone could see. "I kept this safe. This feather blew into my cave via the hole in the ceiling. I sensed a special magic attached to this feather." A single black feather, scorched at the tip, was presented to them in the box. Clover inhaled sharply. "Eve," Hazel nodded, "it's the last remnant of her spirit before she was bound to the witch's ash tree. We can use it, but only once." Julie's voice was soft. "What happens if we free her?" Hazel met her gaze. "She will return in full form. In flame." Velina looked up, "And what if we fail?" "Then John becomes unstoppable," Orenda answered. "He has already taken Ted's body. He's already fed on the essence of countless poor people. If he destroys the only thing that can kill him, he'll raise a second smoke army, one we cannot banish."

Pearl stepped forward, her hands in fists by her side, "Then we don't fail." Hazel laid out pieces on the table, assigning each item to a person in the cave. "Clover will lead the ritual at the witch's ash tree to free Eve, using the feather and her ghost-wielding power to call Eve from within this dimension she is caged in. Velina and Pearl will hold the perimeter until you are needed to form the power circle. Velina, with your barriers and pearl with your water, you are our formidable defence whilst the ritual starts. Julie will break the illusion John has cast around the battlefield, making any traps he set useless, using her growing seer gift. We now have an idea what he is planning. Orenda and Axel will lead the ground fight. Orenda, with earth-shattering power, and Axel will lead the ghost army. When you are all in the power circle from the outside, I will intervene only if something starts to go wrong." Hazel drew a symbol in dust on the cave floor, a circle inside a burning tree, flanked by a large raven with its wings outstretched. Clover sat still for a while; the others moved around her, discussing tactics and strategies. Her fingers curled around the scorched feather, its texture strange and ancient, like something that had witnessed the birth of magic itself. She could feel Eve, sleeping, burning, waiting. Axel knelt beside her. "You don't have to carry this alone, wicky," she looked up at him, "wicky?" "That's

261

the name for a witch, isn't it?" Clover laughed and felt lighter from his blunder. "You mean a wicca?" he laughed and pulled her in for a hug. "You're my wicky kiddo." She laughed again and said, "I can feel it in my blood. She's been waiting for someone to bring her home for a long time now." Axel nodded, "Then let's bring her home, Wicky."

Hazel took the centre of the room, the fire burning bright behind, silhouetting her long, flowing cream dress. "You've trained. You've grown. You've grafted. But now you will rise. Not as scattered witches. Not as a survivor. But as a coven, a family. ONE FIRE. ONE PURPOSE. ONE FINAL STAND". The fire they felt inside them all made them call out and scream in cheers, ready for a fight, ready to bring Eve home and destroy the Molthera for good. Time went by from that night, and they still practiced their magic in the grounds of Antler Manor to make sure they were in tune with their crystals they now wore around their necks. Axel fell back into family life, keeping close to Clover's magic so he could pick up and read a book in the library again, play with Jasper. He missed Tex, but knowing his remains were buried with his gave him comfort. The halls of Antler Manor were quiet, their silence broken only by faint creaks of the old beams shifting in the autumn wind. Moonlight spilled through the tall windows, laying pale patterns across the floorboards. Axel Brinford wandered there, his ghostly form drifting between shadows and light, boots making no sound upon the wood that had once echoed with his confident stride. His hand brushed the banister as he moved up the grand staircase, though the railing passed half through his palm, insubstantial. Still, memory filled in what the present denied. He recalled the nights of laughter when guests poured through these halls, the clink of goblets raised in cheer, the weight of Velina's hand tucked warmly into his arm. For a heartbeat, it almost felt real. But the manor had grown too quiet without him. The portraits on the walls watched with still eyes, and every corner whispered a reminder of a life he could no longer claim. Axel paused at the landing, staring into the great hall below where he once danced with Velina, all his family and friends around him, where he toasted victories, where his voice had filled the space with easy humour. Now, only emptiness answered him. And then it came, that pull. Subtle at first, like a thread tugging at the edge of his soul. A call from the other side, beckoning him towards rest. He felt it in his chest, a hollow ache that urged him to let go to drift into eternal peace. His green eyes dimmed; part of him longed to answer it, to lay down the weight of unfinished battles, of love left behind. Yet another part clung to Antler Manor, to Velina, to the Brinford name that still burned in blood and legacy. "Not yet," he whispered to the silence, his voice carrying like wind through the rafters. His form flickered, caught between the yearning pull of the other side and the relentless tether of the world he knew and loved. So, Axel wandered on, a ghost bound to his family and home, torn between the rest he craved and the love he could not release. He came across Orenda's old room. He pushed the door open and peered inside, memories flooding back to him. The room was filled with canvases of paintings Orenda had done over the years. He started looking through them all and realised they were paintings of Orenda's life before Clover and after she arrived. Paintings of her prom night at school, getting her degree in art and photography, and her becoming Halloween spooktacular Queen are memories that Axel had missed through the years. He was smiling at himself, looking through each image when he found one of him helping souls onto the back of the stag. He could not believe that Orenda's visions could see him doing that. He had an idea that he wanted to do for Orenda before the battle was to come.

As the sun rose over the golden and orange-leaved trees, it was the day the battle was to take place. There was a nervous energy running through the house. Before everyone awoke, he caught sight of Dean, who was always up early to go to work with his family at Hunter Manor to finish his normal human day before the supernatural one took over. "I need you to do something for me. It's a surprise for Orenda," Dean agreed. "Of course, anything you need, just say, mate." He placed a hand on Axel's shoulder and followed him into his old office. "In my time sitting in spirit, I would sit out front of the bakery. I have seen a shop that has been empty for a year. The front of this is right across from the bakers, and the back of the shop runs parallel with the river that runs past the entrance of the village. I want you to go find Shelly the vicar who is selling it and buy it." Dean nodded and took the cash from the safe that Axel opened. He had saved up a lot of spare cash that he kept locked away in the safe for emergencies behind a large painting of Tex that hung over the fireplace. Dean ran into the village, spotting Shelly just leaving the bakers with a warm loaf in hand. "SHELLY, SHELLY, WAIT!" Dean called out. Shelly turned around and smiled to see Dean running towards her. "I want to make an offer and buy your empty shop from you. The one opposite the baker's," she smiled and led him to the shop door. She fumbled around through all her keys until she found the right one. When she pushed the door open, it was dark inside due to the heavy metal shutters being closed, but he could see how large the space was. Shelly turned to Dean and said, "There are two floors with working bathrooms on the lower floor and upper, a fully functioning kitchen and staff room upstairs, two large windows on either side of the shop, one overlooking the baker and one overlooking the river, with two doors to enter and exit. I'm selling this place for twenty thousand pounds. It's going into my retirement fund," she giggled to herself.

Dean opened the bag to check what he had taken from the safe. "I have twenty-five thousand here, please take this amount. I would love this shop; the space has so much potential." Shelly was very thankful for the extra five thousand and handed Dean the keys to the shop. Dean locked up behind him and went back to Antler Manor, excited to tell Axel he had made the purchase. As he walked down the drive, where he saw Axel sitting on the front step waiting, he looked up and saw the smile on Dean's face as he waved the keys out to him. "The shop is bought she is going to love it, I have tried to get her to pursue her painting, but she just never really went for it". Axel took the keys and placed them in his pocket before racing into the house, calling out for everyone to come on a little outing with him. Everyone arrived at the main hall entrance, seeing Axel and Dean trying to act nonchalant, but they could see they were up to something. They all left the house together, making sure Orenda was at Axel's side. When they entered the village together, Axel hid behind Dean, making sure no one could see him, as he was under Clover's magic. Without her power over him, he was invisible. As they walked in front of the bakers Orenda just became more and more confused "are we going to be eating out together? what's going on?" Axel lifted a blind fold up and placed it over her eyes "you will see my dear" he put his hands on her arms and gently turned her around to face away from the bakers and pushed her in the direction of the new shop, Dean had the keys as he tried to stay as quiet as possible to mute the jingle as he pushed the key into the lock. Everyone had figured the surprise out now, and the excitement grew between them all, knowing that Orenda would be very happy here with her artwork.

They all funnelled in, followed by Axel guiding Orenda through the door.

She steadied her feet as Axel let go of her. She could smell something like old dust, but every now and then, she could smell cooking from the bakery blowing through the door they had just entered. Everyone stepped away from Orenda, as Axel instructed her to remove the blindfold. She pulled it from her face, focusing her eyes on everyone staring at her, and she was still confused as to why they were standing in an empty, dark shop. Dean walked over to the shutters on either side of the room and unlocked the catch, flinging them open to let the light into the room. Axel walked up to Orenda, "This shop is yours, my dear, to fill with your paintings and photography to sell or a gallery, you can do whatever you want with this space, it's all yours." He walked over to an open cupboard, spotting a tin of blue paint. He popped the lid off, hoping it was still in date. It smelt bad, but the consistency was ok. He dipped his hand in and walked to an empty spot on the white painted walls and placed his blue hand print clear and firm, leaving his palm print behind. Everyone followed behind him, doing the same; even Jasper's paw print was put on the wall with everyone's. "Orenda my dear when it's my time for me to pass on which I will have to eventually you will have a bit of me here with you in this shop" Orenda smiled through tears thanking him and Dean for the amazing Surprise, she already had so many ideas she wanted to do with the space "before I get carried away with all the ideas I have for this place we need to defeat John first I can't thank you enough I love it" They locked the shutters back down and washed the paint from their hands as they all agreed to visit the bakery to get something to eat together to celebrate for the future they were sure they would have after killing John and locking his vile soul away inside the black crystal Hazel had given Clover to keep safe until the battle.

As they entered the bakery, the smells of fresh bread and cakes filled their senses. Clover removed her magic from Axel so he could silently become invisible and sit with them, enjoying and watching the happenings as they stuffed their faces with cake and pumpkin bread. Orenda walked over to the till to pay for all the food when she noticed the little pony she had given Ruth the baker all those years ago when she was a child. She smiled and picked the small pony up, and asked Ruth if she could have it back. Ruth laughed, "You can have it back, dear. This little pony has kept me company for a long time, thank you." Orenda thanked her and placed the pony in her pocket and left with her family to go home. When they got back they all decided they would get ready for the battle ahead and Hazel the elder white witch appeared in the kitchen door that led into the hallway "I have something for you all if you want to fight as a witch you also need to look the part" She led them down the grand staircase into the ball room that was flooded with natural light from the large patio doors. Five mannequins were displayed in front of them; each had an outfit designed for it. Clover's was a black vest top with skull laced sleeves, the black leather trousers that had reinforced black skull knee guards. The corset that was placed over her was lined with black chainmail to keep her safe. Velina's was more practical to protect her older body more; hers was a black long-sleeved jumper with a black chainmail vest that buttoned over the top. Deep red roses were stitched down the arms of her jumper. The trousers were again black leather with reinforced knee guards in the shape of red roses.

Pearls again had to be more practical for her older body. It was a black chainmail corset with a short leather shrug that was sewn to the corset to protect her arms. There were black leather trousers, but hers had a protective skirt over the top, falling from the corset. The hem of the skirt had waves sewn into the black leather fabric, which looked like it danced every time she moved.

Orenda was next, hers was an all-in-one black cat suit with silver spikes that jutted down her lower arms for blades. Dark green vines were stitched into the boots that continued up the leather trousers over her body and down her right arm. The body of the catsuit was also installed with black chainmail. Julie's battle outfit was designed remarkably similar to Velina's, with the black chainmail vest covering the jumper, but on the legs of her leather trousers was the all-seeing eye stitched up the side of them. Hazel looked to Dean, "I haven't forgotten you, good sir," she waved her hand, and a sixth battle outfit appeared draped over another mannequin. It was bigger and looked heavier. "As you are human and not a witch, yours is more safeguarded than the ladies', as their powers are also their weapons." Dean's was black armour on the top with dark brown leather trousers and a black sword. Hazel said she had enchanted it to cut through the smoke demons when they began the fight. Dean took a gulp and walked forward to examine the armour, his tight jaw clenching under his stubble in amazement as his eyes ran over the armour, tapping the metal plates. The sound echoed around the room. She took Clover to one side, eyeing her over with pride, seeing the power that now burns inside her. "Clover, there's one last thing that your power can summon: it's a beast of death in battle born of magic. With your powers on the battlefield, summon the beast to keep you safe. Her name is Whispermane, a spirit-bound phantom steed that will only answer to your rage and power. Clover's eyes widened at the concept of summoning such a creature to battle with her. "How do I do it?" Hazel placed a hand on her shoulder and felt how tense Clover was. "When she is summoned, don't fear her, she will blend your essence and soul with hers to fight, to call her place your hand to the Earth, you only must whisper for her to answer to your power. Say Whispermane, I call for you, and she should answer." Clover nodded and took on those words, ready to channel the rage she felt to destroy the Molthera for good.

Chapter Twenty-Five

READY FOR BATTLE

"Go into battle with all your legacy, go with the army of the dead behind you. You are the spell now. Cast yourselves wisely. Do not fear the dark. Only fear of forgetting who you are"

-The elder white witch Hazel.

They all eyed up their battle wear, feeling the weight of the fight ahead, so one by one they took their battle outfits to try them on to make sure there was no weakness in the armour. Orenda tried hers on first as she stepped out from behind the divide. Hazel gave her armour a once over, hovering her staff-tipped crystal over the fabric and chainmail to make sure it was spelled securely to stop any smoke demons attacking her body beneath. Velina stepped behind the divide to try hers on next. She was huffing, trying to pull on the leather trousers, which made everyone have a bit of a giggle. She stepped out from behind the divide and did a spin, "Shall I do?" she asked. Everyone applauded her as Orenda gave her mum a hug saying "when the fight begins stay with and Clover we will keep you safe" Velina laughed out loud "I'm the mum I'm supposed to be protecting you" Clover wrapped her arms around her mum and nan and said "we will protect each other" Pearl was already behind the divide squeezing into her battle outfit as she stepped out the waves on her skirt almost looked like they had a life of their own as she swayed the fabric. Julie replaced Pearl and got into hers with ease, as she was so tiny. Dean took a bit longer as he needed to be strapped into the armour Axel and Orenda were pulling on his straps, making sure it was all placed onto him properly. Finally, it was Clover's turn to put on her armour. Jasper was barking beside her, wagging his tail. She disappeared behind the divide and quickly changed into her armour, and stepped out from behind. Orenda was so proud of her that she would step up into this fight. She had grown up into a young lady overnight, watching her fiddle with her arm straps. She rushed over to help her. "Clover, I am so proud of you, but I wish you didn't need to be in this fight." Clover looked up at her mum whilst she tightened her arm straps. "Mum, I have the gift to free Eve. We will win this with our coven together. Nothing will stop us".

They pulled each other in for a long hug and Clover started crying into her mum's shoulder. "it's ok let it out don't be scared" Clover sniffed and pulled away "I'm not crying because I'm scared, I'm crying because of my rage that is filling my soul, tonight John the Molthera whatever he calls himself, his time is up" The grand ballroom of Antler Manor stood transformed. Once a place of dancing and laughter, it now hummed with anticipation. Velvet curtains hung heavy at the windows, their folds stirring in the faint draft. The great chandeliers' crystals that hung down above cast reflections of rainbows around the room as the light hit just right through the tall windows. The coven came together, each clad in their battle attire, chainmail gleaming, leather reinforced, embroidery catching the firelight like quiet promises of victory in war. At the centre stood Clover. Her breath slowed, steady, as she closed her eyes and lifted her hands. When she opened them again, her ice-blue iris ignited with a spectral glow, casting a pale sheen that shimmered across her face. Power rippled through her veins, the very air thickening around her. Her palm lifted, radiant with ghostly light, threads of silver swirling across her skin like lightning of living crystal. The mirrors lining the ballroom walls began to tremble, their glass surface rippling as though disturbed by unseen water. One by one, they darkened, the light around the room dimming until the ballroom seemed lit only by Clover's glow. From within the mirrors, shapes began to form. Pressed against the glass were the faces of the dead soldiers, villagers, ancestors long passed, each pair of eyes burning faintly, awaiting her command. Their breathless forms crowded the glass, spectral hands clawing faintly at the barrier as though eager to be unleashed. The army of the dead. Clover's jaw tightened, her voice steady though the weight of the magic bent the room around her. "Not yet," she whispered, though her voice carried like an echoed command. "You will have your fight soon. The Molthera will fall". The mirrors pulsed in response, the glass glowing faintly with frost as the spectral army pressed harder, waiting for the moment to spill forth. The gathered warriors fell silent, the air heavy with the presence of countless spirits eager for vengeance. In that dim ballroom, Clover stood as both summoner and sentinel, the bridge between living and the dead. When the final battle came, the undead army would march at her side. Clover stands back from everyone and calls her family together. "I know you're probably feeling apprehensive about the fight ahead. I am too. But fear and worry don't make us weak; they just show we care. We care about what we're fighting for. Our home, our loved ones, our ancestors, the people who live in this world, who will be affected if John wins this fight, which he won't. We're not just a handful of witches and warriors standing against a monster. We're generations of power. I carry the voices of those who came before us. I hear them even as I speak now. Right now, they are with us. Eve's power is with us. My grandfather will lead the spirit army I summon. The spirits of Antler Manor. Every soul that this creature thought he could consume, stand with us. Molthera thinks he can burn us, break us, bury us in smoke. But we are fireproof. We are the storm that doesn't bow. The bloodline that doesn't die. So, when you swing your weapons or cast your magic, do it with every ounce of your power. When we stand, stand like the earth itself holds your feet, because tonight isn't the end. Tonight is the night we end him." Everyone cried out and cheered, the sea of spirits roaring and cheering along with them in the mirrors around the great hall, their war cries echoing through the halls of Antler Manor.

Hazel called everyone together to do some final battle preparation. Clover waved her hands down, and the spirits disappeared back into the mirror like a wave of mist, waiting to unleash them upon John. "Listen closely, all of you. This isn't just a battle of strength or order; timing and trust are key. Everyone here has a role; every role matters. First, we form the power circle. Place yourselves in front of the witch's ash tree. Eve's raven feather will be placed at the centre once the circle is complete. You must raise your energy in unison. No doubt, no fear, just purpose. That energy will free Eve. Without her, we cannot win this fight. Orenda, once Eve is released, you must conjure the bramble wall. Make it thick with thorns of Posin and roots, let the earth rise to protect us. That will buy us time. Clover, once the barrier is in place, you must call upon Whispermane. When she arrives, the spirit army will follow. Axel will be waiting to take the lead. He knows how to fight. Dean, you're our muscle. When that wall drops, you charge, and you will be at the front with the army and Axel, slicing through the smoke demons. Keep the pressure on, no hesitation, we want to weaken and tire the Molthera; the more power he uses, the weaker he should become; he can't rely on the Bloodmoon forever. Pearl, Velina, and Julie, you three stay together. You're our battlefield support and shields. Cast shields where they're needed if anyone gets in a tight spot. Pearl, when the moment is right, I'll call for you. You'll unleash your water magic to push the Molthera back, ready for Clover to make the final strike. You only get one shot, make it count. Eve, when she is released, will be heading straight for the Molthera to take the killing blow with her sharp talons of fire. This is our stand. We do not falter. We do not scatter. We hold the circle; we fight with the dead and end this curse tonight."

The sun hung low behind the blackened trees, bleeding red into the sky like a wound that wouldn't close. Orenda was sitting cross-legged on the ground, eyes closed, palms to the dirt, murmuring an incantation to the roots below. Clover adjusted the skull-laced sleeves of her battle top, the leather already warming with her pulse. It's too quiet, she muttered. Dean was swinging a broad-handled sword that glinted black with every slash of the air, testing its weight. "Quiet's good. Means everyone is focused on the task ahead." Pearl, crouching over a small basin of enchanted water, was drawing symbols with her fingers onto the surface. Ripples spread, dancing with ghostlike images. "They're gathering," she said softly, "I can see it in the water beyond the ridge. We've got until moonrise to get into position," Velina was reinforcing Julie's shield charm, tracing red threads of light up her arms with delicate precision. "Hold still, darling. If I mess this up, it'll backfire like a mule with wings. Bet all those years ago we never thought we would be here doing this?" Julie laughed to herself, "You are my best friend and always will be, we are ride or die." They pulled each other into a hug, promising they would go to the city once this was done and have a very big glass of wine after some retail therapy. Hazel stood at the edge of the hall, watching them all with her arms folded over her staff. Her long white braid swung as she turned to Axel, who was brushing down his jacket and fidgeting uncomfortably. She approached Axel to see if she could ease his stress. "Axel, my spectral friend, what's wrong?" she asked in a gentle voice. "My entire family is going into battle. This is my last stand on this earth. When the fight is over, I must leave, but I don't want to say goodbye".

Hazel knew Axel had wandered this earth too long; he was not at rest, but he stayed for the sake of his family to learn all he could about John to give them the best advantage. We know his power drains if he does not consume. We know how to kill him, but what does he know about us? Does he even know we will be there to stand in his way? Do we have the upper hand, or does he? All these questions whirled around Axel's mind, but he just had to look up and observe his family to feel connected to earth again. Clover took a few steps forward, grabbing a handful of practice staffs from a nearby fallen dead tree. "Alright, let's get warmed up. We've got demons to cut through later, I'm not dragging any of you out if you're too stiff to fight let's limber up" She tossed one to Julie, who barely caught it, and pointed at her dad, Dean stepped forward and caught the second piece of practice wood from Clover. "Let's spar, we need some practice" Julie gulped and turned towards Dean "lets practice but I warn you I won't be easy on you" she said in a mocking tone. Dean raised his brow, "Bring it on." Laughter stirred through the group like a gust of wind through the leaves. It was nervous, but real. The clearing buzzed with low chatter, and the distant whistle from Clover to start the sparing to begin echoed over the grounds. Clover stood with her arms folded, watching her dad stretch his shoulders under the weight of his armour. Across from him, Julie tightened her grip on the practice staff Clover had tossed her, feet planted in the dirt. "Alright, Julie," Dean said, rolling his neck. "Just don't cry when I knock you on your backside." Julie narrowed her eyes, "Just don't blink, or you'll miss me knocking you on your backside first." That eased a bark of laughter from Pearl and Hazel as they settled around to watch. She raised her eyebrow but said nothing; these moments had their own kind of magic.

Dean steadied himself, then lunged first, fast for someone who was clad in heavy Armor. Julie spun to the side, narrowly missing the sweep of his staff. The air cracked with the sound of wood hitting wood as they lunged and hit at each other, trying to disarm the other to win. Julie retaliated with a jab to his ribs. He blocked it, but the impact made his stance shift a step. "Not bad, you've been training," he grunted. Dean growled playfully and dodged left, then pivoted and swung low. Julie leapt over the sweep, twisting in the air and gracefully landing on her feet. "Not bad for a woman in her fifties, and yes, I have been training, I listened when Hazel taught me, you should try it sometime," she mocked playfully. Julie pushed forward, a quick, precise strike aimed at his shoulders and then his legs. Dean blocked most of the attack, but one caught the edge of his thigh. "Ow," he said, "you trying to bruise me?" Julie twirled the staff and smirked, "Only your ego, young man." He came at her harder after that. A flurry of heavy strikes rained down, and for a moment, Julie had to fall back, digging her heels into the earth as she blocked. She felt a surge of power filling her mind, slowing her vision, seeing everything in slow motion as she watched Dean lift both his arms for the killer blow to disarm her. But she saw he had left his legs completely exposed. She dipped fast and swiped Dean from under his feet. Time sped up again as she knocked the staff clean from his hands and pointed the end of her staff at his throat. Dean blinked like he had missed something completely. "Well, damn." Clover and everyone clapped for Julie's win against Dean, "remind me not to get on your bad side." Julie beamed, panting and offering a hand to Dean, who lay on the floor below her. Dean chuckled and took her hand to stand up, "That was badass, Julie." Julie beamed with pride at the feeling of winning the fight, but she knew the real thing lay ahead.

While Dean and Julie caught their breath, Pearl stepped silently into the centre of the clearing, her chainmail corset glinting faintly in the fading light. Her hair was pinned back so she could have unobstructed vision free from runaway hair in the breeze. She gave her wrist a quick roll, then raised one hand. "Velina, little sister," she said in a challenging tone, "let's remind them what power looks like." Velina turned, already smiling, her long gloves dusted from adjusting Julie's shield. "You sure you want to be the one humiliated, big sister?" Pearl tilted her head, "Such arrogance." Velina's soft blue eyes sparkled. "I must get that from you." They stepped into the centre of the makeshift ring without another word. The others took a few steps back to watch from a safer distance. Pearl raised both hands, conjuring twin orbs of rippling water that hovered above her palms. Velina whispered under her breath, runes glowing down her gloves, a soft white shimmer coiled around her like fog. Pearl struck first; she flung one orb forward, reshaping it mid-air into a wave blade that slashed through the air between them. Velina spun, raising a shield of translucent lavender light. The water slapped against it like an angry wave attacking a cliff face, and it splashed out in harmless mist as it connected with Velina's shield. Velina countered with a flick of her hand, three glowing orbs of magic spun through the air heading straight for Pearl. She blasts a wall of water across her body, absorbing the balls of power before they hit her. The tempo rose; water and light flew back and forth in a graceful rhythm. Pearls wave magic struck in curves and spirals, always flowing, adapting. Velina's shields held strong, expanding and shrinking at her will. At one point, Pearl sent a whip of water low along the ground. Velina vaulted over it, landing lightly on her feet and driving a bolt of power downward like a falling star. Inside the steam, Velina laughed, "cheap tricks," "learned them from you sister," Pearl replied in a smug, joking voice. When the steam cleared, the two stood face to face. Just a few feet apart. Neither had landed a decisive blow. But their smiles were wide, their cheeks flushed, and their eyes sparkled with pride. Hazel stepped forward, clapping and laughing, "Enough, you two, save some for Molthera, that was very impressive."

Julie, still holding her staff, looked in awe. "It was like watching poetry fight itself." Dean was in just as much shock as Julie after witnessing so much power. He felt like they could win the coming war with just the two of them alone. The last glow of the sun dipped below the hills. Dusk crept across the grounds like a slow breath held in anticipation. After Pearl and Velina stepped out from the fighting ring, their spell work still crackling off their skin like fading starlight, Clover looked towards her mother. "You ready?" she asked, eyes locked. Orenda straightened from where she'd been adjusting her magic, connecting to the earth beneath in preparation for lifting the bramble wall. Her green eyes shimmered faintly with residual earth magic. "I was born ready, dear," Orenda said, lips curled into a grin that was equal parts pride and challenge. "The question is, daughter, are you?" Clover's smirk flickered, but her stance shifted with weight and precision. Her skull-laced sleeves rippled with a conjured breeze. "You're not going to be easy on me, right?" Orenda stepped into the circle, cracked her knuckles, and rolled her shoulder. "What good would that do?" They faced off, only a few feet between them. The others formed a quiet circle and lit some fire torches for light. Clover moved first, always fast, always direct. She darted in with a low kick towards her mother's legs, followed by a sharp elbow toward her knees. Orenda blocked the elbow and caught the kick, twisting Clover Sideways. "Predictable," Orenda said in a disappointed tone. But Clover twisted mid-air, using the momentum to land behind her and strike a glowing palm towards Orenda's spin. Vines surged up from the earth in response, blocking her hand with a whip and lash that tore her away from her target. Clover jumped back, huffing. Orenda raised an eyebrow. "Stop being too predictable," Clover growled, then clapped her hands together. A flare of haunting mist shot up her arms, spirit energy pulsing like fireflies. She summoned a ghostly echo of otherworldly power that she let loose and sent it slashing through the air towards Orenda.

Orenda stomped power through the ground with her foot hard, a quake split the soil as roots creaked and rose with glowing power to shield from Clover's blow that was hurtling for Orenda. In a thin line between them, the ground opened, forcing Clover to leap. While in the air, she spun, kicked off the brambles and roots that were surrounding her and came down with her hand glowing like a comet as she raced at Orenda with her fist flying out towards her. This time, Orenda caught her. Full stop. Palm to fist. Her earth magic glowed like green emeralds sparking from her hand as it collided with Clover's magic, sending them both flying from each other in a blast of power. The clearing went still for a moment. The only sounds were their breathing. One mother, one daughter, both ready to stand and take a fighting position again. Clover didn't even need to use her limbs to stand; her body began to glow in spectral light as she levitated from the floor, floating in mid-air, her hair blowing wildly around her, her ice blue eye glowing white with fire. She screamed out, sending pulses of pure magic from her entire body that sent Orenda flying back. Clover noticed what she had done in her loss of temper and drew back her magic, landing back on the floor and panicking that she had hurt her mother. She ran to her on the floor, but thankfully, Orenda lifted a shield around herself when she landed. She looked up at Clover and smiled. She placed a hand on her daughter's cheek. "You've grown," Orenda said gently, "you're not just strong. You're ready." Clover blinked, then nodded her jaw tightening, "I had to be, you and dad raised me to be strong." A silence stretched between them. "Let's win this war together."

Chapter Twenty-Six

MOLTHERAS BATTLE PREP IN THE

SHADOWS

*"Let them chant their spells. I will answer with demons and death.
You don't win by being seen. You win by being inevitable. I
watched them build. Now I will become their fall"*

- J.B. Molthera

The sky was still light where the sun clung to the edges of the
world, but within the twisted grove where John stood, all light
seemed to die. Smoke oozed from his fingers as he sat, almost
looking drunk with power. He shifted from his seat of bodies that
had been piled beneath him, all drained of life. Beneath his skin,
glowing red veins pulsed with stolen essence, souls he had
devoured. Behind him, fading in and out between the trees, were
his Demons snapping and biting at each other, dying for a fight.
They were not men. Not anything. Twisted remnants of the lost
and the damned with claws stretching out from their hands and
sharp horns reaching from their heads. John the Molthera now
stood at their front, the wind tangling his charred clothes from
summoning one demon after another using the power he had taken
from the innocent, but he was waiting for the Bloodmoon to rise so
he could siphon even more power to raise his full army. He wasn't
just going to destroy Eve; he wanted the world to burn like he had
been burning all those years. He could still feel Ted's body as a
cocoon, his true form dwelling underneath, but the embers were

burning too hot to keep control anymore. The bones resisted with every move, and the heart stuttered. The man was fully gone; only shadows and smoke remained. In a blast of heat he tore free from Ted's body sending limbs and chunks of flesh scattering to the forest floor as his Molthera form stood tall with deep cavernous cracks across his skin, smoke bellowing out from each spilt, hot molten lava spat from his mouth and the smoke demons he had summoned all bowed to him in pure fear as they dripped from the shadows like oil. They writhed at his command, crawling towards him, informing him of the actions of his enemy's, he sent smoke spies to study them as they prepared for the battle. He ripped a limb from one of the bodies that were piled up, and he used the dead finger to draw a circle of blood on the floor, blood and bone dust, a ritual to twist the battlefield when the time comes. "They prepare their feathers and light," he muttered to the shadows, "they gather their ghosts. Let them. I have the real fire that will burn them to a pile of dust."

He extended his burned palm. A wisp of Eve's stolen essence floated above it, faint, but real. She still resisted him from within the witch's ash tree, but her pain still fed him. He breathed it in. "You will not stop me, witch. Your line ends tonight." The smoke army shifted, sensing the surge of power. The ground cracked and burnt where he walked now, leaving black charred footprints behind him even on bare stone. He turned to the makeshift altar of bodies as he started a second ritual. Deep within the forest, he entered an ancient ruin at the edge of the trees, John the Molthera prepared. The night that drew in was thick with smoke, stars hidden behind a veil of his poison, the air so heavy it seemed to bow beneath his presence. He drew a circle of black ash around himself; every mark scorched into the earth by his burning hands. Before him lay the pile of bodies his smoke carried them inside the ruins, and piled them before him, their essence was stolen. Around them, he scattered bones charred black, the marrow still whispering with trapped life. He raised his hands, long fingers trembling with a mix of fury and triumph, and he began the chant. The words were guttural, ancient, each syllable dragging like iron chains through the air. The circle flared, ash rising in a spiral as if the ground itself recoiled from the power, shadows of what he could become. From his hollow eyes leaked trails of molten tears, searing the soil where they fell. His chest heaved as he breathed the smoke back in, feeding it into himself. The fire swelled, engulfing the pile of bodies before him as he inhaled more and more stolen essence. It filled him, threatening to crack him open, but he forced it down, binding it with will and rage. When the ritual peaked, the bones ignited, releasing their last fragments of stolen soul. John opened his arms wide, smoke wings stretching out, and the earth trembled.

"The power," he growled, his voice carrying like a furnace roar, "I will call upon it when they force my hand. And when I do… they will know a god of smoke and fire stands against them". The circle dimmed, its embers sinking into the soil, waiting. Bound to him, hidden but ready, the ritual was now a weapon, one he could ignite in the heart of battle to make himself larger, stronger, and unstoppable. As the sun started to lower behind the trees and the skies started to darken, he rejoined his small army to wait for the Bloodmoon to appear. He dived into his bag of supplies, removing an incredibly old piece of paper that he had kept for a very, very long time. The journal page was torn; soot stained the edges, curled as if the very words on it resisted being read. But John held it carefully, reverently, like a relic because it was one. The page had come from Axel Brinford's Journal, Eve's husband.

He read the words slowly, his cracked lips twitching. "If you are reading this, the flames have taken me. Please live on, Axel, find love again. I will never stop loving you. Orenda is safe, hidden and bound. Her spirit lingers there still, waiting. As long as her soul remains inside, he cannot touch her. But listen to me, once she is born again, once her soul is free, the ring must be protected by love. Only love can shield her from the final tether. If the ring is destroyed after rebirth... she will die. From your love."

John ran his blackened fingers down the page. "This will be sweet revenge, kill the daughter she fought so hard to keep safe, to keep safe from me, knowing what she was going to turn me into. She underestimated me I turned this curse into my power" He remembered taking the ring and concealing it in the loft keeping it safe in case Eve had anymore tricks under her sleeve but on the night of the fire when she turned him into the Molthera the ring would sit in that loft for a very long time, until Ted found it and sold it to Axel. "So, they have the ring. I know the wife wears it and never takes it off. I will have to remove her hand or kill her. I would be happy with either of those outcomes." John laughed to himself and his scheming in preparation for the fight, the field air around him started to change a tone of red as the Bloodmoon rose above the trees. He stepped out into the field with his arms out wide, soaking in the power, the energy and the smoke consumed the woods, demons falling out from the dark mist multiplying again and again until the woods were black, filled with roars and growls and clawing at the trees as they became wild and more aggressive with each passing minute. As he turned to the field with his dark hoard behind him, he had an idea, "I will not destroy the ring outright. No, I will crack it first, just enough, in the heat of battle. Let her feel its pull. Let it distract her. Let her soul panic as the distortion will make her suffer, as the diamond's structure weakens, I will rip her apart." He turned to his smoke demon army, and in his palm, he conjured a shadow replica of the ring, a cursed echo, built from soot and spite. "Bring me this ring, it's on the hand of the wife, Velina, I think that's her name. I'll hold that star in my hand... and crush them."

He knew that none of them knew about the ring's connection to Orenda. "She would not wear it so carelessly. Eve must not have told them, which works in my favour. Eve. Eve. Eve. Tut tut for making such a huge mistake. Maybe I will let them bring her back so she can watch me as I kill her daughter in front of her." Back at Antler Manor, the grounds started to turn a glow of red. It was time to leave and head for the witch's ash tree. Orenda stood apart from the others, near a thick patch of bramble that hadn't been summoned by her will, just part of the wild. Her breath still came steady from sparring, her limbs loose and ready. But something buzzed beneath her skin. She looked down at the palm of her hand and traced the lines of a star in her palm. Velina placed a hand on her shoulder, which made her jump. She spied the star-shaped ring on her hand, and she felt sick for some reason, but could not understand why. She took her mum's ring hand and held it; it felt warm. She frowned in confusion. She examined the ring by turning the band slowly around her finger, looking to make sure the ring was whole and not damaged. Velina pulled her hand away and asked if Orenda was ok. She looked shaken, and she turned away. Pearl was approaching, soft-footed, a gentle seriousness in her eyes. "The wind just shifted," Pearl said quietly, "Do you feel it?" Orenda looked towards the reddening sky; there was no breeze. And yet the brambles rustled behind them. "Yes," she said softly. Then forced a smile, "Let's make a move, we need to get there and get organised." Pearl gave a faint nod, but glanced once more at Orenda, feeling concerned for her. Orenda closed her eyes and lifted her head to the skies; a vision sparked in her head of a star exploding. She felt it was a bad omen, but she could not let it distract her. She kept her worries to herself and followed everyone out of Antler Manor towards the road that took them to the Witch's Ash Tree.

As they walked, all they saw above them were flocks of Ravens squawking and flying overhead as if they were joining in on the fight also.

As they left the soft glow of the streetlights behind them from the safety of Hollow Wood, they followed the dark country road out towards the large Witches Ash Tree that loomed ahead of them. Hazel informed the group that she would bring up a domed shield over the battlefield to protect the village from the sounds of battle. "They don't have to know, they don't have to worry, but they will know if we fail tonight. John won't stop with us; he will take his smoke demons and unleash them on everyone everywhere." Dean took a deep breath, "Please stop adding more pressure, we get it, it's the end of the world if we fail," he said in a humoured, sarcastic tone. Hazel giggled to herself at his remark. They walked onto the clearing of the field. Hazel walked to the centre and lifted her staff to the sky. The sky churned overhead, the Bloodmoon looming like a watchful eye. Behind her, the group stood together and observed her magic take shape. Hazel's presence at the battle was not to fight but to guard the world from the war about to come. She knelt on one knee, placing her palm flat on the cold ground, feeling grass between her fingers. Her staff hovered just above the soil, its tip humming with ancient magic. With her free hand, she drew a triskelion in the dirt. "Let this veil be woven from root and wind," she murmured, her voice like the hush before a storm. "Let no child see the blood. Let no mother feel the scream. Let Hollow Wood rest in silence." From the drawn symbol beneath her hand, golden lines spread out in all directions, weaving between trees, flowing across rocks, rising slowly into the air like threads of silk. They arched high above the treetops, joining into a vast dome that shimmered only when it caught the wind. A barrier of light and silence. As the final strand sealed into place overhead, the sounds of the world fell away, distant now, as if through a closed window. She exhaled. "It's done," Hazel whispered, "let the village sleep. We'll face the nightmare head on".

Chapter Twenty-Seven

BRING FORTH VENGEANCE

"I may be young, but I have the strength of powerful women's blood running through my veins. Eve, I will not let you down. We miss you; we need you."

-C.B.

They say the Fire Raven is not born of the skies, nor summoned from the elements. It is born from within, from the very soul of a witch whose magic runs pure with wild, untamed passion, unbroken by fear, untouched by corruption. It sleeps in silence, curled deep within, waiting to be unleashed. Waiting not for rage, but for resolve. Not for violence, but for justice. Only when the witch stands at the edge, betrayed, broken or bound and chooses not to break, not to bend, but to burn bright with purpose, only then does the Fire Raven stir. Its wings, large and unyielding, do not scorch the world in wrath. They shine with the fire of truth, or transformation, or reclamation. I did not summon the Fire Raven. It rises from within. When the flames dance upon the midnight feathers, embers reflect in the large talons, an inferno blazing deep within the eyes. The flame is not our fear. It is our power to transform into something new.

John lingered in the shadows of the trees where the ashen smoke turned the air thick and the trees bent as if afraid. Smoke curled through the cracks in his skin, slow and constant, like breath from something long dead. His hollowed eyes, empty save for the leaking threads of shadows, fixed upon Hazel. "So old, so sure, so foolish." He could feel the pulse of her magic stretch outwards, warm, golden, alive. The dome was built not to imprison the battle… but to protect the innocents beyond it. His cracked lip curled. "Let her wrap the war in light whispers. Let her sing her prayers to the ground. None of it would matter. Not when the screams begin." He let her finish. That was the thing about hope: it tasted sweet right before it was shattered. He waited in the haze, the smoke curling tighter and thicker, hungrier. His fingers flexed, behind him, his demons took shape from ash and hate, horns rising, mouths stretching. "Not yet. Not yet. Almost time." He would strike when her back was turned, "when her strength was spent, sealing her sacred shield. And then… we will burn her name from memory." He watched them intently, seeing their movements, watching for weakness that he could exploit when the battle began. He spied Velina wearing the star ring. He knew then that that was his first target. To destroy the ring and kill Orenda, but he wanted Eve to be summoned first before he even made a move towards them. Clover stepped forward, the Raven feather gripped tight in her hand. It was warm now, pulsing like it remembered. Like it knew. The witches' Ash Tree loomed at the edge of the battlefield, its blackened trunk veined with silver cracks that hummed faintly in the presence of magic. Hazel gave her a firm nod from the edge of the circle, her shield cast and her duty done. Now it was time for Clover to step into her own legacy. Orenda, Velina, Pearl, Julie, Dean and Axel each took their place in the circle in front of the base of the tree. They held their crystals in their palms, connecting each as each hand grasped the person next to them. Hazel etched runes into the ground around them to boost the power circle's energy to ensure its success. The curling lines of the runes glowed a light blue with ancient intention. Spirit flickers danced just outside the lines like small fireflies, waiting to be unleashed.

Clover closed her eyes. Her heartbeat was hard in her chest. She could feel it… she could feel Eve's power rising. She broke the circle, placing the Raven feather in the centre. It quivered on its own, the black strands of the feather catching a red glint of fire from the blood moon above. Clover rejoined the circle, standing between her mum and nan. "I call you," Clover whispered, her voice steady despite the sting in the wind, "by feather, fire and blood. I'll bring you back." The feather flared with flame. Tiny sparks lifted into the air and hovered between them, forming a spiral of glowing heat. The tree groaned behind them, its branches twitching. Clover's ice blue eye began to glow, the other green. "COME BACK, EVE," she called out louder, "WE CALL YOU BACK TO US, WE FREE YOU TONIGHT UNDER THE BLOOD MOON." The feather lifted from the ground, the embers growing in intensity, forming a small tornado of burning fire. The tree cracked behind them, a few large branches plummeting to the ground that Velina shunted away with her shields. A sound like splitting bone echoed across the field. In the centre, the heat grew hotter as the circle broke apart and everyone fell back, leaning away from the swirling inferno in front of them. They could see the shape of a woman's body dancing in the flames. The glow deepened. Orange turned gold. Gold to molten red. Flames are licking upwards into the air, forming a tighter spiral of crackling heat. The wind howled inwards, drawn to the growing vortex, until power exploded from within, wild, radiant, alive.

The others ran back away from the violent swirling heat growing in front of them, but Clover rose and stood firm. Her eyes blazed, one green, one ice blue, reflecting the inferno before her with her hands raised, supplying Eve with her magic to come forth. Within the heart of the flaming vortex, a huge dark shadow began to take shape, enormous wings outstretched, feathers forged from

Flame, talons forming in sparks, a beak glowing like smelted steel. A shape rising not from flesh, but from wrath, fury and vengeance. A loud, earth-shattering scream pierced the air. Not human. Not a creature. The Ravens cry reborn in flame. The group gathered behind Clover, her legs shaking, exhausting her power. They each placed a hand on her shoulder and back, feeding their power through her in turn to keep the power and energy flowing. They recited Eve's ballads together out loud, "In fire she fell, but ash bore wings. The mother lost, the raven sings. Her love undone, her soul unbowed, she walks the winds, no longer cowed. They feared her hands, they feared her name, so they cast her body into flame. But witch fire burns beyond the pyre, and vengeance wakes within wings of fire. Eve… Eve Longbow… they whisper still through broken trees and breathless chill. Protecting one, avenging all, she answers every pistice call. So mark the night and heed her cry, she is the wind, the wrath, the woe, the fire they sparked… long ago" when the final word was spoken and all their magic channelled into the vortex from the heart of the firestorm burst Eve, The Fire Raven, her massive wings unfurling with a thunderclap that sent the trees shaking. She circled above them, a blazing silhouette against the blood red sky, leaving trails of fire in her wake, a burning omen, a protector returned.

From the shadows of the battlefield, the Molthera's patience snapped like a fraying thread. The shield was cast. The fire Raven had risen. "No more waiting," he growled, smoke pouring from cracked skin like venom. "Let them choke on what they've unleashed." Behind him, his demons' stirred, massive beasts of black vapour and hatred, they surged forward, thundering out from the darkness and also bringing the darkness with them. The ground rumbled beneath them and sounds of roars and groans echoed across the space between them. John walked upon a large boulder to get a bird's-eye view of his creation. As he outstretched his arms to the Bloodmoon, drawing in more power, he formed and bent and cracked as his limbs grew longer and his body formed rock-hard lava for armour around him. He grew monsteras, throwing smoke comets from his palms as they hit the ground, and another smoke demon rose from the impact to join the dark army hurtling towards the coven. They could hear Eve in the sky scream as she dived down, flaring her wings, barrelling into the smoke army, taking a chunk of them out, making a beeline for the Molthera.

Clover's eyes widened. "They're coming," Orenda spun towards the oncoming tidal wave of smoke demons. "Get behind me," She slammed her boot into the earth, large cracks and splits forked out from the impact of her stamp, glowing green light spilling from the webbed breaks as they split and raced across the field. Vines writhed and twisted, snapping outwards in a jagged line with deadly sharp thorns as long as a lamp post, growing faster with each pulse of magic. The smoke demons collided with it, and Sonic booms and screams cried out as thorns laced with magic pierced through their chest, splitting shadows apart. The bramble wall held, groaning, cracking, but not breaking for now. Orenda's voice shook as she strained, "I can't hold them forever, Clover, it's your turn, you can do it". Clover stepped forward, still feeling a bit shaky from freeing Eve.

Clover lifted her hands, her eyes glowing brighter now as she summoned every ounce of magic she had. "Spirits of the fallen. You who remember. You who wait," She reached into her pocket and pulled the second item, the black crystal that would be John's prison, which she put around her neck with her clover. The air thickened, humming with otherworldly presence. "I summon you," the wind howled around her as a heavy mist started to form in the distance. Row after row of people started to appear, translucent warriors, glowing from the mist within as it got closer and closer to them, hearing the battle cries from the lost souls who were taken by John and others who wanted to help in the fight. Behind the warriors, the wind spiralled, then a blue light burst from the centre of the mist, heavy hooves echoed racing ahead of the spirits, its mane and tail trailing spectral fire, came Whispermane, a ghostly steed clad in ghostly armour made of wind and soul. It reared beside Clover, shrieking like a storm. She mounted on a leap, the army forming behind her like a tidal wave. "They wanted war," she said coldly, "let's bring them death". Axel and her dad, Dean, joined her up front, readying themselves for when Orenda lowered brambles that were now beginning to falter as the smoke demons just pushed through, breaking it apart. John, watching this happen before his eyes, kept summoning more and more demons to his army to increase his chances of winning this fight. "They were supposed to scatter," He watched the bramble barbed wall tearing into his demons. Then the spirits pale and endless, crawling from the mist like forgotten oaths come to collect. He watched Clover Brinford, one eye glaring green, the other lit with unnatural blue fire. She rode a beast not born of flesh, a thing of mist and storm, hooves never quite touching the ground. The whispermane shrieked with a sound that shattered his memory. It knew her, and so did she as it reared up, blowing steam from its nostrils.

A scream tore through the clouds of smoke. He turned just in time to see The Fire Raven streaking towards him like a burning comet. Wings of flames cut through smoke and ash, her body a fireball of vengeance. "Eve," he said through gritted teeth. She was coming straight for him, a blazing bolt of hatred with talons bared. John's chest cracked wider, his molten wounds leaking blacker smoke. He snarled, raising his arms, forming a bodyguard of smoke demons around him. "Let them come, I will burn them all," But for the first time since he clawed his way back into this world, he wasn't sure of the outcome ahead. Orenda's arms trembled, her fingers outstretched, vines still pulsing from the ground, replacing the ones that faltered. The bramble wall groaned under the weight of smoke demons slamming against it, twisted horns ripping them apart, causing the wall to become thinner. Her breath came in gasps. "Now," she called through gritted teeth, "now, Clover," from behind her, the sound of spectral hooves and the rumble of rallying ghosts rose like a storm tide. Clover gripped Whispermane's reins tighter. She turned to her father and grandfather, Dean beside her in his black armour, sward glowing faint with witch silver and Axel, eyes locked on the battlefield, face calm but resolute. Clover gave one sharp nod to her mother, "Bring it down, we are ready." Orenda let out one deep breath and released her magic as she toppled to her knees. The bramble wall exploded outwards in a thousand snapping thorns and smoking vines, the remains hissing as they fell into ash. The path was clear. And through the mist, the dead charged.

Axel led the way, his blade gleaming with spirit light. Spirits swarmed behind him, swords and axes and all kinds of weapons held up at the ready. He signalled the archers to step forward to nock their arrows and let loose. The sky filled with glowing arrows that littered over the smoke demons. Dean followed on foot, slicing through the straggling demons with brutal precision, his black forged sword cleaving shadows like butter. He glanced up, seeing Orenda still kneeling on the floor, her power spent as a massive demon started barrelling towards her; she was unable to move; she was frozen in place, feeling weakened. The demon was on top of her. Dean was slicing his way through, trying to reach her, trying to save her, but he could not get there quick enough. He pushed and pushed, not giving up until he saw Velina run and dived behind Orenda, throwing her hand up forming a shield around them as the demon's claws ricocheted off the shield of glowing power. Dean launched his body up towards the demon, plunging his sword into the beast's side, splitting it into two. He knelt as Velina dropped the shield when Hazel appeared at their side out of nowhere, giving Orenda a liquid to drink that would help give her a boost. She took the drink, hastily gulping down the liquid when she felt a spark of energy come back to her. She stood slowly, seeing Clover riding down the battlefield, wielding a spirit sword, directing waves of ghosts to attack, whilst Whispermane was kicking and biting her breath, blue fire from her mouth. Hazel was gone in an instant, leaving them to stand together as they were joined by Pearl and Julie wielding their weapons panting out of breath from fighting. Clover, her eyes glowing, riding like the commander of a storm, locked on John, who had his demons around him, seeing Eve diving for him with her talons out. She raised her voice, loud enough to shake the bones of the living and the dead."

FOR THE FALLEN. FOR THE LIVING. FOR THE BLOODLINE". The spirit army howled with her, a sound not of fear, but fury.

Chapter Twenty-Eight

THE HEAT OF BATTLE

"For The Bloodlines"

-C.B.

Before witches, before any mythical beings were born, before those who walked the whispering path between worlds, there were those born with the gift of spirit-wielding, the rarest of all callings. These were not seers, nor mediums. They did not simply listen to the dead. It is said the first spirit wielder was a child, her name was Elowen, born in a time when ghosts walked openly through forests, forgotten and furious. But Elowen did not fear them. She spoke to them like kin, soothed them with lullabies older than memory, and when they clung to her soul, she carried their grief with grace. The spirits wished to give her compassion, so they gifted her with ever seeing sight by giving her an eye of ice to glance into the world beyond and an eye of green to see the world as it should be. For the spirit wielder, they raised her a guardian, a guide, a bridge between the seen and unseen. From the bones of the first buried war horse, from the wind's breath, from whispers of thousands of spirits, they created Whispermane. A pale mare with eyes of deep silver, her mane flowing like moonlight and mist. She leaves no hoofprints, but where she walks, the veil thins. Her breath can stir ashes into voice; her gallop can outrun death itself. But Whispermane is not summoned. She cannot be tamed. She chooses. She comes only to those who carry the burden of spirits with reverence. To those who listen with their soul, not just their ears. She appears in silence, sometimes through dreams, sometimes through grief, sometimes in the moment just before a soul slips away. When she comes, the air stills. The spirit's hush. The true journey begins. Many have called for her. Few have seen her. Fewer still have ridden her back from the shadowlands. But those who have… bear a silver thread through their soul forever.

The battlefield quaked as they crashed forward, light colliding with smoke, memory against oblivion. Yes, it's time for Eve to strike like divine retribution from above. Her presence is fire and fury, ancient and unstoppable. The sky tore around her. Eve's wings left trails of flame in the air, the very clouds parting in her wake. Every beat of her mighty wings cracked with fire. She saw the battlefield below the swirling mass of smoke demons, the glowing wall of spirits, Clover charging ahead on Whispermane. But her eyes locked on him. John the Molthera, or what would be left of him. That thing of cracked skin and hollowed smoke. The man she'd once trusted and cursed to suffer to be judged now a mockery of life, his soul long since burnt to cinders. She dove faster. Flames burst around her as she spiralled downward. Faster than a scream, talons outstretched and burning white hot. He saw her coming. Good. He raised both arms, shadows swelling around him like wings on rot. A demon's cry echoed from deep inside his hollow chest, no longer the voice of a man, but something ancient and broken. "This ends with me and him," her voice rang through the minds of every fighter below. She slammed into him with force, wings wrapping them both as fire exploded in all directions. The impact sent a shockwave across the battlefield. Demons screamed and scattered. The earth cracked. For a moment, there was only fire, spinning in the centre of the smoke like a sun dragged to earth. Then Eve rose from the blaze, her feathers scorched black, her talons dripping in molten ash. John staggered, his chest torn open, smoke spilling from fresh fissures in his skin. He growled, but it shook with pain. Eve hovered above him, eyes glowing embers. "You crawled out of the fire once." She said, voice like thunder, "But now you burn on my terms".

The fire clung to him. Eve's strike had torn his chest, a crater of blackened bone and scorched soul. Smoke gushed from the wound, hissing like steam from a boiling cauldron. He staggered but did not fall. He never fell. He had burned before and survived it. John let out a roar that split the night, not a cry of pain… but defiance. The shadows around him swelled, thickening like oil. His cracked hands clawed at the sky, dragging down the darkness, feeding it with every ounce of hate still coiled inside his ruined frame. "You will not take this from me!" he bellowed. Eve circled above, fire ripping from her wings, ready to strike again, but it was too late. John thrust his arm outward, and the smoke erupted. It surged upward like a geyser of shadow, a cyclone of blackness and broken souls. It wrapped around Eve mid-flight, dragging her down with chains of vapour. The sky itself dimmed. She shrieked, flames battling against the choke of darkness, but the smoke siphoned her fire, swallowing the heat, drinking it. John smiled, eyes like twin pits, "You cursed me," he said through clenched teeth, his voice layered with too many voices, "but you made me this way." He slammed a hand to the earth. A wave of black smoke burst outward in every direction, knocking back the spirit army, tossing Whispermane into the air, and splitting the ground beneath Dean's feet. Clover reeled, her vision flickering as the undead around her faltered. John rose in the centre of it all, taller now, his body wider, splitting with fresh cracks glowing with inner flame, like magma leaking from a living fault line. He pointed to Eve, now grounded in a ring of choking smoke. "No more flying, bird," he growled, "now you burn with me".

Clover had hit the ground hard when she fell from Whispermane. The shockwave from John had knocked her pretty hard mid-charge, the ghostly steed scattering into vapour was reforming a few yards away, pacing in a spiral of ash and wind. All around her, the spirit army falters. Some flickered like candles in the wind. Others lay motionless, their forms struggling to pull back together. Dean was down on one knee, coughing from the smoke. Axel stood over him, blade raised, shielding them both from a charging smoke demon. "Eve!" Clover cried. She could barely see her. The firebird, once soaring, is now grounded and wrapped in writhing coils of shadow. Her wings beat furiously, but the smoke fed off her flames like leeches. Clover gritted her teeth and forced herself to her feet. "NO," she yelled, "YOU DON'T GET TO WIN". She reached for Whispermane. The steed galloped back to her, eyes glowing like twin stars. As she took hold of her reins, her body hummed with energy, not her alone, but something older, something passed down. Her hands glowed, her ice-blue eye igniting again. "Spirits!" she shouted, her voice echoing unnaturally. "Do not fall! Rise!". A wave of energy pulsed from her chest, rippling through the air; the spirits around her froze… the flickering stopped as they reformed. One by one, they stood taller, brighter, more defined. Their eyes glowed with unity. The army of the dead stood shoulder to shoulder again. Clover turned towards John. "You think fire and smoke scare us?" she spat, lifting her blade once more. "I've walked among the dead. I've spoken with them. Now is their time for revenge as well." Whispermane reared, "CHARGE," she roared. The army answered. They surged forward again, spectral weapons raised, battle cries echoing from hundreds of forgotten souls towards the heart of the storm where the Molthera waited.

The battle at the edges was no quieter than the storm in the centre. Velina stood with her back to Pearl and Julie, flanking her as smoke demons circle, probing for weak points. Her breath came steadily, even as her pulse pounded in her ears. She extended both arms, her palms glowing as twin arc-shaped shields of golden energy shimmered into place. The embroidered roses on her sleeves glowed faintly red, pulsing in time with her heart. "Hold," she said calmly. A smoke demon lunged. Velina turned, pivoted her body and slammed her shield into its face. The creature screamed, a shriek like glass dragged across bone.

Another replaced it. "Julie. You're left," Pearl called, hurling a whip of water across the battlefield, slicing a demon in half. Julie moved in tandem, her slicing her daggers at the demon. Velina wasn't focused on the numbers anymore. One demon stood still among the chaos. Taller. Watching her. Its eyes burned brighter than the others, but focused. Why wasn't it attacking? It was waiting. Then she felt it, a pulse on her hand that felt like a warning. She glanced down. Her ring, a slender, woven silver band with the star diamond atop it, was glowing. The demon hissed and stepped forward. Velina's lips parted, "You're after this." The thing didn't speak. It didn't need to; it raised one long, smoke-wrapped claw and pointed directly at her hand. Pearl noticed it too late. "Vee, shield." But the demon struck faster than expected, claws slashing not for her throat, but for the ring. Velina stumbled back, blocking the blow, sliding down the curve of the golden light, hitting the ground in a burst of sparks. Her ring flared. "He's trying to separate me from my ring." Julie cursed, "That's not just a smoke demon, that's something else different." Pearl stepped forward, slamming a water barrier between them and the creature. Velina lifted her shield again, this time drawing it into a full barrier dome around the three of them. "You'll have to go through me to get to her," Pearl yelled at the creature. The demon tilted its head, its red thick scales glistening, its mind calculating and stalking. Then it attacked again.

Velina's breath caught; she staggered mid-strike, red mist halting her, her senses heightened, there was something very wrong. Her chest ached not from pain, but from something deeper. Something tethered. Then she went out cold. Orenda spun towards the edge of the battlefield. But she was too far. Too late. Velina, Pearl and Julie lay still, collapsed within a dome of thin glowing red mist that hissed as it dissipated. The demon was gone in a heartbeat. Across the battlefield, John stood taller now, through his wounds still glowing, he raised a twisted, burned hand. The red smoke demon reformed beside him, rising like a shadow in reverse. In its clawed hand was the ring. "So delicate," he muttered, "and yet this simple trinket binds her heart. Her strength". At the sight of the ring in Molthera's hand, Eve went into a thrashing panic under the strain of the smoke that was holding her down. He lifted it into the air as the battle slowed. Clover reigned in Whispermane, the spirit army halting behind her, noticing her nan's ring in his hand. She panicked, eyes searching around the battlefield that had stilled before her. Axel and Dean stood ready, but none dared to strike as John held the ring aloft. "I know how to break her now," he snarled. "I'll shatter the tether between them. Crush the vow, Orenda will fall, and Eve, I want you to have a front row seat". He looked at Clover, "You, my dear, will kneel in the ashes of your mother". He clenched his fist and parted his demons, calling Orenda forward. She approached him slowly. Everyone halted, not knowing what to do. Then John squeezed hard on the ring, causing a crack to appear across the top. Orenda fell to the floor screaming as he squeezed the ring again, causing another crack. He laughed, hearing Eve behind him flapping and stomping, trying to break free.

Clover called out for her mother but was blocked by a large smoke demon as Whispermane bucked at them. Orenda was dying. With a crack of light, Hazel appeared before Molthera, stepping out from thin air. She walked through a seam in the world. She drove her crystal-tipped staff straight into his chest, deep. The point of her staff was buried through his burnt flesh. John's howl tore the sky. Smoke blasted outwards from the wound, his body flickering with darkness. The ring flew from his grip, spinning through the air. One rough landing could cause it to break and

finish Orenda off for good. Clover saw the ring heading in her
direction as she lunged forward, flying past the smoke demons. As
she hit the floor right before the ring was to fall and shatter, she
stretched her hand out and caught it in her palm. She held it tight to
her chest to keep it safe, as she scrambled for her mum, who was
limp on the floor. John staggered backwards, falling to one knee,
coughing smoke and flames. Hazel stood over him, expression
unreadable. "That's for Orenda," she whispered. John looked up,
and with his last ounce of hatred, formed claws from the smoke
swirling around his forearms. He drove them into her chest. Hazel
gasped but didn't scream. She leaned forward, resting her forehead
against his, their faces barely inches apart. "Magic… always
finds… its next flame", she whispered. Her eyes turned white.
Then she fell, collapsing to the ground, the staff clattering beside
her, its crystal still glowing faintly. Everyone cried out and ran for
her, but the smoke demons were making it very hard. Clover was
crying as she held her mum's limp body in her lap. Just the quiet
magic remained from Hazel; her blood pooled at her side as it
began to shimmer from her. A tiny mote of glittering white light
rose from her skin as her body dissolved into air. The dust rose
slowly at first, swirling upward in spirals, carried not by wind, but
by intent.

Still pinned, the Fire Raven struggled against the smoke
binding her to the earth. Her wings flared but faltered. The black
fog hissed with every flap. But then Hazel's glitter-like essence
settled around Eve, one speck, then hundreds, then thousands. The
smoke around Eve burned away on contact. The magic wove
around her feathers, her talons, her molten eyes. The white glow
gathered in rings, curling through the air with grace, until it
wrapped completely around her form. The fire exploded outwards,
not in violence, not angry, but pure magic. From that ring of

burning white gold flames, Eve's shape began to change. The raven's body glowed, each feather unravelling into brilliant light and reforming, not as a bird, but as her old human self. Young again, whole, strong. Her arms extended outward, hands open, as flame sliced across her skin like markings of destiny. Her hair, once ash and grey, now flowed long, shining and glossy black as midnight with edges glowing like living diamonds. She hovered above the battlefield in absolute silence. The air stilled, and the demons froze in place. Even John, still on one knee, looked up with trembling lips, his strength leaking in streams of smoke. Clover whispered, "Eve." Eve slowly opened her glowing eyes and spoke, her voice now layered, deeper, no longer just her own. "The white witch still lives in me". She hovered there for a moment, the large black wings spread from behind her back, keeping her aloft with strong beats against the wind, catching the updraft, holding her there as the wings glowed with fire.

Chapter Twenty-Nine

WINGS OF POWER

"Even when the world tries to burn you down, you rise from the ashes and fight. love is the flame that cannot be extinguished, fight for it, and you will never fall" **- E.L**

Great black wings veined with molten gold and glowing with fire at every beat. Each movement stirred the air into embers. The smoke demons, sensing the new white witch's rebirth, howled in fury and desperation. They surged forward, a tsunami of shadow and shrieks. Eve opened her arms. The wind quieted around her. She flexed and spread her wings wide and snapped them downwards. Flame gusted out like a living storm, sweeping the battlefield in ribbons of fire and light. The wings were not just wings; they were weapons, conduits of elemental retribution. Wherever the flames touched, smoke demons were reduced to ash mid-scream, their forms unravelling back into the void. Repeatedly, Eve struck the air, wingbeats like thunderclaps, each gust whipping dozens of the creatures from existence. She moved like a living storm, like prophecy unleashed. Her expression was focused. This wasn't cruelty. It was cleansing. The earth trembled beneath her power. All that remained was John. The Molthera. He watched the last of his army burn away, smoke curling from his mouth, cracks deepening across his volcanic skin. The molten light within him pulsed violently, unstable. Still, he stepped forward. "You've become what I was accused of." He growled, voice like grinding stone. "A monster of flames. A god of judgment. You are no better than me". Eve's feet touched the scorched soil. Her wings curled behind her, glowing like twin blades. "The difference", she said softly, "I never wanted more power. I just refused to burn at the stake you tied me to; I fight for my family; you fight for greed and want". She stood over John, who was on his knees, barely able to meet her gaze. Eve looked down at him with a snarl, curling her lip as she spun to Pearl, "Now," she whispered, "finish him".

That was when Pearl stepped forward, still feeling a little groggy from the red smoke demons' poison. But she stood tall with Velina and Julie at her side, hands trembling, her eyes bright with sea-glow. She raised both arms. The clouds thickened above them, a torrent of pure, ancient water fell, drawn from the veil, summoned by lineage and desperation. It struck John with the force of a storm, searing into his Molthera body. He roared in agony as his lava began to cool, crack and harden. Steam hissed into the air as his form began to petrify like obsidian sealing itself under pressure. His movements fractured and slowed. Then Clover stepped forward. She wore the black crystal around her neck that pulsed. It had once been a trinket; now it was a vessel. She held it tight and bellowed the spell, "You don't belong here. This is not your world anymore". John froze mid-roar, trying to speak. But Clover plunged the crystal into his chest, and the battlefield flashed white. A suction of spirit surged out. The crystal drew John's essence like smoke through a funnel, spiralling inward with a scream of wind and molten rage. Then, silence. The crystal dimmed, the spirit sealed. John the Molthera was gone. Forever. Smoke still curled low over the scorched earth, but the battle was over. The once writhing sky was now clear with stars shining, and the Bloodmoon even looked softer. The ash settled gently like snow across the field, quieting the land. Clover stood in the centre, still holding the black crystal, now cool and silent in her hand. She looked down at it, at what it contained; it felt strange in her palm. Behind her, Whispermane lowered her head in friendship. As her eyes met Clover's, she felt a warmth come over her as she nodded toward Whispermane in thanks. The ghostly steed faded gently into the mist, her duty complete, but her bond felt strong.

Clover approached Eve and took her hand, tears falling down her face as she looked back at her mum, still limp on the floor with her family around her, trying to bring her back. Dean cried out, "I don't feel a pulse." Clover could sense her mum's spirit, but she could not see her. Panic glazed her eyes as she took Eve's hand. "Eve, we have missed you so much. I'm sorry we took so long to free you, but please help my mum, bring her back to us." Eve pulled Clover into a hug, then bent down to pick up Hazel's staff from the ground. She flared her wings and walked towards Orenda, lifeless on the floor. She took her hand and placed the tip of the crystal at the end of the staff over her heart. "I can feel her; she is still in there, but she is far away from life and closer to death." Eve took a deep breath, letting the air fill her lungs as the white witch power rushed through her veins. The crystal on her staff began to glow as Orenda sputtered and lurched up, coughing and grabbing her chest. She locked eyes with Eve now in her human form as she grabbed her and pulled her into a hug. Eve squeezed her shoulders as she stood and sat near the remaining ashes of where Hazel had last stood. Her wings hung low, the last flicker of flame tracing their edges before fading entirely. She stared at the scorched soil for a little while. Clover approached and knelt beside her. "She gave it to you," Clover said softly, "because she knew you'd carry that power with love, not pride". Eve didn't speak at first. She nodded. "She always said fire was a teacher. I just never thought the final lesson would come like this".

Clover placed a hand on her shoulder. They sat in silence together, listening to the wind, the breath of the land slowly returning. Around them, the others gathered. Velina, her hand still singed from the ring, was helping Orenda to her feet. The two locked eyes for a long moment, one scarred by grief, the other by survival and hugged without words. Pearl, quietly crying, let the last of the summoned water soak into the roots of the battlefield. She murmured something to the soil, perhaps a goodbye, perhaps a blessing. Julie walked among the carnage left behind by the smoke demons, seeing spirits looking exhausted and finding comfort in each other. Dean's blade, still stained by the black blood of the demons, came to Clover's side. "You did it," he said, voice hoarse. "He's gone". Clover shook her head gently. "No, dad… we did it". She looked to the horizon, "But the world still has shadows. We're the ones left to carry the light". As dawn began to claim the sky, the Bloodmoon had fallen behind the trees. Ash still marked the earth where the fiercest fighting had taken place. Clover looked to her army of spirits as they all gathered around her, "Thank you for your bravery in winning this fight. Go now and be at peace". As the sun began to rise in golden quiet, the pure damage and destruction showed in the light of dawn. Cracks in the soil bore the memory of the battle. In the very centre, where Hazel had last stood, the ground remained bare. No one spoke when Eve stepped forward. She wore no crown, no armour, only a simple cloak tied with a lavender sash and a plain white dress. Her large black raven wings sat calm at her back, softly brushing the floor behind her. Her hair, still long and black, flowed free down over her shoulders. She lifted her face to the warmth of the dawn sun, feeling the light over her eyelids, the soft breeze blowing her feathers.

She knelt; one hand pressed to the blackened earth. "She taught me everything," Eve said, voice quiet but clear. "I was a child when I found her cave. Lost. Afraid. The plague had taken my parents. But she… Hazel… she looked at me and said, Magic will make you strong, you have fire in you, child". Clover stood behind her, flanked by Orenda, Velina, Pearl, Julie and Dean. Axel stood back. No one interrupted. The air itself seemed to hold its breath. Eve closed her eyes and whispered a spell. "From ash to root, from silence and gloom, where pain once lived, let peace now bloom. Where fire once burned, let healing grow. Let lavender cover what once was home". A quiet hum pulsed through the earth, Hazel's magic now flowing through Eve's hands. From beneath the cracked soil, vines emerged not thorned, not twisted, but gentle and green. They spiralled outwards in every direction, weaving over wounds in the land like soft bandages. Where the vines touched, lavender sprouted, tall, fragrant and vibrant. The scent filled the air, calming the wind, stilling the hearts of all who saw. Within moments, the entire battlefield was transformed into purple. What had once been scorched and stained was now a field of soft lavender waves, stretching out like a sea of amethyst beneath the rising sun. At the centre of it all stood a single white stone, unmarked and simple. No need for names, as everyone knew who it was for. Eve rose, tears trailing down her cheeks. "She saved us all and today… I now claim her magic and carry on her memory". Clover stepped forward, taking Eve's hand. The circle formed one by one, and they joined hands. Velina, Pearl, Orenda, Julie, Dean. But Axel's spirit flickered behind them, silent. They surrounded Hazel's memory with the lavender she loved most, they whispered their goodbyes, not as warriors but as family.

Chapter Thirty

GOODBYE

"It's not goodbye forever; it's goodbye for now."

-A.B.

The lavender field whispered in the morning breeze. The battle was over, the land once scorched now swayed with calm, fragrant life. The white memorial stone stood at the centre of it all, glowing faintly as the first fingers of dawn reached over the horizon. They came one by one. Each witch warrior and survivor carried the small crystal Hazel had gifted them. No two alike, each humming with the unique thread of magic. A piece of her trust. A piece of her legacy. Velina stepped forward first. Her crystal, a pale rose quartz wrapped in silver vines, trembled in her hand. She pressed in gently on the white stone. The crystal sank into the surface without force, as if the stone had been waiting for it. A soft pulse of pink light shimmered, then stilled. Velina placed her hand on the white stone and smiled, tears falling down her face. Next came Pearl, her hands weathered but steady. Her sea blue crystal merged beside Velina's, forming a gentle spiral. Orenda, still bearing the scars of near-death, stepped forward with her deep green crystal. As it fused into the stone, Vines etched themselves across the surface, connecting the crystals like roots in a shared tree. Julie, Dean and Axel followed. One after another, each pressing their crystal into the growing mosaic. As they did, the stone began to change, not just glowing but shining a soft hum that resonated with exact harmony Hazel had used in her protective chants. The field felt alive. Finally, Clover approached the stone holding her crystal, a shimmering white opal threaded with colourful flecks. A gift Hazel had given her in private, saying, "This is not just power. It's for guidance, when you feel lost in your own light". Clover placed it in the very centre. A burst of white light ripped outwards, and the stone sealed the crystals in place. They remained visible, like stars in a pale sky, locked in a constellation.

Eve approached the stone and brushed her hand on a bare section as letters engraved under her hand as she swiped across the flat surface, "she is not dead, just sleeping". Silence settled, and then a faint wind stirred the trees. They turned. Axel stood at the edge of the field, glowing faintly in his spirit form. He looked distant than he had before, his cheeky smile returned to his lips, soft and sincere. Clover moved to him. "You're leaving, aren't you?". He nodded. "I've guided long enough, watched enough. The dead have their place. It's time I left the living". The lavender parted as everyone moved around him. From between the trees, bathed in the first golden rays of the morning sun, stepped the white stag. Its antlers shimmered like crystal, its hooves silent on the ground. It carried no ill will, only peace. Its eyes met Axel's with ancient knowing. Axel turned back one last time. "You've all made me so proud I'm going to miss my little family, until we meet again in the beyond, I will be waiting for you all." Orenda reached for him, but he was already climbing on the back of the stag, light bleeding gently from the edges of his form. With quiet reverence, Axel placed a hand on the stag's neck. Velina ran to his side; she had to say goodbye properly this time. When their eyes met, she stepped forward without a word, the space between them closing as if pulled by gravity. For a moment, time softened. All that remained was memory, the sound of laughter in Antler Manor's halls, midnight dances under the ballroom chandelier,

whispered promises on winter mornings. She lifted a trembling
hand to touch his cheek, her finger then passed through his spirit
form, but he leaned into the motion anyway, eyes half closed as if
he could still feel the warmth. "You came back," she whispered,
her voice thin. "You always come back to me. "Always," he
replied. A tear slipped down Velina's cheek. "You don't have to go
yet. Just a little longer. "I do," he said gently, brushing her hair
with a flicker of light. "The living needs to live. Your story… it
isn't done yet".

Velina's breath hitched. "How do I go on without you?". Axel
leaned down towards her. His voice was steady, but his spirit
flickered with the weight of parting. "You're stronger than you
know. You've always been fire wrapped in lace. When the time
comes…" he leaned in more, their foreheads nearly touching, just
enough for her to imagine the warmth of his lips. "When it's your
time, I will be waiting for you at the end of the driveway… with
the stag". His voice softened to a whisper, the kind she used to
hear when they lay in bed, stars beyond the window, pain. "I will
find you in the stars, my love". Velina closed her eyes as the wind
stirred her hair. "I'll come when it's time". Axel nodded, his own
eyes shimmering now. "I will be there". He leaned away from
Velina, the white stag moved towards the trees. Velina placed a
hand over her heart, where once he had laid his vows. The white
stag began to turn, antlers shimmering in the light as Axel prepared
to ride into the trees, into peace. But before he could move, a voice
rang out after him. "WAIT". She ran through the swaying
lavender, hair trailing behind her, boots crushing beneath her. Her
breath caught in her throat, not from the run but from everything
she hadn't said. Axel turned, his spirit glowing finally gold in the
rising sun. She slowed as she neared him, unsure what to do now
that she was before him. "You weren't supposed to leave yet," she

said, voice cracking. "Not before I said it. Not before I told you I forgive you". Axel's smile faltered. He leaned down towards her, "I never meant to leave you, Orenda. Not when you needed me most. I thought I'd have time… gods, I thought I'd have more time." Orenda looked up at him, her eyes the same green as his. "I was angry for a long time. At you. At mum. At magic. But after the battle, all we have been through together to have that time with you. The one who carried me on his back through hollow wood when I was scared of the shadows". Axel's spirit shimmered, unsteady. "Orenda, you are my light. That little girl has grown into a strong, magical woman, and I couldn't be prouder. Clover is a credit to you and Dean," Her chin trembled.

Axel glanced around at his family, seeing them safe and together. Dean lifted his middle finger to him and laughed. Axel laughed out loud, throwing his head back as he returned the gesture. He turned away, not looking back, knowing they would lead a full and happy life. The stag turned towards the sun that was bleeding through the trees as he gracefully walked away into the light, and with a flash of bright ray of light, they were gone. Everyone cried together but also could not stop laughing, feeling happy for the memories they had made in Antler Manor and in Hazel's cave, the picnic atop the hill and for Orenda to start filling her gallery. After seeing the white stag vanish with Axel into the sun, Eve flared her wings behind her, her hands glowing faintly with power. The battlefield had been sealed off since the battle began. A great shimmering shield of light was cast by Hazel herself before. It kept the ground and horror of battle hidden. Eve raised her arms, "shield of gold, fall with grace. The battle is done, let peace take its place". The air rippled like heat above a flame. Then, with a single soft chime like glass chiming together, the shield collapsed, folding inward like wings at rest. Where war once scarred the earth, lavender bloomed, stretching to the edge of the trees. The wind danced through it, carrying the scent of Hazel's favourite flower all the way to the hills. The witches stood in silence for a moment longer, letting the stillness settle over them. Then Clover turned "Let's go home".

The path back to Antler Manor was quiet. No words were needed. Just the rustling of clothes and the clink of Armor, the soft thump of tired boots, the occasional breathy sigh when someone stumbled from the weight. The house stood just as it always had, weathered, grand and deeply familiar. Its windows caught the morning sun like welcoming arms. Inside, the corridors were warm. Velvet drapes had been drawn open. Tea already steeped in the kitchen, likely prepared by the manor's loving staff. No one has gone to their rooms yet. Instead, they drifted one by one out to the garden terrace behind the manor. Eve took her leave and flew from the terrace to the cave. There, a circle of old garden furniture sat waiting, a long wooden bench lined with comfy cushions and single chairs placed around a wooden garden table. Armor fell away piece by piece. Velina was the first to slip off her reinforced boots and sink into a chair with a groan. She pulled her gloves from her hands and dropped them onto the table, then leaned back, eyes closed. Pearl followed, undoing the hooks of her chainmail corset with a wince. Julie took off her stained sleeves and laid them gently over the chair, then poured cups of tea for everyone into the cups left on the table. Orenda, still tear-streaked, sat on the bench and pulled her knees to her chest. Her brambled sticked armour was battered, but she didn't seem to care. Clover sat cross-legged on the bench beside her, the black crystal resting on the table before her, now dormant and still. Then she got pounced on by Jasper, licking her face in excitement to see her. Dean removed his heavy chest Armor and plopped down next to Orenda; he placed a supportive arm around her. Steam curled from the cups of tea. Everyone took one and sipped quietly. The soft aching breath of witches who had given everything they had and lived to tell the tale. After a long silence, Dean finally broke it, "God, we all look awful." Laughter broke through the coven as they all looked at each other.

Velina raised her cup of tea, "to looking like crap and feeling like it too." The others followed and laughed out loud. Then Clover raised her cup again, "to Hazel", then Orenda lifted hers, "to dad, we will see each other again". No more monsters. No more screams. Just lavender and tea and the sounds of a world beginning to heal. Days had passed since the battle. Antler Manor was peaceful, its halls no longer echoing with the sounds of war, but with quiet voices, firelight and the comforting rustle of pages. The Brinford line was safe. The smoke had cleared. The spirits had been honoured. But Eve Longbow was not one for stillness. Not for long. She rose before the sun one morning, cloaked in white and grey, her raven wings resting atop the fabric. The lavender field shimmered with dew as she passed, the path to the cave calling her like a final whisper. No one followed. This was her walk alone. The entrance to the cave hadn't changed. Hidden among the wild trees on the hill and stone-laced ground. Its mouth was dark and soft-edged, still framed with vines that Hazel once enchanted to bloom only in moonlight. Eve stood at the threshold for a long moment. She placed her hand on the rock beside the entrance. There, carved deep into the stone, was the symbol Hazel had once taught her to trace as a child. "To those who are lost, come home". She stepped inside. The cave smelled like damp herbs and old firelight just as it always had. Her footsteps echoed gently. The walls were lined with ancient carvings and half-burned candles. Each one carrying years of stories, of lessons whispered over steam and flame. At the back, the small stone hearth still held the remains of Hazel's last fire. Cold ash but not dead. Eve knelt there. She didn't speak for a long time. Just sat in the silence, breathing it in. The chaos of her younger self still hung in the cave's memories; she was a child crying on the stone floor. When she settled, she would watch Hazel grind mugwort, learning how to listen and how to use her powers.

A smile touched her lips, "You made a white witch out of me," she whispered. "A real one. Not the kind they burned… the kind who lived." She reached into her pouch at her side and pulled out a handful of lavender fresh from the field, Hazel's unknowingly chosen final resting place. Eve scattered the lavender gently into the hearth, then snapped her fingers together. Sparks exploded from the snap and scattered over the dried wood. It ignited into a healthy burning fire, casting shadows on the walls, and the smell of lavender filled the cave. Then she spoke not a chant, not a spell, just a truth. "I'm going to open this place again. For the girls who are scared. For the women who are hunted. For those who dream in silence." She looked up at the smoke curling into the ceiling. "Your cave won't be a secret anymore, Hazel, it'll be a school, a sanctuary, A place to become more". In that moment, a breeze stirred through the cave, and it smelled of rosemary, of lavender, of Hazel. Eve smiled, then stood and placed a new crystal at the end of her staff, one that spoke to her soul, that she connected with its energy. The fire burned low in Hazel's old hearth. Eve stood before it, palms raised, eyes closed. Her wings flared once, silent, shadowed, edged with dim flame. She spoke, not a spell of destruction, but of creation. "From shelter to strength, from stone to sanctuary, let what was hidden become a home. Let the cave become a haven." The magic surged upwards in glittering tentacles. Magic hummed through the rock around her. The very bones of the cave trembled; they shifted not in collapse, but in rebirth. The walls expanded outwards, stretching into corridors and halls. Roots wove themselves into archways. Stone reshaped, smoothed, curved like the hand of an artist across clay.

Chapter Thirty-One

REBUILD

"Things old can be made anew"

-E.L.

The entrance, once narrow and shrouded, now stood open and proud, still carved into the side of the hill, but now towering wide. The original stone arch remained, preserved at the heart of the new structure, Hazel's carving still etched into its side. To those who are lost, come home. But now beneath that arch stood a tall, commanding door of dark wood, bound in black iron and centred upon it is a great metal raven door knocker, its wings outstretched, eyes gleaming amber, mouth parted in mid-cry. It wasn't just a symbol. It was a promise. The Raven rises. The witch protects. Inside the manor, bloomed with purpose is a grand hearth where flames danced, each flicker whispering an ancestor's spell or a shadow's song. Dormitories carved into stone, each with runes carved into the windows and soft linens made on black cotton, four-poster beds with black lace curtains draped around them. A spiral tower opens to the sky where stars could be read. A long dining hall where laughter could one day echo louder than grief. A teaching chamber centred around Hazel's original stone seat, now draped in lavender in her memory. Eve walked the hallways in silence, bare feet against the stone, until she reached the front door. She looked at the raven knocker and placed her hand over its iron beak. "You'll guard them now," she murmured, "you'll call them home." Behind her, wind moved through the manor like breath, whispering through empty halls. Soon, it would be full of young witches. This time, they would not walk alone. She raised her staff and summoned a fallen tree, its wood creaking as the magic formed it into a lavish sign with the words etched into it, saying Unkindness Academy that took its place above two large iron gates that had swirls of leaves and wildflowers shaped in iron. On either side were two large pillars with two stone raven statues placed atop them, welcoming anyone who wished to enter.

UNKINDNESS
ACADEMY

Eve walked the grounds of Unkindness Academy, seeing the large water fountain in the courtyard that had a large raven perched atop it with black water that flew from its beak, filling the fountain below. She walked to the edge of the woods, looking back at the impressive home that she crafted with her magic. She turned back to the woods and raised her hands, squawking into the wilderness, summoning all the ravens to her side. As the sky turned dark with black beating wings and the hills echoed with chattering and squawks, she slowly held a finger to her lips and shushed the birds' excitement. They all stopped and focused on Eve. She spoke to them, and they understood every sound she made as they listened intently to her, "My friends, I need your help in finding young ladies who need our help and sanctuary." The birds blinked and ruffled their feathers in agreement. Eve raised her hand, a woven basket materialised at her feet filled with black ribbons tied into a necklace and a black Raven metal Sigel with the name of the academy beneath it. She called each bird forward one by one, placing the ribbons over their necks. "Fly far and fly wide, use your senses to find them and bring them here, give them this Sigel, it will place a message in their mind of the academy and how to fund us". The birds took flight, turning the skies dark again with the beats of their wings as they disappeared beyond the trees out of view, until the final Raven left Eve standing alone. She outstretched her wings, taking flight to the skies, soaring above the tree canopy, examining the academy from above, seeing the tall twisting tower and large windows, the courtyard and grounds, feeling excited for the future that her magic had built before her. She glanced over the distance and spied Antler Manor's roof. She dived lower, sweeping the tops of the trees, heading towards the Manor. She glided over the grounds of the Manor, spotting an open place to land, also seeing Clover sat outside in the sun with Jasper, reading a book.

She gracefully descended and landed with a light thud, her bare feet falling into the grass. Jasper jumped up in excitement, bounding towards her. Eve leaned down and scratched his head softly. "Clover, my dear, I need to speak with you and everyone else. Can you call everyone here for a talk?". Clover stood and left Jasper with Eve as she walked through the Manor, calling the family out. Everyone came rallying outside and took a seat at the garden table. Eve stood at the head of the table. "I have some news for you, but I also need your help with something big that I have done." Everyone looked intrigued, focusing on Eve as she fidgeted and relaxed her wings behind her. "Look to the horizon of the trees, what do you see?". Everyone turned their eyes skyward, seeing the tops of black tiled roofs peeking over the treeline. Clover stood, "What is that?" Eve lifted her hands in calming motions. "That is Unkindness Academy, my new home and the future for young ladies to come who need sanctuary and help to harness their powers. I can feel them out there, I can sense them. So, I have built that sanctuary from Hazel's cave repurposed and reimagined in a new image". Everyone fell silent for a moment looking around at each other. Eve felt a little awkward with the silence until Orenda rose to her feet. "Whatever help you need we are here to assist you, how can we help?". Eve relaxed her shoulders and started to explain her vision "I need your help in teaching the girls when they come, I can give you a tour of the academy so you can familiarize yourselves with its halls and rooms". Everyone agreed to meet Eve the following day in the morning to have a full tour of the new Academy and find out what roles they will be given. As the following morning came around, they started the trek up towards Unkindness Academy, walking through the woods up to the rock that looked like the head of a horse, then turned left on the stone pebbled path until they saw the large black gates.

Eve greeted them at the gates, and with a wave of her staff, they flew open as iron creaked. They look on in awe, seeing the grand Gothic design of the building in front of them. Recognizing the large stone arch, which was once the entrance to the cave, now a large dark, rich wooden door hangs there with a black raven knocker. "Everyone, please follow me." They all fell in behind Eve, following her through the large, dark wooden door, seeing the grand hall open in front of them. The shining black marble floor gleamed from the light of the large, tall windows overlooking the entrance grounds. Hallways and corridors snaked off in all directions, leading to dorm rooms, classrooms, the grand dinner hall, the courtyard, the kitchen and the medical room. Eve took Velina and Orenda to one side, leaving everyone sitting in the grand dining hall lined with long benches, large flags hung around the room with the Academy's Sigel of a large black raven holding a piece of lavender in its beak stitched onto a deep navy-blue flag. As you walked towards the end of the hall, it opened onto a large open stone balcony overlooking the woods and a large lake below. Eve led Velina and Orenda down a short, thin stone hallway that led into a massive greenhouse with black iron framing the large, green-tinted panels of glass. They looked around in amazement, seeing all kinds of plants and herbs already growing. "I would love for you both to teach plant taxonomy when the girls get here. If you are both together, you can combine your knowledge and lead a very skilled class." Orenda and Velina smiled in agreement as Eve left them to explore the greenhouse. As she returned to the main dining hall, she spied Dean peering out the balcony overlooking the lake, "Dean, can I borrow you next?". She led him up a flight of twisting stairs to a hallway, and at the end was a large brown door that she opened with a wave of her staff. As they stepped inside the training room with crash mats scattered across the floor and a practice dummy hung from the ceiling, Eve turned to Dean. "As you have hunter's blood and a good eye for targets, I would love for you to train the girls in self-defence and weaponry?". Dean stood there for a moment, spying all the weapons, "hell yeah, I'm your guy". Eve smiled and left him in there to examine all the tools and equipment.

Eve made her way back to the dining hall to call forth Julie, who was sitting warming herself by the large stone fireplace, hearing the cracking and popping from the wood as it burned. Eve manipulated the fire, making a bird dance in the flames to get her attention. Julie's eyes watched the bird's wings for a moment, then turned to Eve. "Julie, can you follow me, please?". She stood and followed her out of the main hall through the entrance and down a hallway to a large black stone classroom, where the original cave paintings decorated the walls. "Julie, I would love for you to show the girls the joys of capturing beauty through a Lens?" Julie smiled wide and agreed, looking at all the different cameras from different periods of time. Eve left her in her classroom to go find Pearl, who was now also on the balcony, lifting her hand and making the water dance beneath her palm. She felt totally at ease. Eve joined her side, "This is your classroom, there will definitely be more water witches that need your guidance". Pearl nodded her head in agreement and saw the wooden decking built over the lake and a large wooden gazebo atop it with benches. Pearl smiled and gave Eve a hug. "I have hidden my gift for so long, and now I can use it and help others, thank you, Eve". Eve's focus turned to Clover, who had found a book and was sitting at the bench reading, "Clover, my dear," Eve called for her. She closed the book and placed it on the bench to follow Eve as they descended down a spiral staircase to a classroom deep blow the Academy, "Clover your gift is very unique not many witches over the centuries have had the power to call upon Whispermane let alone befriend her, so I would love you show the students your gift of spirit wielding and teaching them the dangers of meddling in such things". Clover walked around the tall, vaulted room with the fire lit in the hearth, heavy metal ball lanterns hung around the room, her own large desk placed next to the fireplace and carved into the stone floor was a giant Ouija board. Eve left her there as she went to the courtyard, seeing some of the Raven's return without their ribbons on their necks, she knew that the girls were on their way.

Pearl was sitting under the wooden Gazebo, soon to be her classroom, overlooking the still water, seeing swans floating by and fish splashing in the lake. She sat and took a deep breath, feeling completely at ease. She stood from her chair as she walked and took a seat at the edge of the decking, letting her feet hang over the edge of the wooden deck. She looked down at the water, concentrating her power. She took a step down onto the water's surface, but she did not sink. She could see the fish swimming beneath her feet; she laughed out loud to herself and began to run as water splashed under her toes. It was the freest she had felt in a very long time. Orenda and Velina were sitting opposite each other in their new greenhouse classroom, writing down class plans and coming up with fun ways to help them learn. They felt the old spark reignited for their passion for plants and herbs and the natural magic they bring. Dean was up in his classroom with all the large windows open, punching one of the punching bags, sweat dripping down his back as something very strange echoed inside him, but he shook the feeling off and carried on training. Julie was already walking around the Academy with one of the cameras, taking all different kinds of pictures, so she could spend some time in her dark room developing them. Clover was sitting in the middle of her rune circle cross legged, breathing deeply and meditating as she saw a flash of a vision, a great hideous beast with deep red fur and long white whiskers and eyes that glowed like rubies, and a long red bushy tail with a white tip at the end. As fast as the vision started, it was over. Her eyes shot open, and she felt confused, but the feeling of foreboding about the creature washed over her. She rose to her feet, needing to tell someone, anyone, about what she had seen in her mind.

Clover found Eve sat in the courtyard on the edge of the fountain with a few dozen Ravens that had landed around her, Clover sat next to her when Eve turned to her "will you look after these for me" Clover took the black box from her "these are the badges the girl will earn when they master certain aspects of their power, there are nine to collect. The first is the Corvus Corax pin this is earned after the first week of being a part of this family, the second pin is for using your powers for the first time, the Principalis pin, the third is for a streak of hard work and good behaviour, the Sinuatus pin, the fourth is for helping your fellow witch and showing team work, the Clarionesis pin, the fifth is for after your first year of being here, that one is the Varius pin, the sixth pin is for attendance in class and extracurricular activities, this one is called the Tingitanus pin, the seventh pin is what you gain when you befriend your familiar, this one is the Canariensis pin, the eighth pin is for recognising your respect and cleanliness of your uniform and dorm room, this is called the Corax pin, finally the ninth pin is what you gain when you graduate, this is the Hispanus pin. I will get more made for when they come". Clover opened the lid and looked at the shining pins. They looked beautiful as they glinted in the light. She closed the lid and asked

Eve to listen. "I have had a vision, and I don't know what it means, but it felt very wrong." Eve took her words in "I saw a large beast that almost resembled a large beefed-up fox with red glowing eyes." Eve went quiet for a moment, then a look of panic washed across her face. "I need to confirm my thoughts on something. For now, don't worry, I will get back to you once I have done some research." Eve stood and left Clover alone with the Ravens, thinking about what she had seen and what it was. Eve burst through her door and slammed it behind her, seeing a wall filled with old, crumbling books and scrolls. She pulled a book from the shelf with a symbol of a fox on the spine. It was a journal Hazel had made not long after she had made the cave.

Chapter Thirty-Two

WELCOME TO UNKINDNESS

ACADEMY

"Welcome, girls. Please make yourselves at home. I will show you to your dorms."

-E.L.

Eve slammed the book shut, holding onto the information to herself as she was panicked by what she had learnt. A large Raven landed on her windowsill, pecking at the glass excitedly. Eve knew immediately what the Raven was excited about; the girls were here. She rose, took a brush to her hair, grabbed her staff and ran for the door to welcome them in. As she approached the front door, she straightened her long white dress and waved her staff for the large wooden door to swing open, revealing seven young ladies before her. They looked nervous as they glanced up at the large Gothic building, and Eve stood there with her tall staff. "To those who were told you were too much. To those who were told you were nothing. Welcome home." Eve waved her hand to them to follow her as she led them to the dining hall. They took seats at the end of the long benches, closer to the stone balcony with the shining light reflecting in from the lake. "Girls, sisters, daughters of power, you stand where many before you could not. Not because they lacked strength, but because the world feared what they were. You carry the gifts of the old ways, of spirit, earth, sky and soul, and you have been brought here not to hide them, but to awaken them. This is Unkindness Academy, a sanctuary, a school, a coven born from survival and risen from the ashes of judgment. We do not teach obedience here. We teach resilience. We do not demand silence. We teach you to speak, to scream, to sing with your truth. Here, you will learn to shape your magic, not shrink from it. You will train with your fellow witches who once fought for their lives. You will find yourselves here within these walls and friendships along the way. You are not here to become someone else. You are here to become more yourself than you've ever been allowed to be. So, take a breath. Look around at those beside you. These are not your rivals. These are your sisters. This is your Unkindness for ravens never fly alone. Now… let's begin".

The girls sat there feeling warm from the inside for the first time in their lives. "How about we go around and introduce ourselves? My name is Eve Longbow, the white witch, and your headmaster". She gestured to the first girl sitting at the edge of the bench, who had her arm in a sling. She was a tall, skinny girl who looked like she needed a good meal in her. She had a very pale complexion with dark circles under her eyes and long flowing red hair of fire. "My name is Henly. I came here from a coastal village about a five-hour walk for me." Everyone looked at her in shock, finding out how far she had walked. "I'm here because I'm lost and need a path". She lifted the ribbon around her neck examining the Raven Sigel in her pale fingers "this feels like home and I'm thankful it exists, my arm is in a sling because the landlord at the women's hostel I was staying in, he broke my arm when he accused me of stealing money from him, I never went anywhere near his money, let alone him he gave me the creeps, so I ran and slept rough for a few weeks when this raven landed in front of me with this ribbon and now I'm here." Eve took a deep breath and pulled her into a hug but careful not to hurt her arm. "we will have someone tend your arm dear and get that mended" She took a seat as the next girl stood she had deep coloured skin with bright blue eyes under a mass of candy pink curls, "my name is Trix I was disowned by my religious family they claimed I was a demon because I can shapeshift my face, but I have no control of it sometimes, it's like if I really connect with someone my features just morph onto there's" she took a seat quickly feeling awkward. Eve turned to Trix "that is an extraordinary gift we will help you with it". Eve looked to the next girl who stood. She was a short curvy girl who kept her head down and arms folded with mousey short hair "my name is Brenda I was kicked out of my town being called a freak and a witch" her introduction was short as she sat back down fast on the bench. Eve shuffled towards her and took her hand, "you my dear are the best kind of freak, own it, find power in it. Those who choose to be different and stand out are braver than the sheep who fall into line". She lifted her head to Eve and smiled, some tears falling down her cheeks.

The next girl stood she was a very well-mannered girl who held herself well but she had quiet shyness about her she had deep brown eyes and long brown hair with a warm complexion "my name is Leyla I have come here because my parents don't know what to do with me, they fear me I think, I have the power to manipulate water I accidentally nearly drown a boy who kept bullying me" she looked to Eve who had a smile on her face "I have the perfect teacher for you who you will meet soon but let's get you settled first, you were protecting yourself from a bully don't every apologies for that" Leyla took a seat and the next girl stood "my name is Misty and I can disappear into mist and reappear somewhere else I have been homeless for a while but I have been surviving by forming my mist portal and transporting myself into hotel rooms to keep warm and safe" Eve looked amazed at her gift "that is amazing you must show me once you are settled". The next girl stood she was pale and tall with long black hair that was platted behind her back, she had the matching dark circles under her eyes like Henly but she was leaned into the look with her black lip stick and large skull rings "my name is Denna and I'm here because I just am" she slumped back down looking unbothered, Eve could see she was a soul that needed care but she didn't push "Denna you will blossom here, learn to trust and let go of the hard shell" Denna looked up to the sky as if she was holding back tears. The final girl stood, a very bright girl with long eyelashes hiding hazel eyes, she wore pink head to toe with platinum blonde hair in piggy tails "my name is pony and I can talk to animals, I love life, I love animals, I bloody hate humans though, not you guys, you guys are cool" she could not get her words out quick enough. Eve giggled to herself, seeing the seven girls sitting in front of her. "Girls, I will take you to your rooms".

She led them up the main staircase, turning right as bright hanging lanterns lit their way. She asked the girls to pair up in twos and one room of three. Henly and Misty entered their room together, Brenda, Leya and Denna entered their room, and finally Pony and Trix joined up and skipped into their room with excitement. Before the doors were closed, Eve informed them that it was lights out by ten o'clock and not to wander the Academy without a guide. With a wave of her staff, she closed the doors behind them, hearing laughing and giggling behind the doors. She walked away with a smile on her face as she went to speak to Clover about what she had found. She found Clover sitting outside on the balcony of her room in the academy with Jasper as she joined her. "I have something to tell you," Eve said, Clover sitting up straight. "What have you found?" "I have read through Hazel's journals; she had encountered these cursed creatures in her time as the elder white witch when she put together the first coven together". Clover took a deep breath. "Here, take this book and have a read. I will find you later," Eve opened her wings and took flight over Unkindness Academy as Clover opened the book to read. The page was titled the Crimson Maw of Hollow Wood.

It has the likeness of a fox, but not one the woods would ever claim. Its fur was coarse red with black smudged socks and a white tipped long tail. Its eyes are twin rubies, glowing like gems in the dark. Its jaws could crush bone like stale bread, its breath smelled of scorched flesh and blood. The creature had a name whispered in the forests, Crimson Maw. It had no soul, only a purpose to track witches by scent, the scent of magic itself. No glamour could fool it. No spell could tame it. The Crimson Maw would chase a witch across realms if needed, growing faster and hungrier the more potent her magic got. They say it was born from the stitched remains of hunted witches, blood-soaked garments, plucked hair, shattered talismans, all stitched together into a pelt and set ablaze in a forbidden ritual under a bleeding moon. From that cursed fire, the beast emerged, growling not like an animal, but like a woman in pain. But the beast is not mindless. It remembers. They say it knows the names of every witch it has ever killed, and one day, it will say, "My job is done now, every witch and scrap of magic is dead". As the night drew on, Dean was up alone in his classroom training again, and he felt like he had so much unburnt energy that nothing could drain it. The moon hung low in the sky, casting Hunter Manor in a sticky glow in the distance. The wind carried a strange weight that night, one of memory and mourning. Dean stood at the edge of his classroom, feeling hot and panting. The scent of crushed sage lingered in the air. Dean took a seat, his head in his hands, and the academy was silent. It was long past curfew, the halls dimly lit by flickering lanterns. Dean remained; his hands were smudged with chalk from punching the punch bag until his knuckles turned red. He couldn't sleep. Couldn't stop thinking about the others, his family and the new students. He exhaled sharply and leaned back in his chair, rubbing his face with both hands. That was when he felt it.

A burn beneath his skin, on the back of his right hand. At first, it was subtle, like the ache of a healing bruise. But it grew quickly, hotter, sharper, crawling up his veins like fire given form. Dean gasped, looking down. The skin on the back of his hand blistered and rippled, then burned open. He screamed. A shape began to emerge from the skin, not carved, not inked, but branded. A fox, long-bodied and lean, with fangs bared and tail coiled like a flame. Its eyes were twin red rubies; they glowed with a light that was not of this world. "What the hell?" He rasped, gripping his wrist. But the mark only pulsed stronger. Then came the memories. Not his. Flooding in like a dam had broken inside his skull, faces twisted in agony, forests filled with screams, the chanting of rituals in cold candlelight. The sound of growls. The smell of burned herbs. His ancestors, generations of hunters forgotten, each one wearing the same fox mark, each one murdering witches in the name of righteousness. Dean collapsed against the wall, clawing at his scalp, eyes wide and glowing red. He saw his ancestor's hands drenched in blood. The mark still burning, the echo of a hunter's oath trembling through time. His voice broke as he whispered, "I don't want this," But the blood didn't care what he wanted. From the corner of the room, a mirror cracked. The shadows deepened. Somewhere, in the darkest parts of the forest beyond the academy walls… The Crimson Maw lifted its head. It had felt the mark awaken. And now, it was coming.

Bonus Page:

THE RAVEN'S OMEN

I have carried the curse and the gift of fire. I have walked through ash and ruin, and yet, I remain. But I am no longer only a witch bound to survive; I am a flame that must light the path for others. There will be girls who are hunted. Girls who are feared. Girls who are lost. They will need a place to belong, a place to grow strong, a place to stand unbroken. I see it already in my mind: walls rising like wings, voices ringing through hidden halls, a sanctuary born from magic. The Ravens will guide them to me, and when they arrive, they will not walk alone. The legacy does not end here. It begins.

Book Two

The Ravens Legacy: The Unkindness Academy

347